Joss knew ~~what~~ was going to ~~happen.~~

And oh, at that ~~moment she wanted him to~~ kiss her.

Wanted him to guide her back onto the sofa cushions, to press his big, muscled body so tightly against her, to hold her so close and kiss her so long, and so deep and so thoroughly that she would forget…

Everything.

The mess that was her life. All the ways her plans and her world had gone haywire. All the things she somehow had to fix, to make right, though she really had no idea how to do that.

She wanted to tear off all her clothes and all of his, too. She wanted to be naked with him, skin-to-skin. Naked with her new best friend— who happened to be a man she'd only met the day before.

She wanted forgetfulness. And she wanted it in Jace's big arms.

Dear Reader,

Former player Jason "Jace" Traub isn't sure what he wants out of life anymore. He's out of the family business and determined to leave his lifelong home of Midland, Texas, and start anew somewhere else. In the meantime, he's spending a week or two at the annual Traub family reunion in Thunder Canyon, Montana.

Runaway bride Joss Bennings is enjoying her *un*-honeymoon at the Thunder Canyon Resort courtesy of that cheating rat she almost married. When Jace meets Joss, it's best friends at first sight.

Nothing serious. They're just great buddies.

Or so they keep telling themselves. But every moment they spend together draws them closer to the realization that there's a lot more going on there than friendship.

I love it when best friends become so much more. I think Joss and Jace are meant for each other. And I totally enjoyed writing their story.

Happy reading, everyone!

Yours always,

Christine Rimmer

THE LAST SINGLE MAVERICK

BY
CHRISTINE RIMMER

All the characters in this book have no existence outside the imagination of the author, and have no relation whatsoever to anyone bearing the same name or names. They are not even distantly inspired by any individual known or unknown to the author, and all the incidents are pure invention.

All Rights Reserved including the right of reproduction in whole or in part in any form. This edition is published by arrangement with Harlequin Enterprises II B.V./S.à.r.l. The text of this publication or any part thereof may not be reproduced or transmitted in any form or by any means, electronic or mechanical, including photocopying, recording, storage in an information retrieval system, or otherwise, without the written permission of the publisher.

This book is sold subject to the condition that it shall not, by way of trade or otherwise, be lent, resold, hired out or otherwise circulated without the prior consent of the publisher in any form of binding or cover other than that in which it is published and without a similar condition including this condition being imposed on the subsequent purchaser.

® and ™ are trademarks owned and used by the trademark owner and/or its licensee. Trademarks marked with ® are registered with the United Kingdom Patent Office and/or the Office for Harmonisation in the Internal Market and in other countries.

First published in Great Britain 2012
by Mills & Boon, an imprint of Harlequin (UK) Limited,
Eton House, 18-24 Paradise Road, Richmond, Surrey TW9 1SR

© Harlequin Books S.A. 2012

Special thanks and acknowledgment to Christine Rimmer for her contribution to the Montana Mavericks: Back in the Saddle continuity.

ISBN: 978 0 263 89472 1
ebook ISBN: 978 1 408 97148 2

23-1012

Harlequin (UK) policy is to use papers that are natural, renewable and recyclable products and made from wood grown in sustainable forests. The logging and manufacturing processes conform to the legal environmental regulations of the country of origin.

Printed and bound in Spain
by Blackprint CPI, Barcelona

Christine Rimmer came to her profession the long way around. Before settling down to write about the magic of romance, she'd been everything from an actress to a salesclerk to a waitress. Now that she's finally found work that suits her perfectly, she insists she never had a problem keeping a job—she was merely gaining "life experience" for her future as a novelist. Christine is grateful not only for the joy she finds in writing, but for what waits when the day's work is through: a man she loves who loves her right back, and the privilege of watching their children grow and change day to day. She lives with her family in Oregon. Visit Christine at www.christinerimmer.com.

For my readers.
You are the best!

Chapter One

Family reunions. Who needs them?

Jason Traub didn't. He realized that now. And yet somehow, a few days ago, he'd decided that a trip to Montana for the annual summertime Traub family get-together would be a good idea.

Or maybe he'd just wanted to escape Midland, Texas, and the constant pressure to return to the family business. He should have realized that in Montana it would only be more of the same. Especially given that the whole family was here—and still putting on the pressure.

And why was it that the reunion seemed to get longer every year? This year, it began on the Saturday before Independence Day and would go straight through the whole week to the Sunday after the Fourth, with some family event or other taking place daily.

That first day, Saturday, June 30, featured a late-afternoon barbecue at DJ's Rib Shack. Jason's cousin DJ had Rib Shacks all over the western states. But this one happened to be at the Thunder Canyon Resort up on Thunder Mountain, which loomed, tall and craggy, above the small and charming mountain town of Thunder Canyon.

"Jace." The deep voice came from behind him. "Glad you could make it."

Jason, seated at one of the Rib Shack's long, rustic, family-style tables, glanced over his shoulder at his older brother Ethan. "Great party," Jason said. And it was. If you didn't mind a whole bunch of family up in your face in a big, big way.

His brother leaned closer. "We need to talk."

Jace pretended he didn't hear and held up a juicy rib dripping Rib Shack secret sauce. "Great ribs, as always." With the constant rumble of voices and laughter that filled the restaurant, how would Ethan know if Jace heard him or not?

Ethan grunted—and bent even closer to speak directly into his ear. "I know Ma and Pete want you back in Midland." Pete Wexler was their stepdad. "But you've got options, and I mean that. There's a place waiting for you right here at TOI Montana."

TOI—for Traub Oil Industries—was the family business. The original office was in Midland, Texas, where Jason and his five siblings had been born and raised. Pete, their stepdad, was chairman of the board. And their mother, Claudia, was CEO. Last year, Ethan had opened a second branch of TOI in Thunder Canyon. Jackson, Jason's fraternal twin, and their only sister, Rose, and her husband, Austin, were all at the new office with Ethan.

"No, thanks," Jace said, and then reminded his brother— as he kept reminding everyone in the family, "I'm out of the oil business."

Now it was Ethan's turn to pretend not to hear. He

squeezed Jason's shoulder—a bone-crushing squeeze. "We'll talk," he said.

"No point," Jace answered wearily. "I've made up my mind."

But Ethan only gave him a wave and started talking to the large elderly woman on Jace's right. Jace didn't hear what they said to each other. He was actively *not* listening.

A moment later, Ethan moved on. Jace concentrated on his dinner. His plate was piled high with ribs, corn on the cob, coleslaw and steak fries. The food was terrific. Almost worth the constant grief he was getting from his family—about work, about his nonexistent love life, about *everything*.

Across the table, Shandie Traub, his cousin Dax's wife, said, "Jason, here's someone I want you to meet." The someone in question stood directly behind Shandie. She had baby-fine blond hair and blue eyes and she was smiling at him shyly. Shandie introduced her. "My second cousin, Belinda McKelly. Belinda's from Sioux Falls."

"Hi, Jason." Belinda colored prettily. She had to practically shout to be heard over the din. "I'm so pleased to meet you." She bent closer and stuck her hand out at him.

Jace swiped a wet wipe over his fingers, reached across the table and gave her offered hand a shake. She seemed sweet actually. But one look in those baby blues of hers told him way more than he needed to know: Belinda wanted a husband. As soon as she let go, he grabbed an ear of corn and started gnawing on it, his gaze focused hard on his plate. When he dared to glance up again, she was gone.

Shandie gave him a look that skimmed real close to pissed off. "Honestly, Jace, you could make a little effort. It's not like it would kill you."

"Sorry," he said, even though he didn't feel sorry in the

least. He only felt relieved not to have to make small talk with sweet Belinda McKelly.

To his right, the large elderly woman Ethan had spoken to a few moments before said warmly, "Such a lovely young girl." The old lady's warm tone turned cool as she spoke directly to Jason. "But I can see *you're* not interested." He kept working away at his ear of corn in hopes that the large old lady would turn and talk to the smaller old lady on her other side. No such luck. "I'm Melba Landry," she said, "Lizzie's great-aunt." Lizzie was Ethan's wife.

Resigned, Jason gave the woman a nod. "Pleased to meet you, ma'am. I'm Jason Traub, Lizzie's brother-in-law."

"I know very well who you are, young man." Aunt Melba looked down her imposing nose at him. "I was married to Lizzie's great-uncle Oliver for more than fifty years. Oliver, rest his soul, passed on last October. The Lord never saw fit to bless us with children of our own. I moved to Thunder Canyon just this past April. It's so nice to be near Lizzie. Family is everything, don't you think, Jason?"

"Yes, ma'am. Everything." To his left, he was vaguely aware that the second cousin sitting there had risen. Someone else slipped into the empty spot.

And Aunt Melba wasn't through with him yet. "Jason, you know that we're all *concerned* about you."

"Kind of seems that way, yes." He got busy on his second ear of corn, still hoping that putting all his attention on the food would get rid of her. It had worked with Belinda.

But Aunt Melba was not about to give up. "I understand you're having some kind of life crisis."

He swallowed. The wad of corn went down hard. He grabbed his water glass and knocked back a giant gulp. "Life crisis? No, ma'am. I'm not."

"Please call me Melba—and there's no point in lying

about it. I'm seventy-six years old, young man. I know a man in crisis when I see one."

"No, ma'am," he said again. "I mean that. There's no crisis." By then, he was starting to feel a little like Judas at the last supper. If he just kept denying, maybe she would go away.

"I asked you to call me Melba," she corrected a second time, more sternly.

"Sorry, Melba. But I mean it. I'm not having a crisis. I am doing just fine. And really, I—"

"There's a lovely church here in town that I've been attending. Everyone is so friendly. I felt at home there from the first. And so will you, Jason."

"Uh…"

"Tomorrow. Join us. The Thunder Canyon Community Church. North Main at Cedar Street. Come to the service at ten. I'll be watching for you. There is no problem in this wide world that a little time with the Lord can't resolve."

"Well, Melba, thank you for the invitation. I'll, um, try to be there."

"Get involved, young man," Melba instructed with an enthusiastic nod of her imposing double chin. "That's the first step. Stop sitting on the sidelines of life." She opened her mouth to say more, but the white-haired lady on her other side touched her arm and spoke to her. Melba turned to answer.

Jace held his breath. And luck was with him. Melba and the other old lady had struck up a conversation.

He was just starting to feel relieved when a hand closed on his left thigh and a sultry voice spoke in his ear. "Jace, aren't you even going to say hi?"

He smelled musky perfume and turned his head slowly to meet a pair of glittering green eyes. "Hi."

The woman was not any member of his extended family

that he knew of. She had jet-black hair and wore a painted-on red tank top. "Oh, you're kidding me." She laughed. "You don't remember? Last summer? Your brother Corey's bachelor party at the Hitching Post?" The Hitching Post was a landmark restaurant and bar in town.

"I, uh…"

"Theresa," the woman said. "Theresa Duvall."

"Hey." He tried on a smile. He remembered her now—vaguely anyway. For Jace, the weekend of Corey's bachelor party and wedding had been mostly of the "lost" variety. His twin, Jackson, had still been single then. The two of them had partied straight through for three days. There had been serious drinking. Way too much drinking. And the night of the bachelor party, he'd gone home with Theresa, hadn't he? Somehow, that had seemed like a good idea at the time. "So, Theresa," he said, "how've you been?"

Her hand glided a little higher on his thigh. "I have been fine, Jace. Just fine. And it is so *good* to see you," she cooed. "I had *such* a great time with you." Theresa, as he recalled, was not the least interested in settling down. In fact, the look on her face told him exactly what she *was* interested in: another night like that one last summer.

He *had* to get out of there. He grabbed another wipe, swabbed off his greasy fingers and then gently removed Theresa's wandering hand from his thigh. "Excuse me, Theresa."

"Oh, now," she coaxed in a breathy whisper, "don't run off."

"Men's room?" He put a question mark after it, even though he knew perfectly well where the restrooms were.

Theresa pointed. "Over there." She gave him a low-eyed, smoldering glance as he pushed his chair out and rose. "Hurry back," she instructed, licking her lips.

It wasn't easy, but he forced himself not to take off at

a run. He ambled away casually, waving and nodding to friends and family as he headed for the restrooms—only detouring sharply for the exit as soon as he was no longer in Theresa's line of sight. A moment later, he ducked out of the Rib Shack altogether and into the giant, five-story clubhouse lobby of the resort.

Now what?

Someplace quiet. Someplace where he could be alone.

The Lounge, he thought. It was a bar in the clubhouse and it was exactly what he needed right now. The Lounge was kind of a throwback really—a throwback to earlier times, when cattlemen had their own private clubs where the women didn't trespass. In the Lounge, the lights were kept soothingly low. The bar was long and made of gleaming burled wood. It had comfortable conversation areas consisting of dark wood tables and fat studded-leather chairs. Women seemed to avoid the Lounge. They tended to prefer the more open, modern bar in the upscale Gallatin Room, or the cowboy-casual style of the bar in the Rib Shack.

The Lounge was perfect for the mood he was in.

He found it as he'd hoped it might be—mostly deserted. One lone customer sat up at the bar. A woman, surprisingly enough. A brunette. Jace liked the look of her instantly, which surprised him. As a rule lately, it didn't matter how hot or good-looking a woman was. He just wasn't interested. Not on any level.

But *this* woman was different. Special. He sensed that at first sight.

She had a whole lot of thick, tousled brown hair tumbling down her back. In the mirror over the bar, he could see that she had big brown eyes and full, kissable lips. She was dressed casually, in jeans and a giant white shirt, untucked. She wore very little makeup.

And the best thing about her? She seemed so relaxed. Like she wasn't after anything except to sip her margarita and enjoy the quiet comfort of the Lounge.

She saw him watching her in the mirror over the bar. For a second or two, their eyes met. He felt a little curl of excitement down inside him before she glanced away. Instantly, he wanted her to glance at him again.

Surprise. Excitement. The desire that a certain woman might give him a second look. These were all emotions with which he'd become completely unfamiliar.

Yeah, all right. It wasn't news that he used to be something of a player. But in the past six months or so? Uh-uh. He was tired of being a ladies' man—like he was tired of just about everything lately. Including finding the right woman and settling down.

Because, yeah, Jason had tried that. Or at least, he'd wanted to try it with a certain rich-girl swimsuit model named Tricia Lavelle.

It hadn't worked out. In fact, the whole experience had been seriously disheartening.

A cell phone on the bar started ringing. The brunette picked it up, scowled at the display and then put it to her ear. "What do you want?" She let out an audible sigh. "You're not serious. Oh, please, Kenny, get real. It's over. Move on." She hung up and dropped the phone back on the bar.

Jace took the stool next to her and signaled the bartender. "Jack Daniels, rocks." The bartender poured and set his drink in front of him. "And another margarita," Jace added. "For the lady."

"No, thanks." She shook her head at the barkeep and he left them alone. Then she turned to Jace and granted him a patient look from that fine pair of enormous brown eyes. "No offense," she said.

"None taken."

"And don't even *think* about it, okay? I'm on a solo vacation and right now, I hate men."

He studied her face. It was such a great face. One of those faces a guy could look at forever and still find new expressions in it. "Already, I really like you."

"Didn't I just say I hate men?"

"That makes you a challenge. Haven't you heard? Men love a challenge."

"I'm serious. Don't bother. It's not gonna happen."

He faced the rows of liquor bottles arrayed in front of the mirror over the bar and shrugged. "Okay, if you're sure."

She shot him a look. "Oh, come on. Is that the best you've got?"

He leaned his head on his hand and admired the way the dim barroom light somehow managed to bring out glints of auburn in her thick, wavy dark hair. "Uninspired, huh?"

She almost smiled. "Well, yeah."

"Story of my life lately. I've got no passion for the game."

"What game?"

He shrugged again. "Any game."

She considered that. "Wow," she said finally. "That's sad."

"Yeah, it is, isn't it?"

She frowned and then looked at him sideways. "Wait a minute. Stop right there, buddy. I'm on to you."

"Oh? What am I up to?"

"You sit there looking gorgeous and bored. I find I have a longing to bring some life back into your eyes. I let you buy me another margarita after all. I go home with you. We have wild, hot, incredible sex. But in the morning, you're looking bored again and I'm feeling cheap and used."

He decided to focus on the positive. "You think I'm gorgeous?"

"That was not my point. It was a cautionary tale."

"I think *you're* gorgeous," he said and meant it. "And that's kind of a breakthrough for me."

"A breakthrough." She was not impressed. "You're kidding me."

"I am as serious as a bad blind date. You're the first woman I've felt attracted to in months. Who's Kenny?"

She shook a finger at him. "You listened in on my phone call."

"Not exactly. I *overheard* your phone call."

"I'm just saying it was a private conversation and I don't even know your name."

"Jason Traub. Call me Jace." He offered his hand.

She took it. "Jocelyn Marie Bennings. Call me Joss."

It felt good, he realized, just to hold her hand. It felt… comfortable. And exciting, too. Both at once. That was a first—for him anyway. As a rule, with women, it was one or the other. He didn't want to let go. But in the end, it wasn't his choice.

She eased her hand free. "My wedding was supposed to be a week ago today. Kenny was the groom."

"Supposed to be? You mean you *didn't* marry him?"

"No, I didn't. And I should have backed out long before the wedding day. But Kenny and I were together for five years. It was going to be a beautiful wedding. You should see my wedding gown. I still have it. I couldn't bear to get rid of it. It's fabulous. Acres of beading, yards of the finest taffeta and tulle. We planned a nice reception afterward at my restaurant."

"You own a restaurant?"

"No. I mean the restaurant I was managing, until I quit to marry Kenny. I gave up a great job for him. Just like I gave up my cute apartment, because I thought I wouldn't need either anymore."

"But then you didn't marry Kenny."

"I already said I didn't."

"Just wanted to be sure. So what went wrong? Why didn't you marry the guy?"

She ran her finger around the rim of her margarita glass. "Who's telling this story, Jace?"

He gave her a nod. "You are, Joss. Absolutely. Carry on."

"It was going to be the perfect wedding."

He nodded once more, to show her he was listening, but he did not interrupt again.

She went on. "And after the wedding and the lovely reception, there was the great getaway honeymoon right here at the Thunder Canyon Resort. Followed by a move to San Francisco. Kenny's a very successful advertising executive. He just hit the big time and got transferred to the Bay Area." Joss paused. She turned her glass by the stem.

He wanted to prompt her to tell him what went wrong, but he didn't. He waited patiently for her to go on, as he'd promised he would.

Finally, she continued. "I got all the way to the church last Saturday. Camellia City Methodist in Sacramento. It's a beautiful church. And I was born and raised in Sacramento and have lived there all my life. I like my hometown. In fact, I didn't really want to move to San Francisco, but I was willing to support my future husband in his powerhouse career. And I would have gone through with the wedding in spite of my doubts."

He'd promised to let her tell it her way, but still. He had to know. "What doubts?"

She shook her head. "Kenny used to be such a sweet guy. But the more successful he got, the more he changed.

He became someone I didn't even know—and then I caught him with my cousin Kimberly in the coat room."

"Hold on, you lost me. What coat room?"

She shook her head again, as though she still couldn't quite believe it. "The coat room at Camellia City Methodist."

Jace let his mouth fall open. "Kenny canoodled with Kimberly in the coat room on the day of your wedding?"

"Oh, yeah. And it was beyond canoodling. Kimberly was halfway out of her hot-pink satin bridesmaid's dress and someone had unzipped Kenny's fly. Both of them were red-faced and breathless. Kind of ruined the whole experience for me, you know?"

He made a low noise in his throat. "I guess so."

Joss picked up the cell phone, studied it for a moment and then set it back down. "So I threw his engagement ring in his face and got the heck out of there—and I'm here at the resort anyway. Having my honeymoon minus the groom."

He tipped his head at the phone. "But Kenny keeps calling."

"Oh yes, he does."

"What a douche bag."

She sipped her margarita. "My sentiments exactly."

"I hate guys like that. He blew it already. He should show a little dignity and leave you alone. But instead it's, 'Joss, *please*. I love you. I just want to work this out. Come back to me. I'm sorry, okay? And that silly thing with Kimberly? It meant nothing and it will never happen again.'"

Joss laughed. She had a beautiful, husky, warm sort of laugh. "How did you do that? You even captured the slightly wounded, whiney tone of his voice. Like *I'm* the one with the problem."

Jace stared at her wide, soft mouth in unabashed admiration. "I like your laugh."

She gave him her sternest frown. "Didn't I tell you not to go there?"

He was about to argue that he wasn't "going" anywhere, that he only liked the way she laughed. But before he could get the words out, Theresa Duvall sauntered up behind him and took the stool on his other side.

"Jace." Theresa's hand closed over his arm. He looked down at her fingernails, which were long and done up for the holiday with glittery red stripes and tiny, sparkly little stars. She leaned close and purred, "I'm a determined woman and there is no way you're escaping me."

Okay. He knew he only had himself to blame if Theresa considered him the perfect candidate for another no-strings night of meaningless sex. But he really liked Joss. And he'd never have a chance with her now, not with Theresa pulling on his arm, eyeing him like a starving person eyes a steak dinner.

And it wasn't even that he *wanted* a chance with Joss. Not *that* kind of chance anyway. He just liked her a lot, liked talking with her, liked hearing her laugh. He didn't want her to leave.

Shocked the socks off him when she *didn't* leave. Somehow, she picked up on the desperate look he sent her. And not only did she stay right where she was, she wrapped her arm around his shoulders and pulled him away from Theresa, drawing him close to her side.

Wow. It felt good—*really* good—to have her holding on to him, to feel her softness and the warmth of her. She smelled like soap and starch and sunshine and roses. And maybe a little tequila.

"Sorry," she said to Theresa, her tone regretful. "This one's taken."

Theresa blinked. And then she let go of his arm and scowled. "Jace, what *is* your problem? You should have told me you were with someone. I want a good time as much as the next girl, but I would never steal another woman's man."

He was totally lost, awash in the superfine sensation of having Joss's arm around him. But then she nudged him in the side and he realized he was supposed to speak. "Uh, yeah. You're right, Theresa. I'm an ass. I should have said something."

Joss clucked her tongue and rolled her eyes. "We had a fight. He's been sulking."

Theresa groaned. "Oh, I know how that goes. Men. I don't let myself get serious with them anymore. They're just not worth it."

Joss pulled him even closer. And then she kissed his ear. It was barely a breath of a kiss. But still, with her arm around him and her lips close to his ear, he could almost forget that he had no interest in women anymore. He was enjoying every minute of this and he wished she would never let go. "I hear you," she told Theresa, her breath all warm and tempting in his ear. "But when it's true love, well, what can you do?"

Theresa just shook her head. The bartender approached. Theresa shook her head at him, too. And then, without another word, she got up and left.

Instantly, Joss released him and retreated to her own stool. Jace felt kind of bereft. But then he reminded himself that he should be grateful. She'd done him a favor and gotten Theresa off his back. "Thanks. I owe you one." He raised his glass.

She tapped hers against it. "Okay, I'll bite. Who *was* that?"

"Her name is Theresa Duvall. Last year, she was working at the Hitching Post—it's this great old-time bar and grill down in town, on the corner of Main Street and Thunder Canyon Road."

"She seemed like she knew you pretty well."

"Not really." He didn't want to say more. But Joss was looking at him, a look that seemed to expect him to tell the truth. So he did. "I had a thing with her last summer. A very short thing."

"A thing."

"Yeah."

"What, specifically, is a thing?"

He tried not to wince. "See, I knew you would ask that."

Joss accused gently, "You slept with her."

"Only once. And technically, well, there was no sleeping."

She laughed again. Really, she had the best laugh. "Jace, I believe you're a dog."

He tipped his drink and stared down into it. "Maybe I was. Not anymore, though. I have changed my ways."

She made a disbelieving sound. "Right."

"No, seriously, I'm not the man I used to be. Too bad I'm not real clear on who, exactly, I've become. I lack… direction. Everyone says so. I'm not interested in women anymore. I don't want to get laid. Or married. Also, I've given up my place in the family business and my family is freaked over that."

"You live here in Thunder Canyon?"

"No, in Midland, Texas. Or I did. I have a nice little spread outside of town there. But I've put my place up for sale. I'm moving. I just don't know where to yet. In the meantime, I'm here for a weeklong family reunion—a reunion that is going on right now, here at the resort, over at DJ's Rib Shack."

"I have another question, Jace."

"Shoot."

"Is there anything you *do* want?"

"That, Jocelyn Marie, is the question of the hour. Please come with me back to the Rib Shack."

She was running her finger around the rim of her drink again. "You didn't answer the question of the hour."

"All right. There is nothing that I want—except for you to come back to the Rib Shack with me."

Her smooth brow furrowed a little. "And *I* would want to go to *your* family reunion because?"

"Because only you can protect me from my family and all the women who want things from me that I'm not capable of giving them."

She shook that head of thick brown hair and sat straighter on her stool. "Before I decide whether to go with you or not, I need to get something crystal clear."

"Fine."

"I want you to listen very carefully, Jace."

He assumed a suitably intent expression. "I'm listening."

"I'm. Not. Going. To. Have. Sex. With. You."

"Oh, that." He waved a hand. "It's okay. I don't care about that."

"So you say now."

"Look, Joss, I like you. You're the first bright spot in my life in months. I just want to hang around with you for a while. Have a few laughs. No pressure. No drama. Nothing hot and heavy. No big romance."

She stared at him for several seconds. Her expression said she still wasn't sure she believed him. Finally she asked, "So you want to be…friends? Honestly? Just friends?"

"My God, I would love that." He put some money on the bar. "The Rib Shack?"

She downed the last of her margarita. "Why not?"

Chapter Two

Joss surprised herself when she agreed to go with Jace.

But then, she got what he meant when he said that he *liked* her. She liked him, too. And not because he was tall and lean and handsome with thick, glossy dark hair and velvet-brown eyes. Not because he smelled of soap and a nice, clean, subtle, probably very expensive aftershave. Not because he was undeniably hot.

She didn't care about hot. Her life had pretty much crumbled to nothing a week before. Finding a hot guy—or any guy for that matter— was the last thing on her mind.

Jocelyn liked Jason because he made her laugh. Because, even though he carried himself like he owned the world, she could see in his eyes that he really was flummoxed by life, that he used to be one guy and now he wasn't that guy anymore. That he wasn't all that familiar with the guy he was now. Joss could relate to that kind of confusion. It was exactly the confusion she felt.

She entered the Rib Shack on Jace's arm. The casual, Western-themed restaurant was packed. Jason Traub, as it turned out, had a very large family.

"Jason, there you are," said a good-looking older woman with a slim figure and sleek light brown hair. "I was starting to wonder if you'd already left."

"No, Ma," Jace said, his charming smile not quite masking the wariness in his eyes. "I'm still here."

Jace's mother turned a bright glance on Joss. "Hello."

Jace made the introductions. Joss smiled and nodded at his mom, whose name was Claudia.

Claudia asked, "Do you live here in town, Jocelyn?"

"No, I'm from Sacramento."

Jace said, "Joss is staying here at the resort."

"With your family?" his mom quizzed. Claudia had that look, Joss thought, the look of a mother on the trail of every bit of information she could gather about the new girl her son had brought to the family party.

"I'm here on my own," Joss told her. "Having a great time, too. I love the spa. And the shopping in the resort boutiques. And I'm learning to play golf." All of it on Kenny Donovan's dime, thank you very much.

An ordinary-looking man a few years older than Jace's mom stepped up and took Claudia's arm. Claudia beamed at him, her golden-brown eyes glowing with affection. "Darling, this is Jocelyn, Jason's new friend. Jocelyn, my husband, Pete—we're staying here at the resort, too. A romantic getaway, just us two old folks in the Governor's Suite."

Joss was in the Honeymoon Suite, but she didn't say so. It would only be asking for more questions than she was prepared to answer at the moment—which was kind of amusing in a dark sort of way. She hadn't even hesitated to tell Jace that she'd run away from her own wedding. But somehow, with everyone else, well, she didn't want to go there. And she really appreciated that Jace was keeping his mouth shut about it.

He seemed like a great guy. And his parents were adorable, she thought. So much in love, so attentive to each other. There should be more couples in the world like Claudia and Pete.

Claudia said, "I hope you'll join us for dinner tomorrow night, Jocelyn. It will be at the home of Jason's twin, Jackson, and Jackson's wife, Laila. They have a nice little property not far from town."

"Yeah, you should come," Jace said with enthusiasm. "I'll take you."

Joss gave him a look that said he shouldn't push it and asked, "You have a twin?"

Claudia laughed. "A fraternal twin. Jackson is older by an hour and five minutes. That makes Jason my youngest son. I also have one daughter, Rose. She's the baby of the family. Dillon, Ethan and Corey are the older boys."

Joss did the math. "Wow, six kids. I'm jealous. I was an only child. My mother raised me on her own."

Claudia reached out and touched Joss's shoulder, a fond kind of touch. "Sweet girl," she said softly. And Joss felt all warm and fuzzy inside. "You come to dinner tomorrow night," Jace's mom said again. "We would love to have you join us."

"Thank you," Joss said, and left it at that.

A few moments later, Jace led her out onto the Rib Shack's patio where the band was set up but taking a break. They found a reasonably quiet corner where they could talk without having to shout.

"My mother likes you," Jace said.

"You say that like you're not sure if it's good or bad."

"Yeah, well, Ma thinks I got my heart broken and she

really wants me to be happy. She's decided I only need to meet another woman, the *right* woman, so I can get married and settle down like my brothers and my sister. Now she'll be finding all kinds of ways to throw us together."

"We'll resist, of course."

"Of course we will."

"Who broke your heart, Jace?"

He hedged. "It's a long story."

"I told you mine," she teased.

He looked distinctly uncomfortable. "Well, you know, this isn't the place or the time."

She got the message. "You don't want to tell me—and you know what? That's okay."

"Whew." He made a show of wiping nonexistent sweat from his brow. "And even though I hate to give my mother the wrong idea about us, I think you ought to come to dinner at Jackson's tomorrow. You know, just to be social."

She gave him a slow look. She knew he was up to something.

And he was. He admitted, "I also want you there because I like you."

"Uh-huh. What else? Give it to me straight, Jace."

"Fair enough. If you come, everyone will think we're together—I mean *really* together, as in more than friends. And that means my family will stop trying to set me up."

"You want me to pretend to be your girlfriend?"

"You don't have to pretend anything. If you're with me, they'll assume there's something going on. It doesn't matter if you tell them that we're just friends. They won't believe you. It doesn't matter that *I* will tell them we're just friends. They'll only be certain we're in denial about all that we mean to each other."

"Still, it seems dishonest."

"Is it our fault if people insist on jumping to conclusions?"

Strangely, she found that she *wanted* to go to dinner at his brother's house. "I'll think about it."

"Good. And don't let my mother get you alone. She'll only start in about the family business and how she needs me in Midland and she hopes that *you* will be open to the idea of moving to Texas because she's already hearing wedding bells in our future."

"What *is* the family business anyway?"

"I didn't tell you? It's oil. Except for my oldest brother, Dillon, who's a doctor, we're all in oil."

She laughed. "Knee-deep?"

"All the way over our heads in it, trust me. We're Traub Oil Industries. I was a vice president in the Midland office. I quit the first of April. I was supposed to be out of there by the end of May. My mother and Pete kept finding reasons why I had to stay. I finally escaped just this past Wednesday. I'm never going back."

"You sound determined."

"Believe me, I am."

"How come you call your dad Pete?"

"He's my stepdad. My father, Charles, was something of a legend in the oil business. He died in an accident on a rig when I was little. My mom married Pete about two years later. Her last name is Wexler now. None of us were happy when she married him. We were loyal to our dad and we resented Pete."

"We?"

"My brothers, my sister and I. But Pete's not only a good man, he's also a patient one. He won all of us over eventually. Pete had a heart attack a couple of years ago. We almost lost him. That really taught us how much he means to us."

"It's so obvious he's head over heels in love with your mom."

"Yes, he is. A man like that is damn hard to hate." He took her arm. "Come on, I want you to meet my brothers."

They wandered back inside. Joss met Dillon and Ethan and Corey and Jace's twin, Jackson. The two did look a lot alike—meaning tall, dark and handsome. But it wasn't the least difficult to tell them apart. Joss also met the Traub boys' only sister, Rose, and Rose's husband, Austin, and she visited with the wives of Jason's brothers. She liked them all, with Lizzie, Ethan's wife, possibly being her favorite.

Lizzie Traub was tall and sturdily built, with slightly wild-looking dark blond hair and a no-nonsense way about her. She owned a bakery, the Mountain Bluebell, in town. Everyone said that Lizzie baked the best muffins in Montana.

And beyond Jace's brothers and sister and their spouses, there were Traub cousins, too: DJ and Dax and their wives Allaire and Shandie. And also Clay and Forrest Traub, two cowboys from Rust Creek Falls, which was about three hundred miles from Thunder Canyon.

Joss was starting to wonder how she was going to keep all their names straight when a woman named Melba Landry, who was Lizzie Traub's great-aunt, caught up with them. A big woman with a stern face, Melba possessed a truly impressive bosom. Joss tried not to laugh as the energetic old woman cornered Jace and insisted she wanted to see him at her church the next morning.

"Of course he'll come," Joss told Melba. "There's nothing Jace enjoys more than a good Sunday service."

Beside her, Jace made a low groaning sound.

And Melba turned her sharp hazel eyes on Joss. "Excellent. I want to see you there, too, young lady."

"Well, now, I don't exactly know if I—"

"We'll be there," Jace promised. Joss elbowed him in the ribs, but he didn't relent.

Aunt Melba said, "Wonderful. The service begins at ten." And she sailed off to corner some other unsuspecting potential churchgoer.

The party continued. It really was fun. Joss forgot her troubles and just had a good time. She spotted Theresa Duvall dancing with a tall, lean cowboy, one of Jace's cousins from Rust Creek Falls. Theresa clung to that cowboy like paint. She didn't seem the least upset that things hadn't worked out for her with Jace.

Joss and Jace danced. He was a good dancer. Plus, he kept to their agreement about just being friends. He didn't hold her too close. She swayed in his arms and thought how good it felt to be held by him. His body and hers just kind of fit together. He was a great guy and if things were different she would definitely be attracted to him. Really, the longer they danced, the more she started thinking that she wouldn't mind at all if he did hold her closer....

But no. That wouldn't be a good idea. The last thing she needed right now was a new man in her life. She liked Jace as a person, but still. He *was* a man. All man. And she wasn't trusting any man. Not now.

Not for a long, long time, if ever.

It was after ten when the party broke up. She and Jace were among the last to leave. They wandered out to the lobby together and then kind of naturally turned for the elevators side-by-side.

The Honeymoon Suite was on the top floor. The doors opened and they left the elevator.

At the door, she paused, key card in hand. "If I let you in, you have to promise not to put a move on me."

He looked hurt. "Joss, come on. How many ways can

I tell you? I need a friend. You need a friend. That's what we've got going on here. It's *all* we've got going on here."

She chewed her lower lip for a moment. "All right. I believe you." And then she stuck her key in the slot and pushed the door wide.

He followed her in, through the skylit foyer area into the living/dining room, which had floor-to-ceiling windows with a spectacular view. "Nice."

"Hey, only the best for Kenny Donovan's runaway bride." She headed for the wet bar. "How about a little champagne and caviar? On Kenny, of course."

"Got a beer?"

She gave him one from the fridge and grabbed a ginger ale for herself. "Make yourself at home." He took a fat leather easy chair and she shucked off her shoes and curled up on the sofa.

And they talked. About his family. About the party at the Rib Shack. About how they both thought Lizzie was great and how Lizzie's aunt Melba cracked them up.

"So how long are you here for?" he asked.

She thought how much she liked his voice. It was deep and warm and made her want to cuddle up against him—which she was *not*, under any circumstances, going to do. Ever. "Another week. As long as Kenny doesn't put a stop on his platinum card, I am having my whole two-week un-honeymoon."

"And then?"

"Back to Sacramento. To find a job. And a new place to live."

"We have so much in common," he said. "I'm here for a week, too."

"You told me. The family reunion. And then after that?"

"I suppose I'll have to get a life. But I'm not even going to think about that yet."

"Jace, I like the way you completely avoid anything remotely resembling responsibility. Aunt Melba would *so* not approve."

"Thank you, Joss. I do my best." He tipped his longneck at her. "I'm glad we're friends. Let's be *best* friends."

"All right. I'm up for that."

"Best friends for a week," he declared.

She held up her index finger and reminded him, "No benefits."

He looked at her from under his thick dark brows. "You know you're killin' me here. Have I, in any way, put any kind of move on you?"

"Nope, not a one."

"Then can we be done with the constant reminders about how I'm not supposed to try and get you naked?"

She saluted him with a hand to her forehead. "You got it. I believe you. You are not going to make any attempt whatsoever to get into my pants. Even if you *are* a man."

"Your trust is deeply touching."

The phone rang. It was on the side table next to the sofa, so she reached over and picked it up. "What?"

"Jocelyn, honestly. Is that any way to answer the phone?"

Without even thinking about it, Joss lowered her feet to the rug and sat up straighter. "Mom, hey." She ran a hand back through her hair. "What's up?"

"How can you ask me that? You know I'm worried sick about you."

"I'm fine. Really. Don't worry."

"When are you coming home?"

"I told you. A week from tomorrow." She sent Jace a sheepish glance and mouthed the word *Sorry*.

He shrugged to let her know it wasn't a big deal. Then he got up and went over to the wall of windows. He stood gazing out. She indulged in a long, slow look at him, from his fancy tooled boots, up over his lean legs and hips in crisp denim, his wide shoulders in a beautifully tailored midnight-blue Western shirt. His hair was thick and dark. She had no doubt it would be silky to the touch.

A great-looking guy. And a considerate one. It was kind of him to pretend to admire the view to give her the space she needed to take this unwelcome call. There ought to be more guys in the world like him.

Her mom said, "This is all just a big misunderstanding. You realize that, don't you? Kenny would never—"

"Mom." She struggled to keep her voice calm and even. "I *saw* him with Kimberly. There was no misunderstanding what I saw."

"Kimberly is terribly upset, too. She's hurt you would think such horrible, cruel things about her."

"Oh, please. Don't get me started on Kimberly. I don't want to talk about this anymore, Mom. I really don't."

"Kenny came to see me this evening."

Joss gasped. "He *what*?" She must have said it kind of loud because Jace glanced back at her, those sexy dark eyes full of concern. She shook her head at him. He turned to face the window again and she told her mother, "He has no right to bother you. None. Ever again."

"Honey, he's not bothering me. He loves you. He wants to work things out with you. He's crushed that you left him at the altar the way you did. You've humiliated him, but still, he forgives you and only wants to work things out so you two can be together as you were meant to be."

There was a crystal bowl full of expensive chocolates on the coffee table. Joss resisted the blinding urge to grab it and fling it at the far wall. "Mom, listen. Listen carefully. I am not going to get back together with Kenny. Ever. He and I are done. Finished. As over as it gets."

"If only your father hadn't left us. You wouldn't be so mistrustful of men. You wouldn't ruin the best chance you're ever going to get with a good man who will give you the kind of life you deserve."

She replied through clenched teeth. "There are so many ways I don't know how to respond to that."

"Just come home, honey. Come home right away."

"Mom, I'm hanging up now. I love you very much and I'll be home in a week."

"Jocelyn. Jocelyn, wait..."

But Joss didn't wait. She hung up the phone. And then she stared at it hard, *daring* it to ring again.

But apparently, her mother had come to her senses at least minimally and decided to leave awful enough alone.

For tonight anyway.

At the window, Jace turned. "Bad?"

She covered her face with her hands. "Yeah, beyond bad."

He left the window and came to her, walking softly in those fancy boots of his. She only heard his approach because she was listening for it. "Want to talk about it?"

"Ugh."

"Come on."

She lowered her hands and met his waiting eyes. He was standing across the coffee table from her, his hands in his pockets, accepting of whatever she might say, willing to listen. Ready to understand. She tipped her head at the cushion beside her. He took her invitation, crossing around the low table, dropping down next to her, stretching his arm out along the back of the couch in an invitation of his own.

An invitation she couldn't pass up at that moment. With a sad little sigh, she leaned her head on his shoulder. He smoothed her hair, but only lightly, and then draped his big arm around her.

It was a nice moment. Comforting. He was so large and warm and solid. And he smelled so clean and manly. And she really needed a strong shoulder to lean on. Just for a minute or two.

She said, "That was my mom."

"Yeah, I got that much."

"I told you she raised me on her own, didn't I?"

"You mentioned that, yeah."

"My dad disappeared when I was two. My mom says he just told her he was through one day and walked out. We never heard from him again."

"That's rough, Joss. Really rough." He squeezed her shoulder, a touch that comforted, that seemed to acknowledge how hard it had been for her. "It can really mess with your mind, to lose your dad when you're only a kid. It can leave you feeling like you're on the outside looking in— at all your friends and their happy, *whole* families. You grow up knowing what normal is. It's what all the *other* kids have."

She realized he was speaking from personal experience. "How old were you when your dad died?"

"Jackson and I were six."

"So at least you knew him, your dad."

"Kind of. He was always working, making his mark on the world, you could say. But yeah, we all looked up to him with stars in our eyes. We felt safe, just knowing he was our dad. He was one of those guys who really fills up a room. Rose always claims it was worse for her than for us boys. She never knew him—well, at least she doesn't remember him. She was two when he was killed."

"Same age I was when my dad left. And I don't remember him either. All I have is the…absence of him."

She pulled away enough to meet Jace's eyes. "You really don't need to hear this. You're sweet to be so understanding, but it's old news and it's got nothing to do with you."

He reached for her, pulled her back down to him. She started to resist, but then, well, why not, if he was willing to listen? She gave in and sagged against him, settling her head against his shoulder again—and yeah, she'd promised herself she would never cuddle up with him. But this wasn't cuddling. This was only leaning. And there was nothing wrong with a little leaning when a girl needed comfort from a friend.

"Keep talkin'," he said. "What's your mom's name?"

"RaeEllen. Her maiden name was Louvacek, but she kept my father's name, never changed it back. She always said she only wanted a good guy to stand by her. But I don't think she went looking after my dad left. It was like she…gave up when it came to men. She never dated when I was growing up, not that I can remember. She worked at Safeway, eventually moving up to managing her own store, which she still does to this day. And she took care of me. She was a good mom, a strict mom. And she always wanted the best for me. To her, Kenny seemed like a dream come true."

"So for some reason, she decided she could trust the cheater?"

"He was always good to her—kissing up to her really, it seems to me, in hindsight. When she would have us over for dinner, he would bring her flowers every time and fall all over her praising her cooking. And she knew how well he was doing at work, getting promotions, one after the other. She just…bought Kenny's act, hook, line and sinker. She refuses to believe that the thing with Kimberly even happened. Kenny's convinced her that I've blown an 'innocent encounter' all out of proportion."

"Convinced her? You're saying she's *speaking* to him, after what he did to you?"

"Because she doesn't believe he did anything bad, I guess she figures she's got no reason *not* to speak to him."

"She's your mom and I won't speak ill of her. But I will say she ought to get her loyalties straight."

"Hah, I wish. When it comes to Kenny, she's got on her rose-colored glasses and I've yet to convince her she really needs to take them off. I try to see it from her point of view. She finally decided to give another man a break, to trust Kenny—for my sake. And now she just can't bear to admit she got it wrong again."

"I guess it's understandable," Jace said. "But still. You're her daughter. She should be backing you up."

"Yeah, I wish. You know how I told you I had doubts about Kenny before I caught him with Kimberly?"

"I remember."

"Well, I went to my mom and confided in her. I told her that Kenny wasn't the guy I loved anymore, that sometimes I felt like I didn't even know him, he was so different from who he used to be. She was the one who convinced me my fears were groundless, that I only had a very normal case of pre-wedding jitters, that Kenny was a wonderful man and it was all going to be fine."

Jace touched her hair again, gently, an easing kind of touch. "So your judgment about the guy was solid. And your mom couldn't—and still can't—let herself see the truth. I'm betting she'll get the picture in time."

"I hope so."

"And the main thing is that you didn't go through with it. You had the guts to turn and walk away. You're a strong woman. And you're going to be fine."

Joss could have stayed in Jace's arms all night. But she'd had her head on his shoulder for several minutes now—too long really. She needed to pull herself together, no matter how good it felt to lean on him.

She sat up and retreated to her end of the sofa. That time, he didn't try to stop her, and she was glad that he didn't. If she was going to have a man for a friend—even just for a week—it was nice to think he was the kind of guy who would know when to put his arm around her. And when to let her go.

"Mostly," she said, "I think I'm doing pretty well, you know?"

He gave her a slow nod, his dark eyes steady on hers.

"I tell myself I'm getting past what happened last Saturday. But every time my mom calls, she just brings the whole mess into painful focus all over again. Her blindness to the reality of the situation makes me see way too clearly what a huge mistake I made." She held up her thumb and forefinger, with just a sliver of space between them. "I got this close to marrying a guy who cheated on me on our wedding day—and with my own cousin, no less."

"But you *didn't* marry him. Focus on that, Joss."

She braced her elbow on the sofa arm and rested her chin on her hand. "You're right, I didn't. But I did quit my job for that rotten, no-good cheater. I gave up my cute apartment. When I go home, I'll be starting all over again."

"Maybe you can get your job back."

"Maybe I can. We'll see." She straightened her spine. What she wanted right now was a long bath accompanied by an equally long, totally self-indulgent crying jag. "Thank you for listening—and I need to stop whining."

He gave her a slightly crooked smile. "I have the strangest feeling you're giving me the boot." He picked up his beer from the coffee table and downed the last of it.

"It's only, well, lately talking to my mom really brings me down." She tried to think of something snappy and charming to say, so they could end the evening on a happier note. But right then, she was all out of snappy, totally bereft of charming.

He rose. "It's the great thing about a best friend. Even a best friend for a week. You don't have to explain anything. All you have to say is good night."

Jace thought about Joss all the way out to Jackson and Laila's place.

He hoped she was okay. And he hoped he'd done the right thing by leaving when she asked him to.

What else could he have done? She'd had that look. Like all she wanted was to get into bed—alone—and pull the covers up over head. He'd figured the best thing he could do for her right then was to get lost.

Jackson and Laila had ten beautiful, wooded acres with a big two-story farmhouse, a barn and a paddock where they kept a few horses. When Jace pulled up in front of the house, the lights were off upstairs. But through the shut blinds of the front room's picture window, Jace could make out the faint glow of the flatscreen TV. He figured he would find his brother in there, channel-surfing, waiting up.

Jace was right.

Jackson sat in his favorite recliner, the mutt he and Laila had adopted from the animal shelter snoozing at his feet. Jace entered the room and Jackson turned off the TV. "Beer?"

"No, thanks." Jace dropped into the other recliner and popped out the footrest. "Good party at the Rib Shack."

Jackson grunted. "Ethan get after you?"

"Yeah."

"He thinks he's going to talk you into coming in with us."

"It's not gonna happen."

"Yeah." Jackson set the remote on the table by his chair. "I told him that. More than once. But you know how he can be when he gets an idea in his head."

Jace closed his eyes. He felt comfortable. Easy. It was always like that with him and Jackson. Even when they fought—which they used to do a lot when they were younger—there was a certain understanding between them. They didn't need a lot of words. They just accepted each other.

The mutt's collar jangled as he scratched himself. The dog's name was Einstein. He wasn't much to look at, but Jackson claimed he was really smart.

Jackson said, "You know, I thought you said you'd sworn off women. But you're in Thunder Canyon barely twenty-four hours and already you've got a girl."

"No, I don't." Jace gave the denial in an easy tone, knowing his brother wouldn't believe him.

"Shame on you, Jason. Lying to your own twin brother."

"Joss is great. I liked her the first minute I saw her. But it's not like that. We're just friends."

Jackson chuckled. "Yeah, and if you think I believe that, I've got some oceanfront property in Kansas to sell you."

"I mean it. We're friends. She's here for another week. I'll be hanging around with her if she'll put up with me, but nothing's going to happen between us."

"Hey, whatever you say. I'm just glad to see you taking an interest in a woman again. And she seems like a great girl to me. Laila liked her, too. So did Ma."

Jace made a low noise that could have meant anything and hid his smile. His family—including his twin—were all so predictable. He showed up with a woman at his side, and they couldn't believe there was nothing but friendship going on.

Which suited him just fine.

Jackson spoke again, gruffly this time. "And it's good, that you came back to Montana finally."

Jace knew he'd hurt his brother's feelings by not coming to Thunder Canyon over the holidays—and worse, he hadn't been there for Jackson and Laila's Valentine's Day wedding.

Time to try and get that behind them. "I'm sorry, Jackson, that I didn't come for the holidays when you invited me. And missing your wedding? That was the worst. I know it was wrong of me not to be there."

Jackson didn't answer for a full sixty seconds at least. Finally, he grunted. "I was pretty miffed at the time—especially that you didn't show to be my best man. But I'm over it."

Jace confessed, "I didn't know my ass from up for a while there. I didn't come at Christmas because of Tricia." He said her name and waited to feel miserable. Instead, he realized, he felt perfectly okay. Apparently, he really was putting all that behind him. "The last thing Tricia said she wanted was to 'head for the sticks over the holidays'—her words, not mine. I didn't even argue with her. I was gone, gone, gone. It was 'Whatever Tricia wants, Tricia gets,' as far as I was concerned. And then it all went to hell. For a couple of months after New Year's, I was operating strictly on autopilot. I went to work and I went home. Then you and Laila decided you wanted a Valentine's Day wedding. I was a mess. I just wasn't up for it."

"Sounds like you're better off without Tricia Lavelle."

"I am. A lot better off. I see that now. But at the time, I was one-hundred-percent certain it was the real thing with her. You know how I've always been. Not a guy who ever gets serious over any woman. So when I actually thought it was love, I went for it. All the way. How wrong could I get? It was a rude awakening when it ended, let me tell you."

"Rough, huh?"

"Bad love will do it to you every time—not that it *was* love. Not that I even have a clue what love is."

Jackson slid him a cautious glance. "The whole family kind of wonders if you're really over her yet."

Jace tried to picture Tricia's face in his mind. Somehow, the image wouldn't quite take form. And then he thought of Joss—her great laugh, how much fun it was just to talk to her, those big brown eyes and all that gorgeous cinnamon-shot coffee-colored hair. He had no trouble picturing his new best friend at all. "Oh, yeah," he told his twin. "I'm over Tricia. I'm ready for a brand-new start."

Jackson chuckled. "Good. You quit your job and you don't want to live in Midland anymore, so it looks to me like a new start is exactly what you're going to get."

Chapter Three

The phone by the bed was ringing.

With a groan of protest, Joss lifted her head from the pillow and squinted at the bedside clock. Nine-fifteen in the morning. Not what you'd call early. Unless you'd lain wide awake until the wee hours, stewing over your bad choices, angry at your mother, wondering what you were going to do with your life....

And the phone was still ringing.

Surely, eventually, it would cycle back to the front desk, because she didn't want to answer it. Who could it be except her mother calling to beg her to come back to Kenny—or Kenny calling to demand she stop being "petty" and quit making such a big deal over a tiny little incident that had meant exactly nothing?

Hah.

She reached over and grabbed the phone and barked into it, "I do not want to hear another word about it. Do you understand?"

The voice of her new best friend answered, "Aunt Melba is going to be disappointed. You know she was really looking forward to seeing you in church."

Joss dragged herself to a sitting position and swiped her tangled hair back off her face. "Ugh. And wait a minute. Did I actually tell her I would be there?"

"No," Jace admitted. "You hedged. Aunt Melba assumed. *I* said you'd be there."

"So thoughtful of you to make my commitments for me."

"Did I mention I brought coffee?"

"Brought? Where *are* you?"

"Waiting in the hallway outside your door."

She grinned. She couldn't stop herself. "That is so not fair."

"Vanilla latte. Just sayin'."

"All right, all right. You sold me." She hung up, grabbed her robe and belted it as she hurried to let him in. When she opened the door, he held out the tall Starbucks cup. She took it, sipped and gestured him inside, shutting the door and then leaning back against it with a sigh. "Yum. Thank you."

"You're welcome." He gave her one of those knock-your-socks-off smiles of his. Really, he was looking great, freshly showered and shaved, in a different pair of expensive boots, tan slacks, a button-down shirt and a nicely cut sport coat.

She grumbled, "At least *someone* got a good night's sleep."

He took in her blenderized hair, the robe, her bare feet—and her grumpy expression. "Sorry to wake you up."

"No, you're not."

"You're right. I'm not." He took her shoulders, turned her around and pointed her toward the bedroom. "Go on.

Get ready. We don't want to be late. Aunt Melba would never forgive us."

"Who's this 'we,' cowboy?" She muttered over her shoulder, but she went. And she took her latte with her.

Twenty minutes later, she emerged feeling church-ready in a pink silk blouse and an oyster-white skirt, with a favorite pair of low-heeled slingbacks in a slightly lighter pink than the blouse. She'd pinned her hair up loosely and worn the pearl earrings her mom had given her when she graduated from high school.

Jace said, "You look amazing."

She realized she felt better. A lot better. Jace seemed to have that effect on her. He cheered her up, had her looking on the bright side, thinking that something exciting and fun could be happening any minute. She grabbed her pink purse and off they went.

Thunder Canyon Community Church, Jace explained, was in what the locals called Old Town, with its narrower, tree-lined streets and buildings that had stood since pioneer times.

Joss loved the church on sight. It was, to her, the perfect little white clapboard church, with tall windows all along the sides and a single spire in front that housed the bell tower. A mature box elder tree shaded the church steps and the small square of front lawn.

The doors into the reception area stood wide as the church bell finished chiming. Inside, the organist was playing something suitably reverent, yet inviting. People smiled and said hello. Melba was there, wearing a blue flowered dress and a little blue hat, standing guard over the open guestbook. She greeted them with an approving smile and showed them where to sign.

Joss signed her name and "Sacramento, California,"

for her address. She felt a little tug of glumness, to be reminded that she didn't have a place to call her own anymore, that all her household possessions were packed up
in boxes and stacked in a rented storage unit, waiting for
her to figure out what to do with her life.

But the glumness quickly passed when Jace took her
arm. They entered the sanctuary and the organ music
swelled louder. The sun shone in the tall windows and
Jace's brother Ethan signaled them up to a pew near the
front. Lizzie, on Ethan's other side, leaned across her husband to greet them as they sat down.

The service was as lovely and comforting as the little
white church itself. Joss even knew the words to a couple
of the hymns. The pleasant-faced pastor gave a sermon on
God's grace, and somehow all of Joss's problems seemed
insignificant, workable. Just part of life.

After the service, Lizzie reminded them that she would
love to treat them to free muffins at her bakery. Meanwhile, Ethan said he wanted Jace to take a tour of his
Thunder Canyon office building.

Jace said, "No, thanks. Gotta go," and herded Joss toward the exit.

Melba was at her post by the guestbook. She told them
how glad she was that they had come. "And I want to see
you both at the Historical Society Museum very soon. I've
been helping out there several times a week. Thunder Canyon is a fascinating place with a rich history. While you're
in town, you might as well learn something."

Joss only smiled and nodded. Jace ended up promising
he would drop by the museum soon.

From the church, they went over to Lizzie's bakery,
where they split a complimentary blueberry muffin and
each had a ham and egg croissant and a tall glass of fresh-
squeezed orange juice. Jace seemed to know everyone. He

introduced her to a guy named Connor McFarlane and his wife, Tori, who was pregnant and just starting to show. Tori taught at the high school. Connor was not only the heir to the McFarlane House hotel chain, but he was also a major investor in the resort.

Joss also met Grant Clifton, his wife, Stephanie, and their little boy, AJ. The child was seventeen months old and adorable, with golden curls and a sunny smile. Stephanie let Joss hold him. He was so sweet and friendly, dimpling at her, laying his plump little hand against her cheek, even leaning his blond head on her shoulder. Joss gave him back to his mom with a little tug of regret. She wished she could have several little ones just like him.

Maybe someday…

Grant Clifton seemed vaguely familiar. When he explained that he managed the resort, Joss realized she'd seen him behind the front desk once and another time at the resort's best restaurant, the Gallatin Room.

That was the great thing about a small town like this one, Joss thought. You could get to know almost everyone. And when you walked down the street, people just naturally smiled and said hi.

After they left the bakery, Jace took her hand. They started strolling west down Main Street, enjoying the sunshine, looking in the windows of the quaint little shops. It felt good to have her hand in his. Really good. Maybe *too* good.

She let him lead her along for another block before she realized they were going the wrong direction and hung back. "Hey, wait a minute. Your car's that way." She pointed over her shoulder. They'd left his fancy SUV back near the church.

"So? It's not going anywhere." He tugged on her hand. "Come on, I want to show you the Hitching Post—you know, that great old bar and restaurant I told you about yesterday?"

She eased her fingers from his grip. "Right, the one where you hooked up with Theresa Duvall."

He stood there on the corner, his dark hair showing glints of bronze in the sun, and looked at her reproachfully. "What did I do?"

She hung her head and stared down at her pretty pink slingbacks. "Not a thing. Sorry, that was low."

"Yeah, it was. But I'll get over it. Hey, look at me."

Reluctantly, she raised her head. His eyes gleamed. With just a look, he made her want to smile at him. But she didn't.

On that corner was a homey-looking restaurant with flowered café curtains in the windows. The restaurant was closed. He stepped into the alcove by the door and tipped his head at her, signaling her to join him.

"We can't stand here on the corner forever," she groused, as an older couple walked past her and went on across the street.

He chuckled. "*We're* not standing on the corner. *You* are." He waved her into the alcove with him. "Come on. Come here…"

Reluctantly, she went. "What?"

He whispered in her ear, "I love the Hitching Post."

"Whoop-de-do." She spun her index finger in the air. "Joss, about your attitude?"

"Yeah?"

"Lighten up."

She knew he had a point. "Okay, okay. So why do you love the Hitching Post?"

He sat on the wide window ledge next to the door. "Good memories, that's why. When I was a kid, we always used to go there every time we came to town. My dad would take us. We'd get burgers and fries and milk-shakes on the restaurant side, where they allowed kids, and it was a special thing, with all of us together, with my dad relaxed and really *with* us, you know, focused on the family? He used to call us his little mavericks. I thought that was so cool. It seems to me that we went to the Hitching Post often, even though I know that we couldn't have. I was only six when he died. And we only got to visit Thunder Canyon now and then in the summer. But I do remember clearly that on our last visit here before he died, my dad took me to the Hitching Post alone, the two of us. For some reason, Jackson didn't even get to come. It was just me and my dad and I was the happiest kid on the planet." He rose from the window ledge. His eyes holding hers, he took a few stray strands of her hair and guided them back behind her ear. A small shiver cascaded through her and she wanted to move even closer to him—at the same time as she knew she ought to step back.

"Okay," she said softly. "I get it now—why that place is so special to you."

"Good." His caressing tone hovered somewhere on the border between gentle and intimate. "I mean, nothing against Theresa, but she's not what I think about when the Hitching Post comes to mind."

Joss felt rotten, and not only for razzing him about Theresa. There was also the uncomfortable fact that she was starting to wonder what it might feel like to kiss him. Plus, she was flat-out envious of him.

He had a great big, terrific family. And he'd had a dad, a *real* dad, until he was six, a dad who hadn't left him willingly. Then, when he lost his dad, he'd gotten kind Pete Wexler as a stepdad. Her dad, on the other hand, had walked out before she even had a chance to know him.

Her family consisted of her and her mom and right now, her mom only lectured her.

He was grinning again. "So come on, let's go to the Hitching Post."

"I don't know. It's past noon. Maybe I should just go back up to the resort."

His grin faded. He blew out a breath. "Okay, Joss. what's up with you?"

"I just…I feel low now, that's all."

"Why? A few minutes ago you seemed to be having a great time."

"I was."

"So what happened? You realized you were having too much fun?"

She opened her mouth to tell him how off-base he was, but then she saw that he might actually have a point. "I keep thinking I can't just hang around in Montana doing nothing forever."

"You're right, but there's no problem. You're only hanging around in Montana doing nothing for another week. Then you can go back home and knock yourself out finding another job and a new apartment."

Now she felt hurt. Really, her emotions were all over the map today. "How can you make a joke of it, Jace? It's not a joke."

"I know it's not." He said the words gently. And then he asked, "Are you bored?"

"No!" She wasn't. Not in the least. "Are you kidding? I'm having a great time—or I was, just like you said, until a few minutes ago. And then, I don't know, all at once I felt low and cranky."

Jace stuffed his hands in his pockets. And then he just stood there next to the glass-topped, café-curtained door of the closed restaurant, watching her, waiting.

She busted herself. "Okay, my life's a mess. And right now, I feel guilty about it. I mean, at least up at the resort I'm busy being defiant, you know? Having my un-honeymoon, hating all men. But here, with you…" She didn't know quite how to explain it.

Jace did it for her. "Here, with me, you're having a good time. And you don't feel you have the right to have a good time. And not only are you having a good time when you don't have the right to, but you're also having it with a *man*." He widened his eyes and spoke in a spooky half whisper. "A man you just met…yesterday." She didn't know whether to laugh or punch him in the arm. Then he put on a look of pretend disapproval. "Face it, Joss. Your mother would never approve."

"This is not about my mother." She said it with way too much heat. "And I really, well, I just want to go back to the resort now. Please."

He gave her a long look. And then he nodded. "All right, but would you do one little favor for me first?"

She resisted the sudden need to tap her foot. "Fine. What?"

"The Town Square's back there about two blocks. It's that small park we passed after we left the bakery?"

"I remember it. What about it?"

"We'll stop there, sit on a bench under a tree and talk a little bit more. And then I'll take you back up Thunder Mountain."

She folded her arms across her middle and looked at him sideways. "Talk about what?"

"I don't know. The weather, the Dallas Cowboys, the meaning of life…"

"Oh, very funny."

"We'll just talk, that's all, about whatever subject pops

into our heads. And not for long, I promise. Half an hour, max. Then it's back to the resort for you."

She accused, "I know you're going to try and make me feel better about everything. Don't deny it."

"I wouldn't dream of denying it. Yes, Jocelyn Marie, the ugly truth is I am going to try and make you feel better. That is my evil plan. So what do you say? The Town Square? A measly little half hour of your time?"

He didn't wait for her answer, but only reached for her hand again.

The little park was a lovely, grassy, tree-shaded place. They found a bench under a willow, the drooping branches like a veil, hiding them from the rest of the world.

"Nice, huh?" he asked her, after brushing a few leaves off the bench seat and gallantly gesturing for her to sit first. She did, smoothing her skirt under her, crossing her legs and folding her hands around her knee. He dropped down next to her. "Kind of private. If we whisper, no one will even know we're here."

She laughed. He really was so charming. "How *old* are you, ten?"

"Only at heart. Tell me a secret."

She gave him a deadpan stare. "You first."

He thought it over, shrugged. "Once I kissed a toad."

"Eeww. Why?"

"Jackson dared me. He was always a troublemaker. And I was his second banana, you know? He would come up with these wild-ass ideas and I felt honor-bound to go along. But then, somehow, if there was something gross involved, he would always manage to get me to go first. Then he would mock me. Once I kissed the toad, he told me I was going to get warts on my lips."

"Oh, that's just mean."

"He could be, yeah. But he's also…the best, you know?"

"How?"

"He'd take a bullet for me. For anyone in the family. That's how he is. You can count on him. Even in the old days, when you never knew what stunt he was going to pull next, you always knew he had your back."

"So you're saying he's settled down, then—from the days when he made you kiss that toad?"

Jace nodded. "He was the bad boy of the family. He drank too much and he chased women and he swore that no female was ever going to hogtie him. But then he met Laila. She changed his tune right quick. Now he's got a ring on his finger and contentment in his heart. I've never seen him as happy as he is now." He studied her face. His gaze was warm. She thought how she was kind of glad he'd insisted they come here before he took her back up the mountain, how being with him really did lift her spirits. "Your turn," he said. "Cough up that secret."

"I always wanted to get married," she heard herself say. "Ever since I was little. I wanted…a real family. I wanted the family I never had. A man I could love and trust. Several kids. Growing up, it was always so quiet at home, with just my mom and me. My mom likes things tidy. I learned early to clean up after myself. So our small house was neat and orderly, with a hushed kind of feeling about it. I dreamed of one of those big, old Craftsman-style houses, with the pillars in front and the wide, deep front porch— you know the kind?"

"I do."

"I dreamed of bikes on their sides on the front lawn, of toys all over the living room floor, of spilled milk and crayon drawings scrawled in bright colors on the walls, because the children who lived there were rambunctious and adventurous and couldn't resist a whole wall to color on. I dreamed of a bunch of laughing, crying, screaming, chattering kids, everybody talking over everybody else, of music on the stereo and the TV on too loud. And I saw myself in the middle of all of it, loving every minute of it. Me, *the Mom*. And I saw my husband coming in the door and stepping over the scattered toys to take me in his arms after a hard day's work. I pictured him kissing me, a real, hot, toe-curling kiss, the kind that would make our older kids groan and tell us to get a room."

"Wow," he said. "That's a lot better secret than kissing a toad."

A leaf drifted down into her lap. She brushed it away and confessed, "I always felt guilty about my dream for my life, you know? My mom did the best she could. But all I wanted was to grow up and get out of there, to find my steady, patient, good-natured guy and start having a whole bunch of rowdy kids."

"Joss." He touched her hair again, so lightly, guiding a hank of it back over her shoulder. "I'm beginning to think there is altogether too much guilt going on in your head."

"Yeah, probably. But my mom tried so hard, she *worked* so hard, to do right by me, to make a good life for me."

"Just because you dreamed of a different way to be a mom doesn't make your mom's way bad."

She gave a low chuckle. "You amaze me, you know that?"

"In a good way, I hope."

"In a great way. When I met you I thought you were just another hot guy trying to get laid. But instead, you're a shrink and a philosopher, with a little Mahatma Gandhi thrown in for good measure."

He arched one of those thick, dark eyebrows. "Just don't tell Jackson, okay? Not the part about Mahatma Gandhi anyway. He would never let me live it down."

She uncrossed her legs, folded her hands tightly in her lap and stared miserably down at them. "I have another secret. A bad one."

He teased, "*Really* bad?"

"Yeah, really stinkin' bad. I'm beyond embarrassed to admit it."

He didn't say anything. He just waited, not pushing her.

So she told him. "For the first two days I was here, staying at the resort, I was fully planning to work things out with Kenny, take him back and marry him anyway, in spite of what he did with Kimberly in the coat room." She paused, waiting for him to say how he couldn't believe she would ever give a jerk like that another chance.

But he only sat there, waiting, his expression unreadable, giving her a chance to tell him the rest.

So, grimly, she continued. "Within an hour after I ran from the church, I was already thinking of how I was only going to make Kenny suffer for a while, make him grovel at my feet and beg me to give him another chance. And then, once he'd admitted what a complete jackass he'd been, once he'd sworn never to do anything like that again, I would take him back. I was thinking that he could give me that big Craftsman house I wanted. I was thinking that with him, I could afford to have all those kids. I was thinking that I had chosen him and been with him for five whole years because he was the one to help me live my dream. I told myself all that, even though long before the wedding day, I already knew very well that he wasn't the sweet guy he used to be, that he'd changed, become a smug jerk I didn't even like being around. But still, I had bought my mom's pep talk and gone ahead with the wedding anyway. Because I'm almost thirty and if I didn't settle for Kenny, I might never find anyone better." Deeply ashamed, Joss fell silent.

Jace was silent, too, sitting there beside her on the bench under the drooping branches of the willow tree. Somewhere in the little park, she heard children laughing.

A child called, "Mama!"

And a mother answered, "Right here!"

"Watch me swing high!" the child commanded.

"I'm here. I'm watching…."

Jace asked, "So what changed your mind?"

She'd come this far. She might as well admit the rest. "Kenny failed to grovel. He called six times those first two days. And every time he called, it was only to say the things he said yesterday—you know, in the Lounge, when you overheard me talking to him? He self-righteously explained to me that *I* was being unreasonable, that *I* had completely humiliated *him*, that *I* had it all wrong. That there was nothing between him and Kimberly and I ought to realize there wasn't and quit acting like *I'm* the one who got messed over." She crossed her legs again. "By the end of the second day, I finally had to admit that there was no salvaging things with Kenny, that it was Over, capital *O*, and I was going to need to make myself a whole new life."

"So…would you take him back now, if he wised up and was honestly sorry for cheating on you, if he got down on his knees and swore you were the only woman for him? If he promised he would never even look at another woman again, that he would do anything—*anything*—for one more chance with you?"

She didn't even have to think about it. "No way. I'm through with him. Done. That ship has sailed. It's as Over as Over gets."

He stood. "Well, all right, then." He held down his hand to her.

She stared at those long, tanned fingers of his, puzzled. "What?"

"I'll take you back to the resort now."

A certain wistfulness curled through her. She tipped her head back to look up at him. "Now you want to get rid of me. You're disappointed in me."

"Hell, no. I think you're terrific. You were with that guy for years. Makes sense it took time to accept that it wasn't going to work out. And in the end, you made the only workable decision about him—after giving him a chance to come clean and make things right. There is nothing to be disappointed about in that. But I did promise you that after we talked for a while, I would take you back up the mountain." He still held out his hand.

She took it. Really, she could get used to holding Jace's hand. He tucked her fingers over his arm and led the way out from under the willow tree, across the grass to Main Street, where they turned back the way they'd come, toward the car.

Twenty minutes later, he pulled into the turnaround beneath the porte cochere at the side of the resort's clubhouse. A valet stepped up to open the door for her. She waved him off and turned to Jace behind the wheel. "I have to ask, did you study psychiatry in school?"

He grunted. "Are you kidding? Petroleum engineering, with a minor in business."

Softly, she told him, "Thank you—for keeping after me until I told you what was bothering me. For listening."

"Hey, what's a best friend for?"

"I had a really good time. At that beautiful little church, at the bakery. Even sitting under that willow tree telling you things you don't even need to know. That part wasn't fun exactly. But it was very…therapeutic, I guess you could say."

He nodded. "Happy to help."

She was suddenly absolutely certain he only wanted to

get rid of her now. And why wouldn't he? She had totally blown it with her sulking and feeling sorry for herself, with her icky revelations about how she'd actually thought she might marry Kenny anyway, even if he was a cheating SOB, because he had money and could give her the life that she wanted. Her throat felt tight. She coughed to loosen it. "Ahem. Well, I'll…see you later, then."

"Later."

She hooked her pink bag on her shoulder, pushed on the door and the valet appeared again to open it all the way for her. "Uh, thanks," she said, and got out. The valet gave her a friendly smile and shut the passenger door. Joss stood there, feeling forlorn, as Jace drove away.

His Range Rover had disappeared from sight when the awful realization hit her like a smack in the face. His family was "in oil." He drove an eighty-thousand-dollar car. The price of a pair of his fancy boots would have paid the rent on her lost apartment for a couple of months at least. True, like her, he was between jobs. But Joss Bennings being out of a job and Jason Traub quitting the oil business were two completely different things.

Jason Traub was a rich guy. A very rich guy. She would bet her whole savings account on that—her significantly reduced savings account. There had been a lot more a year ago, before she'd paid for the wedding and the reception that hadn't happened after all. But even if she hadn't spent all that money on her nonwedding, her total savings still wouldn't be more than chump change to someone like Jace. She knew he had to have an inheritance and a nice, fat stock portfolio. He didn't really *have* to work.

And now that she'd told him the truth about her goals, what could he think but that she was trolling for a good provider so she could buy a big house and raise a bunch of boisterous kids? He must be wondering if she'd set out to get her hooks in him. He'd probably decided that she'd been giving him an act, pretending to hate men when she was really looking for a guy with big bucks to replace the no-good cheater she'd left at the altar.

Joss let out a small moan of misery. She *liked* Jace. A lot. She really did want to be his friend. She *loved* being his friend. And she'd been looking forward to spending more time with him before she went back to Sacramento and got to work picking up the pieces of her life.

But now she'd gone and ruined it with him. She just knew that she had. She tipped her head back and let out another moan.

"Ma'am?" asked the valet, looking worried.

She pulled herself together, pasted on a smile and shook her head. "I'm okay. Really."

Another vehicle rolled under the porte cochere and the valet stepped forward to open the passenger door. With a heavy sigh, Joss turned for the glass doors that led into the clubhouse.

Chapter Four

In her suite, Joss tossed her purse on the table in the foyer and went straight to the bedroom, where she shucked off her shoes and fell backward across the bed. As she stared blindly at the peaked ceiling, she tried to make up her mind whether to call Jace and swear to him she wasn't after him in any way, shape or form—or if the wiser course would be to leave bad enough alone.

And then she realized she didn't even have his number, so the question of whether to call didn't matter anyway.

The phone on the nightstand rang. Joss told herself not to answer it. The last thing she needed right now was another lecture from her mother or more crap from Kenny.

But then, as always, she couldn't stand to let it ring. She reached over, picked it up and put it to her ear. "What now?"

"You're my best friend for the whole week and I don't have your cell number. How wrong is that?"

"Jace." She breathed his name like a grateful prayer. Tears blurred her eyes and clutched at the back of her throat. "Hey."

A silence on his end, then gruffly, "Are you all right? Did something...happen?"

She blinked, swallowed, let out a slow breath. And told him the truth. "I was sure that I'd totally freaked you out. That you had to be thinking I'm some kind of gold digger."

He made a bewildered sound. "Whoa. Wait. *Why*?"

"Okay, now I hear your voice, it all seems completely ridiculous that I could have thought that."

"Joss, why?"

"Because of what I told you. About marrying Kenny anyway, even though he cheated and I caught him in the act, marrying him because he had money and could, um, support me in the style to which I hope to become accustomed."

"Oh, right." He was smiling. She could hear it in his voice. "The big, messy house and all those loud, undisciplined kids who really shouldn't be allowed to color on the walls."

"You can get special paint, you know. Washable paint. And yeah, that would be it—the style to which I can't wait to become accustomed."

"Listen to me, Joss. Are you listening?"

"Yes."

"I don't think you're a gold digger. Not in any way. Got that?"

"Yeah."

"So can I have your cell number?"

She rattled it off. "And can I have yours?"

"Absolutely." He gave it to her. She rolled over and scribbled it down on the complimentary notepad by the phone. "And about tonight," he said, "dinner at Jackson and Laila's? I'll pick you up at five-thirty."

She grinned to herself. She'd never actually told him she would go, but so what? She *wanted* to go, and she was going to go.

"I'll be waiting," she promised. "Outside, under the porte cochere, where you dropped me off just now."

Jackson's house was wall-to-wall family and friends.

To Jace, it looked like just about every Traub in the state of Montana was there, not to mention all the Traubs from Texas. And there were other well-known Thunder Canyon families represented. There were Cateses and Cliftons and Pritchets, all of them related to the Traubs—if not by blood or marriage, then by the bonds of longtime friendships.

Friends and family filled the big living room, the kitchen and spilled out onto the wide front porch and into the tree-shaded backyard. Jackson had a professional-sized smoker barbecue going along with an open grill. The mouthwatering aromas of mesquite-smoked ribs, barbecued chicken and grilling burgers filled the air.

Jace had arrived with Joss just a half hour ago. She was a knockout in dressy jeans that hugged every curve and a silky shirt the color of a ripe plum. He'd whistled at her when she got into the car at the resort. Hey, even a best friend could show his appreciation when a woman was looking good.

His plan had been to keep her close at his side all evening, so his mother wouldn't have a chance to start working on her, pumping her for information about "how things were going" between them, trying to convince Joss that she would love living in Midland, Texas. But within fifteen minutes of their arrival at Jackson's, Laila had dragged Joss off to look at some old picture albums. He'd tried to stick with them, but Jackson had called him outside to help him flip burgers.

And now Ethan had caught up with him. "We need to talk. Come with me," Ethan commanded.

Jace shouldn't have followed, but he knew he was going to have to face his big brother down at some point. Might as well get it over with. Ethan led Jace to the edge of the yard, to a secluded spot beneath a cottonwood tree, where he commenced to put on the pressure.

"I just want you to drop in at the office for a few hours tomorrow," Ethan coaxed. TOI Montana had its offices on State Street not far from the Town Square. "Let me show you around. You can see how far we've come in the past year." Ethan had made the move to Montana only the summer before. "The shale oil operations are surpassing even my expectations."

"I know you're doing a great job, Ethan. I've seen the reports, but tomorrow's a busy day. Remember? We're all taking off in the morning, going riding up Thunder Mountain for that family picnic."

"That's right." Ethan frowned. "I forgot about the damn picnic. Tuesday, then—or come in early tomorrow. The ride up there doesn't get under way until ten or so. We won't have a lot of time, but at least I can show you the corner office that has your name on it."

Jace thought how he'd be happy to admire the new offices. But if he did, Ethan would only be all the more certain that he could talk Jace into coming back to TOI. "I'm out of the oil business, Ethan. I know I've told you that more than once."

Ethan blinked. "Aw, now, Jace. You know you don't mean it. You're an oilman to the core."

"I *was* an oilman. Not anymore."

Ethan reached out and hooked his arm around Jace's

neck, getting him in a headlock, then fisting his free hand to scrub a noogie on Jace's head—like he was five again or something. "Snap out of it, little maverick," Ethan muttered, using the pet name their father used to use on them. "What else you plan to do with your time? We Traubs might have more money than we know what to do with, but that's because we're hard workers. We earned every cent and we *keep* earning until they lay us in the ground."

"Let me loose, Ethan." Jace said the words quietly, but he'd had about enough.

Ethan let go. "I didn't mean to get you all riled up."

Jace ran a hand back over his hair. "Oh, right. Put me in a headlock and pull a noogie on me and then say you didn't mean it."

"I'm only trying to help you get your head on straight."

"It's my head. And it feels plenty straight to me."

Ethan gentled his tone. "All I'm asking is for you to come and have a look at what we've built here."

"And I would be more than happy to do that, if that was all you were up to."

Ethan's lip curled, and not in a smile. "You calling me a liar, kid?"

Jason really wanted to pop his big brother a good one, but he valiantly managed to keep his fists at his sides. "In case you've forgotten," he said way too softly, "I'm thirty-three years old. I haven't been a kid for a long time now."

"Well, stop acting like one, then. Ever since you tangled with Jack Lavelle's little girl, you've been moping around, throwing your life away, acting like you don't care about anything anymore."

Again, Jace reminded himself to hold his temper. "Ethan, you don't know what you're talking about."

"The hell I don't."

"You're here in Montana. And I've been in Texas. And

Ma and Pete have been filling your head full of their own assumptions about what's been going on."

Ethan demanded, "So what *was* going on?"

"Nothing the least mysterious. I want to find a different kind of work, that's all."

"And Tricia Lavelle didn't break your heart?"

"It's a long story. I don't want to go into it."

"Hah. She did a number on you. You're the last single maverick in the family and it's getting to you."

"Will you stop it with the maverick talk? I'm not six anymore. And Ethan, you're not Dad."

"You fell for Tricia, thought you'd finally found your woman. But she dumped you flat, crushed your hopes and walked all over your tender heart. Admit it."

"I'm not admitting anything. Get off my back."

But Ethan just kept on. "You *love* the oil business. You always did. You love it the most of all of us in the family—next to me, I mean."

"People change."

"I don't believe that," Ethan insisted. "Not for a minute. You got your heart broken and that set you on a downward spiral and all I'm trying to do is help pull you out of it."

"Look, Ethan, how many times do I have to tell you? You've got it all wrong. You've been listening to Ma and Pete. And they don't know what they're talking about."

"They know you were going to marry Tricia Lavelle. And then suddenly, it was over. And you were dragging around like someone shot your favorite hound dog, saying how you were through with the oil industry and getting out of Texas."

"It's not their business. And it's not yours either. Give it up."

"I'm only explaining that I get the picture, loud and

clear. You're a mess, Jason, and what you need is to come back to work."

"I have *been* at work. Until last Wednesday, as a matter of fact. I have remained at work well past the time I was supposed to be finished because Ma and Pete pulled every trick in the book to get me to stay. But I'm done now. And I am not going back."

"A man needs to work."

"And I plan to work. Just not for TOI."

"Then doing what, Jason?"

"Something completely different. A business of my own, something hands-on."

"TOI is hands-on. It's *our* company."

"Listen, Ethan, I don't know another way to say it. I'm done at TOI and I don't know yet what I'll be doing next."

"You don't know yet," Ethan echoed in a smarmy sing-song. "Well, that's okay, because *I* know. You're coming to work for *me*, here, in Thunder Canyon."

They were head to head by then, and Jace knew exactly where this discussion was headed. Nowhere. As always, Ethan thought he knew it all. And Jace was not about to be bullied into going back to work doing what he *didn't* want to do anymore. "Back off," he said. "I mean it. Let it go."

"You're my brother. And I love you. And I'll bust your fool head open before I let you ruin your life."

Jace's fists burned to start flying. But what would hitting Ethan prove except that, along with all his other shortcomings, he couldn't control his damn temper even stone-cold sober? They were grown men, for pity's sake. Well beyond the age of imagining they could settle a problem with a brawl. There was nothing more to say here. He turned to walk away.

Apparently, Ethan got the message at last. He spoke wearily to Jace's back. "Aw, come on, Jace…"

Jason wanted to keep walking, but what good was that going to do either of them? Ethan could be a pushy, over-bearing SOB, yes. But his heart was in the right place. Jace made himself face his older brother again.

Ethan said ruefully, "You know I only want to help."

"Well, you're *not* helping."

Ethan threw up both hands. "I only thought…a little tough love, you know?" He shook his head. "Lizzie warned me to stay out of it. You have no idea how much I hate it when she's right."

Jason almost grinned. "Why? Because she's right most of the time?"

"She's one hell of a woman, my wife. But she's too damn smart."

"You know you wouldn't have it any other way." His brother's mention of Lizzie had Jace thinking of Joss. He really had to go and find her before Ma did. He said, "The truth is, I'd been thinking about making some changes for a while now—since before I met Tricia, as a matter of fact."

"I…didn't realize that."

"Well, now you know. Ma and Pete hate to see me go. They're going to be on their own in Midland and even though they still want to run the show there, they don't like it that all of us have pulled up stakes and moved on."

"Yeah," Ethan said gruffly, "I get that. They didn't like it much when I left either."

"Whatever they've been saying, I really have changed my mind about the family business. I want another line of work. Something completely different. No, I haven't fig-ured out what yet, but I'm not coming back to TOI. And I really need to go find Joss now."

One side of Ethan's mouth quirked up. "You thinkin' Ma's gotten hold of her?"

"I seriously hope not. Gotta go." He scanned the yard

as he headed for the back door. No sign of a hot brunette in snug jeans and a purple shirt. And no sign of his mother either.

He went up the back steps and into the kitchen. "Do you know where I can find Joss?" he asked Laila, who was arranging the food buffet-style in the breakfast nook on a long, wide table covered with a red-and-white striped tablecloth, decorated with flags and red, white and blue candles and sparkly little red, white and blue Uncle Sam hats.

Laila flashed him her dazzling beauty-queen smile. "Did I tell you I really like her? She's fun and down-to-earth."

"Yes, she is." .

"And she loved looking at the pictures of all you Traubs as little kids. She told me she appreciated getting to see some of the old photos of your dad—Charles, I mean. She said you have his killer smile."

"I'll bet she did," he muttered drily. "But where is she now?"

"You know, I think I saw her in the dining room a few minutes ago. She was chatting with your mom."

Jace stifled a groan. "Thanks." He made a beeline for the formal dining room. No sign of Joss in there—or of Ma either. He moved on to the living room.

And spotted them right away, sitting on the sofa, their heads bent close together. His mother was saying something. Joss was laughing and nodding. She didn't look the least overwhelmed. Whatever Ma was filling her head with, apparently it wasn't all that scary.

But still. Joss was kind of jumpy about men—and for good reason. He didn't need his mother freaking her out with too many personal questions and a boatload of assumptions about what was really going on between the two of them.

He headed over there to rescue her.

His mother saw him coming. She gave him a big, wide smile. Joss turned to meet his eyes. He breathed a sigh of relief to see she looked completely at ease.

Maybe Ma was minding her own business after all.

But then he got close enough for her to speak to him. "Jason," his mother said, suddenly looking way too innocent. "Ethan really needs to talk to you. He's been looking all over for you."

"He found me." Jace tried not to scowl. "We had a nice, long talk. I think I cleared up a few...misconceptions for him."

"Oh?" Claudia gave him the arched eyebrow. "What misconceptions do you mean?"

"Long story, Ma. But the upshot is, Ethan understands now that I'm not going to stay in Midland and I'm not going to work at TOI anymore—not in Texas, and not here in Montana."

His mother shot Joss a nervous glance. "Jason, really. This is neither the time nor the place to go into all that."

Oh, right. Now things weren't going the way she'd planned, suddenly it was better if they didn't talk about it now. *Way to go, Ma.*

And he had to give Joss credit. She simply sat there looking gorgeous and completely unconcerned about whatever antagonistic undercurrents might be churning between him and the woman who'd given him life.

He said cheerfully, "Just clueing you in, Ma." And then he bent and kissed her still-smooth cheek.

She grabbed his arm and held him close enough that he could smell the light perfume she always wore. Softly, she told him, "I love you very much. You know that."

"I know. And I love you, too, Ma." He rose to his height

again and spoke to Joss. "Hungry? The food's on." He held down his hand.

She took it and rose to stand beside him and he felt like a million bucks suddenly, just holding her slim, smooth fingers in his. "Great getting a chance to visit with you, Claudia," she said.

His mother was all smiles. "I'm so glad we were able to talk a little. And don't forget we would love to have you ride up Thunder Mountain with us tomorrow. The picnic will be such fun, and the views from up near the tree line are stunning."

"Thank you for inviting me," Joss said. "But...didn't you mention that you're riding *horses* up there?"

"Yes, we are. It's a beautiful ride."

"I've never ridden a horse in my life."

"First time for everything," Ma said brightly. "And there are always calm, even-tempered horses available from the resort stables, mounts they keep especially for beginners."

"I'll, um, talk it over with Jace."

"Wonderful." His mother beamed.

He asked, "You coming to eat, Ma?"

"I think I'll find Pete first."

"Well, all right, then." He guided Joss ahead of him. She led the way toward the kitchen. After a few steps he caught up with her and spoke low so only she could hear. "So are you moving to Midland?"

She laughed, a soft, enticing sound. "It was suggested."

They entered the dining room. He pulled her over to a quiet corner where they could talk for a moment or two undisturbed. "What else was 'suggested'?"

"Your mother said she thinks I'm lovely—her word—and she's so glad you and I met and she really has a wonderful feeling about me."

"Well, three things Ma and I can agree on at least."

"Hey, at least *your* mom knows she's meddling."

"Don't be too sure about that."

"But I *am* sure. She wants you back in Texas, but she knows she's out of line to keep after you. She gets that you're all grown up and that it's your life."

"She said all that?"

"Well, not exactly. But I can see it in her eyes."

"Why am I not reassured?"

"You should be. You should take my word for it. Backing Claudia off is going to be a piece of cake—unlike someone *else's* mother I could mention."

Jace wasn't so sure. "Ma filled Ethan's ears with a whole bunch of complete crap about me. He decided he had to come to my rescue with a domineering attitude and some 'tough love.'"

"Yikes. Just now, you mean?"

He nodded, admiring the pretty arch of her eyebrows, the juicy curve of her mouth. She really was easy on the eyes. He'd never had a best friend so good to look at—but then, all his other friends were male and looking at them didn't do a thing for him.

She said, "I hope it all worked out."

"It did. I only *wanted* to punch his lights out."

The brown eyes widened. "But you kept your cool."

"Yes, I did, surprisingly enough. Ethan and I are on the same page now. And I have to agree that siccing Ethan on me was probably Ma's main move. That didn't work, so she'll be about out of ways to get me to come to my senses and get back into life as I've always lived it. But don't kid yourself. She's not finished working on *you*."

Joss tugged on the collar of his shirt. He leaned down even closer. Her warm, sweet breath teased his ear as she whispered, "If she knew the truth about me she might actually believe that we really are just friends."

He whispered back, "Are you saying you're planning on telling her the truth?"

She held his gaze. "Are you?"

"I *have* told the truth, that you and I are just friends. Is it my fault that no one will believe me?"

"I guess not."

"I'm glad you see it that way." Leaning close to her, breathing in the tempting scent of her perfume, it would be so easy to wish for more than friendship. "As for *your* truth, well, it's not mine to tell."

She smiled up at him then, causing his heart to beat harder in his chest. "I appreciate that, Jace. Because I don't want to go into it with everyone. It's too embarrassing."

"That's A-okay with me. I won't say a word."

"Thanks." Now those big brown eyes looked at him trustingly. He felt minimally guilty about that. After all, he did find her way hot. And if she just happened to decide she wanted some benefits in this temporary friendship after all, well, every moment he was with her, it got harder to remember why a few benefits wouldn't be a cracker-jack idea. "For some weird reason, I don't have any trouble telling *you* all my secrets—even the shameful ones." Her cheeks flushed pink and she lowered her gaze so she was looking at the second button of his shirt.

He couldn't resist using a finger to tip her chin back up. He stared at her mouth. How could he help it? She had the softest, widest mouth he'd ever seen. He wanted to kiss her. A lot. But he wouldn't. He said, "There's nothing shameful in wanting your dream so much you're willing to compromise to get it."

"That depends on the compromise. Even letting myself *imagine* I might get back with Kenny after he betrayed me with my own cousin…uh-uh. *That* was shameful."

"Listen to me, Joss. I want you to stop beating yourself up about that."

"It's only…"

He put a finger against those soft lips of hers. "Take it from your new best friend. It's over with the cheater. You *didn't* go back to him. That's what matters." From the corner of his eye, he saw everyone filing past, moving toward the kitchen. His brother Corey and his wife, Erin, glanced their way. Erin whispered to Corey. He could just guess what she was saying—something about how Jace had found someone special.

Which was great. It fit into his plan just fine.

He and Joss would have a good time together, enjoying each other's company, taking each day as it came. And his family would leave him alone to pursue what they all hoped was the beginning of a "meaningful" relationship, a relationship that would help him get over Tricia, whom they were all so damn certain had broken his heart.

"Everyone's heading for the kitchen," Joss whispered. "Shouldn't we join them?"

He draped an arm around her slim shoulders. "Let's go."

Chapter Five

"No way. I'm not going anywhere on a horse," Joss informed Jason for what seemed like the hundredth time that evening.

By then, they were back up at the resort in her suite, eating chocolate from the complimentary bowl on the coffee table. She added in a tone she intended to be final, "I'll just take a pass on the family picnic, if you don't mind."

"But I do mind." He put on a needy expression. The guy had no shame when it came to getting his way. "You'll break my heart if you don't go."

She had the bowl in her lap. She fished around in it and found what she wanted. Swiftly, she unwrapped the tempting square of lovely, smooth bittersweet perfection. A groan of pleasure escaped her as she popped it into her mouth. It was fabulous. Too fabulous. Shiny wrappers littered the coffee table in front of them. "Your heart," she said, "is way too easy to break."

Now he looked noble—in a soft-eyed, far-too-appealing way. "It's true. Please. Don't hurt me any more than I've already been hurt. Come to the picnic with me tomorrow. Save me from my family. I'm begging you, Joss."

"So how exactly have you already been hurt?" She *was* kind of curious about that woman who had apparently dumped him.

He actually stuck out his lower lip. "It's just too painful to talk about."

"You know you're totally full of it, right?"

He dug in the bowl for another candy. "What? Full of chocolate, you mean?"

She gave him a slow look of great patience. "You're not going to tell me, are you?"

"One of these days…"

"Which day? By my count, we have five days left and I'm outta here."

"Yeah, but we've been best friends for only about twenty-four hours. I need a little more time to…let down my guard."

"Hah." She kept after him. "So, tomorrow, then? You'll tell me tomorrow?"

"Do you really *need* to know?"

"I'm curious, okay?" And growing more so the longer she hung around with him. "Then again, what does it matter if you tell me all about your recent bad romance, or not?"

"So then, you don't *really* need to know."

She gave it up. "No, Jason. I don't need to know."

He beamed. "Great."

She started to root around for another piece of candy—but no. She really didn't need another piece of candy. Resolutely, she handed him the bowl. "Don't let me near that again tonight."

"Count on me to save you from yourself—and come to the picnic tomorrow."

"Do you *ever* give up?"

"No, I don't. It's not in my nature." He dug in the bowl and pulled out a nutty caramel chew. "Damn, these are good."

"You had to remind me." She reached for the bowl.

He jerked it away. "Uh-uh. Remember? You're not having any more."

"Just one."

"You won't respect me if I don't hold my ground here." He actually put his hand over the top of the bowl, as if she might try to reach in.

Which was exactly what she'd planned to do. "You can be so annoying. You know that, right?"

"It's for your own good," he said oh so nobly. "You said not to let you."

"Well, I *meant*, don't let me until I *want* you to let me."

He cast those bedroom eyes heavenward. "Women. They have no idea what they want."

"Men. They think they know everything." She scooped up the scattered candy wrappers and started firing them at him.

"Hey, knock that off." He ducked and held up the bowl as a shield.

She fired more wrappers. One got stuck in his hair. "Gimme that candy," she demanded, trying really hard to sound scary.

But he only set the bowl aside—his *other* side—and knocked the wrapper out of his hair. "Sorry. No can do." He deflected with his hands that time.

She was out of wrappers. Laughing, she lunged for the bowl.

He caught her by both wrists before she got there. "Behave," he commanded.

"Let me go." She tried to pull away.

He held on. "Say you'll behave."

"No way."

"Say it. Promise."

"Uh-uh. Forget that."

They were both laughing by then, as she struggled to free her wrists and he held on. She got one hand free and she went for it—reaching across him, grabbing for the bowl.

She made it, too. She shoved her fingers in and came out with a nice, big handful. "Got 'em!" she crowed in triumph, holding her prize high.

"Put those back," he instructed in what could only be called a growl.

"What, these, you mean?" She opened her hand and let them rain down on his head.

He sat very still—for a moment anyway—as the candy bounced off his thick hair and broad shoulders and fell to the sofa cushions and down to the floor. Then, frowning thunderously, he glanced around them. "Look at this mess. Wrappers and candy everywhere."

"It's your own fault. You should have given me the candy when I asked for it."

He let go of her other wrist, but then he only captured both of her arms and made a big show of baring his gorgeous snow-white teeth at her. "You're a brat, Jocelyn Marie. You know that?"

"Yes, I am. And proud of it." She tossed her hair and held her head high.

He leaned in, playfully threatening....

And right then, in the space of an instant, everything changed.

One second, they were tussling like a pair of ill-behaved third graders—and the next second, they weren't. One moment she was laughing and teasing and giving him a hard time—and the next, she wasn't.

Out of nowhere, her breath snagged in her throat. Her pulse spiked and her skin felt sensitized and too hot. All at once, she was acutely aware of his big, warm hands gripping her arms, of his dark, dark eyes and the beautiful, way-too-kissable shape of his lips. Of the scent of him, that was a little spicy and a little green and also electric somehow, the way the air smells right before a thunderstorm.

She watched his eyes—saw them track. From her eyes, to her mouth, back to her eyes again…

She knew what was coming. He was going to kiss her.

And oh, at that moment, she *wanted* him to kiss her.

Wanted to feel his powerful arms banded around her, wanted his breath in her mouth and the rough wet glide of his tongue.

Wanted him to guide her back onto the sofa cushions, to press his big, muscled body so tightly against her, to hold her so close and kiss her so long, and so deep and so thoroughly that she would forget…

Everything.

The mess that was her life. All the ways her plans and her world had gone haywire. All the things she somehow had to fix, to make right, even though she really had no idea how to do that.

She wanted to tear off all her clothes and all of his, too. She wanted to be naked with him, skin-to-skin. Naked with her new best friend who happened to be a man she'd met only the day before.

She wanted forgetfulness. And she wanted it in Jace's big arms.

But then, very softly, he asked, "Joss?" And his eyes were different, clearer somehow, seeking an answer from her.

And she liked him so much then. She liked him more than she wanted the temporary escape his lean, strong, male body offered her.

He was doing the right thing by her. He was giving her the moment she needed.

The choice she needed. The chance to stop now. To say no.

She swallowed, slowly. She pressed her lips together and gave an almost imperceptible shake of her head.

That was all it took.

He let go of her arms and sank back against the cushions. She did the same. Her heart still pounded too hard, her breath came too fast and her body still yearned. But that would pass.

It wasn't going to happen. And that was…good.

Right.

For a long, silent moment, they simply sat there, among the scattered candy and empty wrappers, not looking at each other.

And then, without a word, by a sort of tacit agreement, they both rose and began gathering up the pieces of chocolate. She went and got the wastebasket by the wet bar and they threw the wrappers away.

Finally, he started to turn for the door, but then he stopped and faced her, where she stood by the sofa, still holding the wastebasket, feeling forlorn.

"Tomorrow," he said. "You're coming. Don't argue. Wear old jeans and bring a jacket. Tennis shoes if you don't have riding boots. Do you have a hat?"

Gladness surged through her. Suddenly, she desperately wanted to go. "You'll be sorry. I meant what I said. I do not know how to ride a horse."

"Then it's time you learned." His voice was gentle. Fond. And yet, somehow, an echo of heated excitement seemed to cling to him, to thicken the air between them.

She looked in those dark eyes and she almost wished… but no. It was better this way. Safer. Saner. And lately, she could use all the safety and sanity she could get. She said, "I bought boots and a hat the first day I was here. And a cute Western shirt, too, as a matter of fact."

"I'll be here to get you at nine."

"I think this is a bad idea," she said the next morning when she opened the door to him and he stood there looking one-hundred-percent authentic cowboy in faded jeans and rawhide boots, a worn blue Western shirt with white piping and a blue bandana. He had his hat in his hand.

He gave her a crooked smile that made her feel all warm and fuzzy inside. "You're going to have a great time."

She made a doubtful sound and frowned at his hat. "Is that a real Stetson?"

"Resistol."

She assumed that must be a brand of hat. "Well, all right. Good to know."

He took in her red plaid shirt with its crochet trim and rhinestone studs. "Aren't you the fancy one?"

She tugged on her pant leg, revealing more of her boot. "And don't you love these boots?" They were red, too—beautiful distressed red leather embroidered with hearts and wings and scroll-like flourishes.

"Very stylish."

"As long as I'm going to make a fool of myself, I figure I might as well look good while doing it."

"You look terrific." His eyes said he really meant that. The memory of that almost-kiss last night seemed to rise up between them. She felt suddenly shy and looked away. "Thank you."

"Joss," he said gently, "it's going to be fine. Ready?"

"No, but I can't seem to convince you what a bad idea this is, so we might as well get going." She grabbed her jean jacket and her brand-new hat and off they went.

They got to the resort stable before the rest of Jason's family arrived, which was great. She would have a little time to practice riding before they started up the mountain.

The horse the groom led out for her was white with brown spots. Already saddled and wearing a bridle, it seemed somehow a very patient horse. It stood there, flicking its brown tail lazily and making gentle huffing noises as Jace checked the strap that held the saddle on and adjusted the bridle.

Joss stood well away from the animal. "Um, does it have a name?"

"Cupcake," said the groom. He was maybe twenty years old, deeply tanned with freckles and a space between his two front teeth.

Joss cleared her throat. "It's a she, then?"

"Nope. Gelding," the groom answered. So very cowboylike. Never use a whole sentence when a word or two will do.

And okay, now she looked, she could see the, er, residual equipment. "Ah, yes."

Jace thanked the groom. The fellow tipped his sweat-stained hat and ambled back to the stable.

"Come on." Jace held out his hand to her.

She eyed that hand warily. "I don't know. I have a bad feeling about this."

"Come on," Jace insisted. He refused to lower his hand. So she took it.

He showed her which side to mount from and boosted her into the saddle. Cupcake made a soft chuffing sound but didn't move a muscle. Cautiously, she patted the side of his warm, silky neck. "Okay. Can we be done now?" she asked hopefully.

Jace didn't answer. He adjusted the stirrups. Then he gave her some instructions: how to hold the reins, how to use her legs to help guide the animal. And a bunch of other stuff she immediately filed under the general heading, *Things I'm Too Nervous to Remember.*

He took the reins and led her around in a circle for a while, just so she could get a feel for being on a moving horse. It didn't seem so bad really. Cupcake was a prince. He walked along calmly, never once balking or trying to go his own way.

Within a half hour, she was holding the reins and riding Cupcake in a circle, using her knees the way Jace had showed her. She decided that maybe this wouldn't be so bad after all.

His family started arriving in pickups, some of them towing horse trailers. Jace went off to saddle his own horse and Joss kept practicing, continuing in the circle and also stopping, turning and going the other way. Really, it wasn't so terrible. She was actually getting the hang of it, more or less. On a sweetheart like Cupcake, she might even enjoy herself. When Jason's mom, looking trim and young in snug jeans and a yellow shirt, called out a greeting, Joss raised her hand in a jaunty wave.

At a little after eleven, they were all mounted up and ready to go. They formed a caravan and took the road that led to the resort condos farther up the mountain. But before they reached them, Dax Traub, in the lead, turned off onto a tree-shaded trail.

The rest of them followed. It was nice, Joss thought.

Not bad at all, riding along at a steady pace beneath the dappled shadows of the trees. There was a gentle breeze blowing and the air smelled fresh and piney. She followed directly behind Jace, who rode a big black horse named Major. A proud-looking creature, Major tossed his head and pranced and required a lot more handling than Joss ever could have managed.

She much preferred the calm-natured Cupcake. With him, all she had to do was stay in the saddle and lightly hold the reins. Every now and then, Jace would glance back at her and she would give him a big smile, just to show him that she was doing okay.

Piece of cake. Seriously. She kind of had a knack for this. Who knew? *Jocelyn Marie Bennings, horsewoman.* It had a nice ring to it.

The trail narrowed, but that didn't seem to faze the sure-footed Cupcake. The mountain, closely grown with tall trees, rose steeply to her left. On the right, the drop-off was dizzying, even with all the trees that might help to block a fall. Joss made a point not to look.

Jace called back to her, "You doing okay?"

"Fine. Absolutely. Doing gr—"

She didn't get a chance to finish saying *great*, because Cupcake took his next step and the downward side of the trail crumbled out from beneath his hooves.

Joss let out a strangled shriek and grabbed onto the saddle horn for dear life. She caught one last look at Jace's stunned face and then she and Cupcake were off, heading straight down the mountain, kicking up a cloud of dust in a high-speed, utterly terrifying slide.

Chapter Six

With both hands, Joss clutched the saddle horn for all she was worth. There was a rushing sound in her ears and her heart beat so hard it hurt. She closed her eyes. She closed them really tight.

Why look? She knew she was done for, that poor Cupcake would lose his precarious balance as they skidded down the mountainside. He would topple and roll and she would roll with him—*under* him. Oh, it was definitely not going to be pretty.

The brave horse stumbled. She lost her seat and felt herself starting to go airborne. But somehow, even though her arms felt wrenched from their sockets, she managed to hold on. Her butt hit the saddle again, knocking the wind out of her, sending a sharp crack of pure pain zipping up her tailbone, jangling her spine.

She might have screamed. She wasn't sure. It was all happening way too fast and she was so far from knowing what she ought to do next to try and maybe improve her odds of surviving the next, oh, say, twenty seconds.

At least Cupcake remained upright and she was still in the saddle. So far. She dared to open her eyelids to slits, saw the blur of trees as they flew by, heard the sharp retort of hooves beneath her that told her the brave spotted horse was actually running now instead of sliding, that by some miracle, he had gotten his legs under him and started galloping in a zigzag pattern, sideways and downward, switching back and forth, one way and then the other, weaving between the trunks of the tall trees.

And…was it possible? Were they slowing down a little?

She felt dizzy and realized she'd forgotten to breathe. So she sucked in a quick breath and forced her eyes open wider and wished she hadn't dropped the reins when she first grabbed for the saddle horn. Right now, she didn't dare let go long enough to try to get hold of them again.

Knees. She was supposed to use her knees, wasn't she? Kind of press them together to let Cupcake know that stopping would be really, really good—no. Wait. That was to go faster. She really didn't want to go faster.

She needed the reins, but she didn't have them.

All she had was her voice. She used it. "Whoa," she said, "Whoa, Cupcake." It came out in a croak, but the horse actually seemed to hear her.

Triumph exploded through her as he slowed even more with a low snorting sound. She had her eyes open all the way by then and she could see a sort of flat space up ahead, between two fir trees.

She went for it, letting go of the saddle horn, groping frantically for the reins. And she got them! She tugged on them, saying "Whoa, whoa…"

It worked. It totally worked. Cupcake came to a dead stop right there between those two trees.

Actually, it was a really fast stop. Maybe too fast. And maybe she'd been a little rough with those reins. Cupcake rose on his hind legs and let out one of those angry neighs like the wild, mean horse always makes in the movies.

She really should have grabbed for the saddle horn again.

But before she remembered to do that, she was already sliding—right off the backside of Cupcake.

She landed hard on the same place she'd hit when she bounced high in the saddle that one time Cupcake stumbled. Her poor backside. It would never be the same. She let out a "Whoof!" of surprise as she hit the ground, followed by a low groan of pain.

And then she just flopped all the way down onto her back and stared up at the blue sky between the branches of the two big trees as she waited for the agony to finish singing up and down her spine.

Cupcake, making soft chuffing, snuffling sounds, turned around and stood over her. He nuzzled her temple, snuffling some more.

She groaned again and reached up and patted the side of his spotted head. "Good job," she told him, and then qualified, "basically." Reassured, he backed off a little and started nibbling at the skimpy grass between the trees.

"Joss! My God, Joss!" It was Jason. Judging by the sound of swift hooves approaching, he must have taken off down the mountain after her.

She really ought to sit up and show him that she was okay.

And she would. Very soon. Right now, though, well, her butt really hurt and she didn't have the heart to sit on it yet.

A moment later, she heard him draw to a stop a few feet away. He was off that black horse and kneeling at her side in about half a second flat.

His worried face loomed above her. "Joss…Joss are you…"

"I'm okay," she groaned.

He didn't look convinced. "Can you…move your arms and legs?"

She reached up and touched the side of his face, the same way she had done with Cupcake. "Honestly, I'm fine—well, except for my backside. That could be better."

"I'm so sorry." He looked positively stricken. "I made you come today. I never should have—"

"Shh." She put her fingers against his soft mouth. She really did love his mouth. She almost wished she'd kissed him last night after all, even if it was a bad idea. "It's fine," she said. "*I'm* fine. Cupcake is fine." She laughed a little. "And I have to tell you, *that* was exciting."

He grunted. "Yeah, *too* exciting."

She gave him her hand and he pulled her to a sitting position as she heard more horses approaching.

"She okay?" Ethan asked. Joss glanced over her shoulder and saw Jace's older brother, with Lizzie right behind him.

"Everything works," Joss told them, gathering her legs under her, only moaning a little, as Jace helped her to her feet. "But I'm guessing there will be bruises." She leaned on Jace. He put his arm around her. That was nice. She felt safe and protected, all tucked up close against him.

He said, "There's a doctor available back at the resort. Can you ride back? He can take a look at you."

She put a hand to her head. "My hat…"

"It's halfway between here and the trail," Lizzie said. "We can grab it on the way back up."

Joss stared from Jace to Lizzie and then to Ethan. "I can't believe you guys rode down here on purpose—even to come to my rescue."

Ethan chuckled. "It's really not that bad."

"It only seems that way when the trail breaks out from under you," Lizzie added. "Lucky they gave you a steady-natured mount."

Joss cast an appreciative glance at Cupcake who continued happily munching the sparse grass. "He's a champion, all right."

"Can we cut the chitchat?" Jace insisted, "We've got to get you to the doctor."

She reached back and felt all the places that ached. "Really, it's just not that bad."

"Joss, you could have been—"

"Don't even say it. What matters is I *wasn't*. Cupcake saved the day and I might end up with a bruise or two and there is no way I'm missing the picnic now I've come this far."

"But you—"

She stuck her index finger in the air. "Wait. Watch."

"Joss—"

"I mean it. Wait."

He looked at her like he wanted to strangle her, or at least try to shake a little sense into her. But he did shut up.

She peeled his hand off her shoulder and stepped away from him. "See? Upright and A-okay." She took a step, then another. It hurt a little. And she bet she was going to be sore the next morning. But she was absolutely certain the damage was only superficial. "Really, I'm okay. See?" She held her arms out to the side. "Ta-da!"

"I don't like it," he grumbled.

"Well, too bad. It's my butt and I say it's going to be fine."

Ethan laughed and shared a knowing glance with his wife. "Give it up, Jace. That woman has made up her mind."

* * *

The trip back up to the trail was nowhere near as thrilling as the ride down. In fact, going upward, it seemed steep, but not scarily so. And they found her hat about midway, as Lizzie had promised.

Jace jumped down and retrieved it for her, scowling up at her as he handed it over. "You *sure* you don't want to see the resort doctor?"

She gave him her widest, most confident smile as she settled her hat back in place on her head. "I am absolutely certain. And tell you what, you don't have to ask again. If I change my mind, I'll let you know."

"What if you have internal injuries?"

"Thank you for getting my hat. And will you please stop worrying?"

"It's only that…" He pressed those fine lips together. "If you end up in a coma, I'll hate myself forever and I'll never forgive you."

"A coma? Maybe you didn't notice. It wasn't my head I landed on."

"You know what I mean."

"Hey, you two! Get a move on," Ethan called from several yards ahead.

Jace just waved a hand at him and kept looking up at Joss, a focused, intense, almost angry kind of look. "If anything happened to you, I couldn't stand it…."

His words warmed her. They…touched her, because he really meant them. He really did care. About her safety, her well-being.

Maybe her life was a mess, but at least she'd found Jason. And he truly was her friend.

"Shh." She bent down to him and she kissed him, softly, quickly, on those perfect lips of his. They felt good, his lips. Even better than she had imagined they might. "Stop worrying," she whispered. "That's an order."

He stared up at her for a moment. He didn't look so angry now. Was that a flash of heat she saw in his dark eyes? But then he frowned. "You're fine? You mean that?"

"I am. Yes."

Shaking his head, he turned and mounted the black horse and they continued upward.

At the trail, the rest of the Traubs were waiting. They congratulated Joss on her excellent handling of a dangerous situation. She laughed and told them that her current good health was all due to Cupcake.

They started moving again, following the narrow, winding trail up the side of Thunder Mountain. It was a gorgeous ride. And Joss appreciated it more fully for having survived the headlong tumble down the cliff. She felt a lot easier on Cupcake, too, a lot more confident that even if she was a complete greenhorn, her horse could handle just about anything that fate might throw his way.

Eventually, they emerged from the trees at a higher elevation, where the wind blew brisk and cool and you could look down and see the lower hills and valleys spread out for miles and miles. From up there, the town of Thunder Canyon looked picture-postcard perfect. She could even see the little white church she and Jace had attended two days before. It really was a beautiful little town.

The Traub women had packed a light meal in their saddlebags. They spread blankets in the sun and enjoyed a leisurely lunch. Joss ate heartily. The headlong race down the side of the mountain had given her an appetite.

Jace stayed close. He seemed to be watching for a sign that she might need a doctor after all. She would glance over and catch him looking at her in that same concerned, attentive way. Every time he did that, she felt all warm and good inside. Protected.

Cared for.

She was starting to see that she really would be okay in the long run. Funny how a near-death experience can snap the world into sharper focus. She was young and smart and strong and she had enough money in her bank account to get by until she found another job.

And hey, after knowing Jace, she had to admit that there were still a few good men left in the world. Not every guy was a cheating jerk.

At three, they were back at the resort stables. Lizzie turned Cupcake over to the groom and felt a little sad to watch him amble away.

Jace said, "I think you like that horse."

"He's the best."

He put his arm around her and she leaned close to him with a sigh. He said, "We can ride again, you know, before the week is out."

"Yes," she agreed, and looked up to meet those velvety brown eyes. "Let's make a point to do that."

That evening Ethan and Lizzie had the big family cookout at their place. Melba Landry was there. She told both Joss and Jason that she was expecting them at the Historical Society Museum.

"Tomorrow, in fact," Lizzie's great-aunt instructed.

Joss had a great time that evening. She helped Lizzie and Rose Traub Anderson in the kitchen. Lizzie was not only a baker but also an excellent all-around cook.

Joss told her about the restaurant she'd managed in Sacramento. "I loved that job," she said. "I hated to leave it. There was something new happening every night. A little bit glamorous, you know? All the customers dressed for a night out, the snowy tablecloths and the good china, floating candles and an orchid in a cut-crystal bud vase at every table. It was a really nice dinner place, with an excellent wine list and to-die-for desserts. I loved the camaraderie between the front and back of the house. And the chef, Marilyn, was a wonder. Not only super creative with a great reputation, but also the calmest, most even-tempered person I've ever met. People say chefs are temperamental. Not Marilyn Standall. I never once heard her even raise her voice, no matter how crazy things got in the kitchen."

Lizzie asked the next logical question. "Why did you quit?"

Joss almost told her. Lizzie would be easy to confide in, but it would have been a downer to get into all that. So she only shrugged. "Time for a change, I guess. I like running a restaurant, though. Most likely I'll find something similar when I get back to Sacramento."

Later, after most of the Traubs had gone home, Joss and Jason stayed to help bring in the extra chairs from outside and stack the dishes by the sink. Lizzie had a housekeeper who would be in to take care of the rest in the morning.

It was after eleven when they climbed into Jace's Range Rover for the drive back up to the resort.

"Did you have a good time?" he asked.

"The best."

"Mind a little detour?" He started the engine.

She glanced over at him and felt a warm glow move through her. "I'm open. Let's go."

Jace's heart sank as he pulled into the parking lot at the corner where Main Street turned sharply north and became Thunder Canyon Road.

The sodium vapor lamp overhead lit a whole lot of

empty asphalt. And the rustic, shingled two-story build-ing stood dark in the eastern corner of the lot.

He turned off the engine and leaned on the wheel to stare out the windshield in disbelief. "Not possible. No-body said a word to me..."

"A word about what?" Joss asked.

He gestured at the darkened building. "The Hitching Post. Looks like it's closed."

"Just for the night, right? It's after eleven."

He shook his head. "In the summer, it used to be open Monday through Saturday till two in the morning."

"Maybe they changed their hours? I see a couple of lights on upstairs."

He leaned closer to the windshield until he could see the glow in the second-floor windows. "There are apart-ments up there..."

She flashed that gorgeous smile at him as she pushed open the passenger door. "Come on. Let's have a look, see what's going on."

They walked across the empty parking lot together, their footsteps echoing in a way that sounded sad and lonesome to his ears. At the sidewalk, they turned for the front of the building, with its wide, wood-pillared porch and the big wooden sign between the windows on the second floor. The block letters were a little faded but still legible in the streetlamp's glow: THE HITCHING POST.

And the long rail was still there, at the sidewalk's edge, the rail that had given the place its name back when it first opened as a bar and grill in the 1950s. To the present day, folks still used that rail to hitch their horses.

Or they used to, at least last summer, when he'd come to town for Corey's wedding.

There was a big white sign tacked to the doors. FOR

SALE, it proclaimed in red letters large enough they were visible even in the shadows of the darkened porch.

Twin signs in the windows that flanked the door proclaimed CLOSED INDEFINITELY in letters as big and red as those on the sign offering the place for sale.

Jace stood on the sidewalk looking at all that darkness, at the sad little glow in one of those upstairs windows. "Closed indefinitely. How is that possible? They did a bang-up business. Everybody in town loved this place. I don't get why it would close. And I can't believe no one even *told* me."

Joss slipped her hand into his and he felt a little better. He was glad for the contact, glad she was there. She said, "You sound like you just lost an old friend."

He turned his gaze to her. There was plenty of light, both from the streetlamp and from the nearly full moon. She'd tipped up her pretty face to him, her big eyes amber-colored right then, and soft with sympathy. Gruffly, he confessed, "I feel like it, too. Damn. I was looking forward to showing you around inside, seeing if that bartender I liked, Carl, was still there. I've been wanting to tell you all about the Shady Lady."

"What shady lady?"

"She was a local legend. Her real name was Lily Divine. She lived in Thunder Canyon back when the town was first settled. They called her the Shady Lady and she owned a saloon by that name, a saloon that stood right here, where the Hitching Post is now. Come on…." He tugged on her hand and she went with him, up the steps, into the shadows of that wide, deserted porch.

She whispered, "Tell me you're not planning a break-in."

He chuckled. "It did cross my mind. But no, I promise. We're not breaking in. I just want a closer look at the For

Sale sign." He read the smaller print at the bottom. The Realtor was Bonnie Drake at Thunder Creek Real Estate. Her name was familiar. Hadn't Ethan mentioned her in the past? Maybe she was the Realtor Ethan had used when he bought the building on State Street for TOI Montana.

Joss asked, "Why? You going to buy yourself a bar and grill?"

"Don't laugh. I just might."

She pulled on his hand until he turned and faced her. "You're kidding."

He busted to it. "Well, yeah. What would I do with a bar and grill?" He joked, "Unless you want to show me how to run one?"

She tipped her dark head to the side, and even through the shadows, he saw the ghost of a smile haunting her way-too-kissable mouth. "It's kind of a nice fantasy. Living in this great little town, running the place where all the locals love to hang out…"

A slight wind ruffled her hair, brought the scent of her perfume to him. She always smelled so good. It occurred to him that if he ever tried again, *really* tried, with a woman, he hoped that maybe she would smell as good as Joss did. Clean and sweet, both at once.

She frowned a little. "What?"

He bent closer, whispered teasingly, "I didn't say anything."

She was studying him. "You had the strangest expression on your face…"

"I was thinking that you smell good, that's all. That I like your perfume."

"Oh." Did her cheeks get pinker? Hard to tell in the darkness, but it seemed that maybe they did. "Well, um, thank you."

"The pleasure is all mine, believe me."

Her eyes seemed so wide right then, and filled with amber light, even in the deep shadows of the dark porch. "Jace?" She sounded slightly breathless.

He encouraged her, "Yeah?"

"You know today, when you came down the hill after me and found me flat on my back?"

"Yeah?"

"I thought how I wished I had kissed you last night." Her words sent a flare of heat moving through him. She added, almost shyly, "I mean life is too short, right? You never know what might happen."

He touched the side of her face. Her skin was so soft. And damn, was she trying to tell him something? "Joss, are you okay? Are you in pain? Do you need to see a doctor?"

She cut him off with a low, sweet laugh. "Stop. I'm fine. That wasn't my point." And then she grew serious again. "It's only, well, in life it always seems like there's plenty of time. But is there really? What if I died and I hadn't even kissed you?"

He gazed down into her upturned face and he never wanted to look away. A moment ago, he'd been kind of depressed, to think that the Hitching Post was closed up, with a For Sale sign on the front door. But suddenly, he didn't feel bad at all anymore. The world seemed full of promise. And hope. Of good things. And every single one of them was shining in Joss's big brown eyes.

"I really don't want you to have any regrets," he said, his voice low, maybe a little rougher than he'd meant it to be.

"But I do have regrets. You know that. About a thousand of them. I've made a lot of mistakes and I—"

"Shh." He touched her sweet lips with his fingers and instructed solemnly, "I want you to let those regrets go."

"I'm working on it."

"And the little problem that we never kissed?"

"Yeah?"

"That's easily fixed."

"You're right," she whispered, tipping that tempting mouth up to him like an offering. "So very easily…"

"We can fix it right now. Here. Tonight."

"Yes." Those bright eyes had a naughty gleam in them. They told him she could be bad—in a very good way. "I think we should."

"Joss…" It wasn't a question. Not this time.

But she answered it anyway. "Yes. Oh, yes."

He lowered his head and tasted her lips for the first time.

Chapter Seven

Joss knew that she shouldn't be kissing Jace.

She was almost thirty, for crying out loud. Old enough to know that nothing messed up a perfectly great friendship as fast as sex could. And what did sex start with?

Kisses.

Kisses like this one. Slow, delicious kisses. Kisses that began so gently, with Jace's wonderful soft mouth just barely brushing hers, with the warmth of his big, lean body so close, but not quite making contact with hers.

Yet.

Kisses that led to touching—oh, yes.

Touching just like Jace was doing right now, his big hands cradling her face, holding her mouth up to him. Wonderful hands he had, strong and slightly callused, and warm.

So warm…

He let them wander.

She knew that he would. She welcomed the slow twin caresses along the sides of her neck as his fingers skimmed downward. Oh, she could easily get used to this, to kissing Jace.

For five whole years, she'd never kissed anyone but Kenny. Really, what had she been thinking?

She'd been missing out, big time.

Jace clasped her shoulders. His lips moved on hers, coaxing. She knew what he wanted.

She wanted it, too. She parted her lips for him and let him inside.

He groaned, a soft, low, pleasured sort of sound. She felt it, too. The beginnings of arousal. Already, her body was kind of melty and heavy in the most lovely, delicious sort of way.

She swayed against him and he gathered her in.

Oh. Yes. Perfect. Her breasts were now pressed against his hard chest. They ached, a little, already. A good, rich, exciting ache. An ache that promised to deepen in the best sense of the word.

His arms were nice and tight around her and she felt cherished and safe and very, very good. And his tongue was doing beautiful things inside her mouth, stroking, exploring. Learning all her secrets—well, a few of them at least.

He lifted his mouth from hers. She made a frantic little sound, not wanting it to end. Not yet.

Oh, please. Not yet....

And then, what do you know? It didn't end. He simply slanted his amazing lips the other way and kissed her some more.

Yes. *This*, she thought in a lovely, foggy, heated wordless way. This was it. *The* kiss. The one she'd known she couldn't afford to miss....

Jace's kiss...

He wrapped her even closer, so tight against him.

Tight enough that she could feel his growing hardness, pressing into her. Her response was immediate. She sighed against his warm lips and pressed herself even closer, lifting her hips to him, eager.

For more.

For sex.

With Jace.

Sex...

Oh, she did want to...

But then what?

The annoying question echoed in her brain, stealing her pleasure in this special moment, reminding her that her life was all upside-down and an affair on the rebound was not a good idea. Her world was way too complicated already. She didn't need to make it more so.

He must have felt her withdrawal. He raised his head and he smiled down at her, so tenderly, his dark eyes low and lazy. "You messed up and started thinking, didn't you?"

"Guilty." She put her hands against his chest. She could feel his heartbeat, strong and steady.

He peered at her more intently. "You okay?"

She nodded. "You are a totally amazing kisser."

And he smiled. "Likewise."

"I would kiss you some more, but..."

"...it's not what we're about," he finished for her. His strong arms fell away and she carefully kept herself from swaying back against him. He offered his arm. She took it. "Come on," he said, "I'll take you back up to the resort."

"Not coming in?" she asked, when he pulled up under the porte cochere.

Jace was thinking he would like to go in. He would like

it a lot, but it seemed too dangerous after that kiss. She'd felt just right in his arms. And the sweet taste of her lips…

That had been something. The way she'd cuddled up close against him had really gotten him going. They might be best friends and not going there. But he had to be realistic. She did it for him. In a big way.

And he needed a little distance. Tonight, he could too easily be tempted to try and put a real move on her. And he got that she wasn't up for anything hot and heavy with him—or with anyone. Not after what she'd been through.

"Not tonight," he whispered. "Breakfast? We can go down to the bakery and maybe—"

"Yes." She smiled an eager smile. And he was glad. They'd shared an amazing, mind-blowing kiss, but it wasn't going to mess things up between them.

The valet opened her door. She got out and then turned back and leaned in to ask, "Nine tomorrow morning? Pick me up right here, under the porte cochere?"

"You got it."

The valet shut the door. Jace watched her turn for the entrance, admiring the easy sway of her hips, entranced by the way all that lush, shiny hair tumbled down her slim back.

During the drive to Jackson and Laila's place, his mind kept circling back to the kiss. To the way she filled his arms, to the feel of her breasts against his chest, to the way she pressed her body to him, lower down, to her soft mouth opening under his…

He thought about kissing her again.

He thought about doing a lot more than just kissing.

The house was dark when he let himself in. He went straight up to the guest room and took a shower. A very cold shower, for a long, long time.

When he got out, his teeth were chattering and his lips

were blue. But the shower had done the trick. He was freezing and sex was the last thing on his mind.

And he'd learned his lesson. He was not kissing Joss again. He was not even *thinking* about kissing Joss again.

Uh-uh. No way….

In the morning before he left to pick up Joss, he joined Jackson and Laila in the kitchen.

"So," he asked his twin, "how long's the Hitching Post been closed?"

"Since March," Jackson said.

"You never a said a word." Jace tried not to sound accusing, but it did kind of bug him that no one had told him. "*Nobody* said anything. Joss and I stopped in there last night and everything was dark."

Jackson sipped his morning coffee and answered with a shrug. "It was a shock when it happened. But you were more or less refusing to communicate at that point."

That was true, Jace had to admit. In March, he'd still been pretty down after the whole mess with Tricia. Half the time, when Jackson or any of his siblings called, he would find some excuse to get off the phone fast, and then not bother calling them back. He hadn't felt like talking to anyone—and he certainly hadn't felt like answering any questions as to what the hell was the matter with him.

"Sorry about that," he said and meant it.

"Hey." Jackson gave him a grin. "You finally seem to be coming out of it. That's what matters."

At the stove, Laila asked, "You want some bacon and eggs, Jace?"

"Thanks, but no. I'm picking Joss up and we're going to the Mountain Bluebell." He asked his brother, "So what's the story? I always thought the Hitching Post was a moneymaker. Why would they suddenly close down?"

"Lance O'Doherty died," Laila said somberly.

Jace blinked. "No." O'Doherty and his wife Kathleen had owned the Hitching Post since it first opened in the 1950s. Kathleen had passed away some years back.

"Yeah," Jackson confirmed. "Lance finally went to meet his maker. The old guy was in his eighties. And he was still going strong right up to the end. Story goes that he went to bed on March first and never woke up on the second. There was no one to take over for him."

"I thought there was a daughter..."

Jackson nodded. "Noreen. She's in her fifties. Plays the harp for some symphony in San Diego. Never married, no kids. Has zero interest in coming back to Thunder Canyon to run her dad's bar and grill. So she shut it down and put it up for sale, cheap. At first, we were all sure that someone would snap it right up. I think I heard that there were a few offers made, but I guess those deals never went through."

Jason shook his head. "The Hitching Post out of business. That's just wrong."

"Someone will buy it eventually," said Laila. "It's been only a few months since it went up for sale. It's a great location, with plenty of parking. I heard a rumor a cousin of the Cateses from Sheridan was thinking about buying the property and turning it into a farm machinery dealership."

"Farm machinery?" Jace swore in disgust.

Jackson chuckled. "People need tractors, Jace."

"And this town needs the Hitching Post."

Jackson sent him a sly look. "Why don't you buy it?"

He thought about last night, him and Joss in the shadows next to the locked-up front door with the For Sale sign on it. He'd teased her that he would buy it and she could teach him how to run it.

But it was only a daydream. A fantasy, like Joss had said.

Laila fished bacon out of the frying pan and onto a

paper towel–covered platter. "Yeah, that would be great if you moved to town. Your brother misses you, you know? We all miss you. Family matters. It matters a lot."

Jackson and Jace shared a look. Jace had missed his twin, too. He only realized how much now he was coming out of the funk that had gripped him for months.

And Thunder Canyon would be a great place to live. Yeah, it got mighty cold in the winters, but he could deal with that. There were still lots of wild, wide open spaces in Montana. He wouldn't mind exploring them. Plus, he'd have the benefit of being near a lot of the people who mattered most to him. And he *was* planning to move.

But he wasn't ready to decide where yet. And as for the Hitching Post…

"I know zip about running a restaurant," he said.

Jackson got up to refill his coffee mug. "No law says you can't learn."

Joss was moving a little stiffly when he picked her up at nine. But she said she was fine.

She laughed. "Hey, you should have seen me when I first got up. It wasn't pretty. But I'm feeling better now that I've been moving around."

And it did seem to him that her stiffness faded as the day went by. After breakfast at Lizzie's bakery, they walked over to the Historical Society Museum on Pine Street. Aunt Melba was there, behind the little desk in the small lobby area of the old building.

"So lovely to see two young, smiling faces," she said. She charged them three dollars each and then gave them a guided tour.

The rooms were small and dark and packed with treasures from the past. There was a whole display dedicated to Lily Divine, the madam who'd owned the Shady Lady

Dance Hall in the 1890s. They learned that some sources claimed Lily hadn't really been a madam at all, but a hardworking laundress who took in women in trouble and helped them to get back on their feet. There was even some dispute as to whether the famous portrait of Lily, nearly nude but for several strategically place scarves, was actually of Lily at all.

Jace couldn't help wondering if that portrait still hung over the bar inside the Hitching Post. He hated to think of someone turning the place into a tractor dealership.

What would happen to the portrait of the Shady Lady then? Would they dismantle the long, gleaming cherrywood bar that had been built over a century ago?

He decided not to think about it.

Times changed and a man had to learn to roll with the punches. He set his mind to enjoying the time he had left with Joss.

It was going by too fast.

That afternoon, they went riding again. He borrowed Major from Jackson and she rode Cupcake. He took her to a small, crystal-clear lake he knew about on the other side of Thunder Mountain from the resort. It was too cold to swim, but they spread a saddle blanket in the sun and stretched out for a while. She said she was feeling better about her life now, about everything. And she thanked him. She told him she didn't hate all men anymore. And she said that was mostly due to him.

He listened to her talk and drank in her laughter and thought about kissing her.

But he didn't. They were friends. Period. And he intended to remember that.

That night, the family get-together was at Dax and Shandie's. Jace took Joss. They had a great time.

The next day was the Fourth. In Thunder Canyon, that

meant a parade in the morning, a rodeo in the afternoon and a community dance in the town hall at night. He and Joss spent every moment together.

He thought about kissing her a lot that day, especially at the dance. When he held her in his arms, it was all too easy to start remembering how good her lips felt pressed to his.

But he held himself in check somehow. Even though sometimes, in her eyes, he thought he saw an invitation. He had a feeling she wouldn't be entirely averse to another kiss. And when he danced with her, he tried not to read too much into the way her curvy body swayed against him.

That night, he took another long, cold shower before he went to bed. It didn't do a lot of good. His dreams were all about Joss, naked and willing in his arms.

Thursday they played golf up at the resort's golf course. Joss was a really bad golfer.

"I'm worse with a golf club than I am on a horse," she said.

He had to agree. Actually, she had some aptitude for riding. But she was a walking hazard with a golf club. Every time she swung it, turf went flying. The ball, however, rarely budged.

After dinner that night at Corey and Erin's, they returned to the resort and hung out in her suite. He told her he kept thinking about the Hitching Post, that he was actually kind of tempted by the idea of maybe buying the place, of moving to Thunder Canyon and learning how to run a restaurant and bar.

She encouraged him. He was just getting around to hinting that maybe she might consider taking a job managing a restaurant and bar in a great little town like Thunder Canyon when the phone rang.

It was her mother, at it again. He couldn't hear the woman's words, but he could see in Joss's face what she must be saying: Come home to Sacramento and work things out with Kenny. When Joss hung up, her slim shoulders were drooping and all the warm amber light was gone from her eyes. He wanted to take her in his arms and hold her, and promise her that everything would be okay.

But she asked him to leave, said she needed a little time alone. She really was down.

He went back to Jackson's and took another cold shower.

That night he dreamed of Lily Divine—except she had Joss's face. In the dream, he stood at the bar in the Hitching Post and looked up at the painting of the Shady Lady.

And suddenly, the painting came alive. The Shady Lady was Joss, so fine and curvy and mostly naked, lying on her side, braced up on an elbow with her beautiful backside to him, sending him a come-and-get-it look over one bare, dimpled shoulder. He stood there, gulping, hard as a rock.

But then she sat up from the pose she'd been stuck in for more than a century. The scarves that covered her breasts and hips wafted in a warm breeze that had come up out of nowhere—right there in the Hitching Post. She stepped out of the painting and down off the wall, her long hair lifted and coiling seductively around her in that impossible breeze. She reached out her slim, bare arms to him, her eyes gleaming with the promise of untold sensual delights.

And then he woke up.

He lay there in the guest room bed and glared at the darkened ceiling and wondered who he'd been kidding, to think it would be enough for him, to be just friends with a woman like Joss.

She called him at seven Friday morning. "Sorry I was such a downer." Her voice was sweet and husky in his ear.

"Hey," he said a little more gruffly than he meant to, "it's not a problem. You know that."

"I want to go riding one more time before I go…."

Her words hit him like a punch to the solar plexus. *Before I go…*

Their time was ending. Tomorrow was Saturday. And Sunday she was leaving.

A week. It was nothing. Gone in an instant. He'd known that, hadn't he?

So why did it suddenly seem so wrong, so completely unfair, that she would be going, leaving him for good?

He schooled his voice to easiness. "So we'll go riding. Today?"

"Yeah. I thought breakfast first at the Grubstake." That was the coffee shop at the resort. "And then we'd head for the stables. I already asked to have Cupcake ready."

He would need to get the go-ahead from Jackson to take Major again. That should be no problem. "Bring something you can swim in," he said.

"But I thought the mountain lakes were too cold."

"I know a little valley. A wide creek runs through it. It's not so high up and should be warm enough for swimming."

"Sounds wonderful," she agreed.

"The Grubstake, then." His voice was rough again, a little ragged with emotions he didn't even understand. "Give me an hour."

"I'll be there. Waiting."

And she *was* there, just as she'd promised, waiting in the coffee shop, dressed for riding in her red boots and jeans and a blue-and-white checked shirt. They ordered pancake specials, with scrambled eggs and bacon. She was animated and smiling, out from under the cloud of misery that had gotten her down the night before.

"Today and tomorrow," she said, her dark eyes gleaming. "And that's it." Did she have to remind him? "I'm going to enjoy every minute of the time we have left."

Don't go. The words were there on the tip of his tongue. He shut his mouth over them and swallowed them down.

He tried to remember what a tangled mess the whole thing with Tricia had been, that he didn't know his ass from up when it came to relationships. That the last thing Joss needed at this point was another man in her life.

A friend, she could handle.

But more?

It wasn't going to happen. She needed time to get over that asshat Kenny, time to put her life back together, to get on her feet. She didn't need to get involved with some ex-player ex-oilman from Texas who didn't know zip about love and was seriously considering relocating to Montana and trying his hand at running a bar and grill.

They finished their pancakes and headed for the stables. By ten-thirty, they were on their way up the mountain. They rode a different series of trails that day, around the mountain, climbing for a time. But then, using a series of switchbacks, heading lower, down into the little valley he'd told her about.

The land belonged to Grant Clifton, the resort's manager, and his wife, Steph. Last year, when Ethan had invested Traub money in the resort, Grant had been kind enough to issue a general invitation to any Traubs who wanted to swim in the creek there.

"It's beautiful," Joss said, when they spread a blanket under a cottonwood at the edge of the creek.

He had a hard time paying a lot of attention to the trees and the clear creek and the rolling, sunlit land. Joss had taken off her jeans, boots and shirt by then. She wore a little black-and-white bikini that looked like polka dots at first glance, but was really tiny white hearts on a black background. She filled it out real nice. He kept thinking about his dream, where she was the Shady Lady and she came down out of the picture and held out her arms to him.

"Jace?" she asked softly. "You okay?"

"Ahem. Fine. Great. Why?"

She laughed then. "Well, your mouth is hanging open."

He shut it. "Is not."

She laughed again and turned and ran to the creek. He watched her pretty, round bottom bouncing away from him and tried not to think about how much he wanted a lot more than he was ever going to have with her. If she had any bruises from her fall the other day, he couldn't see them.

Hugging herself and giggling, she went into the water. "It's cold!" She bent at the knees and got right down into it all the way up to her neck.

"I can hear your teeth chattering," he teased from the bank, admiring the way that thick, long hair of hers fanned out on the water all around her.

"My teeth are chattering because the water is freezing!"

"Don't be a sissy," he taunted.

"You said it would be warm down here in this valley," she accused. "Brrrr."

"It is warm—compared to the lakes higher up."

She rose to her feet, the water sheeting off her body, her hair falling to cling like a lover to her shoulders and the high, proud curves of her breasts. The sight stole the breath clean out of his body and made all the spit dry up in his mouth.

"Well?" she demanded. "Are you coming in?"

He remembered to breathe and he swallowed, hard. "Yes, ma'am." He dropped to the blanket and pulled off his boots and socks. His shirt followed. Then he stood up again to unbuckle his belt. A moment later, he stepped out of his jeans.

Joss gave him a two-finger whistle. "I never saw a cow-boy in board shorts before—neon orange, no less." He made a show of flexing his biceps and she laughed some more.

And then he took off toward her at a run. She shrieked as he cannonballed into the water. And when he got his feet under him and stood up, she started madly splashing him.

He dived and grabbed for her legs, yanking them out from under her. Flailing and laughing, she went down, but only for a moment. Then she kicked free of his grip and swam for the far bank.

When he caught up with her, she was trying to climb out on the other side.

He grabbed her shoulders and pulled her back in.

She let out a shriek and went under again.

A moment later, she shot upright. She was quick, he had to give her that. She gave him a shove when he wasn't expecting it. He went down on his back, sending water flying. He heard her laughing as the creek closed over his head.

In a few seconds, he was upright again. They started madly splashing each other, both of them fanning the water for all they were worth, really going to town.

Finally, her hair plastered to her face, water dripping from her nose, she put up both hands. "All right. I surrender. You win. You're the champion."

That made him laugh. "The champion of splashing?"

"Yeah." She swiped a hand over the crown of her head, gathering her hair in one thick swatch, guiding it forward over her shoulder so she could wring the water from the dripping strands. "You don't want to be the champion of splashing?"

He speared his fingers back through his hair. "Depends on the prize."

She made a scoffing sound. "Please. You don't get a prize for splashing the hardest."

He stepped up closer. He couldn't resist. They stood in the shallows by then, not far from the bank and their waiting blanket, with the hobbled horses grazing nearby.

She stared up at him, drops of water caught like diamonds in her long, dark eyelashes, her eyes so bright they blinded him. Damn. She was beautiful. "Jace?"

He couldn't stop staring at her wide, soft mouth. "I want to kiss you."

"Oh, Jace…"

"You'd better tell me not to. You'd better tell me now."

Chapter Eight

She drew in a breath—a sharp little sound. And she argued, "But I don't want to tell you not to…"

He took her shoulders. Wet. Silky. Cool. Longing speared through him. Sharp. Hot. "Was that a yes?"

"Oh, Jace…"

"Answer the question."

"Yes." She said it fervently. Eagerly. "That's a yes."

So he kissed her. Kissed her for the second time. Slowly, deeply.

She opened for him and he tasted the sweetness beyond her parted lips. He gathered her close to him, skin to skin, carefully. Tenderly.

The sun was warm on his back and she was so perfect in his arms. He didn't want to let her go.

But he knew he had to. He lifted his mouth from hers with regret. And he opened his eyes to find hers waiting for him.

She searched his face. "Do you know how much I'll miss you?"

Don't go. "Hey, you're not gone yet."

She reached up, touched his lips with her cool, smooth fingers. "That's right. I'm still here. And I'm so glad…" Her eyes shone brighter, wetter. A single tear escaped and trailed down her cheek. He leaned close and kissed that warm wetness away. She whispered, "I'm so glad I met you."

"Me, too." He took her hand. "Come on." He led her up to the bank where he picked up the blanket and moved it out from under the shading branches of the tree.

They lay down side-by-side, faces tipped to the sunlight.

Far off, he heard the cry of a hawk. And then silence, just the rushing whisper of the creek and the wind stirring the cottonwoods.

He closed his eyes. It was one of those moments, so simple. So perfect—him and Joss on a blanket in the sun.

Eventually, they got up and pulled on their jeans, shirts and boots. They ate the jerky he'd brought along in his saddlebag and drank from their canteens. Then they rolled up the blanket and tied it on behind Major's saddle.

They mounted up and started back the way they had come.

That night, they had dinner with the rest of the family at Rose and Austin's. Around eleven, they went back to the resort. He stayed until three in the morning. They talked and they laughed. They ate too much chocolate. They watched two movies on pay-per-view: a romantic comedy for her and an old Western for him.

The whole night he kept thinking, *Don't go, don't go.* After a while it seemed that the words were there, echoing, in every breath he took, in every beat of his heart.

But he didn't say them.

And he didn't kiss her again either. Not kissing her was almost as hard as not saying "Don't go." But he managed both somehow. He went back to Jackson's in the early morning hours, had his usual cold shower and climbed under the covers to toss and turn and dream of her.

He was up at daylight. He showered fast and dressed faster and headed for the resort. Luck was with him. He caught Grant in the office complex down the hill from clubhouse and took care of the business that had been nagging at him.

Then he went up the hill, got two coffees at the Starbucks on the first floor of the clubhouse and took the elevator to Joss's suite. He had to knock twice before she finally answered, looking sleepy and tousled and irresistible, barefoot in a cream-colored terrycloth robe.

"I see you brought coffee," she said in a sleepy voice. "Smart man."

Don't go. "Mornin'." He held hers out to her. She took it and sipped, stepping back at the same time so that he could enter. "I have a confession," he said to her back as she led the way into the sitting room.

She paused to send him a look over her shoulder. "Nothing too awful, I hope."

"I'm afraid you're going to be mad at me."

She turned around then, and faced him in the archway to the sitting room. "Better just say it." She sipped from her cup again.

It made him ache all over to look at her, to think that she was leaving, that tomorrow, she would be gone. "I stopped in and saw Grant this morning—you know, the resort manager?"

"I remember Grant."

"I caught him down the hill at his office…"

"Yeah?"

"And I paid your bill."

She had her cup halfway to her lips again, but she lowered it without drinking. Her face had a set look to it suddenly, and her dark gaze was steady on his. "Jace. No."

"Come on. It's not a big deal."

"It's a lot of money. And no." She reached out her hand.

He looked at it. "I guess if you're offering me your hand, at least you're not *too* mad. Right?"

"I'm not mad," she said softly. "I promise." She grabbed his fingers. Heat shot up his arm and he had to stop himself from yanking her close to him and slamming his mouth down on hers. "Come on." She towed him into the sitting room and over to the sofa. "Sit." He sat. She dropped down beside him and set her cup on the coffee table. "I'm…well, I could really get emotional, you know? It means so much that you would want to do that for me."

He set his untouched coffee beside hers. "Just say you're okay with it."

She blew out a hard breath. "But I'm not okay with it. It's not right."

"Sure it is." He tried to look stern and uncompromising. "I can afford it, believe me."

"That's not the issue. I mean, I get why you would want to. I do. And it's so sweet of you, really."

"It's not sweet, believe me," he muttered. "Not sweet in the least. I don't think you get it at all."

"But I do get it. It's about Kenny, right?"

How did she know that? He admitted, "I don't want that lowlife, cheating sonofabitch paying your way here. I just don't."

"Jace." She put her hand on his arm. For the second time that morning, he had to steel himself to keep from grabbing her tight and kissing her senseless. "Listen," she said, "I agree with you. I've been thinking about it, too.

And I've realized that I really can't have Kenny footing the bill. I don't want *anything* from Kenny."

"Good. There's no problem, then. It's paid."

With a low groan, she let go of his forearm. "You're not listening to me. It's not Kenny's bill. And it's not *your* bill. It's mine. And I will pay it."

He almost wished she'd been mad at him, instead of so firm and sure and uncompromising about it. How does a man get through to an uncompromising woman? "Listen. You like me, right?"

Her eyes held reproach. "Of course I do."

"You even trust me. A little."

"I trust you a lot." She almost smiled. "And a week ago, I would have sworn I would never trust a man again."

"So...can't you think of it as a gift from a friend? From your best friend? When you get settled, with a new apartment and a great job, you can feel free to pay me back if it's that important to you. But maybe, over time, you'll see things in a different light. You'll remember that I said I *wanted* to do this. And I meant what I said. I don't want you owing your ex a thing. I want you free of him. And I don't want you spending every cent you've got to *get* free of him."

She gathered her legs up onto the cushions and tucked them to the side. Then she wrapped the fluffy robe closer around her. "It wouldn't be every cent I've got..." She gave a low, sad little chuckle. "Not quite, anyway."

"Let me do this for you, Joss. Please."

"I really shouldn't..."

"Yeah, you should."

She shut her eyes, hung her head. "Thank you," she said, so softly.

He wanted to touch her, but that would be too dangerous. "Glad to do it."

And then she swayed against him, whispering a second time, "Thank you."

What could he do but exactly what he longed to do? He wrapped an arm around her and drew her close. And when she lifted her sweet lips to him, he kissed her, a light kiss, one he didn't allow himself to deepen.

And then he picked up her cup from the coffee table and handed it to her. "Go on. Get dressed. Let's get some breakfast."

Joss wanted that final day with Jace to last forever, but it seemed to fly by even faster than the ones before it.

They went to Lizzie's bakery for breakfast, and then they dropped in at the Historical Society Museum to say hi to Melba. They took a long drive along Thunder Canyon Road, all the way to the steep, rocky canyon for which the town was named.

That night, they had dinner in the resort's best restaurant, the Gallatin Room. They ran into Jace's parents there. Claudia and Pete were still staying at the resort.

Jace muttered resignedly, "I suppose we should go and say hi to them."

"Yes, we absolutely should."

So they stopped by the Wexlers' table for a moment. Claudia said how she and Pete would be there for at least another week. And Joss confessed that tomorrow she was on her way back to Sacramento.

"I hope you'll get Jason to bring you to Midland one of these days very soon," Claudia suggested.

Joss didn't give her an answer, only said how much she'd enjoyed spending time with the Traub family while she'd been in town.

They moved on to their table shortly after that. It was in a secluded corner, so it really felt like it was just the two of them. Jace ordered a nice bottle of wine and the food was wonderful, better than ever, she thought.

Jace thought so, too. He told the waiter.

The waiter said they had a new chef.

"Give him our compliments."

"I'll be more than happy to."

The waiter left, and the new chef came out to chat with them briefly. His name was Shane Roarke. He was ruggedly handsome, with black hair and piercing blue eyes. Joss had the feeling she'd met him somewhere before.

When he left them, Jace gazed after him, narrow-eyed. "I could swear I've met him somewhere before."

Joss nodded. "You know, I was just thinking the same thing...."

He looked at her then, his dark eyes so soft and warm, his mouth hinting at a smile. "Did I tell you that you look beautiful?"

Her chest felt a little tight and a delicious shiver whispered across the surface of her skin. "You did tell me. Twice—three times, counting just now."

"I like that dress."

It was snug, black, short and strapless. "You mentioned that, too."

He scowled. "I hate that you're leaving."

"I know. Me, too."

"But we can't go on like this forever."

She grinned. "You're so right. We've been having way too much fun."

He grunted. "It's got to stop."

She laughed. "Yep." She picked up her glass of wine. "Here's to a new life and a great job—for both of us."

He tapped his glass to hers. "To all your dreams coming true."

* * *

After dinner, he suggested, "We could go into town. I think there's another dance at the town hall tonight."

She shook her head and took his hand. "Let's go up to the suite."

He must have had a sense of what she was up to because something hot and hungry flashed in his eyes. "Maybe that's not such a good idea, Joss."

She knew exactly what he was doing—or trying to do: the right thing. As usual. "Jace…"

"What?" His voice was rough and low.

"It's our last night. I'm leaving in the morning. We may never see each other again."

"Rub it in, why don't you?"

"Come up to the suite with me." She held his gaze. She refused to glance away, to pretend to be shy about this. She wasn't shy. Not with him. With him, she'd always been able to say exactly what was on her mind.

He muttered something under his breath. She thought it was a swear word, but she wasn't sure.

She kept hold of his hand. "Come upstairs with me. Please."

He touched her cheek, smoothed a few strands of hair out of her eyes. "Are you sure? I don't want you to regret anything about the time you've spent with me."

"I'm sure." She searched his face. "But maybe you're not?"

A strangled sound escaped him. "Of course I'm sure. That's not the point."

"I disagree. I think if you're sure and I'm sure, well, what else is there? And don't start in about regrets again. I will never regret spending tonight with you." She whispered, "Could you stand it if I left without making love to you? I know I couldn't."

He actually groaned. And then he lifted her hand and pressed his warm lips to it. "That does it." He breathed the words onto her skin. "Let's go."

In the bedroom of her suite, they stood by her bed, facing each other.

She felt nervous. Apprehensive.

And yet, at the same time, absolutely sure.

The covers were already turned back. There were chocolates on the pillow.

"Your favorite kind," he said. "Dark and bittersweet."

She grabbed up the candy and set it on the nightstand. "I'll never eat them. I'll save them. To remember tonight…"

He grinned at that. Her heart ached. How would she live without seeing that grin of his? "Uh-uh. You should eat them. I'll feed them to you personally."

She turned her head away a little and gave him an oblique glance. "Now?"

"Later." He growled the word.

She swallowed. Hard. "I'm…on the pill, but I should have bought condoms."

He reached in his pocket and brought out four of them. "Okay," he said roughly. "It's like this. I never planned to put a move on you, I promise you…"

She teased, "But you wanted to be ready, just in case I dragged you up here and wouldn't let you go until you made mad, passionate love to me."

"Right." His dark eyes were bright with humor—and heat. "You being such a total animal and all."

She took the condoms from him and set them on the nightstand next to the chocolates. "So, all right, we have chocolate and condoms. We're ready for anything."

He was watching her so steadily. "Joss."

Her heart stopped still inside her chest—and then started in again, swift and hard. "Hmm?"

He took her by the shoulders, his big hands so warm and firm. And then he turned her around, smoothed her hair to the side and over her shoulder out of his way, and took down her zipper in one slow, seamless glide. Her strapless black dress dropped to the floor.

She looked down at it, in a silky black puddle around her ankles. Now, she wore her strapless bra, satin tap shorts, black high-heeled shoes. And nothing else.

He whispered her name again. "I never had a best friend like you before…" And he traced the bumps of her spine, so slowly, with one teasing finger, from the nape of her neck all the way down to where her tap pants rode low on her hips. "Beautiful." The single word was more breath than sound.

She stepped out of the dress and bent to retrieve it. There was a slipper chair a few feet from the nightstand. She tossed the dress on that chair and turned to him.

His eyes were dark fire, burning her in the most arousing way.

She said, "I'm so glad you're here. In this bedroom. With me." And she reached behind her, undid her bra and let it fall away.

He gasped. She found that ragged sound supremely satisfying, not to mention exciting.

"Your turn," she instructed.

He started undressing. He did it really fast, with a ruthless efficiency, dropping first to the side of the bed to tug off his boots and socks, and then rising again to face her as he stripped away everything else, tossing each article away from him as he removed it.

Within seconds, he was naked. He stood before her, so lean and tall and beautiful—yes. Beautiful. Beautiful in the way only a man can be, a beauty of power, of muscle. Of strength.

He reached for her, gathered her to him. She went with a soft, hungry cry.

His mouth came down to settle on hers and his chest was so hot and hard against her bare breasts, his arms so tight around her.

She kissed him. She opened to him. Her heartbeat, so rapid and frantic a moment ago, settled into a lazier, hungrier rhythm.

He took her face between his two hands, kissing her so deeply, so thoroughly, and then he threaded his fingers into her hair, combing the long strands, following them all the way down in one long stroke. He clasped her waist.

And then lower, grasping the twin curves of her bottom and drawing her up and into him—so tight. He kissed her some more. A dizzying, magical kiss. At the same time, he was turning her, guiding her to the bed, still kissing her as he eased her down. She sat on the edge and he bent to her, his mouth and her mouth, fused in a hot tangle of warm breath, of questing tongues....

He came down to her. She opened her thighs so he could kneel between them.

His strong hands caressed her breasts so gently, at first. He learned the shape of them, cradling them tenderly. He teased her nipples into aching hardness.

She swayed toward him, her mouth fused with his, wanting to be closer, aware of the thousand ways he thrilled her, excited her, made her burn. Awash in sheer wonder, she counted those ways: his touch, the taste of his mouth, the rough rasp of his beard shadow against her palms when she caressed the side of his face.

His dear face...

How had that happened? In the space of a week, he had

become so very dear to her. She could no longer imagine her life without him in it.

No. She couldn't.

Not now. Not tonight.

Facing the loss of him would be for tomorrow. In the harsh light of day.

Tonight was for magic. For beauty. For pleasure. For the impossible—her and Jace. Together.

This one time...

For tonight, she could almost be grateful that her world had come crashing down. That her groom had betrayed her. That her dream for her future was shattered. Gone.

She'd lost the life she'd longed for. She was going to have to start over.

But in the middle of her own personal disaster, she'd met Jason. He'd taken her bitterness and transformed it somehow. Made it something so perfect and good and sweet. He'd given her a week she would always remember.

And now, at the end, he presented her with one final gift: tonight.

He broke the kiss, settled back on his knees.

She gave a lost, hungry cry and tried to catch his mouth again.

But he clasped her shoulders, steadying her. She opened her eyes to find his dark gaze waiting. He almost smiled, but he didn't. Not quite.

He let his hands trail down the outsides of her arms, rousing goose bumps of desire, making her sigh.

"Oh, Jace..."

"I dreamed about you..."

She laughed, low, a secret, woman's laugh. "No..."

"Yeah."

"Tell me."

"You were the Shady Lady. It was you in that painting

over the bar at the Hitching Post. Remember, we saw a picture of that painting, that day we went to the museum?"

She nodded. "The Shady Lady, lying on her side, draped in nothing but a few scarves…"

His caresses strayed downward. He clasped her waist, molded the outer curves of her hips, and lower. He laid his warm palms on her thighs. "You do remember, then…"

"I do." She moaned a little. "You're driving me crazy."

"Good. In my dream, you were the Shady Lady and you came out of the picture and down into my arms. The wind was blowing out of nowhere, lifting your hair around your face, and lifting the scarves, too, so they kind of floated in the air around you."

"Wait a minute."

He frowned. "You want me to stop?"

"Don't you dare." She let out a shaky breath. "But…the wind was blowing in the Hitching Post?"

"It was a dream after all."

"Ah."

He cradled her calves, one in either hand, rubbing them a little. "And the wind was warm…."

She was on fire by then, yearning. "Ah. Warm. What happened next?"

He took her left ankle, raised it and slipped off her high-heeled shoe. "I woke up."

She sighed. "Oh, no."

"Yeah."

"Sad…"

"Yeah." He lifted her other foot, removed the other shoe, set it aside with its mate. And then he was stroking her legs again, but this time moving upward, over her shins, her knees, her trembling thighs.

Breath held, she watched him as he eased his clever fingers under the loose, lace-edged hems of her tap pants.

He touched her, both hands meeting at the place where her thighs joined, delving in, parting her.

She gasped as he caressed her, his fingers moving beneath the black satin. He found her, found her sweetest spot without even half trying. And he worked it, making her burn, making her so wet and ready....

Oh, it was heaven. Jace's touch.

She lay back across the bed and let him torment her so perfectly. She moaned out loud; it felt so right. And she lifted her hips to him, sighing, whispering his name, tossing her head, reaching down to clasp his corded forearms, holding on to him as he stroked her, bringing her higher.

Higher and higher...

"Lift up," he muttered low, pulling on the tap pants, guiding them down.

By then, she was wild with desire, lost in her own building excitement. She moaned and she raised her hips and he slipped the tap pants down and away.

And then he leaned closer. And his fingers were touching her, opening her. She knew she was bare to his gaze and somehow, that only fired her need, made her burn hotter.

"Jace. Oh, Jace..."

And then he leaned closer still. She felt his breath, stirring the dark hair that covered her sex.

His breath.

And then...oh, and then...he kissed her. There. Right there, where she was burning for him. He kissed her and he parted her and his tongue slid in to find that sweet spot all over again. His tongue...

How did he do that? He created sensations that were delicious beyond bearing.

She reached down, threaded her fingers in his dark,

thick hair, pulled him even closer. She called out his name, wildly, as he held her in his endless, wet, perfect kiss.

Oh, she was rising, reaching…

And he went on kissing her, his big hands under her hips, tipping her up to him. She didn't want it to end. Not ever.

But of course, the end came. And it was glorious.

With a cry, she hit the crest and went over.

Her body trembled. He held on, drinking from her, doing something impossibly fine with his tongue so that the pleasure expanded, moving out in waves from the core of her, filling her, overflowing, spreading out and out… until it halted, hung suspended on a thread for a world-stopping moment.

And then at last, receding, drawing back, like a shining, perfect wave, retreating to the center of her, where it continued to pulse so sweetly in delicious afterglow.

She lay there, dazed. Wondering.

He eased his hands out from under her hips. He broke that incredible intimate kiss.

And he rose to his feet.

She asked, softly, "Jace?"

He said nothing. She gazed up at him, over his muscled thighs, over the proof of his desire for her, jutting so hard and proud. Over his hard belly and powerful chest.

Beautiful, she thought again. A beautiful man…

Strange. She'd always thought of him as kind. An easygoing, easy-to-know sort of guy.

But he didn't look all that kind right then. And not in the least easygoing.

She saw a roughness, now. A depth of need and emotion she hadn't known in him before. Something that called to the woman in her.

Something undeniably, excitingly, possessively male.

She wanted to reach for him, to beg him to come back to her, but her arms felt so wonderfully heavy, her body limp with satisfaction. Pliant. Slow.

So she simply lay there, watching him, yearning for him, as he turned to the nightstand and took one of the condoms. He had it out of the foil pouch and rolled into place in an instant.

Only then did he come down to her again. She welcomed him, lifting her arms eagerly then, to wrap around his hard, broad shoulders, pulling him close to her, loving the weight of him as he settled on top of her.

He buried his head in the curve of her neck. And he kissed her there, using his tongue, sucking the skin against his teeth. Not hard enough to leave a love bite.

Just hard enough to make her moan.

"Now," she commanded in a ragged, needful whisper. "Please, Jace. Now…"

His hands swept down, along the outer swells of her hips. He guided her legs up to encircle his waist. She hooked her ankles together at the small of his back, and she felt him there, thick and hard and smooth, right exactly where she wanted him.

In one long, sure stroke, he filled her.

She moaned at the wonder of it, and sank her teeth into his shoulder, but gently. Oh, he did feel so good inside her.

He felt exactly right. He filled her so deep.

She wrapped herself closer around him, tightening her grip with her arms and her legs. She rocked against him.

And he answered her, rocking back, finding first a long, sure rhythm, teasing her with it, bringing her fully out of the soft fade of her own satisfaction.

Into renewed pleasure. Into rising again, this time with him, better even than the time before.

Slow and deep and steady…and then faster, harder, faster still.

And she held on, she went where he took her.

Into the heart of the heat and the wonder. Over the moon, into a velvet black night scattered with bursting stars.

Chapter Nine

Later, as they soaked in the suite's jetted bathtub, he fed her the chocolates the maid had left on her pillow.

Leaning back against his broad chest, trapped between his bare, muscular thighs, feeling loose and easy and totally decadent, she let the lovely bittersweet treat melt on her tongue. "I could get used to this."

"Me, too." His voice was a fine, dark rumble in her ear. And along her spine, she could feel the rise and fall of his chest with every breath he took.

She turned her head to him.

He leaned to the side to reach her mouth. And he kissed her. "Um. Chocolate." He offered her a sip of the champagne he'd ordered from room service. She took it, laughing when some of it spilled, those lovely, fizzy bubbles straying down her chin. He said, "I think I'm getting…ideas."

She laughed again. "I feel you." She wiggled back against him. "Oh, my…"

He groaned. "You'll kill me."

"With pleasure…" She rolled, floating up, settling against him again, but this time facing him. "What have we here?" she teased, as she found him under the water and wrapped her eager fingers around him.

He made a rough, wordless sound.

She kissed him as she stroked him.

That didn't last long. A few minutes later, he was gathering her to him, getting his legs under him, rising from the tub, heedless of the water splashing over the sides. He carried her into the bedroom, where he turned so she could reach the nightstand.

She knew what he wanted her to do. Laughing, she grabbed one of the condoms. "We're dripping water everywhere."

So he carried her back into the bathroom, where he boosted her up onto the long counter between the double sinks.

"Oh, my," she said so softly, as he filled her for the second time.

He captured her lips in a long, sweet, wet kiss as he took her over the moon again.

By two in the morning, they had used the last condom. They were back in the bed by then.

She cuddled up close to him and whispered, "I don't want to go to sleep. I don't want to waste a moment of the time we have left."

They spoke of their childhoods. He told her more about his brothers, about the battles between them and also the good times growing up.

She told him about her best friend when she was twelve. "Her name was Jane Ackerman. She dumped me our freshman year to get in with the popular kids."

"You weren't popular in high school?" He shook his head. "I don't believe it."

"I was shy."

"No way."

"Oh, yeah. And lonely—I told you that the first night I met you."

He answered tenderly. "That's right. I remember."

"I never felt like I fit in, you know? I was something of a misfit, I guess you could say."

"And just look at you now."

She rested her head on his warm, strong chest, where she could hear the steady beating of his generous heart. "You always make me feel so good about myself. Like I could do anything I wanted to do."

"Because you could." His lips brushed her hair.

Her eyelids felt heavy. She let them droop shut. Just for a minute or two...

Joss opened her eyes to sunlight streaming in between the half-drawn curtains.

And to Jason, his strong arms around her, smiling at her sleepily. "Looks like we fell asleep after all."

She snuggled in closer, feeling really good, really relaxed. And really satisfied. "What time is it?"

"Quarter after nine."

"Yikes." She sat straight up and raked her hand back through her tangled hair. "I've got to get moving, get packed. My plane takes off from Bozeman at ten after twelve."

"I'll order room service. You pack. I'll drive you to the airport."

"No need to drive me. I have a rental car."

He looked surprised. "You do?"

She shrugged. "I know. I have taken shameless advantage of you, had you chauffeur me everywhere since that first day we met." She didn't know whether to grab him and hold on for dear life, or burst into tears. "What will I do without you?"

He was braced up on an elbow, looking sleepy and way too sexy. Low and rough, he suggested, "Stay."

Yes! her heart cried.

But then she thought of her mother, of her marriage that hadn't happened, of everything that was so totally up in the air for her. She couldn't run away from her life forever. "Oh, Jace, I wish."

He studied her face for a long, tender moment. And then he said gently, "Well, then you'd better get moving."

She had so much to say to him, but when she opened her mouth, no words came. In the end, she only cleared her throat and answered sheepishly, "Yeah, I guess I'd better." She pushed back the covers. "I'll just grab a quick shower."

"I'll get us some food." He picked up the phone by the bed.

Half an hour later, she was showered and dressed and running back and forth from the closet in the bedroom to the living area, where she had her suitcases spread out on the sofa.

Jace sat at the table by the window, wearing his trousers from the night before and his dress shirt, unbuttoned, in bare feet, putting away a plateful of bacon and eggs. "Come on, Joss. Your food will get cold. Sit down and eat."

She glanced at him, at his beautiful, tanned bare chest between the open sides of his slightly wrinkled shirt. Was there ever a guy as great in every way as Jace? He was smart and fun, thoughtful, kind and generous. Not to mention, superhot and amazing in bed.

Her arms were full of shoes. She wanted to drop them

and run to him, grab him, drag him back to her bed and keep him there all day.

He prompted, "I mean it. Come and eat."

That broke the spell. She couldn't run away from her life anymore. She needed to get back to reality. She was going home to Sacramento today. As planned.

He patted the chair beside him.

She promised, "I will, just a minute," as she dumped the shoes into the biggest of the suitcases and then raced back into the bedroom.

Her wedding gown confronted her. She stopped in the open door of the closet and stared at it, so white, so beautiful— a Cinderella fantasy in the classic ballroom style, with a strapless crisscross bodice sparkling with crystal beading and rhinestones, with endless acres of tulle and glitter net over taffeta that made up the fluffy, cloudlike layers of the skirt.

It was her dream dress.

The one that went with her dream wedding—the wedding she'd run from as fast as she could.

She should just ignore it. Just pack the rest of her things and walk away, leave it hanging there for the maid to find.

But somehow, she couldn't. Somehow, it represented way too much that she hadn't really relinquished. She'd got a great deal on it. But still, it had cost what to her was a small fortune.

She wanted it. She...coveted it. She wanted what it seemed to represent, the life she had planned for herself to which her beautiful, perfect wedding was supposed to be the gateway.

The life she would probably never have after all.

She heard knocking from the other end of the suite. Someone at the door.

Jace called, "I'll get it. It's room service with my extra toast."

She took the dress off the hanger and tossed the bodice over her shoulder, far enough that the acres of skirt were well clear of the floor. Then she took the veil. Cathedral length, it was sprinkled with diamante and edged in lace. She folded it in half and laid it over her other shoulder, so the folded end and the hem end each came almost to the floor in front and in back.

She heard voices in the other room and assumed that Jace was probably overtipping the room service guy.

With one arm wrapped around the dress and the other holding the veil in place, she had all the layers of taffeta and tulle out of the way so that she could see where she was going. She aimed herself at the door to the living area.

She was so busy trying not to trip over all that fluffy fabric that she didn't register Claudia Wexler's voice until she was almost to the sofa and the open suitcases.

"Well, I'm sorry, Jason," she heard his mother say. "I didn't mean to…interrupt."

Joss froze in midstep and glanced toward the arch to the foyer. From where she stood, she could see Jace's back in the open door to the hall and the side of Claudia's face.

Jace said, "Joss is kind of busy, Ma. She's got to get to the airport and she's still trying to pack."

"I only want a word with her."

A word? Oh, Lord. What kind of word? She wasn't up for dealing with Jace's mom. Not right now. Not this morning.

It wasn't even so much that Jace had answered the door barefoot, with his wrinkled shirt wide open, which meant that Claudia had to know he'd spent the night. It was more that Jace's mom would be bound to read more into it than there was—to see it as another proof that Joss and Jace were serious about each other.

And that made Joss feel really bad. Last night had been so beautiful. But look at her now: packing to go. What was she doing with her life? Seriously. Two weeks ago, she'd been about to marry one guy. And last night, she'd done all kinds of naughty, intimate things with another.

Even if he *was* Jace, who just happened to be the greatest guy she'd ever known.

She'd never been the type to go for casual sex.

And last night *hadn't* been casual.

Not exactly.

But it hadn't been the beginning of forever either.

Don't let her see you—or the dress. There was simply no way to explain the dress.

Retreat. Do it now. Joss started to turn.

And Claudia spotted her. "Jocelyn." She craned to the side and put on a too-bright smile. "There you are."

Jace glanced over his shoulder and saw her, too. "Sorry." He mouthed the word.

Joss sucked in a fortifying breath and tried not to think how absurd she must look, buried in a fluffy mountain of taffeta and tulle, frozen in mid-stride just as she was turning to hide. "It's okay, Jace. Really. Claudia, come in."

Now Jace's mom hesitated. Who could blame her? "I honestly didn't mean to butt in."

Jace muttered something under his breath.

His mother glared him. "Well, Jason, I had no idea that you would be here." She aimed her chin high and announced, "Not that there's anything wrong with your being here. You young people have your own ways of doing things. I understand that. I grew up in the seventies. I'm not a complete fuddy-duddy, you know."

Jace stepped aside. "It's all right, Ma," he said resignedly. "Come on in." Looking very uncomfortable, Claudia stepped forward. He asked, "Want some coffee?"

"Oh, no. I won't stay. I have to meet Pete at the Grubstake in ten minutes." Pasting on another smile, she walked past her son and came straight for Joss. "Jocelyn, I only wanted to say—again—that we would love to see you in Midland anytime you care to visit. I have so enjoyed getting to know you. And I'm hoping that even though you're going back to Sacramento, you won't be a stranger. You'll return to see us again and maybe you and Jason…" By then, the fake smile had faded once more. Claudia's voice trailed off. She blinked. "Oh, my goodness." And she stretched out a hesitant hand to lightly brush the frothy skirt of the wedding dress Joss still had draped over her shoulder.

Jace, clearly bewildered at the whole situation, lingered in the arch to the foyer. Joss's frantic gaze skipped from him back to his mother again.

Claudia's face was transfixed. "Is that…" Tears filled her eyes. "Oh, I knew it." She let out a glad cry. And then she was reaching out, grabbing Joss and the Cinderella wedding gown and the endless yards of veil in a hug. "Oh, Jocelyn," Claudia whispered tearfully, her face buried in the dress. "I'm so happy. You two are so right for each other…."

Joss made a sputtering sound. "I, um, well…"

And then Claudia was drawing back, somehow managing to find and clasp Joss by the shoulders, even with the dress and veil in her way. Joss blinked and met the older woman's eyes, which were diamond-bright with happy tears.

"It's a beautiful gown," said Claudia fervently. "Stunning. And I don't really believe in that old superstition that it's bad luck for the groom to see the dress ahead of time. Whatever works, is what I always say. And the two of you…you *work* together. Perfectly. I'm thrilled that you two have realized so quickly how right you are for each other. Jason has been looking for you, Jocelyn—you realize that, don't you? He's been looking for you for much too long now. I think he was giving up hope, if you want to know the sad truth. But now, here you are. Together. In love. Ready to marry and get on with your lives."

"I…uh…." What could she say? How to even begin? *No, see, this is the dress I was going to wear to marry that other guy. As a matter of fact, I've been here on my honeymoon, my un-honeymoon. Maybe you noticed I'm in the Honeymoon Suite….*

"Thanks, Ma," Jace said out of nowhere. He sounded sincere. Joss sent him another wild glance. He met her eyes. Held them. And he smiled. The bewildered look was gone. Now he was totally confident. Utterly sure. "We're pretty excited, too."

We are?

This wasn't happening, not really. It wasn't real. Actually, she was still fast asleep in the bed in the other room.

A dream. Yes, it had to be. She wanted to pinch herself, but the dress and the veil and Claudia were all in the way.

Claudia hauled her close and hugged her again. "Have a safe flight to Sacramento. And hurry back. You must come to Midland soon. I can't wait to show you around."

"We're not living in Midland, Ma," Jace said firmly.

We aren't? Joss blinked three times in rapid succession.

He added, "And I'm out of the oil business for good."

Claudia let Joss go and turned to her son. "We'll talk about that."

"No, we won't. There's nothing to talk about. I'm looking into another line of work. And we're staying here in Thunder Canyon."

Claudia sighed. "Oh, Jason..."

"Be happy for us, Ma." He went to his mother and grabbed her in a hug.

Claudia let out another cry and hugged him back. "Well, all right," she said in a tear-clogged voice. "All right. If that's what you really want...."

"It is." He gave Joss another steady, determined look over his mother's shoulder. Joss gaped back at him and didn't say a word. Why speak? None of this was real anyway.

"Then I'm happy for you," Claudia cried. "I am. So very, very happy."

"Thanks, Ma." He stepped back, releasing her.

Still reasonably certain she'd slipped into a dream world, Joss stayed rooted in place, draped in her wedding finery, and went on gaping at the pair of them.

Claudia pulled a tissue from her pocket and dabbed at her eyes. "Oh, I am just so pleased. So very pleased. I can't want to tell Pete." With a delicate little sniffle, she asked Joss, "The wedding will be in Sacramento, then?"

"We're...still in the planning stages," Jace answered for her.

Claudia waved her tissue. "Of course you are." She laughed, a teary, soggy, happy sound. "And look at me. Butting in like this. I can see you were trying to enjoy your breakfast."

"Well, yeah, we were," Jace confessed.

She stepped close to him again and lifted on tiptoe to kiss his beard-shadowed cheek. "I'll leave you two alone, then."

"Thanks, Ma."

She grabbed his hands. "Just...be happy. That's all I want for you. All I've ever wanted for each of my children."

"We will," he answered solemnly. "I promise."

"That's the spirit." She gave his hands a final squeeze and released them. And then she aimed a jaunty wave at Joss. "See you very soon, dear." She was beaming.

"Ahem. Yes. Bye."

Still beaming, Claudia headed for the door, Jace right behind her.

Joss remained where she was, buried in wedding finery, wondering if she was going to wake up soon.

But then she heard the door click shut and the privacy chain sliding into place.

Jace returned and stood in the arch from the foyer again. "Don't say a word."

She didn't, but she did manage a wild, confused sputtering sound.

He put up hand. "I swear to you, Joss. I have a plan. I think it's a good one. Let me explain."

She found her voice and demanded, still not believing that this could be happening, "A plan? You have…a *plan*?"

"Don't look at me like that. Please. Give me a chance. Hear me out."

About then, she realized she wasn't going to wake up. It wasn't a dream.

Jace had told his mother that they were getting married and moving to Thunder Canyon.

And Joss had just stood there and let it happen.

Chapter Ten

Jace looked into those big amber-brown eyes of hers and knew she wasn't going for it. He felt like a total fool.

But so what? He wasn't giving up yet.

"Come on," he coaxed. "Put the dress down. Eat your breakfast. We'll talk."

She blinked and stared. "I don't have time for talking. I have a plane to catch."

"No, you don't. You don't have to go. You can stay here. With me."

She wrinkled her nose and shook her head in disbelief. "What *planet* are you from? I can't believe that you... I don't... You just..."

He took a step toward her. "Joss..."

"Don't." She lurched away, almost tripping on the veil that hung down her back, but then she stopped. She stared at him, clutching that giant dress, her slim shoulders drooping. And then, out of nowhere she started to cry. "Oh,

Jace." Fat tears trailed down her soft cheeks. "What are we doing? Are we going crazy? What's happening here?"

He felt crappy. Bad. Rotten. And really, for a minute there, he'd thought he'd had a great idea....

And wait. Hold on just a minute. It *was* a great idea. He just needed to convince her of how really perfect it was. "Joss, come on. Don't cry. Please don't cry...." He took another step. She didn't jump away that time, but only stood there, tears dripping from her chin, her nose turning red. "Here," he said gently, "give me all that."

A tiny sob escaped her. "M-my dress, you mean?"

"Yeah. Come on. Give it here...."

She continued to cry, making sad little snuffling sounds, as he eased the big white dress off her shoulder and gently laid it over her suitcases. With a sniffle of pure misery, she asked, "Why did you do that—lie to your mother? It's bad. Very bad. To lie to your mother."

"Give me that, too," he said, and took the giant veil and set it down on top of the dress. He whipped a couple of tissues from the box on the side table and returned to her. "Here, dry your eyes."

She frowned at the tissues, but then she took them. She blew her nose and wiped away the tears. And then she gazed up at him, wearing a shattered expression that somehow managed to be trusting, too. "Now are you going to *talk* to me?"

He took her smooth, slim hand and thought how right it felt in his. She didn't pull away, so he led her to the table and guided her down into the chair in front of her plate. He poured her some coffee, took the warming lid off the plate. "Eat," he said.

She picked up her fork.

And there was another knock at the door.

She stiffened, whimpered, "What now?"

He put his hands on her shoulders, gentling her. "It's nothing. Just the toast I ordered. Eat."

He went to the door, got his toast, tipped the attendant and returned to the living area where Joss was sipping her coffee and staring out the window at the snow-capped peak of Thunder Mountain.

"I'm waiting," she said without looking at him. "This had better be good."

She didn't sound happy, but at least she'd stopped crying.

He set the toast on the table and reclaimed his chair.

She did look at him then. One eyebrow inched toward her hairline. "Well?"

He decided to lay it right out there. "Marry me. We'll buy the Hitching Post. You can teach me how to run it. We'll get a big house with a wide front porch, just like you always dreamed about, on a nice piece of land where we can have a large floppy-eared dog and a couple of horses. And then we'll get to work having a whole bunch of loud, rowdy kids."

She set down her coffee cup and looked at him sideways. "You just want to have sex with me again."

As if he would deny that. "Well, yeah. The sex is great. It's *all* great with us. And come on, think about it. *You* want to get married and have kids. And *I* want you. Here. In Thunder Canyon. With me. And when Ma started in about hearing wedding bells, it all fell into place for me. Why the hell shouldn't we both get what we want? Why should you go? You don't really *want* to go, do you?"

She pressed her lips together and stared out the window again.

He didn't let her off the hook. "Look at me, Joss."

Slowly she turned her head and met his eyes. She wore a

144   THE LAST SINGLE MAVERICK

slightly stunned expression. "What?" Her voice was more than a little bit husky.

He rose from his chair. Just enough to capture her beautiful mouth. He kissed her. Hard. "Marry me."

She stared at him for about half a century, dark eyes huge and anxious in her amazing face. Finally, she sighed. "Your mother. I think she really is thrilled at the idea that we're getting married."

"Yeah, so?"

"We just met. Shouldn't she be warning us to take it slow?"

"Joss, she sees what you do for me. She's relieved that I'm back among the living again after months of dragging around like a ghost of myself. She thinks we're good together. Why shouldn't she be happy at the thought that we're making it legal?"

Slowly, she shook her head. "She's just so different from my mom, that's all. If we, um, do this, my mom is going to hit the ceiling. She's going to go right through the roof and it is not going to be pretty. You can take my word on that."

"Don't borrow trouble. We'll deal with your mom together when the time comes."

"But really, our getting married, it seems crazy. Insane. I mean, yeah, you're right about things being good with us. You...do it for me. You're the absolute best. On so many levels."

He felt triumph rising. "And *you* do it for me."

"But get real. It's been a week. It's not like it's undying love or anything."

"So what?"

She kicked him under the table—not hard, but right on the shin.

He winced. "Ow, that hurt."

She had her soft mouth all pinched up. "I don't like you dissing love, Jace. I happen to believe that love matters."

He reached down and rubbed where she'd kicked him. "Okay, it matters. I guess. If you say so. But I mean, well, what *is* it anyway?"

She glared. "What do you mean, what is it?"

"Well, I mean, you loved Kenny Donovan, right?"

She sat completely still for a moment, her face somber, her eyes unhappy. And then, with a heavy sigh, she slumped back in her chair. "I thought I loved Kenny." She shook her head. "Now, though…now, I only wonder *how* I could have thought that. I look back and the only good thing I can say about him is that he seemed like a nice guy. At first."

"Exactly. That's it. *I* thought I loved Tricia Lavelle. And what did I love really? *Who* did I love? I swear I didn't even *know* her. I saw her at a party, standing by a grand piano, wearing a short, sparkly red dress, her long blond hair shining in the light from the chandelier over her head. She looked really good in that dress. And what did I do? Out of nowhere, on the spot, I decided it must be love." He made a low, disbelieving sound. "Me, Jason Traub, in love. I mean, come on. Where did that come from? Until I got a look at Tricia in that red dress, all I ever wanted from any woman was a good time and for her to go away when I was ready to go to sleep."

Joss's expression had relaxed a little. She reminded him, "Your mother said you've been looking for the right woman."

He grunted. "My mother said I've been looking for *you*."

"She meant the right woman."

"Okay. Fine. Yeah. I guess I have been looking lately— for the right woman, for the things that really matter in life, the things I never realized how much I wanted. But love? I meant what I said a minute ago. I honestly don't have a clue about love and I don't even want to go there. I'm just a guy doing the best I can to make my life a good one, to…get involved."

She pulled a face. "Get involved?"

"Yeah. With my…community, you know? With *this* community. Like Aunt Melba said the first day I met her, *'Get involved, young man. Stop sitting on the sidelines of life.'* I admit, I just wanted to get away from her when she said that, but that doesn't mean she wasn't a hundred percent right."

Joss almost smiled. "So." Her velvety gaze sparked with challenge. "The mystery woman's name was Tricia Lavelle, huh?"

He picked up a piece of toast, and then realized he didn't want it after all. He set it down. "That's right."

She put her hand on his arm. It felt good there. He wanted to scoop her up and carry her back to the bedroom. He might keep her there all day and into the night….

But first he had to convince her that they could be a great team in a lifetime kind of way.

"I want to hear about her, about Tricia Lavelle," Joss said, as he'd pretty much expected she would. "I want the story, all of it."

He groaned. "Now?"

She repeated, "All of it."

He pushed his plate away. "It's pretty damn embarrassing. I acted like an idiot."

"Hey, you're talking to the girl who was going to marry Kenny Donovan, remember?"

He held her gaze. "You're no idiot. You always knew what you wanted. And that cheating creep just had you convinced he was it. And from what you've said, he *was* it. At first."

"Thank you." She said it softly. And then she added, "Now, about the thing with you and Tricia..."

Resigned, he explained, "All that happened with her is that I saw a good-looking girl in a red dress and I had a completely out-there reaction. Instead of admitting I wanted what I always wanted—an overnight, totally *un*-meaningful relationship—I decided that I was in love. Which is a complete pile of crap. I'm just not that deep. I have no idea what love really is and I'm better off not kidding myself that I do. I see now that I need to just go for what works and what's right and leave it at that."

She squeezed his arm. "Tell me about her."

"Ack. You're kidding. You want *more*?"

"I do, yes. More."

He tried to bargain. "Tell me first that this isn't going to ruin my chance of getting you to marry me."

She almost smiled, but not quite. "Talk."

So he did. "I met her through her dad, Jack Lavelle. Jack's rich as Rupert Murdoch, a legendary oilman. He was a real-life wildcatter back in the day. In fact, he was once in partnership with *my* dad."

"You don't mean Pete, do you?"

"No, I mean my birth father."

"And Tricia. Is she in the oil business as well?"

"Are you kidding? She might break a nail. Tricia dabbled in modeling. A couple of years ago, she even made the cover of *Sports Illustrated*. But she's never *had* to work. She has trust funds for her trust fund. One look at her in that slinky sequined party dress, standing by the grand piano in the front sitting room of her daddy's Highland Park mansion, all that blond hair falling in golden waves to her perfect ass, singing 'The Yellow Rose of Texas' for her adoring daddy and all his rich guests, and I was gone, gone, gone."

Joss brushed his shoulder with a comforting hand. "It's not so surprising that you fell for her. She sounds pretty fabulous."

"She did *look* fabulous, I'm not denying that. But what's the old saying about all that glitters?"

Joss smiled at him, a rueful sort of smile. "Go on."

"You sure you haven't heard enough?"

"I'm waiting."

"Fine. All right. We spent the holidays in a series of luxury hotels all over the world. For the first time, I thought I understood what it was to be head-over-heels for a woman. I bought an engagement ring with a rock the size of the Alamo. And on New Year's Eve, I went down on my knees and proposed...." He left it there. Maybe she would let it go.

He wished.

"And?" she prompted softly.

"Tricia got cagey."

"Cagey, how?"

"She said she loved me madly, of course. But she was only twenty-four. Much too young to settle down, she said. Couldn't we just go on having fun? And then, in a few years, when she got old—that's exactly how she put it. 'When I get old.' Then we could talk seriously about getting married. She said I could move to Dallas and get work with her daddy. Because Tricia was never, ever leaving her daddy—well, except temporarily, for a prime modeling gig in New York or to lie around slathered with suntan oil, wearing a bikini the size of three postage stamps aboard a friend's yacht on the French Riviera."

Joss said, "And the last thing you ever wanted to go to work for anybody's daddy...."

He chuckled then, even though he knew the sound didn't have any humor in it. "You got that right. Plus, as I said, Lavelle is in the oil business. And by then I was already thinking I might want *out* of the oil business. I was thinking that I wanted..." He frowned as he let the sentence wander off.

"You wanted what?"

"Truth is, at that point, I didn't really know what I wanted. But it wasn't to spend another five or ten years jetting around the world with some spoiled little rich girl. Suddenly I was seeing my supposedly 'perfect woman' in a whole new—and not very attractive—light. I started wondering what my problem was, wondering what I thought I was up to, generally speaking.

"All the things I'd been sure of in my life—my place in the family business, my no-strings-attached lifestyle—I was all at once itching to change. I'd thought Tricia was the solution to the vague unanswered questions that had started nagging in my brain. But within a few days of her blowing off my marriage proposal, I saw that it was never going to work with her. I realized I didn't even *like* Tricia much."

"So what did you do?"

"I felt so stupid. Here I'd been telling her I would love her forever and now all I wanted was to get free of her. So I tried to be really smooth and subtle. I told her that maybe we ought to cool it for a while."

"What did she say to that?"

"She said that was fine with her. She said that ever since I'd started in on her to marry me, I hadn't been any fun anyway."

"Wow, that was kind of cold."

He grunted. "That was pure Tricia. She's a girl who just wants to have fun—and to live near her daddy."

"So that was the end of it?"

"Yeah. It really bummed me out, you know? But not for the reason my whole family assumes. Not because she ripped out my heart and ate it for breakfast like everyone seems to think. By the end, I didn't give a damn about Tricia—in fact, I'd realized I probably never *had* given a damn about her. I was just glad it was over without any big scenes. But all the questions in my head, about the way my life was going, about my work for Traub Oil, about all of it, those questions were nagging me worse than ever. I realized I had no idea what I wanted. I only knew I *didn't* want the life that I had. I went into a really low period after that."

"A depression, you mean?"

"I don't know if I would call it that. It was just, well, I didn't care about much. I blew off Jackson and Laila's wedding, I was so down. I regret that. A lot. I decided to quit the family business. I had no interest in the things that I used to enjoy."

"Like…casual relationships with women?"

"That's right. Can you believe it? I didn't even care about sex. And before the thing with Tricia, I *always* cared about sex."

She did smile then. "You seemed to enjoy yourself last night."

"Yeah." He drank in the sight of her, those brandy-brown eyes, the lush, delicious curves of her mouth, the thick, cinnamon-kissed waves of her dark hair. "My interest in sex has returned at last. It's a miracle. It started about a week ago. The day I met you."

Her expression turned knowing. "Oh, come on. You told me that day that you only wanted to be friends."

"No, I said I would love to be friends and I accepted the fact that you weren't going to have sex with me. That doesn't mean I wasn't interested. I was. From the first moment I saw you. And that was a great moment for me. It's been six months since it ended with Tricia. And until eight days ago, I had nothin' going on with any woman. No dates, no interest. Not even a spark."

She tried to be cynical. "You're working me, right? To get me to say yes to this wild plan of yours. Next you'll be saying you fell in love with me at first sight."

"No way." He put up a hand, palm out, like a witness swearing an oath. "Uh-uh. I told you already. When it comes to love, I've accepted the hard fact that I have no idea what it is or when I'm in it—that is, *if* I've ever *been* in it, which I seriously doubt. When it comes to love, I'd rather just not go there. The whole subject makes me nervous, you know what I mean? I don't understand it and I prefer just to leave it alone."

She studied his face for several long seconds. "So really, what you're proposing is a practical arrangement."

He knew he was getting to her. He tried not to get too cocky, but he couldn't hide his excitement. "That's right. That's it. You and me—together, a team. Getting everything we want out of life. We…pool our experience and resources. We start a family."

"Wait. *You* want a family, too?"

"Haven't I just been saying that?"

"No. You said *I* wanted a family and you were willing to help me have one."

"Then let me correct that. I *do* want a family. A family with you. Remember when you first told me about your dream for your life?"

"I do, yeah. Sheesh, that was embarrassing."

He didn't follow. "Embarrassing, how?"

"Well, I mean, that even after Kenny betrayed me, I actually considered taking him back…."

"But I told you I could see what you were getting at—that you had a dream, and it was hard to give that dream up."

Her expression softened. "Yeah, you did understand. I really appreciated that."

"And I'm trying to tell you now that when you described your dream to me, I started thinking how great that would be—to be a dad, to be a husband to someone like you, to have a big house with a bunch of kids. I realized something about myself. I was tired of being my family's last single maverick. I knew I could go for just the life you were describing. Seriously, I could. Who knew? But it's true. I think part of what's been eating at me the past several months is I've been wanting what a good-time guy like me never wants and I just wasn't ready to admit that yet. But I'm ready now. I promise you, Joss. I want a great big family. I want that a lot."

Her eyes had that special light in them again. "Oh, this is crazy."

"No, it's not. It's the sanest thing two people can do. To get married because they want the same things out of life, because they're good together in all the right ways."

She picked up her coffee cup, looked into it and then set it back down. "So, if we did this, *when* would we do it?"

"You mean, when would we get married?"

"Yeah." She seemed slightly breathless. "When—I mean, I kind of would like a real wedding, you know? I would like to wear my dress."

He sent a wary glance at the pile of white over on the sofa. "*That* dress?"

She bit her lip. "Tacky, huh? To marry you in the dress I chose to marry Kenny in?"

It did kind of bug him. But come on, what did it matter? It was just a dress. And if she liked it so much, why not? "You want to wear that dress, you wear it."

"Oh, Jace. Are you sure?"

"Absolutely." He stuffed his own discomfort at the thought of her coming down the aisle toward him wearing that dress. "You wear your dress. And we get married right here, at the resort. I'm thinking on the last Saturday of the month."

"*This* month?"

"Yeah. Okay, I know it's quick, but I say we go for it. We put a nice party together for our families and friends in the time we have till then, and after that, we get on with our lives."

Out of nowhere, she jumped up and headed for the bedroom.

He watched her go, too surprised at the suddenness of her leaving to ask her what was up. But then, a few seconds later, she returned with her cell phone. She tapped it a few times. "That's the twenty-eighth? Saturday, the twenty-eighth…"

So, okay. A calendar. She'd brought up the calendar on her phone. She slanted him a sharp look and he realized she wanted confirmation. "Er, sounds about right."

She narrowed her eyes at the screen. "That's twenty days. Tight."

"Joss."

"Um?"

"Is that a yes?"

She glanced up. "Did I mention this is insane?"

"Repeatedly." He pushed back his chair, captured her wrist, took the phone from her hand and set it on the table. "Is that a yes?"

She looked up at him, a little frown etching itself between her smooth brows. "I mean, this would be for real?

This would be a real marriage and we would both give it everything. We would commit ourselves to making it work."

He held her gaze, refused to waver. "That's it. That's the plan."

"You would stick by me always." Tears welled in those fine eyes again.

He knew she was thinking of that bastard Kenny, of how he'd messed around on her. "I would. I swear it. Say yes."

She dashed the tears away. "Oh, Jace...we've known each other only a week. Two weeks ago, I was supposed to be marrying someone else."

"We've been through all that."

"Yes, but—"

"Stop right there."

She blinked. "What?"

"You just said yes. That's the word. Say it again, minus the 'but.'"

"Oh, God, my mother is going to freak."

"Joss, I mean it. Yes or..."

With a little cry, she put her cool, smooth fingers to his lips. "Shh. Wait."

He made a low sound, but he kept quiet. He waited.

And then, at last, she swallowed. Hard. And she nodded. "Yes," she said. "This is so crazy and I can't believe what I'm about to say. But yes, Jace. Yes, yes, yes!"

Chapter Eleven

The moment she finished saying yes, Jace scooped her up and carried her back to the bedroom again.

"You need rest," he insisted.

She laughed at that. She knew that look in his eyes.

And then he started kissing her. She kissed him back, of course. Making love with Jace was a lot more fun than sleeping anyway.

They stayed in bed until eleven or so, which was check-out time. She called the front desk and asked about extending her stay. The clerk said the suite was hers until Thursday. After that, she would have to change rooms.

She hung up the phone and asked, "What now?"

He was still in bed, braced up on an elbow, looking sleepy and sexy and wonderfully manly. "We need to try and reserve a room for the wedding."

So they showered and dressed and went down to the front desk, where the weekend manager was happy to help them out.

As it turned out, the smaller of the resort's two ball-rooms was available. They booked it. The manager told them it would be a simple matter to set up the ballroom for the ceremony first, and then bring staff in again to add tables and reset the room for the reception afterward.

That seemed a little complicated to Joss. Would they have to ask everyone to leave and come back later? Jace said they could talk to DJ, maybe see about having the re-ception at the Rib Shack, if she wouldn't mind the casual atmosphere.

She grinned. "Our first date was at the Rib Shack—sort of, more or less. Remember?"

He laughed. "How could I forget? It was just last week."

"I love that," she said.

"You mean that our first date was only a week ago?"

"No, that our first date was at the Rib Shack, which means it's the perfect place for our reception because it has special meaning for us."

He faked a scared expression. "It makes me nervous when women start talking about special meanings."

She poked him with her elbow. "Get over it—and okay. Speaking more…practically."

He made a big show of looking relieved. "I'm all for 'practically.'"

"Got that, loud and clear. Where was I? Oh, yeah. We can dress up the ballroom really pretty for the ceremony, and then everyone can just go on over to the Rib Shack for the party after."

He agreed. "I'll get with DJ and see what we can do."

They also wanted to arrange for a consultation with Shane Roarke, the Gallatin Room's new chef, to plan a special menu for the reception after the ceremony. Jace said that since the Rib Shack was right there in the resort, it shouldn't be too much of a problem for the Rib Shack and Shane Roarke to work together.

Joss clued him in that top chefs didn't, as a rule, work all that well with others. However, she was willing to go with it, talk to Grant Clifton about the idea. If Grant said it wouldn't be an issue for the resort, then they could approach Roarke about the idea.

They went to the Rib Shack for lunch. And then they made a trip to Bozeman to drop off her rental car at the airport.

Jace insisted on stopping at a jewelry store next. They picked out a ring. It wasn't a hard choice. One look at the one-and-a-half carat marquise-cut solitaire on a platinum band and she gasped. The price brought a second gasp.

Of course, Jace made her try it on, and then decided it was perfect for her. He handed over his credit card and laid claim to the velvet case. The case still held the matching platinum wedding band, which was channel-set with diamonds.

Back in Thunder Canyon, they drove out to Jackson and Laila's house to share the news of their engagement with his twin. As it happened, DJ and his wife Allaire were there. They'd brought their little boy, Alex. Ethan and Lizzie were there too. So was another of Jace's brothers, Corey, and his wife, Erin.

And Laila's single sisters had come. She had three of them—Jasmine, Annabel and Jordyn Leigh. Laila's other sister Abby, who was married to a local carpenter, couldn't make it that day. Neither could her baby brother, Brody.

Everyone was wonderful, Joss thought. They congratulated Jace and really seemed to mean it. They all told Joss that they were so happy to welcome her to the family. The women made a big deal over Joss's ring. She showed it off proudly.

She also spent some time chatting with Laila's sister Annabel, a librarian who owned a therapy dog named Smiley. Annabel and Smiley spent a lot of time at Thunder Canyon General Hospital, working dog therapy magic on emotionally needy patients. Annabel said how great it was to see the last of the Texas Traubs and headed for the altar.

Yeah, okay. Joss felt a little guilty when Annabel said that. Everybody seemed to think that she and Jace had found true love.

But really, what did it matter what everyone else thought? She and Jace had a great thing going. They would have a good life together. A full, rich life, a life they both wanted.

DJ said he'd be honored to host their reception at the Rib Shack. And if Shane Roarke was up for creating a special menu, DJ would see that his staff assisted the chef with whatever he might need from them.

Lizzie insisted that she would bake their wedding cake personally and they agreed to visit her bakery the next day to put in their order. And then Erin launched into a story of how Lizzie had saved the day for Erin and Corey the year before. Ethan's wife had created a fabulous emergency wedding cake at the last minute when the bad-tempered French baker who was supposed to provide the cake skipped town.

Dinnertime approached. Laila insisted they all stay to eat. She had two Sunday roasts slow-cooking outside on the barbecue. There was plenty for everyone.

After dinner, they lingered over coffee and Lizzie's strawberry-rhubarb pie. Joss enjoyed every moment. It was still a little unreal to her that she and Jace were actually getting married at the end of the month. But she could get used to hanging around with Jace's brothers and cousin and their wives. They treated her like one of the family already.

Before they left, Jace went upstairs and packed up his things. From now on, he would be staying with Joss.

He thanked his brother and Laila for their hospitality. Jackson grabbed him in a hug and said again how happy he was for them. She and Jace drove back to the resort in a happy fog of good family feelings.

Kenny called that night.

It was late. Joss and Jace had just finished making slow, delicious love. She'd cuddled up close to him with his warm, hard chest for her pillow and she was fading slowly, contentedly toward sleep.

The phone by the bed rang.

The sound startled her.

Jace wrapped his big arm around her and whispered into her hair. "Don't answer that…"

She kissed his strong, tanned throat. "I have to."

"No, you don't."

"I do. It's ingrained. The phone rings, I answer it."

He chuckled. With some reluctance, he let her go. She reached for it, cutting it off in mid-ring. "Hello?"

"I called your cell twice," Kenny accused. "Aren't you checking your messages?"

She sat up. "Leave me alone, Kenny."

Jace sat up, too. He wasn't smiling. "Can't that jerk take a hint?"

"Who's that?" Kenny demanded. "It sounds like a man's voice."

Jace instructed flatly, "Tell him to get lost." She reached out and silenced him with two fingers against his lips.

He kissed those fingers. "Tell him."

"It is. My God." Kenny was outraged. "There's a guy

with you—in your *room*? Jocelyn, what's happened to you?" He fired more questions at her. "Why is there a man in your room? Why aren't you home? You missed your flight, didn't you?" He heaved an outraged sigh. "This is ridiculous. I've had enough. I thought if I…indulged you a little, you would come to your senses. But this is beyond it. I'm calling my credit card and denying any charges you might incur."

"Go ahead. The bill's already paid."

Kenny sucked wind. "What do you mean paid? I *refuse*, do you hear me? I'm not paying for you to have some strange man in your room. I'll call my credit card company and tell them—"

"I didn't use your credit card."

"What? But—"

"I decided I couldn't stand the idea of taking your money after all."

Kenny made a sputtering sound. Meanwhile, Jace had captured her wrist. He sucked her index finger into his mouth and then ran his tongue around it.

She giggled, mouthed, "Stop that."

He shook his head and sucked some more, using his tongue in a lovely, wet caress. Amazing, really, the things he could do with his mouth. With that tongue…

Kenny demanded, "What is going on with you, Joss? Are you having some kind of breakdown? I don't get it."

She pulled her finger free of Jace's grip—not because it didn't feel really good. It did. But because he made her breathless and she needed all her wits about her to make things perfectly clear to Kenny. "What is going on with me, Kenny, is that I've met someone."

Jace grinned. It was an extraordinarily sexy grin.

"*What*?" Kenny practically shouted.

"I said, I've met someone. He's fabulous. He's asked me to marry him and that is exactly what I'm going to do."

"Joss, you can't. That's completely insane."

Was it? Maybe so. She told herself she didn't care. "Your opinion means exactly nothing to me now, Kenny. I'm getting married the twenty-eighth of this month at five in the afternoon, right here at the Thunder Canyon Resort. As a matter of fact, I'm going to be living here in this beautiful little town with my new husband. We're buying a bar and grill and running it together."

"Wait. No. You're making this up. Just come home. We'll talk. We'll—"

"You're not listening, Kenny. The past couple of years, you never listened. I *am* home. *This* is my home now. I'm never coming back to California, except to get my stuff out of storage and, on occasion, to visit my mother."

"Joss, please—"

"Uh-uh. Forget it. Enough said. Leave me alone. Do not call me again. Goodbye."

"Joss, wait. Don't—"

She hung up the phone. And then she put her hands over her face and let out a groan.

Jace touched her shoulder. "Hey."

She made a vee between her middle and fourth fingers and peeked at him, groaning again. "That was awful. Don't you dare try to cheer me up."

He reached out and pulled her close and settled her head against his shoulder. His beautiful, big body felt so warm and good cradling hers. He even stroked her hair.

She let her hands drop away from her face and allowed herself to lean on him. All of a sudden, she felt totally exhausted. "Ugh. And that reminds me, I should call my mother."

"In the morning."

She let out a short burst of laughter that felt a lot like a sob. "Or maybe never..."

"You just need some sleep," he said. "A little rest and in the morning, you'll feel better about everything."

"What is it with you and all this optimism?"

He chuckled, the sound warm and deep. "It's all going to work out. You'll see."

Was it? Oh, she did hope so. Because seriously, married in twenty days? To this amazing man whom she'd met barely a week ago? Maybe Kenny was right. She'd gone off the deep end—not that she had any intention of backing out of her most recent engagement. No way. If she was crazy, so be it. She wanted to marry Jace.

She sighed. "It's just that we have so much to do."

He captured a swatch of her hair and began slowly wrapping it around his big hand. "Later for all that."

Her mind just kept racing. "And you know, I was thinking that I really need somewhere to stay—we both do, until we find the house want."

"We can stay right here." His voice had gone husky. She knew that dark, hot look in his eyes.

And in spite of her anxious thoughts, a little spark of excitement bloomed low in her midsection. She tipped her head back, kissed his manly square jaw, and insisted, "No way can we stay here."

"Why not?"

"Because it's ridiculously expensive. Plus, the suite is booked starting next Thursday, remember?"

He unwrapped her hair from around his hand only to raise the strands to his face and rub his cheek against them. "So we'll get another suite."

"Jace." She pulled away enough to catch his dear face between her palms. "It's almost three more weeks till the wedding. And it could be months before we find our place. Months at these rates? Forget about it."

He kissed the tip of her nose. "You're worth it."

She lifted up to lightly bite his ear and whisper, "I like the way you say that, but come on, there has to be another option."

He made a low, growly sort of sound. "I'll see what I can do, okay? But now, you should kiss me."

She caught his earlobe between her teeth again and teased it with her tongue. "I know what you're planning...."

"Kiss me."

She blew in his ear. "I thought you said I needed to get some sleep."

"A kiss," he said gruffly. "Then you can sleep."

So she kissed him.

And that, of course, led to more kisses.

Which led to another thoroughly satisfying hour of lovemaking.

It was after three when they finally went to sleep, and six in the morning when the phone rang again.

"Don't answer that," Jace grumbled in her ear.

More asleep than awake, ignoring her hot new fiancé's wise advice and not stopping to think that the call would probably be someone she didn't really want to talk to without advance preparation, Joss groped for the phone.

"'Lo?" she answered groggily.

"Kenny just called me," her mother said tightly. "He is devastated. He tried not to drag me into this, but what could the poor man do? He spent a sleepless night after he talked to you. And in the end, well, he just couldn't help himself. Jocelyn Marie, you have broken a good man's heart. How could you? I ask you, sincerely, what is the matter with you? Have you lost your mind?"

Joss had dragged herself up against the pillows by then.

She must have had a stricken look on her face because Jace was fully awake and watching her, a frown of concern between his brows.

She put her hand over the mouthpiece and whispered, "My mother."

He must have been holding his breath because he let it out slowly. "You want me to talk to her?"

"Oh, no. Uh-uh. I don't think so…"

"Jocelyn, hello?" Her mother's voice grated in her ear. "Are you there? Can you hear me?"

She took her hand away from the mouthpiece. "I'm here."

Her mother huffed. "I asked you several questions. You didn't answer a single one of them."

"Yes, well, Mom, I didn't know where to start."

"Start by reassuring me that this all just a terrible misunderstanding. Tell me you're not marrying some stranger you just met."

Joss swallowed, sucked in a slow breath and counted to five. Jace held out his hand. Gratefully, she took it and wove her fingers with his.

"Jocelyn, will you please answer me?"

"All right, Mom. No, I am not marrying a stranger. I'm marrying a wonderful man named Jason Traub. Jace and I are buying a business together and staying here in Montana to make a new life for ourselves."

Her mother made a tight, outraged little sound. "So it's all true then, what poor Kenny said? You have gone over the edge, lost your mind completely. This is pure craziness. Now, you listen to me…."

"Mom, I—"

"Jocelyn, I'm begging you. I want you to pack up your things and get a flight home. Now. Today. This instant.

Call me as soon as you have your flight number and I will meet you at the airport on your arrival. We can—"

"No!" Joss pretty much shouted the word. By then, she was clutching Jace's hand for dear life.

"What did you say?" her mother demanded.

"I said no, Mom. No. I am getting married right here, in Thunder Canyon, Montana, on the twenty-eighth of July. That's all there is to it. I hope you'll come for the wedding. But if you don't, well, that's your choice."

Her mother scoffed outright. "But this is ridiculous. Impossible. It's just all wrong."

"I'm sorry you feel that way, Mom. I'm sorry that lately we seem to be unable to communicate in any constructive way. The wedding will take place here at the Thunder Canyon Resort at five in the afternoon, with a reception in the Rib Shack restaurant, also here at the resort, afterward. I love you and I hope you'll come. Goodbye."

As usual, her mom was still talking frantically as she gently set the phone back in its cradle. "Oh, my Lord…."

"Come here, come on." Jace pulled her close.

She wrapped her arms around him good and tight. "Why couldn't I have a normal mother—say, one like yours? That would be so refreshing."

He pressed his lips to the crown of her head. "Your mom will come around in time."

"I hope so. I truly do. She's not *all* bad, you know?"

He answered gently, "I know she's not."

"She really does love me. I think she truly believes that she's doing the right thing. She just can't let go of the idea that Kenny Donovan is a knight in shining armor and I have to be out of my mind to walk away from him." She let out a low groan. "I honestly have no clue how to get through to her."

He tipped her chin up and pressed a quick, hard kiss on

her lips. "I know a copy place on the east side of town, in the mall in what we call New Town. We'll put some invitations together today to send out to the family. We'll send one to your mom, too."

"You think sending her an invitation is going to make a difference with her? Frankly, I can't see how."

He kissed her again, lightly this time. "I just think it's good to remind her that we do want her here for our wedding. By the time she gets the invitation, she'll have had a few days to think it over, to change her mind about coming on so strong. I think once she settles down, she's going to realize that you're what matters to her. She'll want to mend fences by then, to make peace with you."

"Oh, if you could only be right about that."

He stroked her hair. She snuggled in even closer, reveling in the warmth of his body, the strength in his big arms, the scent of him that was clean and manly and managed somehow to excite her and to comfort her simultaneously. He asked, "You want try and get a little more sleep?"

"Hah, as if that's an option at this point. I'm so hopped up on adrenaline, my ears are buzzing."

"So okay, let's get some breakfast."

Over bacon and eggs at the Grubstake, they planned out the day.

It was a busy one.

First they went to the New Town copy shop and ordered some simple, attractive-looking invitations. The clerk said their order would be ready the next day, which was Tuesday.

From the copy shop, they moved on to Lizzie's bakery. Aunt Melba was there, just leaving after enjoying a muffin and morning coffee. She chided them for missing church and then congratulated them on their upcoming wedding.

"Lizzie told me the news and I couldn't be happier about it." She insisted on hugging them both and seized Jace first. Holding him tight against her considerable bosom, she announced, "I am so pleased you'll be making your home right here in Thunder Canyon."

"Uh, thanks, Melba," Jace said, easing free of her grip.

She grabbed Joss next. "Oh, I know you two will be very happy here." Joss managed a noise of agreement as Melba crushed her closer. "And we need more nice, hard-working young people in this town." She took Joss by the shoulders and held her away at last. "Our youth, after all, are our future."

"So true," Joss agreed. "We'll be sending you an invitation. I hope you can come."

"I wouldn't miss it for the world, my dear."

Melba waved as she left them. They ordered a couple of large coffees. Lizzie joined them and they chose the cake they wanted *and* learned that the two-bedroom apartment over the bakery was vacant.

Lizzie said Joss and Jace were welcome to it until they found the house they were looking for. She took them up and showed them the place, which was charming and fully furnished, right down to the linens in the bathroom, the pretty old-fashioned floral-patterned dishes in the kitchen and the impressive array of pots and pans.

Lizzie explained, "I lived here for a while before Ethan and I got married. It's all pretty much as it was when I stayed here. I keep meaning to have a big garage sale, get rid of everything and put it up for rent. But then, you know, it's kind of nice to have it available, just in case someone in the family needs a place to stay...."

"I love it," Joss told her. "It's perfect."

Jace whipped out his checkbook, but Joss told him to put it away. He gave her a dark look.

She didn't back down. "Come on, let me cover this at least. Please?"

He wrapped an arm around her and they shared a quick kiss.

After which Lizzie informed them that she wouldn't take money from either of them. She waved a hand. "No way. You're family. I have a successful business *and* a rich husband. I don't need the money. Just take good care of the place, that's all I ask."

Both Joss and Jace promised that they would.

The three of them sat in the apartment's bright living room overlooking Main Street and chatted for a while. Jace told Lizzie about their plans to buy the Hitching Post *and* a new home. Lizzie suggested Bonnie Drake for their Realtor. She said that both she and Ethan had worked with Bonnie before.

But Jace told her that the Drake woman was representing the owner of the Hitching Post and he would rather use someone else. Lizzie whipped out the business card of a guy who came in the bakery every morning early for breakfast.

"His name is Milo Quinn," she said. "An older guy. Seems nice. Steady and dependable. I think you'll like him."

They went to the county courthouse next to see about getting their marriage license. It was a relatively simple procedure, although in Montana, the bride was required to have a test for rubella before the license could be issued. Jace had the solution to that one. He called the family doctor—his brother Dillon—and they drove over to Dillon's clinic to get the test done.

That afternoon, they met with Milo at his office. Tall and white-haired, he wore a Western-cut sport coat, dark brown slacks and tooled boots. He set up an appointment for them to see the Hitching Post the next day. He also said he would find them some houses on acreage.

After that, they returned to the resort and spoke with Grant, who congratulated them on their upcoming wedding and said that he was certain Chef Roarke would be happy to cater their reception. He took them upstairs to meet with Shane. He was agreeable. They set an appointment for 9:00 a.m. on Wednesday to get the menu planned.

And then they went back to Dillon Traub's clinic to pick up the expedited rubella test results. They made it to the county clerk's office again before it closed. When they left the courthouse, they had their license.

That night, they were so tired that they made love only once.

And they were up bright and early Tuesday morning. They grabbed a quick breakfast and went down into town to meet Milo Quinn at the Hitching Post.

Joss loved the bar and grill from the first moment she stepped through the front door. It was as rustic inside as out and had an old-timey feel about it, with the dining room on one side and the bar on the other. There was plenty of space for a dance floor on the bar side and a small stage in the corner where a band could set up. No wonder the place had always been a hit with the locals. It was a great venue. As long as she and Jace provided good food and good service, they probably couldn't go wrong.

Jace was relieved to discover that the painting of the Shady Lady still hung in the place of honor above the gorgeous antique bar. "She is lookin' way hot as always," Jace said with a grin.

Milo assured them that the painting and all the furnishings and equipment were part of the very reasonable asking price. Lance O'Doherty's daughter, it seemed, really wanted to sell. The place had a full, if somewhat dated, restaurant-style kitchen. And off the long hallway in the back, there were restrooms and three smaller dining rooms for private parties.

The building could use some updating—of the kitchen and of the restrooms. The main bar and restaurant could stand a little sprucing, too. The idea was to keep all that old-time Hitching Post charm, but freshen things up, make it brighter and more inviting.

All three of them went for lunch together at a pizza place in New Town and then they followed Milo out to see a trio of four- to five-acre properties. None of them were quite what they were looking for.

That evening, they met Lizzie and Ethan for dinner in the resort's Gallatin Room. Over thick, perfectly seared filets, garlic potatoes and curried spinach, they discussed the potential purchase of the bar and grill. Lizzie and Ethan both offered advice.

Shane Roarke emerged from the kitchen while they were devouring a to-die-for dessert of carrot cake and sweet pea ice cream with lavender caramel sauce. The chef greeted Joss and Jason, who introduced him to Jace's brother and his wife. Shane stayed to make small talk for a few minutes and then moved on.

Ethan stared after him. "That guy reminds me of some-one...."

Joss and Jason both laughed. Joss said, "We had the same feeling the first time we saw him. We just can't fig-ure out exactly *who* he reminds us of."

The food for the reception, they decided when they met with Shane the next morning, would be buffet-style. They went with mostly finger foods. From the resort, they drove to Milo Quinn's office. After lengthy discussion, Jace of-fered the asking price on the Hitching Post.

Once they signed the offer, they picked up their invitations at the copy place and returned to the resort, where they spent a few hours scrolling the address lists stored in their smartphones, filling out the envelopes and sticking on stamps. Joss stuck a little note in the invitation to her mother. The note explained that she and Jace had found an apartment to live in until they chose a new home. She gave her mom the address and the phone number at the new place, although she really wasn't expecting to hear from her mother anytime soon—and not expecting her to come to the wedding either.

Every time she thought of her mom, a gray, sad gloom descended. It was a giant rift that had opened up between them over that jackass Kenny Donovan. Joss appreciated Jace's positive attitude about the situation, but she doubted she and her mom would be making peace for a long time to come.

Jace looked up from the envelope he was addressing. "That was a really sad-sounding sigh."

She pulled a face. "It's just, you know, my mother…"

He reached across the table and put his hand over hers. "Hey, she'll come around."

She turned her hand over and clasped his. And then she got up from her seat so she could lean close to him and share a slow, sweet kiss.

Later, they took the finished invitations down to the front desk where the clerk promised they would go out with the morning mail. Back in the suite, they ordered room service. Shandie Traub called. She invited them to dinner the next night, which was great. They wouldn't have to worry about stocking the cupboards at the apartment on their first day there.

It was their final night in the king-sized pillow-top bed. They made the most of it, enjoying slow, lazy love for hour upon hour.

As always, it was the best. Better than ever, Joss thought, as she sat in his lap, facing him, her legs wrapped around him, holding him deep within her.

Oh, yes! Better every time. Who knew it could be like this? Really, she'd had no idea.

He surged up into her. And she took him. Deeper. All the way. He filled her up so perfectly.

She cried his name. He kissed her, his mouth claiming hers so hungrily as she felt his climax take him.

Seconds later, she joined him. They went over the edge of the world together.

This, she thought. *Yes! Nothing like this. Ever. Not ever in my life before…*

Grant had told them they didn't need to be out of the suite until noon, so they stayed in bed later than usual Thursday morning.

At nine-thirty, as they were lazily dozing and Joss was telling herself they really needed to get motivated and get their stuff packed to move over to the apartment, the phone rang.

Jace said what he always said: "Don't answer that."

And she did what she always did. "'Lo?"

"Is this Jocelyn?"

She sat bolt-upright.

Jace sat up, too. "What the—"

"It's Milo," she whispered excitedly. Then she cleared her throat and tried to sound composed. "Hi, Milo. What's up?"

"You've just bought the Hitching Post," the Realtor announced.

Joss let out a yell and pumped her fist toward the ceiling.

"Give me that." Jace took the phone. "Hey, Milo…"

Milo said something. Jace listened and finally answered, "Great. We'll be there." He handed her the phone back.

She put it to her ear, but the Realtor had already hung up. "He's gone." She dropped the phone back on the cradle. "So?"

"We're meeting him at his office at three today to sign the final agreement, give him the earnest money check and talk about inspections. He also said that if everything goes as planned, we close on the property August fifteenth."

"So fast!"

"It's a little over thirty days. That's about right."

She sat there, mouth agape, heart racing with excitement. "Jace, we did it. This is happening. It's really, really happening."

He chuckled, "No kidding."

She swayed his way and planted a big, smacking kiss in the middle of his broad, handsome forehead. He tried to reach for her, but she ducked back, giggling.

"Get back here," he growled.

"No way. I can't sit still." She shoved off the covers and leaped from the bed.

Jace started to go after her, but then changed his mind. He laced his hands behind his head and grinned—possibly because she was totally naked. "All right," he said. "Have it your way. I gotta admit I'm lovin' the view from here."

She let out another joyous shout and then she grabbed her robe from the floor where she'd dropped it the night before. Quickly, she tugged it on and tied the sash. Then she ran around the room chanting, "We did it, we did it, we bought the Hitching Post!"

He just sat there, beaming. "Gee, Joss. You could show a little excitement, don't you think?"

With a long trill of laughter, she ran back to the bed,

grabbed her pillow and began hitting him over the head with it. "Oh, this is fabulous! Oh, I just can't believe it…."

"Hey," he protested, still laughing. "Knock that off." He grabbed for the pillow and snatched it away from her. Then he used it against her, trying to bop her a good one.

She played along, leaning in as he took aim, then jumping out of the way when he delivered a blow. "You missed! I'm too fast for you."

He clutched the pillow against his rock-hard, gorgeous chest so she couldn't steal it back from him and threatened in the raspy voice of a villain in some old-time melodrama, "That's it for you, beautiful."

"Hah!"

The bad-guy leer vanished. He gave her the bedroom eyes and crooked his index finger. "Come down here. Nice and close…"

"Forget that noise, mister!" Breathing fast, her heart racing with giddy excitement, she started laughing again.

And then, just like that, out of nowhere, her breath caught.

She could not breathe and her heart had stopped stock-still in her chest.

Twin lines appeared between Jace's dark brows. "Joss, you okay?"

She *was* actually. More than okay.

The breath came flooding back into her chest and her heart started beating again and the hotel bedroom seemed so beautiful suddenly. It seemed to glow with golden light. *Happy*, she thought. *At this moment, I am so perfectly, gloriously happy.* Never in her life had she felt exactly like this. Everything just paled next to this.

She saw it all, her life up till now: her lonely childhood with her brave, determined, damaged mother. Her adolescence, during all of which she'd felt awkward and different;

she'd never managed to fit in. And later, through a couple of years of college and her first job in the restaurant business, which she'd discovered she enjoyed. Through her search for a good guy who could help her make the big, loud happy family she'd always dreamed of. To Kenny, who was supposed to be the one, her guy forever, and had turned out to be anything but.

All of it. The whole of her life until she met Jace. It simply couldn't compare to her days and nights with him, to this one shining, perfect moment.

She didn't stop to consider. She just opened her mouth and let the scary words pour out. "I love you, Jason Traub. I love you so much. I never knew that it could be like this, that it could *feel* like this, could fill me up like this, I..." Her throat clogged and the words ran out.

He didn't look happy.

Not in the least. He looked...stunned maybe?

And very uncomfortable.

She felt her face turn blazing red. "Oh, wow." She winced. "More information than you needed, huh?"

Because seriously, hadn't he made it painfully clear upfront that he had no clue what love was, that he just didn't get it and didn't care to get it? That he only wanted to start a business and settle down. That he liked her a lot, but for him, love didn't enter into it.

How had he put it last Sunday when he asked her to marry him?

I have no idea what love really is and I'm better off not kidding myself that I do....

Oh, God. Way to go, Joss. What had possessed her to just blurt it out like that?

He set the pillow aside and sucked in a slow breath. "Uh. Well. Good." And he actually pasted on this fake, too-cheerful smile. "That's great, Joss. I mean, thank you."

"Thank you?"

"Aw, Joss…"

"I say I love you and you say 'Thank you'?"

"Joss…"

She put up a hand. "Okay. Yeah. Bad. Really bad." And exactly what she should have expected, if she'd only had the presence of mind to keep her mouth shut until she'd thought the whole thing through. Duh. Double duh in a big, big way.

"Come on, Joss…" He looked so embarrassed, so totally out of his depth.

And she? Her mouth felt dry as a handful of dust. Her heart felt like a shriveled husk in her chest. She swallowed. With care. And she made herself ask him, "So then, is this going to ruin it for you? Do you want to back out? Because if you do, I would appreciate knowing that now."

"Back out?" He looked totally dazed, beyond confused. And so handsome, she hated him.

Almost as much as she loved him.

Because seriously, he was much too good to look at. It wasn't fair, now she thought about it, how really hot he was. "Excuse me," she said carefully, "are you saying you didn't understand the question?"

He started to push back the covers. "Joss, I—"

"Uh-uh." She leveled a look on him that had him sinking back into the bed. "Do you want to back out? Just say so. Just answer the question."

"No, then. Okay?"

Okay? As a matter of fact, it wasn't. It wasn't okay in the least. "No," she echoed with excruciating care.

"No," he repeated yet again. "It's what I said."

"No, you don't understand? Or no, you don't want to marry me? What are you telling me, Jace? Just do me a big favor and be straight with me about this."

His handsome, square jaw was set. He said, with heavy emphasis, "I *do* want to marry you. I *don't* want to back out."

Relief flooded through her. Yeah, it was tinged with the weight of sadness and mortification and a host of other not-so-fun emotions. But still, it was something. "You mean that? You really do still want to marry me?"

Now he was the one swallowing. She watched his Adam's apple bounce. And then he nodded. "I do. Yeah, it's what I want. You and me. The life we planned. I still want that." He paused. She waited. Finally, he began again, haltingly, "It's just that, well, the whole love thing—"

She cut him off. "Stop. I don't want to hear it, you know? I sincerely do not."

He blew out a slow, cheek-puffing breath. "Wow. Well. Whatever you say."

She wrapped her arms around herself in a meager attempt to give herself the comfort he couldn't—or wouldn't. "It was…a mistake. To even bring it up, the whole love thing. I know that. I don't know what I was thinking. After all, I understand how you feel about it. And it's my bad. It's not like you didn't set me straight right from the first, not like you didn't make yourself perfectly clear."

"Joss…"

She shook her head. Hard. "No, I mean it. Can we just stop talking about it? Can we just let it go?"

Was that relief she saw in those beautiful chocolate-brown eyes of his?

So what if it was? She could relate. They were both relieved—he that she was giving up the love talk, she because he claimed he still wanted to marry her.

Now her mouth tasted like sawdust. And the luxurious bedroom, aglow with golden light moments before, was all at once dingy and dark.

"Joss, you know that I care for you."

She looked away. "Just don't, okay? Just stop. I said I understand. And I do. There's nothing more to say about it."

The covers rustled as he pushed them aside again. "Damn it, Joss…"

Someone knocked on the outer door.

It was perfect timing as far as Joss was concerned. "What now?" she asked bleakly, turning to look at him again. "You think that's your mother?"

He swung his feet to the floor. God, he was so beautiful. "I hope not," he muttered. "I'll get rid of her."

"No, I'll get it." She tied the belt of her robe more securely.

He didn't say anything. He was looking at her sideways, a concerned kind of look.

Well, he could take that look and shove it. She didn't need his concern. He didn't want to go there—and neither did she. Not anymore. They got along great and they knew what they wanted and that was enough for him.

And it would damn well be enough for her. To show him she was fine with the way things were, she sent him a big, defiant smile, after which she whirled and headed for the other room, pausing only to shut the bedroom door firmly behind her.

The knock came again as she reached the foyer. She ran her hand back through her sleep-mussed hair and peeked through the peephole.

Her heart sank. It wasn't Jace's mom out there in the hallway.

It was hers.

Chapter Twelve

With a low moan, Joss rested her forehead against the suite's thick outer door. She did not want to open it. She really, really didn't.

Shutting her eyes, she sucked in a slow breath, peeled herself off the door and fled back to the bedroom.

When she flung the door wide, she found Jace right where she'd left him, sitting on the edge of the bed, wearing nothing but a slight frown.

One look at her expression and he jumped to his feet. "What? Who is it?"

She let out a groan. "You'd better get dressed."

"What's going on?"

"It's my mother."

He dropped back to the edge of the bed. "Wait a minute. Your mother. Here at the resort?"

She nodded. As if on cue, her mother knocked for the third time, five swift, hard raps on the outer door.

Jace jumped up again and came for her. Before she could think to jerk away, he caught her face between his hands. "It's okay. It'll be okay."

"Oh, I'm so glad one of us thinks so." She bit back a sob. His touch felt so good. As good as ever. Was that right? Was that fair?

And then he kissed her, the lightest brushing breath of a kiss. That felt good, too. It comforted her in spite of everything. "Now you go on, let her in," he said gently. "I'll put some clothes on."

She laughed, a slightly wild sound. "Great idea. Ahem. I mean, you know. That you should get dressed…" God, she was babbling. Losing it. Holding on to composure by the tiniest of threads.

"There's nothing to worry about," he said. "It's good that she's here."

"Good?" she whispered desperately. "How can it be good?"

"Well, because it means that you two can work everything out now, all the stuff that's been tearing you apart."

"But I…she's not…we can't…" She sputtered into silence.

"It's okay," he said again. "Go let her in." He took her shoulders, turned her around and gave her a gentle push.

She went. What choice did she have?

Quietly, he shut the bedroom door behind her.

And she kept walking, one foot in front of the other, across the living area, back into the foyer, right up to the outer door. She undid the chain, turned the dead bolt.

And pulled the door back. "Mom, hi." RaeEllen had her two large black rolling suitcases, one to either side of her. She planned on a long stay apparently, "It's, um, good to see you," Joss said. She leaned forward and kissed her mother's cheek. Then she stepped back so her mom could enter.

Glancing suspiciously from side to side, RaeEllen crossed the threshold, pulling one of the suitcases behind her.

Joss stepped around her and brought in the other one. She shut the door. "This is…a surprise."

RaeEllen settled her favorite brown purse more comfortably on the shoulder of her cream-colored summer blazer. "You're not even dressed? At this hour? It's almost ten."

Joss kept her smile in place. "Just leave your purse on the table there. And come on into the living area. Things have been so busy. There's so much to do in such a short time." She was babbling again, and she knew it. But somehow, she couldn't seem to stop herself. "We just heard a few minutes ago that we bought the restaurant we offered on and we're very excited that the deal went through, that our plans are—"

"A restaurant? You *bought* a restaurant?"

"Yes, we did. We're so excited. And we've been looking for a house, *and* getting the invitations out, *and* finding a place to stay in the interim. Plus there's all the wedding stuff—arranging for the cake and settling on the menu. It goes on and on. Today's another big day because we'll be moving to—"

"We?" Her mother's pale blue eyes widened.

"Yeah. Jason, my fiancé, and me. We have to be out of the suite by noon and we're moving temporarily to an apartment down in town. I sent you a note about that, along with a wedding invitation. But of course, you didn't get it yet. And anyway, we were both worn out with all the running around, pulling everything together, so we decided to indulge ourselves and sleep in a little. We were tired, you know? Just beat."

RaeEllen held on to her brown bag for dear life and blinked several times in rapid succession. "He's here, in this room, with you?"

"That's right." Joss reminded herself not to clench her teeth. "Jason's in the bedroom actually. He's getting dressed."

"Oh. Getting dressed. Then you're telling me he…well, I mean, that you and he…"

Joss had had enough. "Come on, Mom. Stop acting like the parson's wife in some Jane Austen novel. Yes, not only are Jace and I getting married, we are already living together. And it's working out great." *Well, except for the fact that I love him and he* doesn't *love me…*.

"It's working out great," RaeEllen repeated in a tone that said it didn't sound the least great to her.

"Yes, that's what I said. We're very happy together."

"But you hardly know this man and only three weeks ago you were supposed to have married Kenny, who is deeply, deeply hurt by your desertion, who only wants a chance to make you happy, to—"

"Mom. Whoa. Stop." Joss waved both her hands in front of her mother's face. "This is kind of a loop we're into here, Mom. Can we please stop going round and round about things we've already discussed and don't seem capable of coming to any agreement on?"

Her mother's mouth drew painfully tight. "Of course. Whatever you say."

Joss focused on her mother's words and tried her best to ignore the angry, disapproving tone. "Thank you. I appreciate that." She straightened her robe, an action that, for some reason, caused her mother to gasp. Joss was trying to figure out what exactly that gasp meant when RaeEllen reached out and grabbed her hand—her left hand.

"Lovely." Her mother sounded sincere as she studied Joss's engagement ring.

Joss tried to tell herself that maybe there was hope for the situation after all, that her mom might actually try to make the best of things. "Oh, I know. I love it."

RaeEllen glanced up, and delivered the zinger. "It looks real."

That did it. Joss withdrew her hand. "I'm not kidding, Mom. I know you've had a long trip and I would like to be glad you've come, but I've had enough."

"What does that mean?"

"It means I'm not going to sit still and let you run over me. I'm not a little girl anymore. I'm a grown woman and I get to determine the direction of my own life, which you *used* to understand perfectly. Either you start *behaving* in a civil manner and treat me like an adult again, or you can just roll those suitcases right out the door and head for home."

Her mother looked stricken. "But I drove all the way here. As you've already mentioned, it was a very long trip and I'm exhausted."

"Then you'd better stop with the mean remarks, hadn't you? Or you'll be on the road again."

RaeEllen assumed an injured air. "You don't want me here? Is that what you're telling me?"

Joss tried valiantly to form an answer to that one. But what could she say? The truth was she *didn't* want her mother there. Not unless she changed her tune.

RaeEllen spoke again, more gently. "It's only, well, I felt I should come. I felt we should…work out our differences."

"And that's admirable, Mom." Warily, she eyed the two

large suitcases. "So…you were thinking you would stay right through to the wedding?"

Her mother pressed her lips together and nodded sharply. "As long as it takes, yes. I have some family leave stored up."

Joss was stuck back there with that first sentence. "As long as what takes?"

Her mother smoothed her short, fine brown hair. "I wonder, could I have a glass of water?"

Joss resisted the overwhelming desire to lay down the law. She'd already made herself more than clear. Going into it all again right this moment would only be hooking back into the loop she'd accused her mother of falling into. "Of course," she finally said. "Come on into the living area."

"My suitcases…"

"Just leave them here for now." She turned to enter the main area of the suite, her mother close on her heels. "Have a seat." She gestured at the sofa and went to the wet bar, where she filled a glass with ice and opened one of the complimentary bottles of spring water.

Jace appeared, fully dressed in nice jeans, a knit shirt and the usual high-dollar boots. He went straight to her mother. "Mrs. Bennings, hello." He laid on the Texas charm, bowing a little at the waist as he reached across the coffee table. "How great to meet you."

Even her sour-hearted mom couldn't completely resist him. She gave him her hand. He cradled it between his two larger ones, and he hit her with one of those lady-killer smiles of his, the kind that could break a woman's heart at twenty paces.

Her mom sniffed. "It's Ms. Bennings, thank you." Delicately, she withdrew her hand.

Joss hurried to Jace's rescue. "But only to strangers."

Jace straightened and slid her a questioning look. Blithely, she went on, "Of course, *you'll* call her RaeEllen." She gave her mother a steely-eyed glance. "Unless you'd prefer 'Mom'?"

"Ahem. Well." RaeEllen nodded at Jace. "Yes. RaeEllen, of course. So nice to meet you." Joss set the glass of ice and bottle of water in front of her. "Thank you, Jocelyn."

Joss nodded, and dropped the bomb on poor Jace. "Mom is planning to stay until the wedding."

Carefully, her mother poured the water over the ice. She said nothing.

Jace said, "Ah. Well, that's great." His smile had slipped a little.

Joss watched him, her heart twisting. She loved him. And he didn't do love.

And now her mother was here with that strange, determined look in her hazel eyes. That couldn't be good.

But she could deal with her mother—if only things didn't go wrong with Jace.

He'd said he still wanted the life they had planned.

But did he really?

Had her passionate declaration changed everything for him? Was he second-guessing now, thinking about how he wasn't really the marrying kind after all? That this was all a big mistake, the two of them? That it had happened much too fast, with her on the rebound—and maybe him, too, when you came right down to it. Because there had been that rich oilman's daughter, Tricia. Even though he said it wasn't love with Tricia, well, he *had* proposed to her. And she'd said no.

And he'd gone into something of a depression after that.

So was he maybe now seeing the future they'd been planning as another trap he needed to escape? Was he...

No.

Uh-uh.

She was not going there.

He'd said straight to her face that he still wanted to marry her. If he'd changed his mind, he could have just said so. She'd given him an opening. A really *wide* opening.

And he'd refused to take it.

If he wanted out, he could tell her. He was a grown man fully capable of speaking his mind.

But what if I want out now? What if I've decided I don't want a marriage without love?

She turned those painful questions over in her mind, and realized that it *wouldn't* be a loveless marriage. At least not on her end.

And she didn't want to back out. Not on her life. She wanted Jace and she wanted everything he offered her—wanted her dream, just as she'd always imagined it might be. Especially now that her dream would include the most important part: the man she loved. He said he still wanted to live her dream with her.

She would have to be crazy to turn her back on that. And she wouldn't. No way.

She let out a heavy sigh.

And realized that both Jace and her mother were staring at her—Jace kind of nervously, her mom in a measuring, calculating way.

Fine. Let 'em stare. "Mom, there's a second bedroom at the apartment where Jace and I will be staying until we find a house. You're welcome to it." She caught Jace's eye and challenged, "Right, Jace?"

She had to give him credit. He didn't even flinch. "Absolutely. RaeEllen, we'd be happy to have you stay with us."

Whatever her mother's real agenda, she had the grace

to hesitate. "Really, I can get a hotel room. I don't want to impose."

Jace stepped right up. "It's no imposition, RaeEllen. You're family, after all."

Milo Quinn's office was only a few blocks from the Mountain Bluebell Bakery and the apartment above it, so Joss and Jason walked to their three o'clock appointment.

An hour later, they left Milo's office with a signed contract on the Hitching Post. Clouds had gathered in the wide Montana sky when they emerged onto Pine Street. A few random drops started falling as they strolled north to Main.

Jace glanced up at the gray underbelly of the thick cloud cover. "We'd better get moving or we're going to get wet."

So they ran around the corner and down the block. They ducked through the bakery's front door just as the sky opened up and the downpour began. One of Lizzie's employees gave them a smile and a wave as they headed up the stairs to the apartment above.

She got to there first. The doorknob wouldn't turn. She sighed. "My mom's used to city life. She's locked herself in." She raised her hand to knock.

Jace caught her wrist before her knuckles connected with the door. "We have to talk." His voice was so deep and more than a little rough.

Her heart did something unsettling inside her chest. And her skin felt all tingly and warm. Her breath snagging in her throat, she turned to him, met those dark velvet eyes that burned into hers, smelled the spicy, green, electric scent that belonged to only him....

"Talk? About what?" She was pleased that aside from a certain huskiness, her voice betrayed none of her excitement. She didn't *want* to be excited by him. Not now.

Not with her new—and unreturned—love so fresh and raw within her.

He looked at her steadily. "It's not the same. You're... distant. Cool to me."

She shrugged. "Be patient. I'll get over it." She wouldn't. But she would get used to it—at least she hoped she would. She'd learn to live with being alone in love.

His gaze burned darker, more intense. "Listen, do you need me to say it? I can just say it if it's what you need."

She took his meaning and whispered low, "You would say that you love me, even though you don't?"

"It's only words."

"To you maybe."

He still held her wrist. And didn't let go. Instead, he guided it back behind her and brought her up close against his broad, rocklike chest. "Whatever you want. Just say it. I'll do it."

Her breasts felt oversensitive, pressing as they did into the hardness and heat of him. Her body burned. And her heart...

It ached. A deep, thick kind of ache. An ache that was almost pleasurable. She didn't have his love. But he did want her. A lot. It was something. Not enough, but still. Better than nothing.

"Okay, Jace. You go ahead. You say it. You lie to me."

His arm banded tighter and he pulled her even closer. What breath she had left came out in a gasp.

And then he said it, roughly, angrily, his breath warm and sweet across her cheek. "I love you, Joss."

She tipped her head to the side, opened her mouth slightly and ran her tongue over her upper lip, openly taunting him. His eyes burned brighter and a muscle jumped in his jaw. "Hmm," she said with a smile that wasn't really a smile at all. "Somehow it doesn't have the ring of truth, you know? And what good is a lie to me? Not a whole lot."

"Joss…" He said her name very low that time. It was a warning. And also, somehow, a plea. "I just don't want to lose you over this, okay? Over three little words. How stupid would that be? No, I don't get the whole love thing. I think it's a crock. You want to be with someone, build a life with someone, or you don't. And the point is, I want a life with you. And you want the same thing with me."

She hitched her chin higher. "I'm not arguing. We're on the same page with this."

"Are we?" He didn't look convinced.

And she was softening. How could she help it, with his fine, big body pressed against hers, tempting her? And his heated words in her ears, reminding her that he did care, that he wanted her, that he had promised to be a true husband to her. And that she believed him on all those points, believed *in* him.

The L-word shouldn't matter so much. It was what a person *did* that mattered.

"Yes." She let her tone go soft as her heart. "Yes, we're on the same page." She reached up with the hand he hadn't trapped behind her back and caressed the slightly stubbled line of his so-manly jaw. "We just bought our business. We're going to find the right house. We're getting married and we're going to have as many kids as the good Lord will grant us."

"It's gonna be great," he said fervently, the contract in his free hand crackling a little as he tightened his fist on it. "You'll see."

"I know." She gave him a real smile that time, even if it was a little wobbly. "Yes, it will be. Great."

"Joss…" He whispered her name as his fine mouth swooped down to cover hers.

Her knees went loose and she sagged back heavily against the door. Oh, that mouth of his—it played over hers, hitting every sweet, hot, perfect note. It was a symphony he created, every time he kissed her. Slow and tempting, fast and hot. He varied the notes and the rhythms. He swept her away on a warm tide of pleasure. She sighed and surrendered to the spell that he wove.

And then, just she was sliding her free hand up to clasp his neck and pull him even closer, the door behind her gave way.

With a sharp little cry, she stumbled backward.

"What the…" Jace growled.

Somehow, she managed to stay on her feet. She whirled to find her mother standing there, hazel eyes wide with pretended surprise.

"Oh!" RaeEllen exclaimed. "Well, I'm sorry. I thought I heard a knock…."

"Not a problem," Joss lied, as she straightened her light summer shirt and recovered her dignity.

Jace actually chuckled. "Caught us in the act, RaeEllen."

RaeEllen only pinched up her mouth and smoothed her hair. "I'm glad you're back. I've made a list of the staples we absolutely must have to function around here. And Jason, I was thinking that maybe you could make a quick run to the local supermarket while Jocelyn and I finish putting our things away."

Joss saw right through her mother. It was divide and conquer time. She was sending Jace away so she could go to work on Joss. Not happening. "We can deal with that later, Mom. We're invited to dinner at Jace's cousin Dax's house tonight."

"But we'll at least need eggs and coffee for breakfast tomorrow."

"Actually, we won't. We can just walk downstairs to the bakery. The breakfast croissants have eggs, ham, sausage—whatever you want in them. And they are to die for."

"That could get expensive."

"Mom, it's one day. We'll shop for food tomorrow, after breakfast, when it's not pouring down rain."

Jace spoke up. "Give me the list, RaeEllen. I'll be happy to pick up what we need right now."

Joss whirled on him. "We should talk." She grabbed his hand. "Come in the bedroom." She sent her mother a withering glance. "Mom, we'll be right back."

RaeEllen knew when to keep her mouth shut. She gave a tight little smile and let them go.

Jace went willingly enough. Joss towed him to the larger bedroom at the back of the apartment, dragged him inside and shut the door.

He went over and dropped to the edge of the old-fashioned double bed with its dark headboard and bright log cabin quilt.

She stayed near the door. "You know what she's doing, don't you?"

He didn't even have to think about it. "She wants to get you alone and tell you all the reasons you shouldn't marry me."

"So why are you letting her get away with it?"

"Because you can't avoid her forever. She's staying right here in the apartment with us. You might as well face her down at the gate, let her know you're not running scared and she'd better straighten up and fly right or she can get back in that big old Buick of hers and head home to Sacramento."

He was right, of course.

But still. "I *have* let her know. It doesn't do any good."

"So tell her to go home."

"I'm…not at that point yet. Close. But not yet."

He got up then. He came to her, clasping her shoulders between his strong hands. "You need to show her she doesn't get to you."

"But that's just it. She *does* get to me—and don't tell me you don't know exactly what I'm going through here. Remember that first day we met? When you practically begged me to go to the Rib Shack with you, to pretend to be your date so your family would stop trying to set you up?"

He grunted. "You *would* have to remind me. They were driving me nuts."

"So all right, then. You understand. And I mean it. Don't leave me alone with her."

"Joss, you're only putting off the inevitable."

"That's right. I keep hoping I'll get lucky and she'll decide to back off and be reasonable."

He shook his head. "She seems pretty determined."

She made a face at him. "She's determined, all right. Determined to put a stop to our wedding. Think about that. Out on the landing a few minutes ago, you were all about how you really, really do want to marry me."

"It's true," he said simply. "I do want to marry you." His words touched her. He was such a big, handsome bundle of contradictions. He couldn't say the L-word without scowling. Yet he sincerely wanted to make a life with her.

"My mother is up to no good," she said.

"Joss, she came all the way here to Montana to try and make it up with you."

She wrinkled her nose at him. "That is so not what she's here for."

He caught a lock of her hair, rubbed it between his fingers. "Talk to her."

She could become seriously annoyed with him. "When

it's *your* mother, you can't run away fast enough. But when it's *my* mom, I'm supposed to hold my ground and talk it out."

"You're a woman. Women are better at all that crap."

"Crap," she muttered. "A truer word was never spoken."

He slid his hand up under her hair and clasped her nape. Lovely sensations cascaded through her. And then he pressed his lips so tenderly to hers. "Talk to her."

Five minutes later, he was out the door.

And she was alone with her scheming mother, who took her hands and dragged her into the long, narrow kitchen and down to the little round table at the far end.

"Sit down," RaeEllen said in her warmest, most conciliatory tones. "Let's catch up a little…."

Reluctantly, Joss sat.

"Jason is very handsome," her mother said carefully, a brave soldier in a dangerous field of hair-trigger land mines. "Very charming and very…compelling."

"Yes, he is."

"And I gather he's got money."

"Yes, he does."

"I can understand how he might have swept you off your feet." RaeEllen paused. Presumably so that Joss could agree with her.

Joss said nothing.

Her mother forged on. "But really, how can he possibly be in love with you, or you with him?"

Love. Joss felt the muscles between her shoulder blades snap tight. The last thing she wanted to discuss with her mother was love. It was way too sensitive a subject right then.

And she didn't want her mother to know that. RaeEllen was trolling for weaknesses. Joss refused to show her

any. She ordered those tense muscles to relax and she kept
her face composed.

RaeEllen kept going, rattling off her list of reasons that
Joss and Jace were doomed to failure as a couple. "You met
so recently. It's just…well, Jocelyn, it's a fling. On the rebound. And the last thing a woman should ever do is marry
a man with whom she is having an affair on the rebound."

Joss couldn't resist. She got in a jab of her own. "Is that
what happened with you and my father?"

RaeEllen stiffened. "I beg your pardon. We are not discussing your father."

"I'm just trying to determine how you're such an ex-
pert on affairs and flings and getting something going on
the rebound. The way I remember it, there was just my
father. And when he left, that was pretty much it for you."

"Jocelyn, this is not about me."

Joss let out a slow breath and shook her head. "Mom,
you're wrong. I think this is very much about you. About
you and your fears and your inability to move on, to try
again with a man after Dad walked out."

"No. No, it's not." RaeEllen put a hand to her chest. Two
bright spots of color had bloomed on her cheeks. "It most
certainly is not. This is about you. About the wonderful
man who loves you and forgives you for making a fool of
him in front of three hundred people on your wedding day."

"I did not make a fool of Kenny. He did that to himself
by rolling around half-naked with my own cousin in the
coat room of the church."

"That never happened."

"Mom, it happened. I saw it with my own eyes."

"What happened is that you got cold feet. I remember
that you were having second thoughts. You confided in
me, don't you recall?"

"Yes, I do recall. Quite clearly. You convinced me that

all brides have second thoughts and I should go through with the wedding. You blew me off."

"No, I did not. I helped you to see that you shouldn't let your unfounded fears get in the way of your happiness."

Joss braced an elbow on the table and rested her forehead in her hand. "This is going nowhere."

"We need to talk about this."

"We *have* talked about this. I have no idea why you're so obsessed with convincing me to get back together with a self-absorbed jerk who cheated on me on our wedding day. But I can't argue with you about this any longer. I am finished. I am marrying Jace and I'm never going near Kenny Donovan again and that's the end of it."

"But you—"

"The end of it, Mom. It's over. Stop."

"But I have to—"

Joss dropped her hand flat, smacking the table. The sound was loud and sharp in the small space. "Enough. I've had it. I can't take this any longer. I'm sorry I can't get through to you. And it doesn't matter what you do, you are not going to change my mind."

"Kenny loves you. He loves you so much. And you are cruel and cold to him. How can you be like that? Why can't you see how horribly you're behaving?"

It was the final straw. "That's it. The end. I want you to go back to Sacramento, Mom. I want you out of this apartment. I've got sixteen days until Jace and I get married. They are going to be busy days. I can't have you at me every chance you get, battering away at me, so sure of your righteousness, so certain that eventually you will wear me down. You *won't* wear me down. What you'll do is ruin what should be a beautiful, busy, exciting two weeks."

"You just want me out of here so you can be alone with that man."

Joss let out a laugh that sounded more like a groan. "You know what? That's right. I do want to be alone with Jace. Why wouldn't I want to be alone with him? Jace is funny and tender and smart." *Even if he isn't in love with me.* "And all he wants is to give me the life I've always dreamed of. What's not to like about that, Mom?"

"What happens when he gets tired of you?"

That hurt. That really hurt. She answered firmly. "He wants to be with me. He's not going to get *tired* of me."

"You are blind. Foolish and blind."

Back at ya, Mom. "I mean it. I want you to go."

Jace returned at twenty after five, his arms loaded with groceries. "There are more in the car. Where's your mom?"

"In her room. Sulking." She took one of the bags from him and turned for the kitchen. "She'll be leaving tomorrow morning." He followed her in there and they set the bags on the counter.

He asked, low-voiced so there was no chance her mother might hear, "You're sending her away?"

"Yes, I am."

"You sure?"

"Yes. I'll make it clear she's still welcome to come for the wedding."

He took her hand, turned it over, wove his fingers with hers. "You okay?"

What happens when you get tired of me? "I've been better."

He pulled her close, into the circle of those powerful arms. She let herself lean on him, breathed in the special scent that belonged only to him, told herself that she wasn't going to let her mother's cruel, misguided words get to her.

But those words were in her head now. Stuck there.

Along with the bald facts: She loved him and he didn't love her.

He'd told her right up front that he'd always been a player, that he'd never been one to settle down, not until his whirlwind affair with the rich oilman's daughter. And now, he was doing it again, with her, with Joss.

Could a man really change that much? Or was this just some phase he was going through? He *thought* he ought to settle down, so he'd swept her off her feet and then proposed, just like he'd done with Tricia Lavelle.

He was the last single guy in his family. Maybe that was getting to him. Maybe he was trying to conform to his family's idea of what a man was supposed to do with his life.

Was it only a matter of time before he realized that marriage and a big house full of rowdy kids wasn't for him after all?

The questions spun round and round in her head. She told herself to ignore them. She wasn't going to let them ruin her happiness.

She held on to Jace tighter. It was going to be all right with them. He wouldn't get tired of her. She believed in him, in what they had together.

Everything would work out fine....

Chapter Thirteen

RaeEllen refused to go with them to Dax and Shandie's that night. She said she was tired and needed her rest. "After all," she added loftily, "I have another long drive facing me tomorrow."

Joss didn't try to change her mind. If her mom didn't want to go, fine. At this point, there was nothing Joss could think of to do to ease the bad feelings between them.

Dax and Shandie's big house was packed. All of Jace's siblings and their spouses were there. And so were Laila's sisters Annabel, Jasmine and Jordyn Leigh. Jace's mom and Pete were still in town, so they showed up, too. And then there was DJ and his family as well.

Joss visited with Claudia, who was all smiles over the coming wedding. Joss tried to take comfort in the way Jace's mom treated her. Claudia welcomed her into the Traub family with open arms. If only her own mom could be so accepting.

And if only the bleak doubts would quit dogging her.

She did worry, the more she thought about it, that Jace wasn't really ready for the life they planned together. If he *was* ready, how hard would it be for him to tell her he loved her and to actually mean it?

With half an ear, she listened to Dax and DJ talk about a couple of local crooks, Arthur Swinton and Jasper Fowler. The two men were in prison. They'd committed a series of crimes, including kidnapping Jace's sister, Rose Traub Anderson. The theory was that Swinton had nursed a grudge against the Traub family for decades because Dax and DJ's mom had turned him down flat when Swinton tried to put a move on her. DJ and Dax still couldn't quite believe that Swinton had gone off the deep end because their mom had turned him down. The more they discussed it, the more they agreed that Swinton's reaction to rejection had been way over the top, that there really had to be more to it than that.

Joss thought she could almost feel sorry for Arthur Swinton. It wasn't an easy thing to love someone who didn't love you back.

It was after midnight when she and Jace returned to the darkened apartment. The door to her mother's room was shut and no light bled out from beneath it.

They went to bed. Quietly. In order not to disturb the bitter, confused woman in the room down the hall. For the first time since they'd become lovers six nights before, they didn't make love. Joss just wasn't up for it, not with her disapproving mother right there in the apartment with them.

But Jace did pull her close and tuck her up nice and tight against him, wrapping that big, warm body of his all around her. Even with her doubts, she felt cherished. Cared for. She dropped off to sleep with a weary little sigh.

Her mom left after breakfast the next morning. RaeEllen and Joss shared an unenthusiastic final hug.

"I sent you a wedding invitation," Joss said. "I hope you'll come."

Her mother held herself stiffly in Joss's embrace. "Of course," she said in the somber tone of someone who'd just been asked to attend a funeral. "I'll be there."

During the first couple of days of the week that followed, Joss and Jace saw five new properties. Wednesday, they made an offer on eight green, rolling acres about two miles from town.

The house would need updating, but it had a little barn and a nice, big pasture for the horses Jace planned to bring up from his place in Texas. On Friday morning, a week and a day before their wedding, they signed the contract on their new home.

Jace took her out to the resort afterward to go riding. She was glad to see Cupcake. The sweet spotted horse seemed to recognize her. He nuzzled the side of her face and kept nudging her hand when she greeted him, urging her to stroke his long, noble forehead.

They rode up the mountain and then down into that valley on Clifton land, where they spread a saddle blanket under the cottonwoods and swam in the creek.

After they swam, they stretched out on the blanket and made out like a couple of horny kids. It was a beautiful day. For a while they lay there side-by-side, staring up at the blue sky, as the horses grazed nearby. They dozed— or at least Jace did.

Joss was wide awake. Her thoughts had turned, the way they did too often lately, to what was missing: his love. She watched a single fluffy cloud float across the blue expanse above and argued with herself, telling herself she really needed to get past this obsession with the L-word. Because, after all, it was just a word and what did a word matter?

"Is something wrong?" Jace asked softly.

"No, not a thing," she said. It was what she'd told him two other times in the past week, when he'd asked if she had something on her mind.

There was no point in going into it again. She loved him. He didn't have a clue what love was. What else was there to say?

Jace waited till they got back to the stables to tell her that he'd bought Cupcake for her.

She threw her arms around him and kissed him long and hard, right there in front of the gaping stable hand. Jace was such a great guy. The best.

Even if he didn't love her.

Even if she kept trying not to worry that someday he would leave her, the way her dad had left her mom.

The next week seemed to fly by. One moment it was Monday and they were making the arrangements for the various inspections at the Hitching Post and on their eight acres of land.

And then suddenly, it was Friday. The day before the wedding.

RaeEllen arrived late in the afternoon. She was actually smiling when Joss opened the door to her.

"Hello, Jocelyn." She held out her arms.

"Mom." Joss made herself smile in return. She acquiesced to the offered hug.

RaeEllen wheeled in her suitcase. "Where's Jason?"

Joss shut the door. "He's out at the new property we bought, following the inspector around. He should be back in an hour or so to say hi. And then he's off to the resort. His brothers and stepdad are throwing him a bachelor party. Tonight it will be just the two of us." Please God, they would get through it without any big scenes. "He'll stay over at his brother Jackson's house. Kind of a nod to tradition. I won't see him till I'm walking down the aisle to meet him tomorrow."

Her mother took her hand.

Joss quelled the urge to jerk away. "Mom, I want this to be a nice evening. Please."

And then her mother said something absolutely impossible. "I've had some time to think about my behavior, Jocelyn. It's been…a lonely time since I left here two weeks ago. And slowly, I've had to admit that I have been losing you, pushing you away by trying to tell you how to live your life. I've had to start facing a few not-so-pretty things about myself. You are the one shining, beautiful thing I've done in all my life. And I've been trying to tear you down."

Joss wasn't certain she'd heard right. "Um. You, um… huh?"

Her mom put her other hand on top of Joss's, so she held Joss's hand between both of hers. "You were right," she said. "It was all about me and what happened with your father. I never trusted a man after him. Not for years and years. And then, finally, I let myself believe that one man could be all right."

"Kenny…"

"Yes." RaeEllen gave a tight little nod. "I couldn't stand to admit that I'd been wrong again. I convinced you to stay with him when you were having second thoughts instead of really listening and trying to understand what was bothering you about your relationship with him. And then I did it again, I refused to hear you when you told me that Kenny betrayed you. I lost sight of what really matters, of what my real job is as your mother now that you're an adult. I treated you like a misbehaving child instead of respecting your decisions and offering my support."

"Oh, Mom…"

"But I want to make things right with you. I want you to know that from now on, I'm not making everything all about me. From now on, I *am* on your side, Jocelyn. It's *your* choice who you marry. And Jason seems like a fine young man. I support you in your choice. I hope—no. I'm *sure* that you and Jason will be very happy together."

Joss's throat locked up and her eyes brimmed. She managed to croak a second time, "Oh, Mom…"

And then they were both reaching out, grabbing each other close, holding on so very tight….

"I love you, honey," her mother said. "I love you and I…support you. Please forgive me for being such a blind, hopeless fool."

When Jace let himself in the apartment an hour later, he heard laughter coming from the kitchen. Joss said something. And then she laughed.

The sound echoed down inside him, warm. Sexy. Good. No one had a laugh like Joss's.

And then another voice answered Joss. Her mother's voice, but lighter than before. Happier. RaeEllen laughed, too.

He followed the cheerful sounds and stood in the doorway to the long, cozy kitchen.

"Jace!" Joss came to him, kissed him.

And then her mother came and gave him a hug and said it was good to see him. She actually seemed to mean it.

RaeEllen, it appeared, had seen the light, which was very good news. It had been so bad the last time she showed up that he'd been kind of dreading her reappearance. Joss had never told him the things her mother had said that afternoon when he'd left them together to have it out. But he knew they couldn't have been good. And he figured RaeEllen must have had a few choice words to say about him.

Sometimes, in the past two weeks, he would catch Joss watching him, a mournful look in her eyes. He figured her mother had filled her head with negative garbage about him, and about the two of them getting married. But when he asked her what was wrong, she said it was nothing.

He didn't believe that. Still, he didn't push her to bust to the truth. There was the whole love thing between them now and he didn't want to get into that again. He knew she wanted—needed—for him to say the words.

And he would. Hell, he *had.* But it hadn't worked out because she read him like a book and knew he didn't mean them.

How could he mean them? He'd told her what he thought of love. He didn't have any idea what love was. But he did want to marry her. He wanted *her,* damn it.

He didn't get why that couldn't be enough for her.

After tomorrow, he told himself, once they were married, things would smooth out. Hey, look what had happened with RaeEllen. She'd had a little time to think over the situation and decided to get with the program and be happy that her daughter had found someone she wanted to make a life with.

It would be the same with Joss. She would see how well things worked out. And she would be happy. He was counting on that.

Jace took a seat at the table and hung around a while. RaeEllen poured him some coffee and he watched the two women bustling between the stove and the counter, putting their dinner together. When he got up to go, Joss followed him to the door.

She whispered, "In case you didn't notice, my mom's come around."

"I kind of had a feeling she might have."

"I still can't believe it. It's like a miracle."

"Hey." He smoothed that wildly curling cinnamon-shot hair of hers. "It's not all *that* surprising."

"It is to me."

"She loves you," he said, uttering the dangerous word without stopping to think about it. "She's figured out that she needs to be on your side."

"Love…" Joss glanced away and then she was tipping her face up to him again, putting on a big smile. "Have fun." She kissed him.

He left feeling strangely regretful. As though he should have said something he hadn't.

As though he'd missed his chance somehow.

The bachelor party went on until after two. It was great, hanging with his brothers and his cousins, getting to know the two Traubs from Rust Creek Falls. Forrest was thirty-one, an Iraq veteran slowly recovering from a serious leg injury. His brother, Clay, was twenty-nine, a single father. They—and Jace—were the only unmarried men at the party. They both seemed like solid, down-to-earth dudes.

But there were a lot of toasts. And Forrest and Clay joined in every one. By the end of the evening, they were both wasted. Jace grinned to himself watching them.

He caught Jackson's eye and knew his brother was re-membering how it had been back in June the year before, when Corey had his bachelor party over at the Hitching Post and Jace and Jackson had really tied one on. Jace hadn't slept at all the night of that party. He'd spent a few energetic hours with the one and only Theresa Duvall and then left her to rejoin his brother. He and Jackson had kept drinking right through Corey's wedding and the reception the next day. It hadn't been pretty. In fact, Jackson had started a brawl at the reception.

Jace doubted that the Rust Creek boys would pull any crap like that tomorrow. But he'd bet they would be nursing a matched pair of killer hangovers. Jace didn't envy them.

And he didn't miss the single life at all.

Ethan raised his glass—again. "To Jace, the last single maverick."

His brothers all laughed, in on the joke, remembering the way their long-lost dad use to call them his little mavericks.

Jace wondered what Joss and her mom were doing.

Which he supposed was pretty damn pitiful. It was only one night away from her.

Well, and then tomorrow. He wouldn't see her in the morning either. The wedding wasn't until five, so he'd be on his own for most of the day.

He really needed to buck up. It wasn't going to kill him to be away from her until the big moment when she came down the aisle to marry him.

In the dress she bought to marry that cheating SOB Kenny.

He didn't like that she would be wearing that damn dress. Every time he thought of it, it bugged him more.

But he hadn't known exactly how to tell her that he wanted her to choose something else. And now, well, it was a little late to do much about it.

She would be wearing that dress. Period. End of story.

He decided for about the hundredth time that he would forget how much he hated that damn dress.

At three in the morning, back at Jackson's place, he said goodnight to his brother, gave the mutt Einstein a scratch behind the ear and headed for the guest room.

It was lonely in there. He missed Joss, missed the way she tucked her round, perfect bottom up against him, how she took his arm and wrapped it around her, settling it in the sweet curve of her waist, before she went to sleep. He missed the little sounds she made when she was dreaming. Sometimes he wondered if he was getting whipped.

Because he was completely gone on her.

Every day, every hour, every time his damn heart beat, he got somehow more…attached to her.

And no. It wasn't love. He didn't know what love was. He was just a not-very-deep guy who'd finally found the right woman for him.

He wanted her with him.

And he would have her.

From tomorrow afternoon on.

At four the next afternoon, wearing his best tux, which he'd had sent up from Midland, Jace arrived at the resort. Lizzie and Laila had taken charge of decorating the small ballroom for the ceremony.

The room was beautiful, set up like a church chapel, with white folding chairs decked out in netlike white fabric, satin ribbons and flowers, a long satin runner for the aisle and a white flower-bedecked arch above the spot where he and Joss would say their vows. Tall vases on pedestals sprouting a variety of vivid flowers flanked the arch, stood at either end of the aisle and on either side of the two sets of wide double doors.

Jace had only Jackson standing up with him. And Joss hadn't chosen any bridesmaids; she wasn't even having anyone give her away. It was going to be short and sweet and simple, which was just fine with Jace. They would marry and head for the Rib Shack to celebrate.

And everything would be good between them. Everything would be great.

He hung around up by the white arch with Jackson and the nice pastor from the Community Church, waiting, nodding and waving at the guests as they entered. He smiled at Laila's single sisters Annabel, Jordyn Leigh and Jasmine. The three came in together, each in a pretty bright-colored summer dress. Forrest Traub limped in wearing his Sunday best, Clay right behind him. As Jace had expected, the Rust Creek Falls Traubs were looking a little green around the gills from partying too heartily the night before.

At five o'clock, almost every chair was taken. Lizzie cued the wedding march. Ma and Pete entered together down the aisle, arm-in-arm, and sat in the front row. RaeEllen came next, escorted by Ethan. He walked her to the front and she sat between him and Lizzie, who was already in her chair.

There was a strange, breath-held moment, when the wedding march played on and Jace's heart seemed to have lodged firmly in his throat and he stared up the aisle toward the small door on the far wall, suddenly scarily certain that Joss had changed her mind about the whole thing. That she'd lifted her white skirts for the second time and sprinted away from the small ballroom and him and the future they had promised they would share together.

But at last, the door opened. And there she was, more beautiful than ever, even if she was wearing that damn dreaded dress. She carried a big bouquet of orchids and daylilies, each exotic bloom more beautiful than the last.

She saw him, there beneath the flowered arch, waiting for her. And she gave him a secret, perfect, radiant smile. And then she started walking, slowly, the way brides always do. Step, pause. Step, pause. He wanted her to hurry. He wanted her beside him. Somehow, as he watched her coming to him, his throat opened up and his heart bounced back down into his chest where it belonged. And he could breathe again.

And still, slowly, so slowly, she came to him. His eyes drank her in and the strangest thing was happening. The craziest, wildest, most impossible thing. The thing that never happened to a shallow, good-time guy like him.

Light. It shone all around her. Golden and blinding, and he couldn't look away.

Why would he want to look away? It was one of those moments. A man like him might not understand it, but that didn't matter. What mattered was that Joss was coming to him, her big, brandy-brown eyes only for him, and there was a light all around her, a light coming from her. She was a beacon, *his* beacon. All he had to do was look for her. Find her.

Follow her light.

All at once, she was there. At his side. And she gave him her free hand and they turned to the nice pastor.

And Jace was *in* the light with her, a part of the light. Should that have freaked him out? Probably. But it didn't. He didn't mind it at all. In fact, it felt great. He knew that being in the light with Joss was exactly the place he was meant to be.

And the pastor started talking, saying the words of the marriage ceremony. Everything was magical and hushed and…more.

More than he'd ever known.

Better than he ever could have dreamed. It was all coming clear to him, all so simple.

And so right.

Until the pastor said, "If there be any man or woman who knows a reason why these two should not be joined in holy matrimony, let them speak now or forever after hold their peace."

And all at once, there was something going on at the entrance, by the twin sets of double doors. The light that held him and Joss was fading.

Joss gasped. And then she groaned. "Oh, no. Not Kenny…and Kimberly, too."

Jace turned toward the doors and saw the tall, fit-looking blond guy in the pricey khakis and the pale blue polo shirt.

"Jocelyn, I'm here," the guy said, noble-sounding as the hero in some old-time melodrama. "Don't do this. Forget that guy. We can work it out. Don't ruin our lives. I know there were…issues. I get that I blew it, but that was weeks ago. We need to get past all that garbage and you need to know that I love you and only you—and look." He gestured at the plump, pretty girl in the yellow sundress, who stood blinking uncomfortably at his side. "I brought Kimberly. She's here to tell you how sorry she is that she's made all this trouble." He jabbed at Kimberly with an elbow. "Tell her," he muttered. "Speak up and tell her now."

Kimberly burst into tears.

Kenny gaped. "Kimberly, what are you doing? Stop that!"

Kimberly cried all the harder. She let out a low wail and covered her eyes with her hands. Everyone in the ballroom was watching them, staring uncomfortably, the way people do when driving by car wrecks.

It was a bizarre moment, so strange that Jace wasn't as angry as he might have been at the sudden appearance of Joss's cheating ex, at the dousing of the golden light.

"Kimberly." Kenny actually took her shoulders and shook her. "Snap out of it. Remember? You're here to help."

"I caaaaan't. I just caaaan't," Kimberly wailed. She

jerked free of Kenny's grip and whirled to face the flower-decked arch and Joss and Jace standing in front of it. "Joss, I'm so sorry. But, you know, I'm *not* sorry. I've always loved Kenny and we've been seeing each other behind your back for the past six months now."

Kenny blinked and shook his perfectly groomed golden head. "Ahem, Kimberly." He tried to reach for her again but she jumped away. "Now, stop that." He cast a frantic glance at Joss again. "Joss, it's not true. I don't know what's gotten into her."

"But it *is* true," cried Kimberly.

"Of course it's not!" Kenny shouted. Then he caught himself. He lowered his voice and spoke out of the corner of his mouth. "You told me you would *help* me. You are not helping. This is not why I brought you here."

"Oh, Kenny, I know it's not. But I just can't stop myself. I'm sick of it, Kenny. Sick, sick, sick. Sick of the lies, sick of my part in this whole humiliating, ridiculous charade. I can see you for who you really are now. I know that you're not worth crap. And you know what? This, today? This does it. I'm through with you. Finished. And I'm glad for Joss. I'm smiling through my tears that my cousin got away without ruining her life and marrying you, you big butthead, creep-faced, yuppie dirtbag, you giant pile of designer-clad trash."

Kenny made a growling sound. "Why you skeevy little bitch…" His face the color of a ripe tomato, he went for Kimberly.

But Kimberly only grabbed a nearby vase of wedding flowers and hurled it at his head.

Kenny ducked.

The vase kept going until it smacked into the side of Forrest Traub's face. Flowers and water went flying.

"Hey!" Forrest lurched upward, trampling the boots of the cowboy sitting next to him.

"Watch it, buddy." The cowboy jumped to his feet and punched Forrest in the jaw. Forrest punched him back. The cowboy fell on the woman sitting next to him. She let out a scream, which caused the man on her other side to leap up and go after the cowboy.

In the meantime, Kenny was chasing Kimberly around the ballroom as Kimberly ran from him, sobbing and screaming and calling him all kinds of imaginative names.

At Jace's side, Joss made a low, sad little sound. "What a disaster...."

That spurred Jace to action. He'd had about enough, too. Kimberly had run down around the other end of the rows of chairs and started up on the far side, coming toward the flowered arch where Joss, Jace, Jackson and the pastor still stood.

Jace waited until Kimberly fled by him, then he stepped forward between the fleeing girl and Kenny. Kenny tried to sprint around him. Jace only slid to the side and blocked him again.

"Outta my way," Kenny huffed.

And Jace drew back his fist and laid the other man flat with one clean right to his perfect square jaw.

Jace stood over the jerk. "Don't get up until I say so."

The man in the polo shirt groaned and tested his jaw and glared up at Jace. But he didn't get up.

By then, the fight in the chairs had spread to every other short-tempered cowboy in attendance. There were more than a few of them, evidently. The men were fighting and the women were alternately shouting at them to stop and screaming "Look out!" and trying in lower voices to settle them all down.

Over by the double doors, Kimberly was still crying.

Melba Landry had gone to comfort her. Joss's cousin clung to Melba and drenched the old woman's flower-patterned purple church dress with an endless flood of desperate tears.

Melba was talking to her in low tones, soothing her, Jace had no doubt. And probably reminding her that there was peace in the Lord.

As quickly as it had started, the brawl wound down.

Things got quiet. Really quiet. The ballroom was in chaos, chairs overturned, vases spilled and shattered, wedding flowers torn and tattered, trampled underfoot. The guests all stood around, clothing askew, hair every which way, looking slightly stunned.

Jace turned to Joss.

But she wasn't there.

"Joss?" And then he spotted her.

She was over by the doors, not far from where Kimberly held on to Melba.

Joss met his eyes. And at that moment, there was no one else in that chair-strewn ballroom. Just him and Joss.

Her eyes shone bright with tears. She said, "This isn't going to work. I can't…" She ran out of words.

"I understand," he answered gently. And he did, though his heart seemed to shrivel to a wasted shell inside his chest. "You're right. It's all wrong."

She threw her bouquet. It sailed over the heads of several shell-shocked guests and into the arms of Annabel Cates, who caught it automatically to keep it from hitting her in the face.

And then, as he'd been secretly fearing she might do for the last couple of weeks now, Joss lifted her froth of skirts, whirled away from him and sprinted from the ballroom.

Chapter Fourteen

RaeEllen appeared at Jace's side. She glared down at Kenny. "Shame on you, Kenny Donovan."

Kenny groaned and started to rise. Jace gave him a look and he sank back to the floor.

RaeEllen turned to Jace. "You have to go after her."

Jace wrapped his arm around Joss's mom. "You okay, RaeEllen?"

Her hazel eyes were dark with concern. "Oh, Jason. I swear to you, I had nothing to do with this. I didn't say a word to Kenny—or Kimberly—about where or when you and Jocelyn were getting married."

Jace patted RaeEllen's shoulder. "I know you didn't. Joss told him, weeks ago, on the phone. She was just trying to get it through his fat head that she really was moving on with her life."

RaeEllen pressed her hand to her heart. "Oh, I just feel terrible about all this...."

"Not your fault," he reassured her. "You and Joss have worked things out. She knows you're on her side."

Jackson, his wife beside him by then, asked, "What do we do now?"

It was a good question. "Hey, everyone," Jace called out loud enough to carry to the back of the ballroom. "Looks like the wedding isn't happening. But there's a party waiting for all of you at the Rib Shack. I want you to head on over there and have yourselves a great time."

People exchanged anxious glances.

Then Clay Traub said, "Great idea, Jace. Come on, everyone, let's head for the Rib Shack."

The guests began filing out.

Jace sent a lowering glance down at Kenny. "*You're* not invited. In fact, you can get the hell out—of the clubhouse, of the resort, of the town of Thunder Canyon. Get out and don't come back. Do it now."

Kenny didn't argue. He dragged himself upright and staggered out.

Jace's brothers, his sister, their spouses and Ma and Pete stuck around to straighten up the ballroom. Kimberly and Melba stayed to help, too, as did RaeEllen. It didn't take all that long. Twenty minutes after they started picking up the chairs, they all left together, on their way to the Rib Shack.

All except Jace. He wasn't going to his own nonreception. Not without his runaway bride.

He found her where he knew she would be—in the Lounge, with a margarita in front of her. She'd taken off her veil and let her hair down. She'd also ordered him a whisky on the rocks.

He almost grinned. "You have a lot of faith in me."

"Yeah," she replied softly, her eyes getting misty again. "I do." She patted the stool beside her. "Have a seat."

He eased her big, fat skirt out of the way and took the stool she offered him.

She picked up her drink and he lifted his. They tapped their glasses together and drank.

When she set hers down, she said, "Got something to say to me?"

"I do." He thought about the golden light, the magic that had happened back there in the ballroom. But then he decided that maybe it wasn't magic after all.

Maybe it was only the most natural, down-to-earth thing in the world. A man seeing what mattered, seeing it fully for the very first time.

A man recognizing the right woman. *His* woman.

And knowing absolutely, without even the faintest shadow of a doubt that she was the only one for him. That he knew what love was after all.

Because he loved her.

"I like you, Joss."

She almost rolled her eyes, but not quite. "There'd better be more."

"There is."

"I'm listening."

"I like you. I want you. You…light up my life. You're the only woman in the world for me. I want the life we planned, want to be your partner in the Hitching Post. I want our eight acres and the house that needs work and the horses and the dog we haven't found yet. I want your children to be *my* children. I want to sleep with you in my arms every night and wake up in the morning with you beside me."

Now her adorable mouth was trembling. "Oh, Jace…"

"There's more."

"Tell me. Please."

"What I *don't* want is to lie to you—or myself—anymore. I not only like you. I *love* you. I'm *in* love with you. It's real and it's forever as far as I'm concerned."

"Oh, Jace…" Her eyes, unabashedly tear-wet now, gleamed like dark jewels.

He dared to reach out to touch her cheek, her shining hair. And he whispered, prayerfully, "Damn if I don't finally get what all the shouting's about when it comes to love and marriage and a lifetime together. It's *you*, Joss. You've shown me that. You've shown me love. I want to marry you. More than anything. I want to be with you for the rest of my life. And I have to tell you…"

"Yes? What? Anything, you know that."

"What I *don't* want is to marry you in that dress you bought to marry Kenny Donovan in—no matter how drop-dead gorgeous you look in the damn thing."

She laughed then, that low, rich, husky laugh that belonged only to her. "Okay." She offered her hand. "Yes, I'll marry you. And I promise I won't wear this dress when I do it."

He skipped the handshake and reached for her, gently sliding his fingers around the back of her neck, under the splendid, rich fall of her cinnamon-shot hair. And he kissed her. "I love you, Joss."

"And I love you. So much. I'm so glad…that you can finally say it."

He cradled the side of her face, oblivious to the bartender who watched them, wearing a dazed sort of smile, from down at the other end of the bar. "I'm sorry," Jace whispered. "So sorry I was such an idiot. So sorry I hurt you…."

"It's okay now."

"I'll say it again. I love you. I'll say it a hundred times a day."

She laughed then. "Oh, I'm so glad. I *was* a little worried."

"I know you were."

"But I'm not anymore. You have put my fears to rest, Jason Traub. You have given me everything—more that I ever dreamed of. And you know what? I love you with all my heart and it means so much to me to be able to tell you so at last without freaking you out. To know that you love me, too." She raised her glass again. "To love."

He touched his glass to hers. "And forever."

"To the Hitching Post. And the house and the horses and the dog."

"And the rowdy kids."

"And to us, Jace."

"Yes, Joss. To us, most of all."

Not much later, they joined the party that was supposed to have been their reception. They danced every dance, enjoyed the great food Shane Roark had prepared for them, fed each other big, delicious chunks of Lizzie's fabulous cake.

It was a beautiful evening. One of the best.

And after all the guests went home, they took the elevator upstairs to the Honeymoon Suite, theirs for that special nonwedding night, courtesy of Thunder Canyon Resort.

They made love. It was amazing.

Better than ever. So good that when they were finished, they made love again. And again after that.

The next morning at a little before seven, Joss woke alone in the big pillow-top bed.

She sat up. "Jace?"

And then she saw him—in the chair by the bed, dressed in a beautiful lightweight suit, holding a handful of wildflowers. He held them out to her. "Marry me, Jocelyn Marie. Marry me today."

She didn't hesitate. She got up, put on a pretty summer dress, took the flowers from him and off they went, stopping only to collect his parents from their suite and her mother from the apartment over the Mountain Bluebell Bakery.

At the Community Church, the nice minister was willing to be persuaded to perform the wedding ceremony that hadn't happened the day before. And there in the pretty white chapel on that sunny Sunday morning well before the regular service, Joss and Jace said their vows.

And when the pastor announced, "You may kiss the bride," Jason Traub knew that he'd finally found what he'd been looking for. He took his bride in his arms and he kissed her.

And when he lifted his head, he whispered, "I love you, Joss Traub. Forever."

"Forever," she echoed.

It was a great moment. The best in his life so far.

For a while there he really had been the last single maverick, wondering where he'd missed out, envious of his brothers and his sister, who had found what they were looking for, had all gotten married and settled down.

He'd felt left out of something important, and left behind as well. That was all changed now by the woman in his arms. He was part of something bigger now.

The last single maverick was single no more.

* * * * *

"I'm so sorry!"

Annabel quickly wound the dog's lead around her palm. "Here, let me help you!"

Dropping to her knees, she started grabbing the loose pages and the manila folders, but the man in front of her mirrored her actions. Their heads collided with a resounding crack.

Annabel swore and fell backward, landing on her butt. She rubbed hard at the stinging at her temple, hoping to erase the pain.

Suddenly, the warmth and strength of male hands, one capturing her rubbing fingers and the other cupping her jaw, caused a shiver to dance over her skin.

"Look at me. Are you all right?"

Annabel blinked hard as her world tilted. She could swear she saw a dizzying array of stars.

Forcing her gaze upward, she found icy blue eyes, serious and probing and perfectly matching his shirt, staring intently back at her.

Forget the stars.

This was a full-blown meteor shower.

Dear Reader,

Have you ever met someone who seemed to show up in your life just when you needed them? Well, Dr Thomas North might not realize it, but he's been waiting for Annabel Cates, and her beloved golden retriever, Smiley, all his life. What he's going to do with this vivacious blonde spitfire, her pup and the upheaval they cause to his well-ordered days is another question!

From the moment Annabel literally runs into the sexy and serious doctor, she knows what this man needs is a strong dose of love, both the human and puppy variety. Finding ways for these two very different, but perfectly matched people to fall in love is what made this story so much fun to write!

Being a fan of the Montana Mavericks for years, it was an honor to be asked to be a part of this amazing series that pays great tribute to the heart-and-home creed of Mills & Boon® Cherish™ with the wonderful families of Thunder Canyon, Montana.

I hope you enjoy their journey to happily-ever-after and please visit me at www.christynebutler.com or e-mail me at chris@christynebutler.com!

Christyne

PUPPY LOVE
IN THUNDER
CANYON

BY
CHRISTYNE BUTLER

All the characters in this book have no existence outside the imagination of the author, and have no relation whatsoever to anyone bearing the same name or names. They are not even distantly inspired by any individual known or unknown to the author, and all the incidents are pure invention.

All Rights Reserved including the right of reproduction in whole or in part in any form. This edition is published by arrangement with Harlequin Enterprises II B.V./S.à.r.l. The text of this publication or any part thereof may not be reproduced or transmitted in any form or by any means, electronic or mechanical, including photocopying, recording, storage in an information retrieval system, or otherwise, without the written permission of the publisher.

This book is sold subject to the condition that it shall not, by way of trade or otherwise, be lent, resold, hired out or otherwise circulated without the prior consent of the publisher in any form of binding or cover other than that in which it is published and without a similar condition including this condition being imposed on the subsequent purchaser.

® and ™ are trademarks owned and used by the trademark owner and/or its licensee. Trademarks marked with ® are registered with the United Kingdom Patent Office and/or the Office for Harmonisation in the Internal Market and in other countries.

First published in Great Britain 2012
by Mills & Boon, an imprint of Harlequin (UK) Limited,
Eton House, 18-24 Paradise Road, Richmond, Surrey TW9 1SR

© Harlequin Books S.A. 2012

ISBN: 978 0 263 89472 1
ebook ISBN: 978 1 408 97149 9

23-1012

Harlequin (UK) policy is to use papers that are natural, renewable and recyclable products and made from wood grown in sustainable forests. The logging and manufacturing processes conform to the legal environmental regulations of the country of origin.

Printed and bound in Spain
by Blackprint CPI, Barcelona

Christyne Butler fell in love with romance novels while serving in the United States Navy and started writing her own stories six years ago. She considers selling to Mills & Boon® Cherish™ a dream come true and enjoys writing contemporary romances full of life, love, a hint of laughter and perhaps a dash of danger, too. And there has to be a happily-ever-after or she's just not satisfied.

She lives with her family in central Massachusetts and loves to hear from her readers at chris@christynebutler. com. Or visit her website, www.christynebutler.com.

To the ladies at WriteRomance,
the best critique partners in the world:
don't know what I would do without you!

And to Susan, Charles and Jennifer...
you all know why

Chapter One

"Do you understand everything we talked about during the drive here?"

Annabel Cates pulled into an empty spot in the Thunder Canyon General Hospital parking lot. "I know these visits are routine by now, but it's important we cover the dos and don'ts every time."

She cut the engine, turned to the backseat of her practically new lime-green VW Bug and was rewarded with a sloppy kiss.

"Smiley!" Annabel pushed at the wet nose of her three-year-old golden retriever, her constant companion since she'd brought him home from the local shelter when he was just a pup. "You could've just nodded!"

An excited bark was her pet's answer.

"Yes, I love you, too." Releasing her seat belt, Annabel grabbed her purse and Smiley's leash and got out of her car, pausing to hold the driver's seat up to allow her dog to exit.

Kneeling, she latched the leash on to his collar then straightened the bright blue bandana around his neck, her fingers lingering over the black lettering on the material. "Just think, buddy, a dozen more sessions and we can switch this In Training bandana for one that reads Certified."

Smiley did the exact thing that earned him his name: he smiled. Many told her it was the natural curve of his mouth, a trait common in golden retrievers, but Annabel could tell when her fur baby was happy.

Which was just about all the time.

Smiley's outgoing, friendly personality, to both humans and other animals, made him a great therapy dog. The two of them had completed the required training, registration and certification over the past few months, but the American Kennel Club required fifty visits before being awarded the title of AKC Therapy Dog.

And Annabel wanted that title for Smiley, which didn't explain this particular visit.

"But this one is special, isn't it, boy?" Annabel gave Smiley a quick scratch to the ears then rose, and they walked across the hospital's parking lot.

Once inside, she stopped at the directory near the elevators. The geriatrics and children's areas were the most familiar to her and Smiley, but today they were headed for a specific doctor's office.

Smiley padded along beside her, staying right at her knee, despite the comments, grins and hellos that greeted them. Then a little boy sitting alone on a bench came into view and Annabel felt the familiar tug on the leash.

Almost by instinct, Smiley was drawn to those who were injured and hurting, but not all injuries were visible. A low whimper and the quickening of his wagging tail made the little boy look up. The beginnings of a smile crossed his face. Annabel slowed and allowed Smiley to work his magic.

After a few minutes visiting, Annabel continued on her way, energized by the boy's improved mood and excited chatter to his mother. They stopped outside the elevators and she eyed the hospital directory on the wall.

"Can I help you?"

Annabel turned and found a pretty nurse standing beside her dressed in scrubs, a short-sleeve shirt and loose cotton pants featuring a dizzying pattern of colorful flip-flops. Perfect for a warm August morning in Montana. "Yes, I'm looking for Dr. North's office."

The woman's eyebrows rose, disappearing into her perfect straight bangs. "Dr. Thomas North?"

"If he's an orthopedic surgeon, then yes, he's the one."

"Is Dr. North expecting you?" Her gaze shifted to Smiley for a moment. "Both of you?"

Living by the motto "it's better to beg for forgiveness than ask for permission," Annabel smiled. "We're here to visit with one of his patients."

"Oh. Well, his office suite is on the second floor, far left corner. I could show you if you'd like."

"That would be great, thanks."

The elevator dinged and seconds later the door opened. Annabel and Smiley waited for everyone to depart before they followed the nurse inside. Once on the second floor, they turned a few corners and moved into an office area. At the end of the long hallway Annabel finally spotted the nameplate for Dr. Thomas North.

"Hey, Marge. I've got a visitor for you."

The older woman sitting behind the desk was obviously Dr. North's secretary. Annabel smiled, not missing the glances between her and the nurse or the way her eyebrows rose in matching high arches, as well.

It was okay. She and Smiley were used to it.

"Can I help you, miss?" Marge asked as a beeping noise filled the air.

"Oh, shoot. I've got to go." The nurse checked her pager and smiled. "I so wanted to stick around and see this. Let me know what happens, okay?"

Marge gave her a quick wink and nodded.

A bit confused, Annabel offered her thanks. The nurse waved it off and then disappeared.

"Miss?"

Annabel turned back to the woman. "Oh, I was wondering if Forrest Traub has arrived for his appointment with Dr. North yet?"

"And you are?"

She opened her mouth to reply, but a low, measured voice came from over her shoulder.

"What are you doing here, Annabel?"

She whirled around, surprised to find the man she'd asked about had somehow snuck up on her. Not usually easy to do with Smiley close by. Annabel then noticed her dog remained sitting at her side, perfectly still, not even his tail moving as he stared intently up at Forrest.

And there was a lot to look at.

Tall, muscular, dark hair and the coolest light brown eyes. Yes, he was very nice to look at. Annabel was sure her sisters would use words like *yummy* and *sexy*. Even the two recently married ones, one of whom was the bride of Forrest's cousin, Jackson, would have to admit good looks ran strong in the Traub family tree.

Too bad the man did nothing for Annabel. No spark, no fizzle.

But that was fine with her. Annabel wanted more. She wanted true love.

The kind of love that came at you like a bolt of lightning and left you dazed, confused and tingly all over. She'd never felt that way in her life, but darn it, after a dry dating spell that had been going on for three years, she was ready for it!

"Hello?" Forrest leaned heavily on a cane with one hand while waving the other in her face. "Annabel?"

"Oh, sorry!" She blinked hard and chased away her dreams. "I…um, I'm here to see you."

His mouth pressed into a hard line as he looked down at Smiley. Annabel did the same, noticing how her pet returned the man's stare with a simple tilt of his head.

She wasn't sure who was sizing up whom.

"How did you know I was going to be at the hospital this morning?" he asked.

Her cheeks turned hot. "I overheard you talking to Jackson at the family barbecue yesterday."

He opened his mouth to say something, but Annabel kept talking. "I know you've been through so much since you got back from overseas. Even before then. And after all that time you spent at Walter Reed Medical Center to still need…well, I thought we could help."

Forrest sighed and directed his gaze to the secretary. "Would it be okay if I—if *we* waited for the doctor inside his office?"

A thrill raced through Annabel. It wasn't a complete victory, but it was a start.

"I'll take full responsibility for them being here," he continued. "And I really need to sit down."

The woman's blue eyes flickered toward the chairs in the corner of the room, but then she said, "Of course, please go in. The doctor is running late, but he should be here soon."

Forrest gestured toward the open doorway with a wave of his hand. Annabel gave a quick tug on the leash and entered the office, Smiley at her side. Forrest followed, and the doctor's secretary stood to close the door behind him.

It was a large room, with a wall of windows behind tightly closed blinds. Two chairs sat in front of a large desk with a more comfortable-looking leather couch along one wall.

Annabel stayed off to the side, not wanting to get in Forrest's way as he dropped into the closest chair. He jammed the cane she didn't remember him using yesterday into the armrest and closed his eyes. His right leg stuck out straight. The bulk of the brace underneath his jeans pulled the worn denim tight around his knee.

This time Smiley tugged a bit at the leash and Annabel released the slack, allowing the dog a bit more leeway while keeping a tight grip on the looped handle. Just in case.

Smiley had been with her yesterday at the barbecue, but he and Forrest didn't interact at all. Considering her pet's reaction to the man a few minutes ago, Annabel wanted to be sure she could pull him away if needed.

Seconds later Smiley was at Forrest's side, instinctively resting his furry head on the man's uninjured leg. Then a deep sigh echoed in the dog's chest.

A full minute passed before Forrest's large hand came to rest behind Smiley's ears, his fingers digging into the dog's thick coat.

Annabel titled her head back slightly and rolled her eyes, upward, pretending a sudden interest in the tiled ceiling. She'd learned it was the fastest way to stop the sharp stinging in her eyes.

Tears, or any sign of pity, were the last thing most people wanted.

The last thing Forrest Traub wanted.

He'd made that very clear while talking to his cousin yesterday about the reason he was in Thunder Canyon for the summer.

"So, Dr. North's secretary seemed a bit hesitant about us being in here." Annabel wanted to talk to Forrest about Smiley being a part of his upcoming medical treatment, but she couldn't just jump into the topic. Not when she'd taken it upon herself to be here instead of waiting for an invitation. "Me and Smiley, that is. Don't tell me your doctor is a stodgy, old curmudgeon who considers his office his inner sanctum?"

"He's not—"

"I'm only asking because the more senior the doctor the more they tend to think the only good medicine is the kind that comes in a pill or from the sharp end of a scalpel." She glanced around for clues, but wasn't close enough to see the graduation dates on the medical degrees hanging from the wall. "Wow, look at all those awards and certificates. Pretty impressive. Then again, this place could use some brightening, a splash of color. Everything in here is brown."

"Annabel—"

"No family photos on his desk. There's not even a plant," she pushed on, afraid if she shut up Forrest was going to kick her and her dog out. "His secretary practically has a jungle around her desk. You'd think she'd put at least one green leafy thing in her boss's office."

"Annabel, stop."

Forrest's soft, yet firm command included an unspoken request for her to look at him. She obeyed, while holding her breath.

"I know why you're here," he said.

She waited a moment, then air became a necessity. "You do?"

"I know all about the work you and your dog do."

"Smiley."

"Excuse me?"

"My dog's name is Smiley, and how do you know?"

"Your sister is very proud of you…and Smiley." Forrest looked down at the dog, continuing to scratch him behind his floppy ears. "But I don't think he can help me."

Annabel had heard those words, many times before and from many different types of people. Young children fighting diseases they couldn't pronounce, the elderly fighting to hold on to their memories and their dignity, and those fighting for the most important thing of all, hope.

"How do you feel?" she asked. "I mean, right now?"

Forrest shook his head. "Forget it, Annabel. I'm not going there."

"I'm not trying to psychoanalyze you." She moved closer. "And I know there's nothing medically we can do—"

"Good. That's my job."

Annabel whirled around at the very deep, very male voice coming from the open doorway.

She immediately cataloged a pair of men's shiny black shoes, dark slacks with a sharp crease down the center of each leg, a cobalt-blue shirt, striped tie and white lab coat.

Dr. Thomas North.

Before her perusal could get past a nicely chiseled jaw, Smiley bounced across the office, pulling his leash to its full length.

Offering an enthusiastic greeting that included a playful bark, her pet rose on his back legs and planted his front paws on the man's midsection.

The move knocked the doctor back against the door frame and sent the paperwork in his hands flying everywhere.

"Smiley!"

Horrified at her pet's unusual behavior, Annabel rushed to help. A quick tug on the collar and Smiley dropped back to all four paws on the ground, but the tail continued to wag up a storm.

"I'm so sorry!" She quickly wound the dog's lead around her palm, pulling him back to her side. "He usually doesn't act like this. I have no idea—" She then focused on the mess on the floor. "Oh, here, let me help you!"

Dropping to her knees, she started grabbing the loose pages and the manila folders, but the man in front of her mirrored her actions. Their heads collided with a resounding crack.

"Oh, fudge nuggets!" Annabel swore and fell backward, landing on her butt. She rubbed hard at the stinging at her temple hoping to erase the pain.

Darn, that hurt!

Suddenly, the warmth and strength of male hands, one capturing her rubbing fingers and the other cupping her jaw, caused a shiver to dance over her skin.

"Look at me. Are you all right?"

Annabel blinked hard as her world tilted. She could swear she saw a dizzying array of stars.

Forcing her gaze upward, she found icy blue eyes, serious and probing and perfectly matching his shirt, staring intently back at her.

Forget the stars.

This was a full-blown meteor shower.

Thomas North knelt on the carpet, cringing at the wrinkled paperwork beneath his feet.

The last thing he'd expected when he hurried into his office, cursing himself for being late thanks to his weekly breakfast date with his grandmother, was to be attacked by an overgrown hairy beast.

Or by the woman who was obviously its owner.

"Hello, miss? Did you hear me? Are you okay?"

"Y-yes, I think so."

Ignoring how her breathy words warmed the inside of his wrist, then transformed into a tremor that raced up his entire arm, Thomas focused on her pale blue eyes. They seemed clear and bright, but her speech was a bit slow.

He waved his hand, holding up three fingers in front of the woman's face. "How many fingers do you see?"

"Two."

Hmm, not good.

His own head still smarted from where they'd

come together with a hard *thunk,* but he didn't have any problem directing Forrest Traub back into the chair he started to rise from or to see the beautiful blonde on the floor in front of him.

Not to mention another blond, with four legs and a wet nose, who was getting in his way.

"And a thumb."

"Excuse me?"

"You're holding up two fingers, index and middle, and your thumb." She laid a hand on the dog's snout, where it tunneled into her loose waves at her shoulder. "I'm okay, Smiley. Please, sit."

The dog obeyed the woman's command, just barely, as its backside continued to shimmy, helped by the rapid wagging of its tail.

Thomas took the paperwork from the woman's grip, added it to the pile he'd shoved back into the top folder. He handed it all to his secretary, who stood over his right shoulder. "Can you put this back into some semblance of order, please?"

"Wow, how did you know she was standing there?" the woman asked, drawing his attention back to her.

"He's got eyes in the back of his head," his secretary quipped as she stepped around them and headed for his desk. "It's something they must teach them in medical school."

Thomas did what he always did when Marge got mouthy. Ignored her. She'd come with the office, having worked for his predecessor for a dozen years, and knew the inner workings of the hospital like the back of her hand. Thomas had only been at TC General two years and he'd be lost without her.

Concentrating on getting the woman back on her feet, he rose and held out one hand. "Do you think you can stand?"

"Of course I can."

She grabbed his wrist with a surprisingly strong grip, and pushed to her feet. He couldn't help but notice the dark polish on her bare toes, the snug fit of her jeans over curvy hips or how the loose ruffled neckline of her blouse had slipped to reveal one bare shoulder.

"Annabel, are you sure you're okay?" Forrest asked.

She turned her head, sending long waves of blond hair flying, covering that shoulder. "Yes, I'm fine."

Thomas swallowed hard and pulled from her heated touch, refocusing his attention on his patient and the reason he was here.

"I don't mind your girlfriend being at your appointment, Mr. Traub—" he moved to sit at his desk, not surprised to find Marge had already left the office, closing the door behind her "—but a dog is a different matter entirely."

"She's not my—"

"Oh, I'm not his girlfriend." The woman dropped

into the second empty chair. "Forrest and I are practically family. I'm Annabel Cates."

Thomas tucked away the news these two weren't
involved, and why he even cared, to concentrate
on finding out what exactly was going on. "Then
what are you and your dog doing in my office, Miss
Cates?"

"Two reasons, moral support and a proposition
you can't refuse."

Chapter Two

"Oh, and please call me Annabel. This is Smiley."

Thomas watched the oversize furball move to sit between her and his patient, ears flopping as it looked back and forth between the two. Then the mutt leaned toward Forrest. Thomas was about to call out, until he saw how the dog rested its chin lightly on Traub's uninjured knee.

"Smiley is a certified therapy dog," she continued. "As his owner and handler, I've been trained and certified, as well. Because of Forrest's injury, and his ongoing treatment, I thought Smiley might be able to help."

He looked back to the woman. "Help how?"

"Therapy dogs are used to assist patients in dealing with the stress and uncertainty that comes with medical issues."

Thomas didn't put much stock in therapy dogs—or meditation, or aromatherapy, or any number of other alternative therapies that floated around out there.

All he believed in were cold, hard facts. And science.

"Miss Cates, I really don't have time for this. Your visit today is not authorized, by me or, I'm guessing, Mr. Traub, and is distracting to say the least."

"Oh, I don't mean to be any trouble—"

"You've already been that." Thomas dropped his hand to the folder in the middle of his desk, drumming his thumb repeatedly on the cover. An action her dog apparently took as a cue to perch its large front paws on the edge of his desk and swat its large, fluffy tail at the shoulder of Forrest Traub.

"Smiley, stop that and get down." She gently tugged at her dog's leash. "I'm so sorry, Dr. North. I promise you he never acts this way. I guess he must really like you."

"I doubt that."

The dog sat again and returned its attention to Forrest. Miss Cates did the same. "I guess this wasn't such a good idea. Maybe you can spend time with Smiley another day."

"I'd like you to stay." Traub laid his hand back on the dog's head. "Both of you."

Surprised by his patient's request, Thomas studied him closely, silently admitting the animal did seem to be having an impact on the man.

He and Forrest had only met twice before, the last time being a week ago when Thomas had performed a thorough examination of the ex-soldier's injured leg. Forrest had been withdrawn and testy, speaking only when asked a direct question.

In the subsequent reading of his military medical records, Thomas had found the former army sergeant had good reason for his surliness, having gone through hell after a roadside explosive destroyed the Humvee he was riding in during his last tour in Afghanistan.

He'd been in and out of hospitals for the past year and still had not regained full use of his leg. Today though, he seemed more relaxed, a hint of a smile on his face as he continued to scratch the animal's ears and neck.

Of course, this had to be temporary. Depression was common in veterans, as was post-traumatic stress, and Thomas couldn't see how patting a dog could counteract such difficult conditions. The only real cure for Forrest was in the skilled hands of a surgeon.

At any rate, the man clearly enjoyed the dog's

company, so Thomas had no choice but to let the mongrel—and Miss Cates—stay.

"Fine." Thomas flipped open the folder. "We planned to discuss my findings and go over recommendations for further treatment. Are you comfortable discussing your condition in front of Miss Cates?"

"Don't worry about me. I've been present at doctor-patient consults before. Confidentiality isn't an issue," the blonde spitfire said with a wave of her hand. "I know how to keep a secret."

Thomas ignored her and waited for his patient to reply.

"Yeah, go ahead," Traub said.

"The results are a bit complex and cover a lot of technical jargon—"

"Get to the bottom line, doc."

Thomas did as requested. "You are going to need surgery. Again."

He waited, but Forrest's only reaction to the news was the fisting of his free hand while the other continued to dig deep into the dog's fur. Thomas glanced at Miss Cates, but her focus was on his ceiling as she blinked rapidly.

"How soon?" Forrest asked.

Thomas looked back at his patient. "The sooner the better. We can schedule you for next week."

The conversation continued for several minutes as Thomas outlined the presurgery preparations, what he planned to accomplish with the delicate procedure and the post-care that would be required.

"Okay, then. I'll see you next week." Forrest finally released his hold on the dog and grabbed his cane. Pushing to his feet, he held out his hand. "I'm betting on you to work your magic, doc."

Thomas rose and returned the man's firm grasp, determined to bring all his skills and knowledge to the operating room, like always. "You can count on it, Forrest."

The man returned Thomas's gaze for a long moment before he released his hand and turned away. "Annabel, I'll walk you to your car if you and Smiley are heading out?"

"That would be great, thanks." Rising, she held out her hand. "Dr. North, it was a pleasure. I would appreciate the opportunity to discuss the possibility of us working together in the future."

Thomas took her hand, the warmth and softness of her skin against his again creating that same zing of awareness he'd felt earlier. "Thank you, but I don't see that happening, Miss Cates."

"I'm sure we can come to a meeting of the minds, not quite as literally as we did this time, I hope." Her full lips twitched and then rose into a playful grin. "Besides, I'm known to be very persuasive when I want something."

For some reason, Thomas believed her. "My schedule is pretty full."

"A half hour." Her fingers tightened around his. "What harm can I do in thirty minutes?"

Thomas cleared throat and released her hand. Seeing her again would be crazy. His mind was already made up. To him, dog therapy was nothing but... fluff. Still, the chance to spend time with this bewitching woman was something he couldn't make himself pass up.

No matter how much his logical side told him it wasn't a good idea.

"Okay, thirty minutes. You can call my secretary to set up a date and time. But be warned, I rarely change my mind."

Once a decision had been made, Thomas stuck by that decision. No matter what. It was something the hospital staff had learned about him in the two years he'd been here.

But agreeing to meet with Miss Cates?

Thomas had seriously reconsidered allowing the meeting to take place many times over the past week.

Thunder Canyon General wasn't a large facility, but thanks to the financial boom that came to town a few years back and the hard work of the hospital administrators—including his grandmother Ernestine North until she finally retired a year ago—the facility lacked for nothing.

Including a thriving gossip grapevine that, until recently, he'd never been a part of. An accomplishment Thomas had worked hard at since accepting his position.

He'd come home to Thunder Canyon determined not to make the same mistake twice. Oh, he knew the staff talked about him. Even after twenty-four months he was still considered the "new" guy around here.

His reputation as a skilled surgeon, and a success rate that was all the more impressive here at TC because of his age, followed him from his previous position at the UCLA Medical Center in Santa Monica.

Thank goodness that was the only thing that had followed.

He also knew some at Thunder Canyon General considered his bedside manner a bit…cold, at least to those who confused emotional involvement with professionalism.

A mistake he wouldn't make again.

But thanks to Annabel Cates and her dog he'd found himself the recipient of even more stares, whispered conversations that ended when he appeared and a few hazing incidents, some subtle and others not so much, starting the day after her visit.

The sweater Marge had worn the other day covered in miniature poodles had been a delicate jab, but the not-so-quiet barking his fellow surgeons and residents engaged in whenever he walked into the doctors' lounge was not.

The old-fashioned glass apothecary jar filled with

dog biscuits and tied with a bright bow he'd found on his desk just the other day had been a nice touch. There'd been no card and Marge hadn't said a word about it. Deciding that leaving it in the break room for someone who actually had a pet would only add more fuel to the fire, he'd tucked the jar into the bottom drawer of his credenza.

All of which had to be the reason why Thomas found Annabel on his mind so much over the past several days. While he could admit, at least to himself, there'd been a spark of attraction, she was definitely not his type.

If he had one.

It'd been a while since he'd dated anyone. The women he'd gone out with in the past, when he found the time or desire, were professionals focused on their careers, much like him.

Of course, his last attempt at a serious relationship had dissolved into such a fiasco he ended up having no choice but to seek another job as far away from Southern California as he could get.

Which meant returning home to Thunder Canyon.

Besides, Annabel seemed…well, a bit flaky, idealistic, pushy. They could not be more opposite. Yet when he reviewed his calendar each morning he'd found himself looking for her name.

It wasn't until after Forrest Traub's surgery two days ago that it appeared with the promised thirty minutes blocked out for Thursday afternoon.

Today.

Annabel—and her dog—should be here any minute.

Not wanting a repeat from last time, Thomas sat behind his desk and tried to edit his latest article for a leading medical journal, but after reading the same paragraph three times he was glad when familiar tapping at the door came.

"Come in," he said, recognizing his secretary's signature knock. "Marge, I'm out of red markers. Could you find me a few more, please?"

"Sorry. I come bearing gifts, but not a red marker in sight."

Thomas looked up and found Annabel Cates standing in his doorway. He immediately noticed she wore her hair pulled back from her face in a ponytail. It made her look younger, though the curves presented in her simple bright yellow top and denim skirt said otherwise. He found himself wondering just how old she was.

He stood, his gaze drawn to her bare legs and toes, thanks to her sandals, this time the nails sporting a matching neon-yellow shade.

Details. Thomas was known for being a man of details, but he realized he'd taken in her entire outfit before he noticed the large, leafy green plant she held in her hands.

And the fact she was alone. No dog in sight.

"Don't tell me my secretary is baby—err, dog sitting."

She smiled and it lit up her entire face. Another detail he remembered from the last time she was in his office.

"Nope, it's just me this time. Disappointed?"

"Not in the least. Please, come in."

She did, closing the door behind her before she walked to his desk and held out the plant. "This is for you. It's a Peace Lily."

"Are we at war?"

"No, but I thought the name was fitting and this place needs a bit of color. Also, they're known for tolerance for low light, dry air and are great indoor air purifiers."

"Well, thank you." Surprised that she went to such lengths to pick out the offering, Thomas took the container, pausing when his fingers brushed over hers. He placed it on the filing cabinet next to his desk. "I can't promise I'll remember to water it."

"I kind of figured you were a busy guy, so I included an aqua globe. See?" She walked around the desk and moved in behind him, pointing out the green shaded globe barely visible among the leaves. Heat radiated off her body and he suddenly felt naked without his lab coat. "You just fill it, turn it upside down and jab it in the dirt. It'll water your plant for two weeks before you need to refill."

"Ah, that's...that's a good idea." Damn, he

sounded like a schoolkid nervous to be talking to the prettiest girl in the class. "Why don't we sit down and get started?"

"Sounds great." Annabel stepped back but instead of taking one of the chairs in front of his desk, she moved to the couch against the wall. Skirting the coffee table, she dropped to one end and patted the spot next to her.

Thomas cleared his throat, but joined her, making sure to keep an empty space between them. Not that it mattered. Annabel simply scooted closer.

He fought against the automatic reaction to lean back and rest his arm against the back of the leather sofa. Instead, he scooted forward and braced his forearms on his knees, his hands clasped together.

"I left Smiley at home because I wanted to be able to talk without any furry distractions." She grabbed a large book from an oversize bag at her feet. "You don't have to feel bad or think you're not an animal person because the two of you didn't hit it off. You just haven't met the right one yet."

His shoulders went stiff. "I never said—"

"Most people love Smiley, which makes him so good at being a therapy dog," she continued, opening the book and laying it flat across her lap. "I started this scrapbook to document our training and all the work we do. There are a number of tests that Smiley had to pass before being certified, such as acceptance of a friendly stranger, walking through a crowd or sitting politely."

Thomas cleared his throat. It then closed up completely when Annabel laughed and reached out, giving his arm a gentle squeeze. "You're a special case."

Her heated touch seemed to sear his skin through the smooth material of his shirt. His fingers tightened against his knuckles until she released him. "Ah, that's good to know."

"Smiley was also tested for basic commands and how he reacted to being around other dogs, children and medical equipment and so on."

"I'm guessing all the animals in this program are required to provide health records?"

"Of course. They have to be tested annually and maintain a good appearance. Grooming is a must." She turned the page and pointed to certificates in both her and her dog's names. "We passed every test with flying colors and have been doing this kind of work for the last six months. I document every visit we make, sometimes with photographs, as we are working toward the American Kennel Club's Therapy Dog title. Smiley's been to schools, group homes, clinics and nursing care facilities. Not to mention a couple areas here at TC General."

Annabel gently brushed her fingertips over the pictures on the next page of a young girl lying in a hospital bed, her head covered in a colorful head scarf and Smiley stretched out beside her. "This is

Isabella. She was the sweetest thing. When we arrived to visit with her she asked me if Smiley was an angel. When I asked why, she said she'd just dreamed that an angel was coming to take her home."

Thomas watched as Annabel paused, pressing her fingertips to her lips, and glanced upward for a moment before she went on. "Her mother told Isabella she was too sick to leave the hospital just yet and the little girl said she wasn't talking about their home. That the angel was taking her to God's house. She died six weeks later, just days after her tenth birthday. That last week Smiley and I were there every day."

He had to ask. "Why do you do that?"

She looked at him, her blue eyes shiny. "Do what?"

"Roll your eyes that way. You did it during the appointment with Forrest when I was discussing his surgery and again just now."

"I wasn't rolling my eyes. Not in the traditional sense."

"Meaning?"

"Meaning I'm not bored or exasperated. You see, I tend to get a bit emotional, especially in some of the situations Smiley and I find ourselves involved with. It's a trick I picked up from another dog handler to stop the tears."

"It works?"

Annabel nodded. "My mom told me that tickling

the roof of my mouth with the tip of my tongue will do the same thing, but I'm usually too busy talking—" She stopped and bit down on her bottom lip. "Well, I guess you've already figured that out."

Yes, he had. What he couldn't figure out was why he liked that about her.

"Should I go on?" she asked.

As if he could tell her not to. "Please do."

Annabel turned the page and his gaze was drawn to the photo of a teenage boy holding himself upright on parallel bars, a prosthetic where his right leg should have been. "This is Marcus Colton. He lost his leg last winter in a snowmobile accident. Like most teenagers, what he did best was give his physical therapists a hard time."

"Let me guess. Smiley changed that?"

"We were at the clinic one day when Marcus was being his usual charming self, demanding no one would get him to make a fool of himself by trying to walk, even though he'd been doing pretty well at his rehab for a month by then."

She pointed to the next picture showing her dog sitting calmly at the opposite end of the bars, Annabel just a few feet away holding his leash. "Smiley allowed Marcus to pet him for a few minutes and then he went and sat there, almost daring Marcus to come to him."

"And he did."

"Not the first visit. Or even the second, but Smiley proved to be every bit as stubborn as Marcus. The boy finally relented and now he's making great progress."

She went on, telling him stories of senior citizens who had no one to visit them but Smiley, of the patients attending their dialysis sessions who welcomed the distraction petting a dog brought and schoolkids finding it easier to practice their reading when their audience was a dog.

With each story came more looks upward, a couple swipes at the tears that made it through and a sexy husky laugh, all of which struck a chord deep in Thomas's gut.

"I'm guessing all of this is to convince me to allow Smiley to work with Forrest during his rehab, if my patient agrees," Thomas said when she finally finished. "But why do I get the feeling you are looking for something else from me?"

"Hmm, now that's a loaded question." She closed her book, a pretty blush on her cheeks. "Yes, working with Forrest was my original plan. I still want to now that he's home from the hospital and ready to start his physical therapy, but what I'd really like is to set up a weekly support group here at the hospital. One that's open to any patient who wants to come, no matter what their illness."

While Thomas still had doubts about her work, he found himself enamored of Annabel's spirit. What surprised him even more was the fact he wanted to see her again.

And not just here at the hospital.

"I'm still not completely convinced, but I'll agree to at least consider your idea."

"Really?" Annabel's smile was wide, her blue eyes sparkling up at him. "That's wonderful!"

"There's just one condition." He could hardly believe the words pouring from his mouth. "You agree to have dinner with me."

Chapter Three

Stunned, Annabel didn't know what to say. Anyone who knew her well would say it was the first time she'd ever been at a loss for words.

Especially after she'd spent the past half hour hogging the conversation with a man who'd put those dreamy and steamy television doctors to shame. Without the standard long white lab coat he'd worn the last time she was here, his purple dress shirt and purple, gray and black striped tie brought out just a hint of lavender in those amazingly blue eyes.

Not to mention what the shirt did for the man's broad shoulders.

He wore his dark hair short, but it stood up in

spiky tufts on top, as if he'd been running his hand through it just before she arrived. The sharp angles of his cheeks and jaw were smooth-shaven despite it being late in the afternoon.

Her breath had just about vanished from her lungs when he'd joined her on the couch, his woodsy cologne teasing her senses. Thank goodness she'd remembered the scrapbook so she had something to do with her hands.

Besides attack the good doctor, that was.

"Annabel? Did you hear me?"

She blinked, realized she'd been staring. "You want to go out?"

"Yes."

Considering how hard she'd tried not to sound like a sap with her endless chatter about the therapy dog program, Annabel now found it hard to put her thoughts into words. "With me?"

"Yes, with you. We can talk more about your program. Unless there's a reason why you can't?"

Was "too stunned to reply" an acceptable answer?

"Do you have a boyfriend?" His expression turned serious again. "I didn't see a ring on your finger, but I don't want to presume you are free—"

"No." She cut him off. He'd actually looked to see if she wore a ring? "I'm free, totally free. Free as a bird."

"Is that a yes, then?"

She nodded. "Yes, dinner sounds great."

"Tomorrow night okay?"

Something to do on a Friday that didn't include her dog or a sibling? Tomorrow night would be perfect. "I work until six, but after that I'm all yours."

Thomas cleared his throat and stood, rising to his feet in one smooth motion. "Where do you work?"

"At the Thunder Canyon Public Library." Annabel mirrored his actions, grabbing her bag and slipping it over one shoulder. "I'm the librarian in charge of the children's area."

He waved a hand at her scrapbook. "So, all the work you do with therapy dogs is strictly volunteer?"

"Oh, yes. I don't get paid for any of my visits, other than Smiley sometimes getting a doggy treat or two." She hugged her book to her chest, peeking up at him through her lashes. "But I love the work. The therapy program is one of my many passions, along with books and my family. I guess I'm just a passionate person by nature."

His eyes deepened to a dark blue as their focus shifted to her mouth. A slight tilt of his head, a restrained shift in his body that brought him just a hint closer.

Her tongue darted out to lick her suddenly dry lips. She couldn't help it. Not that she dared think he might—

Yes, she had thought about the man, probably too much, over the past two weeks. She'd been looking forward to this meeting for more reasons than convincing Thomas to allow a therapy group here at the hospital. One she would be in charge of.

Annabel could admit, at least to herself, she'd wanted to find out if the quivering sensations she'd experienced when they'd first met had been all in her head.

They weren't.

"I know a great Italian bistro, Antonio's, over in Bozeman. Where should I pick you up?"

She blinked again, breaking the spell the doctor seemed to weave around her. Antonio's? A dinner there cost more than she made in a week. "Oh, we don't have to go that far. Any place in town would be fine by me."

"My treat, so I get to pick the place."

His tone was persuasively charming, so Annabel simply rattled off her address. And her cell phone number. "You know, just in case."

Thomas nodded, then gestured in the direction of the door with one hand, signaling the end of their meeting. "Until tomorrow night, then."

Annabel stepped in front of him, sure she could feel the heat of his gaze on her backside as he followed her. She turned when she reached the door, but found those blue eyes squarely focused on her face.

"I'll pick you up around seven?" he asked.

She smiled. "I'll be waiting."

She waited.

And waited and waited.

Palming her cell phone, Annabel paced the length of her bedroom, her bare toes scrunching in the soft carpet. Smiley lay at the end of her bed, watching her stride back and forth like he was a spectator at a tennis match.

She'd changed out of the sundress with its matching knitted shrug and into a cropped T-shirt and yoga pants an hour ago, kicking her cute kitten heels back into the bottom of her closet.

After she'd accepted the fact Thomas had stood her up.

She'd really been looking forward to tonight. Yes, the chance to talk more about her idea of a weekly therapy session with Smiley at the hospital was a big draw, but darn it, getting to know Thomas better appealed to her even more.

"It's after nine thirty," Annabel said softly, eyeing the clock on her bedside table. "Why hasn't he called?"

Smiley offered a sympathetic whimper and lowered his head to his paws until a quick knock at her bedroom door grabbed his attention.

Seconds later, her sister popped her head in. "Hey! We're about to start a Mr. Darcy movie marathon now that Dad has gone off to bed. You coming downstairs?"

Annabel gave Jordyn Leigh a forced smile, knowing the "we" she was referring to was herself, their older sister, Jazzy, and their mother, all of whom shared a deep affection for the beloved Jane Austen literary character.

As did she.

"I don't think so," she said. Not even Colin Firth's portrayal of the dashing hero could lift her disappointment—or erase the tiny flicker of hope she still held.

"You know, Mom said she can't believe the three single Cates sisters are all home on a Friday night." Jordyn Leigh nudged the door wider and leaned against the frame. "Of course, you taking a pass on dinner tonight had us all thinking you had other plans."

"I did."

Her sister eyed her outfit. "Dressed like that?"

Annabel sighed and glanced at her phone again. "I decided to change after he didn't show. Almost three hours ago."

"Yikes. Hoping for the old 'if I get into my sweats the jerk will call' effect, huh?"

"He's not a jerk." Her defense of him came easily, even if she had no idea why.

Her sister frowned, but only said, "Why don't *you* call *him*?"

Annabel had thought about it, but the only number she had for Thomas was his office. The last thing she wanted was to leave a pathetic voice mail for him to find first thing Monday morning.

"I don't have his number," she finally said. "He's

got mine, at least I'm assuming he does. I mean, I gave it to him, but—"

"But he didn't write it down or put it in his phone right away?" Jordyn guessed. "So you're thinking he forgot?"

Her number? Their plans? All about her?

Annabel didn't know what to think.

"Well, you know where we'll be if you decide to join us. Mom's insisting we start with the black and white version of *Pride and Prejudice* featuring Sir Laurence, so you have plenty of time before our favorite Mr. Darcy appears."

With that, her sister vanished and Annabel flopped down on her bed, immediately bestowed with a sloppy kiss from Smiley, who'd crawled next to her.

"Oh, buddy, what am I going to do?" She scratched at her dog's ears. "Maybe I should go back to work. Goodness knows I got zero done this afternoon thinking about tonight. Or do I stay up here and drive myself crazy wondering why—"

An odd chiming filled the air. It took a moment before Annabel realized it was coming from her cell phone. Not her usual ringtone that asked a cowboy to take her away.

She sat up and read the display. Caller unknown. Her fingers tightened around her phone. One deep breath and she pressed the answer button. "Hello?"

"Annabel? It's Thomas."

"Oh." She paused. "Hi there."

"I'm sorry. I didn't mean to be a no-show tonight."

She released the air from her lungs, while the ache in her stomach that she'd insisted was due to lack of food eased. "Did you get lost?"

"I never left the hospital." His voice was low and a bit husky. "I was called into an emergency surgery this afternoon and didn't have time to try to get ahold of you. I didn't expect it to take this long, but there were complications."

Stuck at work. She'd never even considered that. "Was the surgery a success?"

"Yes, it was." He sounded surprised. "Thanks for asking."

"Are you still at the hospital?"

"Sitting in the men's locker room. I called as soon as I got out of the shower."

Trying not to picture Thomas standing in front of a locker dripping wet and wearing nothing but a towel was as impossible as stopping Smiley from hogging the bed at night.

So she didn't even try.

"You must be exhausted," she said. "I can hear it in your voice."

"I am, but it's a good fatigue, sort of like a runner's high after completing a marathon. I feel like I could run ten miles." He sighed. "Not really, but that's the only comparison I can think of."

An idea popped into Annabel's head, so crazy it

just might work. "So, I'm guessing you didn't have a chance to eat dinner either?"

"I'll probably grab a burger at a drive-thru on my way home—wait, did you say 'either'?"

"How about meeting me at The Hitching Post? Say in about twenty minutes?"

"The what?"

"The Hitching Post. It's on Main Street in Old Town. You know the place, right?"

Silence filled the air. Annabel crossed her fingers. On both hands.

"Ah, yeah… I mean, yes," Thomas finally said. "I know where it is."

Annabel jumped up and began rifling through her closet. "Great! I'll see you there!"

Thomas slowed his silver BMW to a full stop at the curb, surprised to find an empty parking space so close to The Hitching Post on a Friday night.

He'd never been here before, but he'd heard his coworkers rave about the local hangout. Once owned by a lady with a questionable past, the place was now a restaurant and bar, a modern-day saloon right in the middle of Thunder Canyon's Old Town, an area that proudly retained its Western heritage.

A section of town Thomas rarely spent time in. Then again, he rarely spent time anywhere other than his condo or the hospital.

Stepping out of his car, he thumbed the button

to lock the doors and set the alarm, then headed for the sidewalk.

He hated to admit it, but his plan had been to take Annabel someplace outside of Thunder Canyon where the walls didn't have ears and the gossip didn't travel at the speed of light.

Things at the hospital were finally quieting down, but to be seen together here tonight… Who knew what kind of rumors would fly?

Asking her out in the first place had been crazy enough. Agreeing to meet her here? That he blamed squarely on the fact she'd surprised him by not being angry at being stood up.

And the fact he wanted to see her again as soon as possible.

He started for the front door then realized the place was completely dark.

Geez, how late was it?

He glanced at his watch and then noticed the sign stuck in the front window. Closed for Renovation. What the heck was going on—

"Hey there!"

He turned and found Annabel standing on the corner, cradling two large paper bags in her arms. She was dressed casually in jeans and a distressed leather jacket, her hair in loose golden waves.

Thomas again felt that familiar zing at the sight of her. "Hey, yourself. Looks like this place is shut down."

"Oh, I knew it was closed. At least temporarily. My uncle Frank and my cousin Matt have been overseeing the renovation for Jason Traub and his new wife, Joss, who are the new owners. I only named it as a meeting place."

Meeting place for what? He must be more tired that he thought. "What's with the paper sacks?"

"Dinner!" Annabel beamed. "A care package chock-full of ribs, chicken and steak fries from DJ's Rib Shack. Come on, I've got the perfect place for us to eat."

He joined her, not knowing what smelled better, the food or that sexy floral scent he'd noticed the first time they met.

"Here, let me take those," he offered.

Annabel handed over one of her parcels. The heat from the cooked food warmed his hands. They headed up the street and Thomas was curious as to where they were going. His first thought had been her place, but she'd given him an address that was on the southeast side of town.

At the end of the next block she crossed the street and walked toward a large two-story stone building.

"The Thunder Canyon Library?" He read the sign as they walked past the front steps. "We're eating here?"

"My second favorite place in town."

"Pardon my ignorance, but isn't it closed, too?"

"Don't worry. I have a key." Annabel smiled and

led him around the corner to a tall wooden fence. He followed her directions to open the gate. "Latch that behind us, okay?"

Thomas did as she asked and they entered a shadowed courtyard. Thanks to a full moon, he could see a grassy area to one side with trees and benches and a wooden jungle gym on the other. Straight ahead was a wall of glass doors covered with blinds.

"This is the back way into the children's section. Don't worry, a security light should come on—" A bright spotlight shined down on them, illuminating the area. "And there it is. Come on, this way."

Annabel punched a code into a hidden keypad and pushed open the closest door. She held the blinds to one side and Thomas followed her, watching as she then did the same thing with another keypad on an inside wall. "The outside light will go off in a few minutes."

"Are you sure it's okay for us to be here?"

"What's the matter, doc?" She turned, that same saucy smile on her face. "Haven't you ever broken a few rules?"

Yeah, an unwritten one about dating a coworker's ex-wife.

Not good, especially when he found out the lady hadn't yet told her husband she'd filed for divorce. The fact that the man had been a senior surgeon while Thomas was fresh out of his residency only added to the mess.

"It's not something I make a habit of."

"Well, you're not doing it now, either. This is my domain, remember? I'm allowed to be here anytime I want and I often work after hours." Annabel hit a light switch, bathing the large room in a soft glow. "Ah, almost like candlelight. No need to go with all the lights just for dinner."

It wasn't the intimate setting like a private corner booth at Antonio's, but Thomas had to admit it was close.

"This used to be a storage area before I took it over three years ago," Annabel continued. "I had the place completely gutted and rebuilt from the ground up, including the wall of glass to the outside area. Now the kids have a place to come where they don't have to be quiet like upstairs. Well, not as quiet."

Thomas looked around, taking in the floor-to-ceiling bookcases, the scattered tables and chairs, most sized for patrons under four feet tall, as well as several large pillows, comfy armchairs and knit rugs covered hardwood floors.

Posters of children's authors and book covers decorated the walls. A curved wooden desk that must be original to the building stood against one wall, and above it hung a framed headshot of a grinning golden retriever that had to be Annabel's dog, with a placard that read Honorary Mascot.

"Come on, grab a piece of floor."

He turned to find Annabel kneeling at a child-size

table, removing a couple of water bottles from the paper bag. She paused to peel off her jacket, revealing a faded Johnny Cash 1967 concert T-shirt that hugged her curves in all the right places.

Thomas had to swallow the lump in his throat before he asked, "You plan on eating right here?"

"Of course." She pushed aside a couple of miniature chairs and grabbed two large character-decorated pillows. "Here, you can have Dr. Seuss, in honor of your profession. I'll take Winnie-the-Pooh."

Shaking his head, he joined her on the carpet, their hips bumping as they worked to empty the bags of their dinner. Thomas edged away, determined to keep this night light and easy. "So, how did you become a librarian?"

"Freshman-year biology."

That got his attention. "Excuse me?"

Annabel opened one of the containers and the spicy tang of barbecue filled the air. "As a kid I was always the one bringing home stray cats or injured birds. I even stole a horse from a rancher who was using inhumane training techniques on the poor animal. My family thought I'd grow up to be a veterinarian or maybe even a doctor. But when I got to high school and was told I had to dissect a defenseless little frog…" Her voice trailed off as she shuddered. "I just couldn't do it."

Thomas grinned. "You do know the frog was already dead, right?"

"Yes, I knew that, but I still didn't understand why we couldn't learn what we needed without killing...cutting—anyway, I organized a protest which pretty much ended my science career. So I got my bachelor's degree in English from San Jose State University, stayed on to get my master's in Library Sciences and here I am."

He was surprised to hear she'd gone to school out of state. "You went to college in California?"

"With the size of my family a full scholarship made it an easy decision." Annabel filled two plates with ribs, chicken and fries. "I loved it. The bay area is so beautiful."

"And yet you came back here afterward?"

"Of course, Thunder Canyon is my home." She pushed a plate in his direction. "This smells heavenly! Let's eat!"

It was a far cry from the refined dinner he'd originally envisioned, but the food was terrific. They ate picnic style with Thomas trying his best to work with the plastic silverware and keep his meal out of his lap.

"You know, messy is the only way to go." Annabel took a barbecued chicken leg in her fingers and attacked it with a large bite. "Mmm, so good."

Thomas smiled. Her lack of pretense impressed him. Most of the women he'd dated seemed to refrain from eating altogether. Annabel approached her meal the same way she approached the rest of her life—with gusto.

Messy gusto.

"And you do know the caveman method to dining will always result in more sauce on your face and hands than in your mouth, right?" Thomas asked, then smiled even wider at the exaggerated indignation on her face. "You've got a large dollop on your cheek."

His breath caught the moment her tongue snaked out, trying to capture the evidence. It should look comical, but Thomas was captivated. "Ah, other side."

She repeated the motion, but still missed.

"Here, let me help…"

He leaned closer, brushing at the side of her mouth with his thumb the same moment Annabel tried again, and was stunned when the quick lick against his skin sent shock waves through his body.

Her blue eyes widened and he couldn't stop himself from dragging the moist digit over her full bottom lip.

Three dates in the past two years, longer than that since he'd even wanted to feel a woman's mouth beneath his, but right here, right now, there was nothing Thomas wanted more in the world than to kiss Annabel.

And damn the consequences.

Chapter Four

For the second time in two days, Dr. Thomas North had left her utterly speechless. Breathless, too. Heck, the only way Annabel knew she was alive was the hot flush burning across her skin and the way her heart was about to jump out of her chest.

Then again, her heart had been rocking and rolling to its own crazy beat from the moment he'd agreed to her spontaneous dinner invitation earlier tonight.

Less than an hour ago, she'd skidded to a stop in her favorite black ballet flats as he'd eased out of his shiny sports car, looking relaxed despite hours spent in surgery, and especially yummy.

His white dress shirt and khaki pants were still fresh and polished. The only concession to his long day were the shirtsleeves folded halfway to his elbows. Even the loafers on his feet gleamed in the streetlights.

She'd used the few moments it'd taken him to notice The Hitching Post was closed to reassure herself that her idea of a take-out meal at her home away from home was a good idea.

Especially after he'd joined her and she'd seen the deep lines of fatigue bracketing his eyes.

Now, however, those icy blue eyes were bright and alive, the exhaustion replaced with longing as they stayed locked on her mouth. The heavenly back and forth friction of his thumb against her bottom lip had her wondering just how amazing it would be to kiss this man.

Should she or shouldn't she?

Despite her flirty and confident attitude, Annabel had no idea how Thomas would react if she threw caution to the wind, closed the short distance between them and pressed her mouth to his.

The barest taste of him lingering on her tongue from where she'd licked his thumb wasn't nearly enough. She wanted more. Did he? The way he continued to touch her, his fingers brushing her neck—

"I'm sorry." Thomas jerked his hand away. Grabbing a napkin, he thrust it at her while managing to effectively put space between them without moving an inch. "That was— I'm sorry."

"No need to apologize." Annabel wiped her mouth, dropping her gaze to the alphabet-patterned rug. Was he sorry about touching her? Almost kissing her? Not wanting to know, she purposely misunderstood his regret. "Messy eating and barbecue go hand in hand, I guess."

"No, I mean I'm sorry about tonight. This isn't exactly the meal I had planned when I asked you to dinner."

"Plans change." Annabel put the chicken leg back on her plate while offering what she hoped was a casual shrug of one shoulder. "Besides, sometimes the best things happen when we least expect it."

"Maybe so, but I'm the kind of guy who likes to have everything fall neatly into place."

That didn't surprise her. He seemed the type who liked to have every *i* dotted and *t* crossed, as her father often said.

Her?

Not so much. Most of Annabel's life had been a crazy, mixed-up mess of spontaneous opportunities and gut decisions that either worked out better than she hoped or provided a much-needed life lesson.

Hoping for the former, she decided to steer the conversation to a safer topic. "I guess your surgery today didn't go as planned either, huh?"

"No, that was another surprise." He took a long

draw on his water. "What should've been a simple lumbar spinal fusion went totally out of whack when we discovered more damage to the spinal cord than we originally believed. Then the allograft was rejected even though a positive match had been achieved beforehand, resulting in us having to take bone from the patient's pelvis—"

Thomas suddenly stopped speaking, the self-conscious grin on his face making his chiseled cheekbones even more pronounced. "I'm sorry. Again." He braced an arm on a bent knee and waved his hand in the air as if to erase his words. "I tend to get carried away when I talk about work."

The change in him was amazing. He'd grown relaxed and animated at the same time. "Oh, please, tell me more." Annabel tucked her legs to one side. "I think it's fascinating."

He did as she asked, going into great detail about the remarkable work he and his surgical team had accomplished today and the more he talked, the more those amazing dimples appeared. Most of the technical stuff went right over her head, but it was fun to listen anyways.

"I'm guessing you didn't have any problem with slicing and dicing back in high school?" Annabel asked.

Thomas's featured softened. "Never even hesitated."

"So how did you end up here in our little corner of paradise?"

"Thunder Canyon is my home, too."

Now that surprised her. She guessed him to be in his early thirties, which would've put him a few years ahead of her in school, but she found it hard to believe someone as good-looking as Thomas had missed being caught on the radar of her older sisters. "Really?"

"Born and raised. Well, born anyway. I started attending private schools when I was around ten. After that it was summer camps or trips abroad until I went to college at seventeen."

"Considering who I'm talking to, I'm going to assume you skipped a year or two in high school and not the more common late-year birthday?"

"I completed high school, college and med school in nine years. Most people take the standard twelve."

Wow, she was impressed. "So did you follow the family business?"

"No, my parents are lawyers. They have a law firm here in town." He looked away, but not before she saw a muscle jump in his cheek. "They probably expected their only child to follow in their footsteps, but I've known what I wanted to do with my life since I was seven years old."

"That young? I was still undecided between being a princess or the presidency." Annabel read the seriousness in his gaze when he turned back to her. "What happened to create such a deep conviction?"

"My grandfather lost both his legs in a car accident that year." Thomas paused, pressing his lips into a hard line. When he continued his voice held a quiet intensity. "He changed after that. Sank into a deep depression that as a little boy I didn't understand. Even though Grandpa Joe lived almost another twenty years, he was never the same man I knew and loved."

A warm, protective feeling came over her. She blinked hard to erase the stinging in her eyes. "Oh, Thomas."

"I remember telling my parents if I was a doctor I could have saved my grandfather's legs. After that, there wasn't any question about what I planned to do with my life."

"And from what I've heard, you do your job very well."

His gaze flew back to hers. "What you've heard?"

"From you. Tonight. When you talked about that surgery I could tell how much you love your work and how good you are."

"Ah, yeah...thanks." Thomas glanced at his watch. "Wow, look at the time. It's almost midnight."

Okay, she could take a hint. "And you've been at the hospital since before dawn."

One brow arched in inquiry.

"You know what a small town Thunder Canyon

is." Annabel shrugged and started to clear up the remains of their meal. "I've heard your name bantered about. Nothing but good things, of course. Like your tendency to work very long days."

"Yes, well, I've heard a few things about you, too." He joined her, collecting the empty containers. "You and your dog are a popular topic at the hospital."

"It's all Smiley. He makes an impression everywhere he goes."

"How did you two get involved in that line of volunteer work?"

"I had a guest speaker here at the library earlier this year who spoke about the special work dogs do, from assistance for the blind and physically challenged to the therapy dog program. I knew right then my sweet little bundle of fur would be great at it."

"That dog isn't so little."

Annabel laughed and headed for her desk. She was glad they were talking about Smiley. Until now she hadn't even thought about her plan to use this time to persuade Thomas to give the go-ahead for her idea. "But he is sweet, gentle and kind. He also instinctively knows when someone is in pain or needs a good dose of unconditional love."

"What my patients *need* is excellent health care, which comes from scientifically proven methods and top-of-the-line medicines."

"I agree." She ducked behind her desk and, hidden from his view for the moment, stuck out her tongue at his lofty tone. Not mature, but it felt good just the same. "But sometimes they need someone who will listen when they talk and love them without expectations."

"Annabel, I don't want you to think I'm a total jerk—"

"I don't think that." Rising, she found Thomas standing in the middle of the room, his hands shoved deep in his pockets. He should've looked out of place, surrounded by miniature furniture and bright colors, but his serious expression made her want to bring back the relaxed one from earlier. "Not totally. At least not yet."

One side of his mouth rose into a half grin. She'd take it.

"Thanks, I think. I'm just not sure that petting a dog can have much effect on a serious medical condition."

"I don't see how it can hurt."

Hmm, silence from the man. Score one for her and Smiley.

"Okay, I'll give you that," he said.

"How about giving me something more?" Annabel offered a sincere smile as she walked back toward him, shaking out a garage bag. "As in a chance to test your theory? Let Smiley and me work with some of your patients, Forrest included, on a trial basis, and we can see how it goes."

"Annabel—"

She pressed her index finger to her lips, the librarian's universal signal for silence. "Just think about it."

It took a lot of willpower, but Annabel allowed her request to hang in the air as they worked together to fill the bag with their trash and headed for the exit. She reset the alarm, locked the door behind them and pointed out the Dumpster on the far side of the building.

Once they were back on the sidewalk, a cool breeze sent a shiver though her. She started to pull on her jacket, but Thomas gently took it from her.

"Here, let me help."

Turning her back to him, Annabel smiled as she slid her arms into the sleeves, enjoying the gentlemanly gesture.

Tugging her hair free, she peered backward at him. "Thanks."

"My pleasure." The weight of his hands rested a moment at her shoulders then they were gone.

As they headed back toward Main Street to their parked cars, Annabel knew this was the end of their evening, and she wanted so much to ask again about the therapy group. But she'd told him to think about it, and pressuring him wasn't giving him time to think. Still she had to capture her bottom lip between her teeth to stop the words from blurting out of her mouth.

Of course, that move only made her think back to the almost kiss.

Would Thomas want to brush his lips across hers as he said good-night? How would he react if she kissed him instead?

"Which car is yours?"

Thomas's question surprised her and she stopped short. They were back in front of The Hitching Post, but on the other side of the street.

Well, she guessed the saying good-night part was already here.

Annabel pointed toward her vehicle. "The little green Bug. Straight ahead."

Thomas headed toward it and Annabel hurried to catch up with him. "Oh, I'm fine. You don't have to—"

"Annabel, don't argue." He motioned for her to continue moving. "Just walk."

She did, digging her keys out of the bottom of her purse. Hitting the button to unlock the driver's side door, she reached for the handle only to have Thomas's hand shoot past hers first.

He opened her door and she stepped off the curb into the space between the door and the driver's seat. Thomas moved in behind her, his close proximity distracting her for a moment.

Should she turn around? If so, would he still be standing on the curb making him appear even taller?

Darn, why hadn't she slipped on her wedged sandals instead? They would've put her at the perfect height to lean forward, balance herself by lightly placing her hands on his chest before she'd lay a quick kiss on his—

"It'll probably take me a few days to secure a room for your group. How about you start two weeks from today?"

She spun around, his words setting off tiny bursts of sparkling happiness—almost as sweet as the kiss she'd been imagining a second ago—that reached all the way to her toes. "Oh, Thomas! Really?"

He stood, one hand braced on the door and the other on the roof of her car looking down at her with a smile that turned those miniature fireworks into a full-blown explosion. "Yes, really."

Kiss him!

Fighting off the internal command to throw her arms around his neck took all of Annabel's strength. She clasped her hands together and held them tight to her chest, just in case.

He took a step backward, his hand coming off the roof. "My secretary will call you with the details. We'll put the word out about your group, but I can't guarantee anyone will agree to come. Or how many sessions you'll have. That all depends on the patients' reactions and your dog's behavior."

Trying to feel grateful he'd saved her from making a fool of herself, again, she concentrated instead on the good news. "I understand. Don't worry. Smiley will be on his best behavior. This is too wonderful for words. I really don't know what to say, but thank you so much!"

"You're welcome."

Deciding to end the evening on an upward note, she dropped into the driver's seat and started the car's engine. She then reached for the door, but Thomas's voice stopped her.

"Thanks for tonight...for dinner."

The pause when he spoke made her look up at him, but he'd moved farther back on the sidewalk, his face in the shadows. "Thanks for meeting me. I had a lot of fun."

He gave her a quick nod in return, then crossed in front of her headlights to his own car on the other side of the street. Pulling out into the road, Annabel stopped at the red light. In her rearview mirror she watched as Thomas made a quick U-turn in the middle of the empty street and headed in the opposite direction, his taillights disappearing into the night.

The light changed to green and Annabel headed for home. As happy as she was about Thomas giving her therapy-group idea a green light, she had to admit his reaction to her reaction did sting a bit.

Had he been able to tell how much she wanted to kiss him?

Heck, he'd started it with wiping the barbecue sauce off the side of her mouth. She'd only been responding to the vibes he'd put out in the cozy setting of the library. Just because she'd been told in the past, by more than a few people, that she tended to leap before she looked, didn't mean she was to blame.

Pulling into the driveway at her family's home, Annabel parked alongside the collection of other cars that belonged to her parents and siblings. She was greeted by a happy, tail-wagging Smiley as soon as she stepped into the darkened kitchen and her victorious feeling returned.

Kneeling, she gave her baby a hug and a treat from his special biscuit jar in celebration. "I did it, sweetie. We're all set for you to work your magic. Provided you follow the rules and do what you're told."

Smiley offered a cheerful bark in return and Annabel hugged him again. So what if her date—if one could even call it that—hadn't ended the way she'd hoped.

"I got what I really wanted tonight," she whispered to herself as much as to Smiley. "That's what counts."

"Hmm, not sure if I like the sound of that."

Annabel's head jerked up at her mother's voice. Evelyn Cates stood in the doorway that led into the family's oversize dining room, flanked by Annabel's sisters.

Jordyn Leigh snapped on the overhead light. "I don't know, Mom, it sounds pretty good to me. So how was Mr. Better-Late-Than-Never?"

"He was fine. I mean, it was fine." Annabel stood. "I told you Thomas got held up in surgery. That's why our plans changed."

"Yet you left and returned with the same sappy grin on your face." Jazzy winked as she headed for the sink with a handful of empty glasses. "And it sounds like you had a better-than-average time on your date, the first one in…what? How long has it been?"

"Refresh my memory." Annabel opened the refrigerator and stuck her head in for no other reason than to escape her sisters' prying eyes. "Which one of us actually had plans tonight?"

"Oh, sis, she's got you there," Jordyn Leigh said, then laughed. "Come on, let's get back to our movie."

"Why do I get the feeling that line 'the lady doth protest too much' fits somehow?" Jazzy shot back. "Hmm, I smell another romance brewing."

"Oh, please. We've already got two bridesmaids dresses hanging in our closet. The last thing we need around here is another wedding."

Annabel jumped at Jordyn Leigh's parting words as her sisters left the room.

Wedding? Who said anything about a wedding?

Grabbing a soda she didn't want, Annabel closed the door. Her mother had stayed behind, her blue eyes filled with the same loving concern she'd shown for all her children over the years.

"Mom…"

"Can I at least ask what it is you got tonight that you're so happy about?"

Annabel explained her plans for Smiley and the therapy group. "This is something I've wanted to do for a long time. Talking about the group and how I want to help Forrest, and anyone else who might come, is the main reason Thomas and I met tonight. I really think Smiley can make a difference."

"I'm sure he will, honey." Her mother smiled. "But I do think your sisters might be right. You haven't been this happy about a date in a long time."

"I'm happy about getting the approval for my therapy group," Annabel said, refusing to allow the memory of the way Thomas had touched her mouth and the desire she'd seen in his eyes come back to life. "Tonight was no big deal. Goodness knows I've had enough missed connections and false starts when it comes to men in the past. I doubt I'll be spending any more time with Dr. North outside of the hospital."

"Okay, dear. If you say so." Her mother leaned in and gave Annabel a quick hug. "I'm going to wash up those dishes before I head to bed. You joining your sisters?"

"No, I think I'll go up to my room. Good night, Mom."

Annabel headed for the stairs, Smiley at her side. She knew her sisters' good-natured teasing was all in fun, and with two recent weddings in their family, Annabel supposed she couldn't blame them for seeing romance where none existed.

She had to admit that Thomas North wasn't anywhere near as stuffy and uptight as she'd first thought. In fact, he was smart, caring and downright sexy. And if asked, and there was no reason why anyone should, she'd also admit the barest hint of his touch sent zingers to all her girly parts.

However, when he had the chance to kiss her tonight—more than once, in fact—he'd backed off.

So what did any of it mean?

Frustrated, she placed the unopened soda can on her dresser and once again flung herself down on her bed and stared at the ceiling. Was the attraction all in her head?

Or was the hunky doctor very good at keeping his feelings under wraps?

Chapter Five

Thomas pushed the button that activated the garage door as he turned the last corner in the condominium complex. When he moved home two years ago he'd been one of the first people to buy in the gated community and had chosen an end unit in the last row, hoping for as much privacy as possible.

At the time there had only been a couple dozen of the two-story condos in the development. Now there were fifty units along with amenities that included a gym, pool and club house, not that Thomas ever found the time, or the inclination, to use them.

He preferred to take his daily runs in private, usually on the many trails crisscrossing the hills behind the complex or the treadmill in his spare bedroom.

Damn, it felt like forever since he'd done his usual five miles this morning.

After pulling his car inside and shutting down the engine, he locked his BMW and closed the garage door. Heading upstairs, he entered the open living/dining room and went straight to the kitchen.

Tossing his keys next to the pile of mail on the granite countertop, he yanked open the refrigerator and pulled out a cold beer. The cap released with a simple twist and he tilted his head back, downing half the bottle without stopping.

Then he dropped his head back against the wall with a resounding thunk.

Nope, she was still there.

Two more thunks and one empty beer bottle later didn't help.

Annabel Cates, with the most delicious mouth he'd even seen on a woman, was still front and center in his head. Not to mention his other body parts that remembered and appreciated her soft curves, the spicy vanilla scent that clung to her skin and the way she got him to open up and talk about himself as if they'd known each other their entire lives.

He'd even told her about Grandpa Joe.

Tossing the empty bottle in the recycling bin, Thomas grabbed a bottle of water and made his way upstairs, pausing to set the security alarm and turn on a couple of table lamps in the living room. He'd learned the hard way to leave the low lights on all night. The chrome, glass and leather furniture he'd chosen was sleek and modern, but it also hurt like heck when walked into while fumbling around in the dark during those times he needed to leave in a hurry.

He entered his bedroom, stripping as he went. Leaving an uncharacteristic trail of clothing behind him, the last thing he did was put his cell phone, wallet, and the water on the bedside table before crawling naked between the cool sheets.

The clock read 12:35 a.m., meaning he'd been awake for twenty hours, fifteen of them spent at the hospital. He should be exhausted, but closing his eyes didn't help.

All he saw was Annabel.

The way she almost glided when she walked, as if her feet barely touched the ground. The way her lips curved upward in a mischievous grin when she'd asked him about breaking rules. The pride in those amazing pale blue eyes of hers as she showed off where she spent the majority of her waking hours.

Pride that melted into kindness and compassion when he'd revealed how a childhood tragedy shaped his entire life.

Damn, it was going to be a long night.

Thomas groaned, remembering his cell phone needed charging. He plugged it in, took it off vibrate and punched up the volume of his ringtone. Just in case.

His fingers paused when he saw the missed-call

icon. He pressed the code for his voice mail, breathing a sigh of relief it wasn't the hospital when he heard the voice of his buddy in Hawaii who'd left a disjointed message, mixed with the sound of crying babies, that ended with Reid's usual "I hate talking to these damn things" tirade.

Grinning, Thomas pressed the button to return the call, figuring out it was only nine-thirty in the Aloha State. Besides, his roommate through medical school and five years of residency had said Thomas should call because he was spending his Friday night—

"Dr. T!"

Thomas smiled at his friend's greeting. "Dr. Gaines, I presume. It's been a while since I've heard from you."

"Well, you know. The life of a busy doctor."

Yes, Thomas did know about that.

He also knew Reid somehow made time for his beautiful wife, a nurse he met a year after graduating from medical school who'd convinced him to return to her native hometown of Honolulu after they'd married. Now Reid was the father of twin eight-month-old boys who he was constantly sending Thomas pictures of via text messages, and the owner of three prized surfboards.

The former San Diego surfer had found his own slice of paradise.

Wasn't that what Annabel called Thunder Canyon earlier?

Maybe for her. But Thomas often wondered if he would've ever returned to his hometown if not for making the biggest mistake of his life—one that forced him to leave behind everything he'd worked so hard for.

"So it's already Saturday in Montana." Reid's voice filled his ear. "Please tell me you were not at work this late."

"Is that any better than what you're doing to-night?"

"Hey, me and the boys, who finally crashed, thank goodness, are watching my beloved Angels getting their butts handed to them by the freaking Red Sox while the baby mama is out with her posse of girl-friends," Reid shot back. "Hopefully the twins will stay asleep until after she strolls in. Then we'll have some real home-run action going on."

"TMI, buddy." Thomas pushed himself up against the padded headboard, refusing to think about the fact he'd passed up the chance to even get to first base tonight. Twice. "Since Gracie was practically a third roommate back in the day, I already know more about your sex life than I ever wanted."

"At least tell me yours has improved since we last spoke. I think you said something about a lawyer who caught your eye?"

It took Thomas a moment to figure out what his friend was talking about. "Yeah, that was almost a year ago."

"Okay, so it wasn't the last time we talked. Sue me. You still seeing her?"

"No."

"Because…"

"Because our careers kept us too busy." The lie fell so easily from his lips. Thomas grabbed the water and took a long swallow. "Doctor. Lawyer. Long hours all around."

"You are the worst liar I've ever met."

"It once served me well."

His friend sighed. "Dammit, you haven't let go of that yet? It's been almost three years."

This time Thomas knew exactly what his friend was talking about. Reid had had a front-row seat to his stupidity and ultimate humiliation after he'd gotten involved with the wrong woman.

The worst possible woman.

Another man's wife. And to make matters worse he'd actually fallen in love with her.

Except he had no idea at the time she was married, with no plans to change her status.

Not that Thomas had been inexperienced in matters of the heart. He'd dated through high school and college, but most girls wanted more of his time and attention than he was willing to give. His studies had been his main focus, especially during medical school, and that focus switched to his work while living the crazy life of a new doctor knee-deep in his residency.

Then he'd met Veronica, in the parking lot of a hospital function no less, which should've been his first clue. But he'd been riding a high after getting his board certification and acceptance into an orthopedic surgery fellowship right there in Santa Monica.

When the gorgeous redhead thanked him for fixing a flat tire by tossing him the keys to her Aston Martin convertible and insisting they drive up the coast until they ran out of gas, he'd been hooked. By the time he'd returned home after spending the entire weekend in bed at a "friend's" beach house, he'd agreed to keep their romance a secret, which had made it even more thrilling. Of course, he'd thought it was great that she didn't try to monopolize his time and understood his long working hours.

Until it all came crashing down on him less than a year later, when they'd gotten caught by her husband.

Thomas soon found their affair the talk of the medical center and any job prospects there had quietly disappeared despite his outstanding record. Thankfully, his grandmother had pulled enough strings to get him an interview at TC General, for the job he now held.

"Victoria Meadows is history, man." Reid's voice jerked Thomas from his memories. "You got played by a coldhearted witch who used you to make her old man jealous. A man she's still with and who made chief surgeon earlier this summer if I read the news correctly."

Yeah, Thomas had read that, too. "Thanks for the history lesson."

"Look, I know your grand plans of making the staff at UCLA Medical flew out the window after everything came out, but you said you were enjoying your work in Thunder Canyon."

"I am." There was no hesitation in his voice and Thomas realized just how true the words were.

Yes, his grandmother had come through with a job for him, but he'd worked harder than anyone on the staff to earn the position. TC General might operate at a slower pace than UCLA, but the work they did was just as important. "Things are going well here."

"Any pretty nurses on the staff?"

Thomas sighed. "You never give up."

"Hey, buddy, I just want you to be as happy as I am."

Reid's words caused the image of blond wavy hair and blue eyes to slide through his head, fully formed and in color, as if he'd had a photograph of her in his hand.

And just like that he was remembering how drawn he'd been to Annabel's warm smile and infectious nature.

He wanted to be irritated that she kept coming to mind, but he had to admit tonight had been more fun that he'd had in a long time. An improvised experience he usually stayed far away from whenever his set plans changed, but something in Annabel's voice had been hard to say no to when he'd called to apologize for messing up their date.

And later he'd seen the bright burst of desire in her gaze making it clear that if he'd wanted to kiss her she would've welcomed his mouth on hers.

If he'd wanted? Who was he kidding? His hand fisted the sheets as he remembered how it'd taken every ounce of discipline he had not to take things to the next level tonight.

Annabel was unlike any woman he'd ever met, nothing like—

Thomas cut off that thought.

Getting involved with someone who'd be a presence around the hospital was the last thing he wanted. And she would definitely be around, now that he'd actually given the okay to put that crazy idea of hers into action.

A mutt that could make sick people well? Who was he kidding? Wait until the hospital gossip grapevine got a hold of *that*.

Thomas scrubbed at his eyes, his bones aching with exhaustion. Chalking up his reaction to Annabel Cates and her dog therapy plan to being overtired was easy to do.

Maybe sleep would be easy now, as well.

"North, did you pass out on me?" Reid asked. "It got real quiet all of a sudden."

"No, still here, but fading fast. I should go."

"Okay, I'll hang up. Oh, but before you drift off

to dreamland I'm going to text you a picture of the newest member of the family."

Thomas must be more tired than he thought. "What? You and Gracie have another kid I didn't know about?"

"No, we agreed to foster a dog from the local animal rescue center a couple of weeks ago, but she's the sweetest pup and fit so well with the Gaines clan we had to keep her."

"Let me guess." Thomas closed his eyes and again dropped his head, the headboard muffling the sound this time. "A golden retriever?"

Reid chuckled. "How the heck did you know that?"

Over the past few days Thomas swore he'd dreamed about dogs every time he closed his eyes.

Being chased by a Great Dane during his daily run. His take-out lunch scarfed right off his desk by a basset hound with ears so long the animal had tripped on them while making his getaway. Performing a knee replacement on a police K9 unit dog, a German shepherd who'd been hurt in the line of duty. These were just a few of the crazy scenarios that invaded his sleep.

He had no idea what all that meant, but he figured it had something to do with the fact Marge had surprised him on Monday afternoon when she'd announced she'd found a meeting room for Annabel's sessions and that they were ready to start this week.

Or maybe it was because over the weekend Thomas had started to do his own extensive research on the results achieved by dog therapy programs. He told himself it had nothing to do with Annabel and everything to do with his responsibility as a staff member at the hospital to know all he could about a program he'd indirectly offered to his patients.

Yeah, right.

So why had he been standing here in the hall on Wednesday afternoon, watching through the open doorway for the past fifteen minutes while Annabel and her dog worked the crowded room? He really needed to get back to his office.

"Dr. North?"

Thomas turned and found a trio of nurses from his surgical team passing him by in the hallway. "Ladies."

"Hmm, that's a new look for you, Doctor." Michelle, the newest of the three and fresh out of the army, had only been at TC General for a month. "Blue is your color."

One of the other nurses quickly elbowed her and the three hurried away, but not before Thomas saw the smiles on their faces.

Glancing down at the standard blue surgical scrubs he wore, Thomas silently acknowledged they were far from his usual attire of dress slacks, shirt and tie. The outfit, complete with thick-soled sneakers that were perfect for long hours on his feet, was comfortable and familiar. He'd practically lived in scrubs during his residency, but now they were something he was never seen in outside of surgery.

Until today.

Now that he thought about it, he'd gotten more than a few stares and smirks since he'd donned the clothes an hour ago. He'd planned to head to his office to change into the spare suit he kept there, but not until he'd completed his rounds.

Then he'd purposely taken a route that brought him right by this meeting room with the idea of observing Annabel for just a moment—

"Dr. North." This time his name was spoken as a statement, not a question and by a voice that held the familiar rasp of maturity and authority Thomas had known his entire life. "I assume there is a fascinating explanation for your current attire."

He turned back and there stood a wisp of a woman at just over five feet tall with steel-gray hair pulled back into a perfect chignon and the same icy blue eyes as him.

"Hello, Grandmother."

She didn't return his greeting as her chin rose a degree while her gaze traveled the length of him.

Thomas straightened his shoulders and stood a bit taller. Force of habit. Despite celebrating her eightieth birthday a few months ago and, more recently, her retirement from her position as a hospital administrator, Ernestine North was still a force to be reckoned with within the halls of TC General.

"And your choice of foot apparel, as well," she finally said with a hint of a smile. "Please don't keep me in suspense."

"I had a patient who had an…er, adverse reaction to his medication while doing my rounds. This was the only choice for me to change into at the time." Thomas relaxed and crossed his arms over his chest. "And I like your shoes, too."

His grandmother leaned on her cane and lifted a foot, offering him a better display of her red-and-white polka-dot shoe with tiny white bows at the ankle peeking from the hem of her navy blue pantsuit. "Yes, they are adorable, aren't they?"

"And a bit too tall. I thought your doctor said no more high heels."

"I'm old. I don't have to listen to him. Besides, the heel is less than two inches." She set her foot down and waved the cane at him. "I don't really need this. I just use it to make myself look authoritative."

More likely because the cane had once belonged to his grandfather, until he had no use for it after his accident. She'd started using it the day of Joe's funeral and Thomas had never seen her without it since. "You're retired, Gran."

"Yes, but many of the staff still fear me in my honorary position. I like it that way."

"Gran—"

"But we weren't talking about me. Did it ever occur to you to keep an extra suit in your office?"

"Of course." Thomas grinned, enjoying the banter. "I'm headed there right now to change."

"No, what you are doing is standing here. Why?" She glanced around, the double take when she spotted Annabel and her dog was slight, but Thomas saw it. "Ah, the dog whisperer."

"She's not a dog whisperer. Annabel Cates is certified in dog therapy and she's doing a weekly session here at the hospital for anyone, including staff as you can see, who wish to stop by."

His grandmother remained silent, the tilt to her head saying more than any words could.

Damn. Had he actually been defending her?

"Yes, I know who Miss Cates is. I read your memo and wanted to stop by and see how things were going." His grandmother stepped closer to him and out of the way as people started to exit the room. "Apparently, I'm not the only one who thought to do so."

Annabel's sweet laughter spilled from the room and Thomas found it impossible not to look.

She knelt in front of a young girl who couldn't have been more than three years old. The child tried to wrap her arms around the furry neck of Annabel's dog, who sat quietly in front of her, his wagging tail the only part in motion. Annabel laid a hand on the dog's shoulder and he bowed his head. The child completed her hug; the woman behind her who was doing her best to hold back her tears had to be the mother.

Annabel smiled when she accepted a hug, as well. She then turned, as if she'd felt his gaze on her, and sent him a quick wink he felt all the way to his toes.

"Thomas?"

It took more effort than it should, but Thomas gave his attention back to his grandmother, not realizing she'd stepped a few feet away to speak with a hospital volunteer. The woman in the pink smock walked away, but Ernestine stood there, a single arched brow that told him she was waiting for an answer to a question he hadn't heard.

"I'm sorry, Gran. What did you say?"

"You seem different, Thomas. Where is that straitlaced, perfectionist grandson I know and love?"

Thomas fisted his hands for a moment, her words delivering a light blow he didn't like. Because it was a direct hit?

"I am not straitlaced."

"Of course you are. It's a family trait. And I asked if you plan to attend your parents' dinner party tomorrow night."

Her question had him wanting to tighten his grip even more, but he relaxed it instead before his grandmother's sharp gaze spotted his reaction. The woman was already well aware of the distance between him and his parents, thanks to having grown up more away from home than with them, but he'd go to their dinner party because his grandmother wanted him there. "Yes, I'll be there."

"And please—" she paused, her lips pursed as if she was holding back a smile "—at least wear a tie."

Unable to hold back his own grin, Thomas didn't even try. "At the very least."

She nodded once, turned and walked away, her steps graceful as always. He watched as she made it as far as the nurses' station halfway down the hall before getting into an animated conversation with another staff member.

"Oh, I love her shoes."

Annabel's soft voice carried over his shoulder, catching him off guard. For a moment Thomas wondered if he should've left when his grandmother did, but Annabel had already seen him. He probably shouldn't have stopped by at all. Being seen with her would only fuel the gossip.

A quick greeting and then he'd leave.

He faced her, noticing the meeting room was completely empty now. A couple of steps and he crossed the threshold before a slight nudge at his knee, followed by another more insistent bump, had him looking down at the dog at his feet.

"Smiley insisted on coming over to say hello."

Thomas considered the dog's expression and

damn if the mutt didn't look like he was smiling, before shifting his attention to its owner. "Did he now?"

"Well, I wanted to talk to you, too." Annabel's eyes sparkled. "Because I realized, despite that first meeting in your office, you and my best bud here haven't ever been properly introduced."

"Annabel, that's not really necessary—"

"Smiley, I'd like you to meet Dr. Thomas North." Annabel gave a gentle tug on the leash as she spoke to her dog. "He's the one responsible for us being here and having such a great first session. Please say hello."

The golden promptly sat and lifted one paw.

Thomas couldn't hold back his laughter as he bent over, accepting the offering with a quick shake. "It's nice to meet you, Smiley."

As he knelt down before the dog and took its offered paw, he was struck by a realization. He, Dr. North, was on his knee shaking a dog's paw. And enjoying it. Just like he enjoyed the dog's unpredictable owner.

Chapter Six

It was silly, but Annabel had to blink back the sudden sting of tears biting her eyes as Thomas interacted with Smiley.

Happy tears, for sure.

Today had been wonderful with all the people who'd come by to meet her and Smiley at their introductory session, but Thomas stopping by to see them made the day perfect.

She'd been so worried no one would show, but then Madge, Thomas's secretary, had called this morning and told her about the buzz the notices for her sessions were generating.

She and Smiley arrived this afternoon to find a

half-dozen patients waiting and, as the hour passed, even more stopped by. Not everyone stayed for the entire session, but Smiley had made sure everyone got some much-needed attention.

Even a few of the hospital staff had wandered in, out of curiosity or looking for a bit of comfort or stress relief, an aspect of dog therapy Annabel hadn't even considered until today.

"Did things go as well as you expected?" Thomas asked as he straightened. "I only caught the last few minutes of your session."

Annabel grinned, watching from the corner of her eye as Smiley heaved a deep sigh that signaled his contentment before he lowered himself to the floor, paws stretched out over Thomas's shoes. "Things went better than we could've hoped for."

"You know, I was worried it might be depressing, so it surprised me at how uplifting and hopeful the session seemed to be."

"Thanks. I think."

He blushed and Annabel's insides fluttered like a mass of butterflies taking flight. She loved it.

"No, that's not what I meant. I was just concerned—"

"Hey, I was only teasing." She grabbed his arm and gave him a quick squeeze. The heat of his bare skin against her fingers set off those tingles she'd missed over the past five days. "I was worried, too, but today was more like a meet and greet. To give people a chance to get to know Smiley a bit and see if regular sessions are something they might be interested in."

Thomas pulled from her touch and folded his arms, stretching the cotton material of the scrubs tight across his chest. His fingers rubbed at the spot where she'd made contact with him. Was that good or bad?

"Well, it looked like you had all the age groups covered," he said. "Who was that last little girl I saw you with? She wasn't wearing a patient band on her wrist."

"No, her little brother was born two months premature and is still in intensive care. Their parents came by to check on the baby and the mother thought her little girl would enjoy meeting Smiley."

"She certainly seemed to."

"I'm glad they stopped by. Of course, the one person I was really hoping to see today was Forrest Traub. Do you know if he was notified about the session?"

A shadow passed over Thomas's blue eyes. "Yes, I saw him on Monday and mentioned it."

Her excitement deflated a bit. "He didn't want to come?"

"He's left town, Annabel."

Confusion swamped her. "What? Why?"

"Something came up at his family's ranch in Rust Creek Falls and he decided to return home."

"But what about his leg?"

"I've done what I can, for now. He's still healing and he assured me that scheduling private sessions with a local physical therapist is one of his priorities."

Annabel didn't like the seriousness of Thomas's tone. Although she was glad Forrest would continue to work toward his full recovery, she was worried about his mental well-being.

"You're concerned about him."

"Aren't you?"

Thomas sighed and nodded. Knowing he couldn't discuss a patient's care in any detail with her, Annabel didn't ask, but made a mental note to check in with her sister and the rest of the Traub family.

Maybe a road trip would be necessary? Rust Creek Falls was only about three hundred miles or so from Thunder Canyon.

Setting that idea aside for now and turning her thoughts back to all the good things that happened today was easy. At least four of today's visitors had expressed interest in coming back on a regular basis and two of those were veterans who'd recently served in Iraq. She was determined to find a way to make those sessions happen.

"Did Marge mention she reserved this room for me for the rest of the week?" The surprise on his handsome face answered her question. "Oh, I guess not."

"You plan on being here tomorrow and Friday? What about your job at the library?"

"It'll take some creative scheduling, but I'll make sure Smiley's sessions don't interfere." Annabel tightened her grip on the leash when the pet responded to his name and rose to his feet between the two of them.

"Once I get a better idea of who's interested in attending, I'm thinking of having two sessions a week. One will be like today, more casual, where people can stop by and stay as long as they feel they need to. Maybe I'll even invite some of my fellow volunteers to stop by." The ideas flowed as she spoke. "The other session should be more private with a limited number of attendees. It's amazing how people open up and talk when their attention is focused on something else."

"Like petting a dog."

"Exactly." She looked down, realizing she'd been scratching Smiley behind his ears this whole time. "See what I mean?"

"Somehow I don't think you need anyone's help to open up."

Annabel laughed then said, "I do tend to talk a lot. The curse of trying to be heard in large family, I guess."

"Sometimes that's hard to achieve no matter the size of the family."

Intrigued, Annabel wanted to ask him what he

meant, but the busy hospital sounds from the hallway grabbed his attention and he took a step backward. "I should head to my office. I want to get out
of these clothes."

Need any help?

Annabel managed to hold back the words, but
took the moment to enjoy the view of how the loose-
fitting top and pants still managed to show off
Thomas's strong arms. "Oh, I don't know. I think
scrubs look really good on you."

"Ah, thanks." A beeping noise filled the air. He
reached for the pager at his waist. "Sorry, I need to
answer this. Are you two heading out?"

Smiley's tail started wagging vigorously, batting
both their legs.

"That's a yes in Smiley speak," Annabel said.
"We'll get out your way now."

"You're not in the way. Come on, we're both heading in the same direction."

Annabel tightened her grip on the leash as they
exited the room and started down the corridor. The
whispers and stares that followed them were pretty
standard, Smiley always drew his share of attention, but Annabel noticed how Thomas's demeanor
changed with every step.

Gone was the easy banter between them and that
wonderful smile of his. They were stopped twice
by people asking about the sessions and by the time

they reached the elevators, she could almost sense his relief.

"Well, here's where we part ways, Miss Cates," Thomas said, his attention focused on the button to call for the elevator.

Miss Cates?

Surprised by his formal tone, Annabel forced her feet to keep moving. She kept her reply breezy and refused to look back. "Thanks, Dr. North. See you tomorrow."

Annabel slid her sunglasses on, to ward off the bright sunshine in the hospital parking lot and to hide from her sister's sharp gaze.

"Okay, spill," Abby said. "You've been tight-lipped about the handsome doctor since Wednesday night. Have you seen him in the past two days?"

"Yes, I saw *Dr. North* yesterday."

Abby took Smiley's leash from Annabel's hand. "So, how did it go?"

"Oh, so well he's pulled a complete vanishing act today."

"Do tell!"

Darn! Annabel should've known she'd regret confiding in her youngest sister. They'd shared a private chat Wednesday after a family dinner while enjoying a glass of wine on the front porch.

Her emotions had been flying all over the place ever since she'd left the hospital—excited about the sessions, confused by Thomas's behavior—and all it took was a simple "what's wrong" from Abby for everything to come pouring out.

"Well, running into him yesterday wasn't planned." Annabel moved to one side of the sidewalk to let an elderly couple walk by. Smiley followed her, of course, and so did Abby. "We'd finished up our second session, and unlike Wednesday afternoon Thomas hadn't show up at all."

"But you'd said you thought he wouldn't after the way he dismissed you the day before."

"I know." Annabel hated that she'd been right. "Anyway, we were getting ready to leave when one of the nurses stopped by. She told me about a patient up on the second floor who she thought could use a personal visit from Smiley."

"The patient didn't come to the session?"

"Mr. Owens broke his hip and leg in three places and is bedridden. He's also a widower with no children, almost ninety years old and, according to the nurse, as mean as the devil."

Abby smiled. "And you just couldn't resist."

"Of course not. So, Smiley and I used the stairs as his room was at that end of the hall. I could hear loud voices coming from his room while we were still in the stairway. Heck, everyone on the floor probably heard him arguing with his doctor."

"Oh, no."

"Oh, yes. You know me, I didn't even hesitate.

Thinking Smiley could take the edge off any situation I just waltzed in, and there stood Thomas."

Her sister's eyes widened. "What did he say?"

"He ignored me at first. Well, not really ignored." Annabel lowered her voice, her gaze on the large expanse of grass and flower beds that led to a low stone wall. The tables and chairs of the hospital cafeteria's outdoor eating area sat scattered on the other side of the wall where a few people gathered, enjoying the late summer afternoon. "I doubt either of them stopped arguing long enough to even notice I was in the room."

"Until Smiley made his presence known."

"By making a beeline straight for Thomas."

"Smiley has always had a good instinct about people," Abby said, giving the dog a quick smile. "He must like Thomas."

"He does," Annabel agreed. "So do I, but the good doctor made it clear he wasn't happy to see either of us. Even after his patient stopped grousing the moment Smiley walked to his bedside and said hello. Of course, I followed to make sure things went okay. The next thing I knew Thomas had disappeared."

"And today?"

"Are you kidding? The man probably took a sick day just to avoid running into— Oh!"

"Oh what?"

The moment he stepped outside, Annabel's eyes were drawn to his steel-gray dress shirt and solid black tie, a calming beacon among the sea of colorful scrubs.

Thomas walked with sure strides to the far corner of the patio and sat alone at a table shaded by a large tree, never once looking up from the paperwork in his hand.

"That's him, isn't it?"

Annabel turned and found her sister openly staring. "Yes, that's Thomas North, M.D., but hey, don't be shy. Just go ahead and gawk at the guy."

"Well, he certainly is something to gawk at." Abby looked back at her and grinned. "Go talk to him."

"What?"

"You like him, Annabel. You just said so and after the way you gushed about meeting him for the first time, your impromptu date at the library, the way he filled out those scrubs—"

"Hey! I wasn't gushing."

"Yes, you were, and don't even think about blaming it on the wine." Her sister waved a finger at her. "Believe me, if anyone knows how hard it is to get a man's attention, it's me. I had to practically throw myself at Cade before the guy finally noticed me."

What her sister said was true, even though Cade Pritchett had been a friend of the family's for years and was now her sister's very besotted husband. "But you two knew each other a long time before things got romantic last year."

"Which only made it harder to get the man to see me as anything but the youngest of the Cates girls. Take my advice, I know what I'm talking about."

With five sisters, Annabel had heard that line many times before. "Famous last words."

Abby laughed. "Trust me."

Unable to stop herself, Annabel gazed across the lawn. "Just jump into the deep end?"

"With both feet and a big splash." Abby blew her an air kiss and crossed her fingers. "Thanks for letting me borrow Smiley. I'll drop him off at the house later. Good luck!"

Annabel stood on the sidewalk as her sister and Smiley disappeared among the cars in the still-crowded parking lot. Checking her watch, she saw it was almost six and Thomas was still here.

Sitting at a table, alone, with his back to everyone.

Giving a tightening tug on her ponytail, Annabel wished for a cuter outfit than her pink cotton blouse and wrinkled khakis, and headed for the stone path that led to the dining area.

She paused when she reached his table. "Hi there."

Judging from the way his head jerked up, she'd surprised him. He stared at her, but thanks to the dark lenses of his sunglasses, she couldn't read anything in his gaze.

"Am I interrupting?"

He closed the folder. "No, of course not."

Without waiting for an invitation, Annabel

dropped into the chair opposite him and went can-
nonball style with her opening line. "I'm sorry for my
unannounced visit to Mr. Owens's room yesterday. It
was wrong of me to bring Smiley to a patient without
asking for permission first. It won't happen again."

Thomas sank back into his chair.

Annabel wasn't sure how to take his relaxed posture. The hard line of his mouth didn't help and she
wished desperately he'd remove the sunglasses,
which probably cost more than her entire outfit, so
she could see his eyes.

"It's just that after I heard about his condition and
his attitude, I thought—"

"How did you find out about him?"

Why did she think he already knew the answer?
"One of your staff mentioned him to me at the end
of Smiley's session. I guess because he's a patient
of yours, she felt it was okay to recommend a private visit." Annabel then remembered her own sunglasses and shoved them up onto the top of her head.
"I didn't know he was your patient until I walked into
the room, but still…that's no excuse."

He stared at her, as still as a statue. It was like
playing the "who will blink first" game and Thomas
didn't know it, but Annabel was the family champion. She'd wait him out if it took all night, but she
wasn't leaving until he accepted her apology.

Yanking off his own sunglasses, Thomas rubbed

at his eyes with the back of his hand before tossing the glasses on the table. "Annabel, I—"

"Hey! It's Smiley's mama!"

Annabel jumped when a cool, sticky hand landed on her arm. She turned and found the little girl whose brother was still in the ICU standing there.

"Well, hello to you." She smiled at the girl, loving her twin ponytails of curly blond hair. "Where's your mother?"

"Suzy!"

Annabel spotted the child's mother waving from across the patio. Rising, she shot Thomas a quick look, surprised to see the slight grin on his face. "I'll be right back."

He nodded.

Taking the girl's hand, Annabel walked her back to her mother and visited for a few moments. She wanted to get back to Thomas, to find out what he was going to say to her, but it felt like an eternity passed before she could. Every time she started moving in his direction, she was stopped by people wanting to talk about Smiley and her program.

She glanced over to make sure Thomas hadn't pulled another disappearing act, hoping his attention was at least on his paperwork.

Each time his attention was on her.

She didn't know if that was a good thing or not, but she liked the warmth that spread throughout her, especially when they made eye contact when she was finally able to rejoin him.

"Whew! Sorry about that, but it is nice to know we're making an impact."

"So, where is Smiley?"

His question surprised her. "That's what everyone else asked me. My sister Abby came by to pick him up earlier. She's taking him to hang out at ROOTS."

"Roots?"

"Haven't you ever heard of it? ROOTS is the hangout down on Main Street for local teens. They have all kinds of programs year-round, but the summers are especially busy. Abby works there while she's pursuing her master's degree in psychology."

"Is she a trained volunteer in dog therapy, too?"

"Smiley's not there in an official capacity. He's just hanging out with whoever might be there on a Friday night."

That got Thomas to smile again. "So he can unofficially work his magic? Like he did with my patient?"

Annabel's breath caught in her throat. "He did?"

Thomas leaned forward, his gaze intent as he laced his fingers together over his paperwork. "I owe you an apology, Annabel. Yesterday was a… difficult one, which seems to be the norm for Mr. Owens since his surgery." His gaze dropped away. "I handled your arrival…badly."

The pain in his voice tugged at her heart. She

reached out and laid a hand over his. "He reminds you of your grandfather, doesn't he?"

"Mr. Owens is like many of my elderly patients, obstinate and scared. But today he actually smiled at the nurses and took his medication without issue." Thomas flipped his hand over and captured her fingers in his. "And when I met with him this afternoon he asked when that beautiful girl and her pup were coming back to see him again."

Annabel gasped, surprised at the man's request. "Oh, I'm sorry we didn't get up to see him. Smiley has an appointment at the vet in the morning, but I can come after— Oh, there I go again!"

Thomas's smile widened. "If you can rearrange your schedule I'd appreciate it if you, and Smiley, came back to visit with him again."

"We would love to." Those familiar bursts of tingling happiness that always seemed to happen whenever she was with him filled Annabel's chest. "Thank you, Thomas, and until Mr. Owens is capable of joining us in the regular meeting room, I'll make a point of stopping in to see him afterward. As long as his doctor approves."

"I do, and thank you."

Annabel gave his hand a squeeze and went to pull away, but he held tight.

"You know, I do believe I owe you a dinner out." Thomas leaned closer. "Are you free tomorrow night?"

Oh, those bursts exploded into a dizzying array of bright colors. It was like last month's Fourth of July was repeating itself all over again. "Yes, I'm free."

"How about we try out the Gallatin Room at the Thunder Canyon Resort?"

"Oh, Thomas, that place is so fancy."

"So, let's get fancy. What do you say?"

Chapter Seven

"Dinner reservation for North."

The Gallatin Room maître d' looked up from his station, then smiled. "Ah, Dr. North. It's good to see you again."

"It's good to see you, too, Robert."

"Your table is ready, if you and your companion will follow me."

Thomas placed a hand at the small of Annabel's back, gently guiding her ahead of him as they walked deeper into the restaurant, enjoying the heat of her skin almost as much as the way she jumped at his touch.

The first time it happened she included a breathless gasp that matched his own when he'd gotten his first look at the wide expanse of skin shown by the open back of her clingy black dress. The lacy shawl she'd casually thrown over her bare shoulders and sexy black heels completed the picture.

Thomas had wanted to stop right there in her family's crowded driveway and kiss her until they were both out of breath.

The hell with the fact her parents and two sisters were probably spying on them from inside the house.

Thomas hadn't picked up a date at her parents' home since his senior prom. And according to Annabel, there were still two more sisters, their husbands and a lone brother that he hadn't met yet!

Well, that wasn't exactly true, but for the moment, for this evening, it was just him and Annabel.

As they walked past tables covered in fine white linen, candlelight and crystal centerpieces of red roses, Thomas acknowledged a few friends of his parents and fellow staff from the hospital, with a quick nod.

He didn't know if the slight kick to his gut was from being seen in the company of a beautiful woman or the fact he'd actually asked Annabel out for another date.

And that she so readily accepted.

Somewhere between the gossip and witnessing the positive effect she was having at the hospital in just a few days, Thomas found himself wanting to spend time with her and damn the consequences. A feeling he hadn't experienced in a long time.

His sudden invite had surprised him as much as it did Annabel. Impulsive decisions had never been his strong suit. Thanks to his scientific mind, he tended to think long and hard about everything, but the moment the words had left his mouth yesterday he knew he wanted tonight to happen.

"Here we are, sir." The maître d' stood to one side at the opening to a private area just off the main room, separated by a slight stairway. "The wine you requested has been laid out for you. Your server will be with you shortly."

"Thank you, Robert."

The man's slight nod told Thomas all of his plans were in place, which didn't surprise him. The Gallatin Room was a five-star eatery and one of the finest dining establishments in the entire state of Montana.

He entered the space behind Annabel in time to hear her gasp again as she stood before the floor-to-ceiling windows that looked out over the entire mountain.

"Oh, Thomas! This is glorious!"

He smiled and walked past the perfectly set table for two and joined her at the curved wall of windows. "Have you never been here before?"

She turned to face him, her hair gliding slowly across her shoulders. "Once or twice for a special occasion, but never in this spot and never with this view." Her gaze moved to the table. "Never this fancy."

"Didn't we agree *fancy* is the chosen word for to-night?" Thomas teased, pulling out the closest chair and waiting until she sat before he moved to the other side of the table.

"I think you and I have different definitions of the word." Annabel accepted the glass of wine he poured for her.

"Maybe so," Thomas said, raising his glass in a toast to her. "So I'll go with another word, *beautiful*. You look very beautiful tonight, Annabel."

Pleasure flashed in her eyes, but before she could respond their server appeared with the first course of their meal. Thomas enjoyed Annabel's confusion as a colorful salad plate was placed before her.

Once they were alone again, he reached for his own fork and dug in, but paused when he noticed Annabel hadn't moved. "What is it? Is something wrong?"

"Ah, no." She opened her cloth napkin and laid it across her lap. "Is that a Caesar salad you're having?"

"Yes, it is."

She looked at her plate again. "Mine's a garden salad without the shredded cheese, croutons or on-ions."

Thomas fought to keep his features passive. "I can see that."

"And the ranch dressing is served in a separate

dish on the side," Annabel persisted, "because there's nothing worse than soggy lettuce."

"That's an interesting reason."

"Thomas, this is exactly the way I like my salads." She leaned forward, her voice a low whisper. "What's going on?"

"Just eat," he replied, matching her tone.

"Thomas—"

He waved his salad-laden fork at her. "I heard your visit with Mr. Owens went well today."

"Yes, it did." Annabel reached for her fork. "He told me the most amazing stories about serving in the navy during the Second World War and how he met his wife in San Francisco after the war ended. Did you know she was a nurse?"

Thomas nodded around a mouthful of food, waiting until he swallowed to speak. "Yes, he mentioned you pointed out how she would expect him to be a better patient."

Annabel laughed. "I did no such thing. He's the one who made that admission. When he told me they'd shared over fifty years of marriage together I agreed that she must've known him better than anyone else in the world."

"Well, I would think so."

"Did you know they fell in love and married within a month of meeting each other?" Annabel paused to take another sip of wine, then sighed. "He told me he knew she was the one for him after their first date. Do you think it's really possible to be so sure that you want to spend your life with someone that quickly?"

"I don't know. My grandparents were married for fifty-five years, after they dated for four years first. Of course, that was because my grandfather was a freshman in college when they met and my grandmother wasn't even out of high school yet."

"My folks have been together for over thirty years. Let's hope long marriages run in the family, huh?"

Thomas's mouthful of salad lodged in his throat.

He coughed and reached for his wine, thankful that Annabel didn't notice his distress due to the amazing sunset outside that grabbed her attention.

"Are you okay?"

Okay, so she did notice. "Yeah—ah, yes, I'm fine."

They finished eating just as the server returned. The empty plates were whisked away and moments later, the main course was served with a flourish.

Annabel's eyes widened as she stared at the offering in front of her. "Surf and Turf?"

"North Atlantic lobster tail with porcini-rubbed filet mignon and apricot-glazed green beans." Thomas provided the specifics as the server silently disappeared again. "Hope it tastes as good as it looks."

"I've only had lobster and steak together a few

times, but I've always considered this combination my favorite meal in the world."

"Yes, I know." Thomas smiled and reached for the wine. "Can I refresh your glass for you?"

Annabel only nodded, holding out her glass toward him, her gaze still on the food before her.

When the idea to create a meal made of her favorite foods first came to him, Thomas wasn't sure it was a good one, but seeing Annabel's reaction was just what he'd hoped for.

"But how?" She finally looked at him after setting her glass down. "How did you know?"

"After you left the hospital yesterday I stopped by ROOTS, introduced myself to your sister Abby, and asked what your favorite foods are." He decided the direct approach was best. "Then I made arrangements to have them served tonight for us."

Annabel's gaze dropped back to the table. The candlelight danced over her shocked features and when she captured her bottom lip with her teeth, Thomas wanted nothing more than to lean across the table and release the fullness from its imprisonment.

And cover her mouth with his.

"Does this mean we're having strawberry chocolate devil's food cake for dessert?" she asked, cutting into the steak.

Thomas laughed, loving the playfulness in her eyes. "You'll just have to wait and see."

The meal was terrific and they talked while they

ate, sharing stories that covered everything from childhood experiences to college escapades. When dessert arrived, Annabel claimed she was too stuffed to eat, but the cake was perfectly sized for two and they managed to make a pretty good dent in it.

"Mmm, that is just too delicious for words," Annabel purred after sliding her fork from between her lips. "This has got to be the best meal I've ever had."

"I'm in complete agreement with you." Thomas signaled for the server, who came into the room. "Do you think we could meet the chef? We'd like to thank him for this amazing meal."

"I'll see if he's available."

A few minutes later a tall man with black hair arrived at their table. "I'm Shane Roarke, the executive chef here at the Gallatin Room."

Thomas introduced himself and Annabel, offering his compliments before his date took over the conversation as only Annabel could, with charm and grace.

"I can't believe Thunder Canyon was able to lure you away from the big city, Mr. Roarke," Annabel said after the man admitted to working in Los Angeles, San Francisco and Seattle before taking his current position at the resort.

Thomas noticed the quick tightening of the chef's jaw for a moment, but then the man blinked and it was gone. "Well, I've only been here since June, but I'm finding I like the slower pace of Thunder Canyon," Shane said. "I'm glad you enjoyed your meal."

The man left and Thomas saw Annabel's gaze follow him as he walked away. A flare of heat raced through him that could only be jealousy, but Thomas quickly squashed the emotion.

"I need to tell my cousin DJ about him," Annabel said, turning her attention back to the dessert. "I think they would get along great."

"Why's that?" Thomas asked.

"DJ owns the Rib Shack, another restaurant here in the resort. Not that he could get Mr. Roarke to work for him, but he'll probably try." She took another mouthful of cake and then laid the fork on the plate. "Oh, this really is so good, but I can't possibly eat another bite. I've probably gained five pounds from one meal."

"How about we work some of that off by dancing?"

Annabel's shocked gaze locked with his. "Dancing?"

The idea surprised Thomas just as much the moment the words left his mouth, but right now he wanted nothing more than to hold this woman in his arms.

"Why not? There's wonderful music coming from the main area and we've got plenty of room." Thomas stood and held out his hand.

"Oh, I'm not the best dancer." Annabel sat back in her chair, the candlelight highlighting the pretty blush on her cheeks. "The whole two left feet thing."

"Maybe you just haven't met the right partner yet." He waited, knowing it wouldn't take her long to match up his words with her earlier declaration about him not having met the right dog. "Dance with me, Annabel. Please."

She placed her hand in his and Thomas gently pulled her to her feet and into his arms. He easily maneuvered her until they were in front of the windows again, the star-filled night sky a beautiful backdrop to the dimly lit room.

Her left hand rested at his shoulder and he tucked her other hand in his and brought both of them to rest over his heart. The softness of her hair brushed against his jaw and he inhaled, pulling her sexy vanilla scent deep into his chest. His hand flattened across her back, seeming to startle her, but he just pressed her tighter to him, her curves wreaking havoc with his attempts at controlling his libido.

Despite all the time they'd spent together over the past two weeks, and the few times they touched, they'd never been this close.

Thomas now knew why he'd worked so hard to keep distance between them. Holding Annabel in his arms wasn't like anything he'd ever felt before.

And that scared the hell out of him.

"You are a liar, Miss Cates."

"Am I?" Her words caressed his neck with warm breaths.

"You're a wonderful dancer." Thomas lowered

his head a few inches until his cheek rested against hers. "I think you like keeping me off balance where you're concerned."

"Now why would I do that?"

He leaned back, hating how their bodies separated, but wanting to see her eyes. "I don't know. I'm normally not a man who likes surprises."

"Well then, what I'm about to say next shouldn't be a surprise," she said, looking up at him, "but I'm going to tell you anyway."

He stilled, having absolutely no idea what she was going to say.

"This has been the most magical night of my life, Thomas." Annabel gazed at him, her eyes wide. "Thank you…from the bottom of my heart."

Annabel had no idea what time it was when Thomas pulled his sleek sports car to a stop in her family's driveway.

The last time she'd looked at the glowing digits of the car's clock it had been almost eleven-thirty. That had been when they left the resort, and as hard as she tried, Annabel just couldn't keep her eyes open during the drive home.

They'd stayed at the restaurant for another hour after her heartfelt thank-you that she'd been so sure would end in a kiss.

Only she hadn't been brave enough to rise up on her tiptoes and press her mouth to his.

Instead Thomas had replied with a simple "you're welcome" and they continued to dance until coffee arrived, which they enjoyed while finishing off the last of that decadent cake.

He shut off the engine and the car stilled. She heard him turn toward her, but again, her eyelids were too heavy even though she'd love to see the expression on his face.

"Annabel?"

He spoke her name in a soft whisper that sent shivers up and down her spine. Something she'd been experiencing from the moment he walked onto her front porch dressed in a charcoal-gray suit that fit him to perfection. Heck, even her sisters had sighed as they peeked at him through the dining-room window.

"Are you asleep?" he asked, his voice back to its normal level, which was still sexy.

"No, but if I lived another mile or so away I probably would be." This time she succeeded in opening her eyes and smiled. "Did I thank you for an amazing evening?"

"Many times."

"Good." She closed her eyes and stretched, pointing her naked toes in a perfect arch. The heels had slipped off the moment she got into his car. The pair were her favorite, but she didn't wear them too often.

Or this dress, because while she loved what the

bandage-style dress did for her curves, it tended to ride up whenever she sat.

Or stretched.

The sound of the driver's side door opening and the inside light coming on had Annabel bolting upright in her seat. She grabbed the hem and yanked it back into place before looking at Thomas, but he was already out of the car.

The interior went dark again when he closed the door, but she'd found her purse, shawl and shoes by the time he walked around the car.

Sliding out of the passenger seat, she gently closed the door behind her. Except for the porch light at the kitchen door, the house was dark and the last thing she wanted was an audience when she and Thomas said good-night.

"I was going to get the door— Hey, you're shorter."

Annabel smiled and held up her shoes dangling from her fingers. "Sore tootsies."

"You okay to walk in bare feet?"

"Of course. I'm outside all the time— Thomas!" Annabel felt the ground disappear beneath her feet as Thomas lifted her into his arms and headed for the side porch.

"We can't—" he paused and cleared his throat, his grip tightening on her bare thighs "—can't take any chances."

She looped her arm around his shoulders, grateful when she didn't knock him in the head with her purse. Moments later, they stood in the soft glow of the light and he gently set her feet to the ground, his arm staying around her waist.

Her hand slid to his upper arm, but she tightened her hold, keeping their bodies close, hating that her other hand was filled with her shawl and shoes.

"There you go. Home safe and sound."

She tried to read the emotion in his gaze, but he dipped his head, the shadows making it impossible for her to see.

Did it matter?

Was he finally going to kiss her?

"Thanks for tonight," he finally said, releasing her and stepping away. "I haven't had… It was a great night."

The lump of disappointment in her throat when he made no move to give her a good-night kiss made it impossible for Annabel to speak. She could only nod as she reached for the screen door.

He stepped off the porch and she spun around, opening the inside door and slipping into the kitchen before he even made it back to the driveway.

Not knowing why she did, Annabel stood at the door and watched through the window as he climbed back into his car and started the engine.

What had gone wrong?

Tonight had been pure magic from the moment he'd picked her up. He'd been gracious with her family, attentive to the point of distraction from the first moment he touched her and that meal—who goes to the effort of making sure they had a private table, finding out a date's favorite foods...

He should've kissed her.

She should've kissed him.

She dumped her stuff on the counter beside her, her hand hovering over the light switch, and still his car stayed.

Was he waiting for her to—

She dragged her fingers downward, flipping the lever and the porch went dark. Then she twisted the lock on the door, the click echoing in the quiet.

Suddenly the car's engine cut off, and Thomas emerged, sprinting back across the drive. She undid the lock, yanked open the door and pushed at screen. Seconds later, he had her wrapped in his arms as he pushed her up against the wall, his mouth covering hers in a searing kiss.

Her hands plunged into his hair, pulling him closer and loving how his kiss was thorough, possessive and exploded with an intensity that had started the moment they met. His hands moved lower until they cupped her backside, pulling her tight to him. He leaned into her, lifted her until their bodies aligned perfectly, allowing her to feel the evidence of his arousal.

She moaned low in her throat, their tongues stroking against each other, eager to share the heat and hunger. He echoed that moan back to her with his own, and regret pulsated through her because she knew they had to stop.

Finally, he lifted his head, his hands sliding back to her waist. He pressed his forehead to hers, his rapid breathing matching her own as her hands moved to lie against the restless rise and fall of his chest.

"Wow." Annabel stole another kiss, thrilling at the groan the quick swipe of her lips over his brought forth. "Please, tell me we are going to do this again. And soon."

Thomas's laugh was husky and warm. "What's that? Go out for dinner?"

"Yeah, that, too." Especially if this man were on the menu as appetizer, main course and dessert because she was already craving another taste of heaven.

Chapter Eight

"I think you're doing what mothers do best, sticking your nose where it doesn't belong."

Annabel stilled as her father's voice carried from the kitchen to the stairway.

Wednesdays were her late days at the library so she'd taken a run without Smiley this morning—his habit of stopping at every tree made it a bit hard to maintain a good pace. When she'd returned she'd grabbed a mug of freshly brewed java and her mail from the basket in the hall before heading up the stairs to her bedroom.

Until her father's pronouncement stopped her in her tracks.

"Annabel doesn't have a lot of experience when it comes to men," came a more feminine voice—her mother. "I'm worried she's going to get hurt."

Unable to resist, Annabel sat on a step and waited, sure her sisters had shown up as well and, like the rest of the family, they'd have no problem stating their own opinions about her love life.

Or anything else, for that matter.

"Then why don't you talk to her?" Zeke Cates said. "No one else is home, including me, because I'm on my way out. You can say your piece without it becoming a major discussion."

Bless her dad. He understood how hard it was at times to be part of a big family. Annabel loved her parents and siblings, and living in the house where she grew up made financial sense, but there were times when having space to yourself and a sense of privacy were sorely lacking.

"But she'll think I'm interfering."

"You are, dear, but that's your right as her mother."

Annabel smiled at her father's parting words, knowing the following silence was her parents sharing a goodbye kiss.

Yep, there was the slam of the kitchen door.

Now, should she go back to the kitchen and find out exactly what was bothering her mother or scoot upstairs and see what Smiley was up to since he hadn't made an appearance yet? She still needed to grab a shower—

"Oh, there you are."

Busted.

Annabel took another sip of coffee, enjoying the surprise on her mother's face. "Here I am. Good morning."

"Good morning, dear." Her mother held on to her own coffee mug with a grip so tight Annabel feared the handle would crack. "How was your run?"

"It was good." Annabel eyed the clock hanging on the wall. She had plenty of time before she had to leave for work. Might as well get this over with. "So, tell me why you're so worried about me."

"Oh, Annabel...I'm sorry you overheard that." Her mother sighed. "I'm just concerned that you're falling too fast for your doctor friend."

Her doctor friend. Well, that was one way of looking at what was happening between her and Thomas. After the way he went out of his way to create such a special dinner—and the way he'd kissed her goodnight last Saturday—she'd like to think he was at least a step above being a friend.

A big step.

"Thomas and I are...getting to know one another. So I would hold off on ordering the wedding invitations just yet."

Her mother walked up the stairs and sat beside her. "You like him."

"Of course I like him. The man is smart, funny, caring and gorgeous. What's not to like?"

"I will admit he was very nice when we met him the other night, even if he did seem a bit serious. Have you seen him since your date?"

Annabel wondered where her mother was heading with that question. "Yes, of course I have."

"At the hospital."

"Yes, at the hospital. I stopped in on Monday to talk about the Tuesday and Thursday sessions I'll be having with Smiley, and I saw him again yesterday after the session."

"Are you planning to go over there today?"

As a matter of fact she was, during her dinner break. Annabel wanted to check on Mr. Owens, whose visit with Smiley yesterday was cut short because the elderly man hadn't been feeling well.

"Yes, I am, but to visit a friend, Mom. Not to see Thomas."

"Don't you think it's strange that outside of your two dates, you've only seen him at the hospital?"

"It's where he works. Not to mention where the therapy sessions take place. Doesn't it make sense that's where we would run into each other?"

"It seems to me you are the one doing all the running into, not him."

Okay, that hit home. Annabel took another sip from her mug, silently acknowledging her mother had a point.

She hadn't heard from Thomas at all on Sunday, even though he'd left with a whispered "I'll call you" after that mind-blowing, body-numbing kiss that really did make her wish she had her own place.

Stopping by his office on Monday to see Marge made sense as the secretary was coordinating Smiley's sessions. Of course, Thomas was there and he did seem happy to see her. They'd even gone down to the hospital café for a light dinner.

At her suggestion.

And he'd walked the two of them all the way to her car yesterday after she'd run into him when leaving Mr. Owens's room.

He'd teased her about parking in the farthest corner of the lot. She'd flirted back that maybe she'd been trying to lure him away from the crowds.

His smile had disappeared when he took a step closer, crowding her against her car. Annabel had been so sure he was going to kiss her again. Until Smiley had broken the spell by noticing a nearby squirrel and uncharacteristically taking off in pursuit.

Okay, so she'd only seen Thomas at the hospital the past few days, but that didn't stop the man from invading her dreams at night.

She wanted to kiss him again. She wanted more than that. The idea of stripping off that starched dress shirt and perfectly matched tie to find out just what those shoulders of his looked like—

"Annabel?"

Wow, she'd gotten lost there for a moment. "Sorry about that, Mom. Did you say something?"

"It's just that your social life has been a bit slow lately and you don't want to rush—"

"Slow?" Annabel cut off her mother's words with a sharp laugh. "Mom, I haven't dated anyone steady in over three years."

"Which is why I'm concerned that you're doing what you always do. You jump in with both feet when you believe in something, without much thought as to how difficult things might become in the future. Whether it's upgrading the children's area of the library or the therapy training with Smiley."

Yes, those projects had entailed a lot of hard work and effort on her part, coupled with more steps backward than forward at times thanks to the said "both feet" habit, but she'd accomplished both goals, quite successfully she might add. "Hey, both of those other ventures turned out fine. Better than fine."

"Well then, what about when you decided to enter the Frontier Days marathon after only running a few weeks? You ended up in the E.R. with a stress fracture. Or that spur-of-the-moment road trip you and Jazzy took last summer that found you in the middle of nowhere with a busted engine?"

Annabel let loose a deep sigh. Boy, what were mothers for if not to remind you of your shortcomings? "So let's add getting a little starry-eyed over a doctor to the list."

"I'm just worried you're setting yourself up for heartache," her mother persisted, laying a hand on her arm. "Doctors are notorious for not having happy, stable marriages. I want you to be happy, just like I want all my children to be."

Surprised at her mother's claim, Annabel could only stare at her. "That's absurd. Where did you hear that about doctors' marriages?"

"I was chatting with Mrs. Banning the other day—"

"You talked about me with the neighbors?"

"Of course not. We were just visiting and she mentioned her daughter's marriage was ending, and in a very messy way. Her husband is a surgeon. He works terrible hours and wasn't there for her or the children. Now he's decided that the woman who supported him all through medical school is too boring to spend the rest of his life with."

"I'm sorry for what Mrs. Banning's daughter is going through, but it sounds as though there are more issues with that marriage than her husband's working hours."

"Mrs. Callahan was with us, too, and she mentioned a friend whose daughter also married a doctor right here in Thunder Canyon, who was crushed when her husband recently announced he was leaving her so he could marry one of the nurses on his staff. A much younger nurse."

"Who needs reality television when the Thunder Canyon gossip mill is alive and well?" Annabel rolled her eyes. "What about Cade and Abby? Cade has his own business and he works all kind of crazy hours."

"Cade works for his family, he can set his own hours. Besides, your sister was in love with Cade for years before she, or he, ever admitted their feelings."

"And Laila?" Annabel pushed harder, bringing up her other recently married sister. "Jackson is an executive at Traub Oil Industries and from what I've heard he travels a lot. Are you telling me Laila should be worried because they only knew each other a month before getting engaged?"

"By the time your sister met Jackson she'd had more experience when it came to men than all of my girls combined, although Jazzy is giving her a good run for her money. When Jackson came to town and swept Laila off her feet, they were both ready for married life."

Annabel stood. She was *ready* for this conversation to be over. Yes, everything her mother said about her sisters was true, but that didn't mean she was heading for heartache.

"Well, you don't have to worry because Thomas and I are…I don't know what we are, but we aren't thinking about anything close to marriage. I appreciate your concern, Mom, but I'm an adult and it's my life and my decision."

"Oh, honey, I just want you to be careful with your heart."

Evelyn Cates pushed to her feet as well, and Annabel saw nothing but love and concern in her mother's gaze.

"I am being careful," she said, leaning over to give her mom a quick kiss on the cheek. "Trust me, I'm not in over my head. And neither is my heart."

Thomas was so far over his head he didn't have a clue what he was going to do.

About Annabel.

Intentionally skipping the "Smiley Session" this afternoon had been the right decision. He was a busy man with a lot of work to do, which was why he was still sitting at his desk an hour after his official workday was over. An hour after Annabel and Smiley had left the hospital, thanks to Marge's report, who was working late herself.

Because of him.

The woman never left the office until he did. He'd told her often enough that it wasn't necessary for her to stay so late. But with her husband gone and her kids moved away, Marge always said the only things waiting for her at home were three cats and they'd survive just fine without her.

Him? She wasn't so sure of.

So most nights he went home with a briefcase full

of work or he'd circle back after grabbing a quick dinner off the hospital campus.

He sighed, leaned back in his chair and scrubbed at his tired eyes. He should get the heck out of here. Reading the same paragraph over and over again in his patient's file wasn't helping the information stick in his head.

Maybe because that space was already filled with images of a perky, bubbly blonde who'd taken his breath away the moment he'd pulled her into his arms and finally kissed her.

He'd thought about little else after they'd danced at the Gallatin Room. No, that wasn't true. He'd been thinking about kissing Annabel from the moment he'd met her, but last Saturday, the need and want had been building all night. Until he couldn't take it anymore.

There'd been so many chances.

Like when they'd walked to his car after leaving the resort or when he'd pulled into her family's driveway and discovered she wasn't asleep like he'd thought. Not to mention, when he'd set her back on her feet beneath the porch light after he'd carried her to the front door, her body brushing the length of his.

He'd taken none of those openings, having decided during the few minutes it took to reach her front porch it was best to keep things simple. Say good-night and leave. He managed to do both, but only made it as far as turning on the engine, before the porch light went out after Annabel got inside.

He'd missed his chance.

Seconds later, he'd been racing across the yard. The way the door opened immediately said she'd been watching him—waiting. It fanned the flames of his desire for her even higher.

The sureness of how it felt to hold her had taken its time to settle in, thanks to the passion of that kiss, but when it had, Thomas knew he had to get out of there. So he'd given a simple promise to call and then left.

Only he'd never called.

He'd seen Annabel on Monday here at the hospital and they'd grabbed a quick bite together down in the café—not the most private venue—and of course he heard about it the next day from a few colleagues. And while he'd purposely dropped by Mr. Owens's room on Tuesday to see how the visit went with Smiley, he hadn't planned on walking her and her dog out to the parking lot.

It'd just been so easy to talk to her. Thomas rose from behind his desk and walked to the window, drawn to the vivid reds and oranges of the setting sun.

No matter what the subject, Annabel made him feel relaxed and comfortable. Not to mention the crackle of sexual energy that seemed to surround her, a deep pulsing pull that called to him every time he saw her.

But late Tuesday night, after he found himself lying alone in his bed, wishing she was with him and, in turn, had berated himself for feeling that way again, he'd realized the simple truth.

Being with Annabel scared him silly.

Not that he was *with* her.

Two dinners and spending time together at the hospital didn't exactly make them a couple. Of course, Marge or some of the staff didn't need much more than to see them together in the hospital café to come to that conclusion.

Getting involved in a relationship again was the last thing he wanted, or needed, at the moment. He still felt he had to prove himself, to right the wrongs of his past, but he was having a hell of time keeping Annabel out of his head.

"So, what'll it be tonight?"

Marge's voice from the open doorway cut into his thoughts. He turned and found her flipping through the notebook she kept of take-out menus from the local restaurants.

"Chinese or Mexican?" she continued, not looking up at him. "Or are you not planning to stick around much longer?"

He didn't get a chance to choose.

"Mmm, go with the Chinese. The kung pao chicken at Mr. Lee's is to die for."

The lilting voice from his dreams drew his attention past his secretary. "Annabel. What are you doing here?"

Silence filled the air for a moment until Marge cleared her throat. "I think I'll just go down to the lounge and get myself a cup of hot tea. Annabel, would you like anything?"

"No, thanks, Marge, but I appreciate the offer."

Marge smiled at Annabel, shot him a quick wink over her shoulder that caused his stomach to drop to his feet and left the office area.

Oh, hell, maybe it was the sight of Annabel walking toward him in a simple cotton skirt, tank top and wedged heels that did that.

Or the fire-engine red polish on her toes.

He bit back a groan and forced his gaze back above her neckline. "So, what brings you this way so late?"

Annabel waved what looked like the remains of a tattered teddy bear in the air. "I had to come back for Smiley's baby."

Her words threw him. "Excuse me?"

"I know it doesn't look like much now, but this stuffed bear came with Smiley from the shelter." As she glanced down at the toy, her long golden curls tumbled over one shoulder. "He carried it around for weeks after I first brought him home. Then he seemed to only need the thing when he went to sleep."

She offered a quick shrug, and continued, "I don't know why he brought it with him to today's session, but once we got home I realized he'd left it behind. I had to run a few errands anyway. When I pulled into the parking lot, I saw your light was on, so I thought I'd stop by and see if you wanted to grab some dinner…"

Her voice trailed off when she looked at him again. Thomas swallowed hard at the mixture of desire and awareness he read in her blue eyes as their gazes locked. And just like that his world tilted off balance as uncontrolled need and want washed over him again.

Shoving his hands deep in his pockets, Thomas broke free and looked away. "Annabel, I'm not sure that is such a good idea."

"What's not a good idea? Chinese? Hey, if you want Mexican, that's fine with me. I'm easy."

Damn it, the last thing she was doing was making this easy.

Control.

He needed to get this situation back under control, back to what he was used to, a place of organization—of having power over one's actions and emotions.

A place that was familiar to him, ever since his mother pulled him aside after his grandfather's accident and told him tears were not allowed. At the tender age of seven, she'd expected him to handle what happened to his grandfather with the same dignity and grace that the Norths handled everything else.

Which probably explained why he'd thrown himself into his studies, determined that when he became a doctor, no one else would suffer the way his grandfather had. Of course, he'd learned the hard way that doctors weren't miracle workers, but he had a pretty damn good track record so far, at least here at TC General.

If his affair with Victoria had taught him anything, it was that he had the tendency of letting a woman's beauty blind him to everything else around. Considering his lack of judgment and having to learn to live with the regret, the last thing he wanted was to make the same mistake.

He faced her again. "I've got a lot of work ahead of me and now that your dog therapy sessions are in place, I don't think— It's just that my free time is going to be very limited."

Barely a heartbeat passed before Annabel offered him a bright smile. "Oh. Well, you've obviously given this a lot of thought." Her cheery tone and calm acceptance were the last things he expected. "I don't want to make things…difficult for you. I'll just go and let you get back to work."

Thomas wanted to speak, even though he had no idea what else to say. Not that it mattered. His throat was so constricted he could barely breathe.

A nod was all he managed.

She quickly backed up until she reached the door. "So, I guess I'll see you when I see you."

Then she was gone.

Thomas stood rooted to the spot, his blood pounding in his temples at he stared at the empty space. Had he really just told a beautiful and fascinating woman he wasn't interested?

He waited for the cool detachment that told him he'd done the right thing to bring relief that it was over. It was nowhere to be found. In its place instead was an overwhelming rush of regret and panic that filled every ounce of his being.

"Dr. North?"

The sharp tone in Marge's voice caused his head to snap up.

How long had she been standing there? How long had he been standing here staring at the doorway like a fool?

He started to ask, but had to pause and clear his throat first. "Ah, I don't know how much of that you overheard, but for some reason I think I should—"

"Go."

With one word the despair shifted to hope. "She has no reason to let me—"

"What she has is a good head start." Marge folded her hands primly over her stomach. "And you're without a car today, if memory serves. Go."

Thomas automatically reached across his desk for his phone and house keys. "I need to shut down—"

"Turning off a computer, the lights and locking your door is within my scope of abilities." She made a show of glancing at her watch. "If you're not back in fifteen minutes, I'm going home."

Sprinting past his secretary, Thomas headed for the stairs. He raced outside and into the parking lot, praying Annabel was a creature of habit and had parked in the same location as before.

He hoped he hadn't ruined his chance with her. If he had, he'd have a lot of making up to do.

Chapter Nine

Annabel couldn't believe how much Thomas's words hurt.

She'd thought things were going so well between them. They hadn't run into each other when she popped in to check on Mr. Owens yesterday, and while she'd hoped to see him today at Smiley's session, it never occurred to her that he'd been avoiding her.

Obviously it hadn't come to mind or she'd have never made the effort to seek him out tonight.

Coming back for Smiley's toy hadn't been an urgent issue. The dog hadn't even noticed it was gone, but Annabel foolishly took it as a sign.

So she'd changed her clothes, spritzed her wrists and cleavage with her favorite perfume and hopped back in her car, daydreaming about more alone time with Thomas and hoping she'd have the good fortune of finding him still at the hospital.

Oh, she'd found him all right.

Shoving the ratty teddy bear in her bag, Annabel marched across the parking lot, proud that she'd at least stayed cool during his little speech and walked away with her head held high.

Okay, so she walked fast once she left his office, but still she managed to keep it together in the elevator, thankful she hadn't run into anyone. She still didn't understand what drove him to say what he did, but the bottom line was the coming days would be empty without him.

The tears began to well in her eyes.

"Hey, wait!"

A voice calling from behind her, followed by hands closing over her shoulders, sent a rush of panic through her. A quick, sharp jab with her elbow was on the mark, punctuated by a male grunt and she was free. Spinning around, keys laced between her fingers, Annabel took a defensive stance ready to scream—

"Thomas!" She dropped her hands, but not before quickly swiping the remaining moisture from her eyes. "Are you crazy? I could have stabbed you with my keys!"

"I'm sorry…didn't mean to scare you." He puffed out the words while rubbing his hand across his mid-section. "That was a stupid…stupid thing to do."

At least the man was right about something to-night.

Annabel folded her arms under her breasts, tried to slow her runaway breathing while telling herself he deserved the hard poke to the gut. "Yes, it was."

"No, I don't mean grabbing you— Well, yes, that was dumb, too." He dropped his hand, but then propped both on his hips. "I'm talking about what happened in my office. I don't know what I was say-ing. I mean, I know what I said. I heard the words coming out of my mouth. It's just that I've been doing a lot of thinking the past couple of weeks, hell, the past couple of years. Probably too much thinking, but I've been that way since I was a kid."

Annabel blinked hard and tried to keep up with Thomas's ramblings. He didn't mean to scare her, but he did follow her out here. Pretty quickly, too, as she'd only walked out of his office less than ten minutes ago.

She ignored the sharp thrill that zinged through her.

"The thing is, I think I was too hasty. It's just that I've been trying to work through some things from the past and what's been going on between us. You know, weighing the good, the bad, lessons learned, and all that stuff. The next thing I knew you were standing there—"

"Thomas, stop!"

Annabel took a leap of faith that she finally understood what this man was trying to say.

He did as she asked, but the silence only made his words a bigger jumbled mess in her head. She didn't want to sort through them right now. Not with him standing right there in front of her.

Grabbing his already loosened tie, and throwing her concerns—and her mother's admonitions—to the wind, she wrapped it once around her palm and yanked him up against her. "Are you going to kiss me or what?"

He blinked owlishly, then relief filled his eyes, his hooded gaze dropping to her lips. "God, yes."

She didn't wait, but instead rose to her toes and covered his mouth with hers before pulling back just enough to gently suck his lower lip between hers.

His large, capable hands circled her waist, holding her in place as a deep groan rumbled in his chest. He quickly took over, ravishing her mouth with hot, deep skims of his tongue against hers. She boldly matched his every move, surrendering to the craziness of the moment.

And it was crazy.

He pressed her up against her car door, his hips brushing in a slow back and forth motion that brought forth a husky moan of her own. A delicious ache for more, much more, filled her, spreading like wildfire until every corner of her body vibrated with need.

His mouth slipped from hers, his lips trailing across her cheek to her ear. "I know how insane this sounds, but I want you, Annabel."

A victorious thrill raced through her and she couldn't hold back the nervous giggle that escaped. "Well, I would say your place or mine, but I'm afraid my father would be blocking your path, his shotgun firmly in hand."

Thomas leaned back, an unreadable emotion in his eyes. Then he blinked and it was replaced with an amused gleam. "Then I guess we'd better go to my place. Problem is my car is in the shop."

Annabel jiggled her keys in front of him. "You know, I'm not even going to ask how you planned to get home tonight. You want to drive or play navigator?"

He gave her a crooked grin as he slipped the keys from her hand. "We can decide that later, but for now, it'll be faster if I drive."

Less than fifteen minutes later they pulled into his condo's garage, located in an upscale complex Annabel had never been to before. When he went to shut off the engine, she slipped her fingers from his, smiling at how they'd became entangled in the first place. Seemed a little teasing finger action back and forth across his powerful thigh was too much of a distraction for the sexy doctor.

But she couldn't help herself.

The man drove her quirky little bug as if it was a luxury car, with purpose and speed. What could she say? It was a turn-on.

"Nice place," she said, popping out of the passenger side as the garage door slid silently closed behind them.

"It's just the garage," Thomas shot back, taking her hand again as he headed for the stairs. "Wait until you see the master bedroom."

At the top of the stairs, he opened a door and wrapping his arm around her waist, pulled her close and kissed her again. She clung to him as he walked her backward into what she guessed was the front foyer.

He broke free of their kiss and flipped on the lights. She blinked as everything came into focus. Then she gazed around in curiosity.

Soft lighting highlighted fine leather furniture and the shiny chrome and glass tables that sat atop an oversize plush Oriental rug her toes itched to dig into. The best "boy toys" money could buy filled the room, as well. An enormous flat-screen TV hung over an empty fireplace while nearby floor-to-ceiling bookshelves held numerous black boxes that must be a high-end stereo system.

Gleaming hardwood floors stretched the length of the room, including a dining area with a table big enough to seat six. Off to the left, she saw a kitchen.

His home was beautiful, but her first thought was "professional decorator." She wondered how much of Thomas was even reflected here.

"Please don't tell me you want a tour." He nuzzled her from behind, his lips warm against her neck, and Annabel was glad she'd secured her hair to one side with a large clip. "If so, let's start with the second floor."

She couldn't agree more, with one minor change.

Facing him again, she dropped her purse to the floor and quickly stripped off his tie, tossing it to one side. "Oh, I think we'll start—and finish—right here."

It seemed to take a moment for Thomas to get her meaning, but once he did, he lifted her in his arms and headed straight for the sofa.

Anticipation flooded her insides as she kicked off her shoes along the way, waiting until he sat, her straddling his lap before she leaned in and captured his mouth again.

Just like she'd hoped to do in his office.

While their mouths tasted and nipped, devoured and shared, her fingers went to work on the buttons of his dress shirt, releasing them all the way to his waist. Yanking the material open as far as it would go, she reveled in the feel and heat of his naked chest, at the way he jumped at her touch.

Time to get serious.

When she lightly dragged her fingernails over

his nipples, his hands gripped her hips, cradling her heated center over the thick ridge of his arousal. The loose swing of her skirt made sure that the only barrier between her nakedness and the silkiness of his slacks were the simple thong panties she wore. Unable to resist, she rotated her hips in a slow circle.

"Damn, that feels good," he rasped, breaking free of their kiss. "You feel good."

Their eyes met and held as he gently pulled her tank top free from the skirt's waistband, his hands slowly sliding underneath and up over her belly. He kept going, taking the material with him until she had no choice but to raise her arms as he tugged the top over her head.

While her hands were raised, she'd reached back and freed her hair, loving the heat in his eyes as her breasts pressed against the bra's lacy cups. Shaking her head sent loose waves flying over her shoulders, but it was the way his fingertips traced the delicate straps of her bra that sent shivers dancing over her skin.

"You cold?" His words came out in rough whisper. "The air-conditioning is pretty strong."

"I think it's more about what you're doing to me than artificial cooling." He proved her point when he caught the lobe of her ear gently between his teeth and another shudder rolled through her. "Oh, see what I mean?"

"Here, let's get you warm." In one swift move, he

had her flat on her back against the cool, soft leather of his sofa as he stretched out over her.

Soft except for the object pressing into her lower back.

"What the—" Annabel reached beneath her and pulled out a large rectangular object covered in buttons of all shapes, sizes and colors.

He took the device from her and tossed it to the side. "It's just my remote."

She gave a half laugh, lowering her voice to a purr. "A remote for what?"

Thomas deftly pulled down the zipper of her skirt while his lips left behind a trail of wet kisses over her collar bone. He then returned his focus to the lace edging of her bra, his tongue dipping inside the delicate border to wet the skin beneath. "Everything."

As sinfully wonderful as his focus was, Annabel persisted. "Everything?"

He groaned and lifted his head, bracing himself on one elbow. "Don't tell me you really want to know?"

Annabel shifted, his erection now in perfect alignment between her thighs. "Mmm, impress me."

"I thought I was."

She laughed, and he joined her, his deep chuckle vibrating the length of her body and at that moment, as sure as if her heart had flipped over and displayed the words *I Belong to Thomas North* etched in a pretty scrolled font, she knew.

She was in love with this crazy, wonderful man.

It wasn't a sentiment she had a lot of experience with, but the pure joy and elation pouring from her heart was something she planned to embrace with both hands and never let go of.

He surprised her when he reached over, picked the remote up and placed it back in her hand. "Press the numbers 3-1-7-3 on the bottom keypad."

Annabel did as instructed, focusing on the device. The last thing she wanted was Thomas to see the newfound emotion going off like skyrockets inside her before she had a chance to examine the feeling.

In private.

As soon as she pressed the last number, a fire blazed to life in the fireplace, blanketing the room with dancing shards of light and a warm glow.

"Oh!"

His lips nibbled up the side of her neck. "Now enter 6-8-7-4-2."

Her fingers shook as she pushed the correct buttons and seconds later a faint beep filled the air, before it was replaced with the smooth strains of classic jazz flowing from the stereo.

"Okay, I'm officially impressed." Annabel blinked hard, refusing to allow her head, or her heart, to even imagine Thomas showing these tricks to someone else. Mentally shaking off that thought, she playfully pointed the remote at him. "Now, what's the magic combination that works on you?"

A smile tipped one corner of his sensual mouth as he took the device from her hand and tossed it farther away this time in the direction of the closest chair. "I think you already know what buttons to press."

He pushed up to his knees and peeled off his shirt. Annabel found herself thankful for the fire's glow that showed off his wide shoulders and washboard abs to perfection. Next was his belt and darn if he didn't take his time letting the strip of leather slide from his belt loops.

Loosening the button at his waist, he reached for the zipper, but she brushed his hand away and slowly lowered the zipper.

She only caught a glimpse of dark boxer briefs and the length of him pressing against the material before he reached for her, tugging gently at her skirt. Raising her hips, he eased the material down over her legs, leaving her in nothing but her bra and matching panties.

"You are perfection, Annabel."

The naked desire in his gaze called to her. She crooked her finger in a come-hither motion and he quickly complied, molding his hard planes with her curves.

He took her mouth again as his fingers nimbly opened the front clash of her bra, his warm hand cupping her breast. His thumb rasped over the hardened bud, drawing it even tighter until he ended the kiss and drew the peak into the moist heat of his mouth.

A blast of shameless need flared deep inside her. Annabel arched, offering him more, and he took, moving his mouth from one breast to the other, leaving behind a shimmering wetness that tingled in the cool night air.

She reached low, her fingers brushing across his stomach as the need to touch him overpowered her. He shuddered when she slipped beneath the cotton waistband and curled around him. She stroked him once, twice, before he pulled her hand away.

"Don't," he rasped. "It's been…a while since I've done this."

His words made her heart soar. He released her wrist and she clutched at his shoulders as his fingers easily moved aside the damp material covering the most imitate part of her before slipping into her wet heat.

"Oh, for me, too. Thomas, please…"

Moments later, the rest of their clothes disappeared and Thomas paused only to sheathe himself with a condom he grabbed from his wallet. Then he was back between her legs, cupping her bottom and tilting her hips. He entered her with a long, slow thrust, capturing her gasp with his mouth.

Their bodies moved together in a natural, instinctive rhythm. A burning caught fire deep inside her, growing stronger and stronger, taking her higher with each demanding stroke.

Those same fireworks she'd felt deep inside from

the moment they met threatened to explode, shattering her heart and soul in a million colorful pieces.

His lips moved to her neck, whispering words against her skin, pushing her even higher as she dragged her nails over his back, demanding the sweet release only he could give.

Then the fuse of her passion ignited, sending her spiraling into the heavens. She clung to him, crying out his name, loving the moment when he gave up his last remnant of control, buried himself deep inside her, joining her.

They lay there together afterward, trying to catch their breaths and failing when he pressed his lips to the pulsing in her neck and she tightened around him.

Annabel had never known a moment like this before in her life. Was it because her heart had already laid claim to this charming, honest and dedicated man?

Her wonder was interrupted by their stomachs suddenly rumbling in sync. She laughed aloud, the sweetness of the moment almost too much to bear. "Boy, I guess you do want dinner."

"I'm starved." Thomas lifted himself off her while flashing a grin of total male satisfaction as he helped her sit up. "Even more so now."

"Chinese from Mr. Lee's still sounds good to me."

"Me, too." Thomas reached for his pants, pulled out his cell phone and hit the speed dial number. "Any special requests?"

"I'm happy with anything."

He rattled off a list of appetizers, his arched brows silently asking for her approval with each item. Annabel nodded in agreement as she scooped up her clothes, suddenly wishing for a light blanket to throw over her naked body.

Not that she was ashamed of being like this with him, but Thomas had been right. The air-conditioning was going at full blast and the air was chilly despite the fire.

Or was it reality setting in?

Goodness knows, she had no idea where things were headed between them now, other than dinner and hopefully more moments like what they just shared.

But what did this mean to Thomas?

She still wasn't sure exactly what he'd been trying to tell her back in his office, or the parking lot. Did he want more? Did he want her? Could he possibly love her in return?

"Okay, we're all set."

Thomas's words pulled her from her thoughts. He stood, the cool air obviously not affecting him, and then before she realized what he was doing, he easily lifted her into his arms.

"Hey!"

"You think I'm going to let some high school delivery boy get an eyeful by staying downstairs? No way." He gave her a quick squeeze. "Besides, we've got twenty minutes until the food gets here."

Annabel laughed again. "You've got to stop carrying me around."

"You feel…good in my arms."

She cupped his face with both hands and placed a chaste kiss, one that carried all the love in her heart, on his mouth. He carried her up the stairs to his bedroom and laid her on the silky comforter. Never breaking eye contact, Thomas lowered his mouth to hers, returning her kiss with one that was just as soft and sweet, even more so because of the slight tremble when his lips met hers.

Sunlight tried to make its way through the room-darkening shades with little success. Exactly how Thomas preferred it on those few mornings when he tried to sleep in.

Like today. Lying on his stomach, he cracked open one eye to focus on his bedside clock: 8:00 a.m.

Blinking hard, he looked again. That had to be wrong. For him, sleeping in usually meant staying in bed until six, six-thirty at the latest.

Nope, the numbers were an eight, a zero and now a one.

He bolted upright, coming to a fast realization of two things. The first, he was alone in his king-size bed, even though that's not the way he'd gone to sleep last night. The second was the aroma of frying bacon hovering in the air.

Annabel.

He quickly grabbed his cell phone from the bedside table, and checked his calendar. He breathed a sigh of relief. Yes, his first appointment of the day wasn't scheduled until noon.

Pulling on a pair of briefs and sweats, he stopped to use the bathroom and brush his teeth. After tossing his toothbrush back into the holder, he paused and stared into the mirror, his reflected image blurring as he thought back to the madness and passion that had consumed him last night.

They hadn't even made it past his living-room sofa that first time. Not that he was complaining. Being with Annabel had been amazing, and afterward, they'd spent the rest of the night in his bed, sharing Chinese takeout, a bottle of wine and each other.

Not the evening he'd thought he'd have after the way he'd fumbled through explaining his "I'm too busy" speech. A decision that hadn't lasted all of five minutes before he chased after her. Did she understand any of what he'd tried to say? Both in his office and in the parking lot?

Hell, he wasn't sure *he* understood the logic and reasoning that still swirled inside his head when it came to her, them.

But she'd dismissed his ramblings with a hard

kiss, and he'd thrown caution, and control, out the window.

Yet again. Letting down his guard like that was something he hadn't done since—

Refusing to confuse things even more with thoughts of the past, Thomas stalked out of the bathroom and followed his nose downstairs. He started across the living room when he noticed a blanket draped over one of the chairs—a patchwork quilt, done up in rectangular-shaped blocks in shades of brown, dark red, black and beige that reminded him of the glass-tile pattern in his kitchen. Tucked into the folds of material was a dog-eared copy of a romance novel featuring a half-naked cowboy on the cover.

"Good morning, sleepyhead." Annabel strolled in from the kitchen, looking impossibly sexy wearing only his wrinkled dress shirt from last night and her long hair pulled back in a messy ponytail. "You saved me a trip back upstairs to get you. Hope you're hungry."

She set two plates piled with scrambled eggs, bacon and buttered toast on his dining-room table, drawing his eye to the vase brimming with daisies perched in the middle.

Daisies?

He hadn't realized he had that much food in his kitchen, but he was quite certain the flowers hadn't been there at all.

"Ah, yeah, I'm starved." Thomas ignored the quick twist in his gut and held up the quilt. "Where'd this come from?"

"I made it." Her voice carried over her shoulder as she disappeared back into the kitchen, and then returned with glasses of orange juice and silverware. "Pretty, isn't it?"

"Yes, but what's it doing here?"

"I couldn't figure out how to lower your air-conditioning when I got up this morning." She sat at the table and motioned for him to join her. "So I grabbed it from my car to wrap around myself. Come on, let's eat before all of this gets cold."

"The food and the flowers came out of your car, as well?"

A piece of bacon stilled halfway to her mouth. "Is that a problem?"

"No, just curious." Proud of his causal tone, Thomas sat opposite her.

"When I went to get the quilt I remembered I stopped at the store last night before coming to the hospital. The flowers needed water and I thought the groceries could camp out in your fridge until I left." She took a bite. "Then I saw the inside of your fridge and figured a healthy breakfast was needed. You do know those things are made to hold food, right?"

He smiled and the knot in his stomach eased.

Everything Annabel said made perfect sense. It

just threw him at how easily those things seemed at home here.

How easily she fit into his home.

And how much he liked it.

Chapter Ten

Three days later, Thomas stepped out of his car, having parked at the far end of the already-crowded driveway at the Cates family ranch.

Tightening his grip on the bottle of wine and the bouquet of flowers he'd brought, he silently counted the number of cars and pickup trucks scattered around.

Six in total, which meant at least two more would be coming. Sunday dinner with Annabel's family.

Her entire family.

Fighting the urge to turn and bolt, he forced himself to keep walking forward, remembering how Annabel had offered the invite just last night.

They'd been lying together on his couch watching their second choice in a classic black-and-white movie night. The screwball romantic comedy featuring Lucille Ball had been Annabel's choice after viewing one of his favorite Jimmy Stewart dramas.

Her words had been casual, not even glancing away from the movie as she spoke, but Thomas could tell by the way her arm had tightened over his stomach how much she wanted him to say yes.

And the sparkle in her eyes when he had accepted.

A thank-you kiss followed, and they never saw the closing credits of the movie. She'd finally left in the wee hours of the morning.

They spent the past three evenings together at his place, but thanks to Smiley, who was like a child to Annabel, she hadn't slept over again since that first night. Not that her family minded taking care of the dog, she assured him. She'd shared the text message she'd sent on Thursday to her sister Jazzy, asking her to make sure Smiley was fed and let outside in the morning, but Smiley was her dog, her responsibility.

Knowing she couldn't stay hadn't cooled their lovemaking; if anything the time they spent in his bed had been hotter and sexier because they didn't have all night to be together.

Still, Thomas found himself tempted to tell Annabel to bring Smiley with her the next time she came over if it meant he could hold her in his arms all night.

And didn't that rock the already wobbly ground beneath his feet?

Walking up to the same kitchen door where he'd kissed her like crazy a week ago, Thomas remembered Annabel's light quip the first night they'd made love about how her father would've been waiting with a shotgun. He hadn't been quite sure if she'd been joking or serious, but now he pushed those thoughts from his head. Thinking about sex and Annabel at this moment probably wasn't a good idea.

Looking down at the wine and flowers in his hands, he wondered again if they were a good idea. Raised by parents who always insisted a gift for the hostess was a requirement, he'd felt strange leaving his house empty-handed.

So he'd turned around and gone back, grabbed a bottle from his private collection and stopped along the way to pick up the flowers, just in case her parents didn't drink wine.

A deep breath, pulled in through his nose and slowly released, helped a little, but not as much as he'd hoped.

Damn, he shouldn't be this nervous.

Having already met half of her family, how bad could it be to spend an afternoon with all of them?

"Psst! Hey, doc. Over here."

Thomas turned and saw Annabel standing at the far end of the porch. She sent him a saucy grin and signaled for him to join her. He did and she took his face in her hands and pulled him close, their lips meeting in a long, slow kiss that Annabel tried to deepen, but he held back.

"Spoilsport," she teased.

"With the size of your family? And your father's shotgun? I think not."

She laughed. "You just keep on impressing me, Dr. North."

Thomas again refused to let his mind wander back to how he'd impressed her on the couch, in his bed and beneath the dual-headed shower over the weekend.

She stepped back and he admired the simple sundress she wore, bright colors splashed in a wavy, tie-dyed pattern that seemed perfect for the hot August afternoon. He was already sweating beneath his collared shirt, despite the short sleeves, but he doubted that had anything to do with the temperature.

"You know, when I invited you here today I forgot to ask you one thing."

The seriousness of her tone got his attention. "What's that?"

"Who's your favorite baseball team?"

That's what she needed to know? "Ah, the Dodgers, I guess."

"Hmm, Dad and Brody are Rockies fans. Well, it should be okay. We're still a few weeks out from the start of football."

"The preseason is already under way."

She waved off his words. "Preseason games don't count. Not around here."

Thomas didn't realize she was such a fan of professional sports. "Tell that to the guys on the field."

"Who's your favorite team?"

He guessed they were still talking about football. "The Broncos, of course."

Annabel graced him with a bright smile and grabbed his arm. "Perfect! Let's go join the others."

Instead of going inside the house, Annabel led him around the backyard and to a large stone patio. Numerous chairs sat scattered around a raised fire pit, piled with fresh cut wood. Two steps led up to the main area where tables, one covered in an array of dishes, and more chairs filled the space.

Another gut check and a deep reach for confidence. How could one family have so many members?

"Dr. North." Zeke Cates, Annabel's father, rose from one of the chairs and greeted them first. "Glad you could make it. It's good to see you again."

Thomas quickly maneuvered the flowers and wine into one hand so he could take the older man's outstretched one. "It's good to see you, too. Thank you for including me, Mr. Cates. And please call me Thomas."

The man's sharp gaze moved between Thomas and Annabel. He tightened his grip and held it for a long moment before releasing him. "You know anything about barbecuing, Thomas?"

Not sure if he remembered Zeke's greeting being quite so strong the first time they met, Thomas resisted the urge to flex his fingers. "Ah, no, sir. Not much."

"That's too bad. Dad can use all the help he can get." A younger version of Annabel's father walked past, a plate piled high with uncooked steaks, burgers and hot dogs in his hands. "Hey, we can use his surgical precision when it comes to slicing the meat."

"That's Brody, one of my many annoying siblings," Annabel said with a grin.

Thomas nodded and acknowledged the younger man he guessed to be in his early twenties with a wave. The flowers started to slip from his grip but then he realized Annabel had reached for them. He released his hold on the bouquet, but held tight to the bottle of wine.

"Oh, aren't these pretty!" She buried her nose in the fragrant stems. "Yellow roses, white mums and my favorites, daisies."

A whisper of unease tagged Thomas as he glanced at the flowers. He hadn't noticed the specific types in the cluster when he grabbed them at the local florist in town.

Daisies again?

"So, you've already figured out my daughter's favorite flowers? How sweet." Evelyn Cates joined them and, thanks to his training, Thomas immediately picked up on the hint of anxiety in her tone. The older woman placed a hand on her daughter's arm. "Annabel, let's go find a vase for those."

"Actually, the flowers are for you, ma'am." Thomas slipped the tissue-wrapped bunch from Annabel's grip and presented them, along with the wine, to her mother. "And this is from a winery that's been in my family, on my mother's side, for years. I hope you enjoy it."

"Thank you." The strain around the woman's mouth eased for a moment, but when she looked at Annabel, the lines deepened and her smile appeared forced. "This was very kind of you."

Still confused, Thomas looked at Annabel hoping she wasn't upset over the flowers, but she offered him a full-blown smile that he felt all the way to his toes as she leaned into him, giving his arm a squeeze.

"Annabel?" Her mother headed toward the double glass doors. "You coming?"

"Don't worry, we won't scare off the good doctor while you're gone." Jazzy, one of the two sisters Thomas had already met, stepped outside through the same doors. "Annabel, I'm letting Smiley out. He started freaking out as soon as he spotted— Oops, watch out!"

The warning came too late as seconds later Thomas let out a rush of air when two large paws landed right on his stomach.

"Smiley!" Annabel cried out and reached for the dog's collar. "Get down!"

"It's all right." Brushing her hand away, Thomas gently lifted the dog's paws, forcing the animal to rest back on his haunches. "Sit," he added, trying for a stern tone, just in case a verbal command was needed.

The dog obeyed, but stayed in the middle of all of them, tail wagging wildly, his attention solely on Thomas, with a few side glances at his owner.

Returning the dog's grin, Thomas reached down and scratched behind his ears. "Hey there, Smiley. Good to see you, boy."

"Well, you seem to have a fan," her father said.

"Oh, Smiley just loves Thomas." Annabel bent and gave Smiley a quick kiss on the snout. "Don't you, baby?"

Annabel's mother whirled around and hurried to the house.

Annabel sighed softly and looked at him. "I better see if she needs any help."

He gave her a quick nod and she left.

"So, what's your poison, doc?" Jordyn Leigh, the other sister who still lived at home and was here last Saturday, too, stood at a nearby table holding a bottle of beer in one hand, a pitcher of iced tea in the other.

The beer would've been great, bathing his dry throat with its tangy coldness but Thomas decided to play it safe. Moments later, he found himself sitting with Jazzy and Jordyn Leigh, a glass of iced tea in his hand and Smiley at his side.

Annabel's dad had joined his son at the oversize grill, keeping watch over their dinner as they argued about last night's Colorado Rockies game and the proper way to cook the steaks.

"Will you two knock it off?" a feminine voice called out from behind Thomas. "Jackson, go over there and play referee."

Thomas stood when four more people joined them, assuming the tall blonde and pretty brunette were the last two Cates siblings.

"Hi, Jackson Traub, glad to meet you." A tall man wearing a Stetson held out his hand, his voice laced with a Texas twang. "I'm Laila's husband and it seems the designated arbitrator for this afternoon's festivities."

"Thomas North." He returned the handshake, liking Jackson's easygoing manner. "And is that really necessary?"

"In this family, you bet. I'm Laila," his wife said, taking Thomas's hand next after handing off a foil-covered bowl to one of her sisters. "It's nice to finally meet the man who's been making my little sister even more bubbly than usual."

"We're all your little sisters," the woman standing beside her said. "Even if Annabel has the market cornered on bubbly. Hi there, Thomas," Abby said. "This is my husband, Cade Pritchett."

Thomas shook her hand first and then her husband's. "Nice to meet you, Cade."

"You're looking a little shell-shocked, North." Jackson Traub grabbed a beer from a nearby ice bucket as his wife and Abby moved away to fuss over the food table. "I remember the feeling well."

Thomas was surprised by the frank assessment. "Is it that obvious?"

"Only to someone who was in your shoes this time last year." The man headed for the barbecue, but then turned back. "Hey, thanks for all you've done for my cousin. The entire family appreciates the surgery you did on Forrest."

"I haven't heard from him in a while. Hope things are going well."

"Me, too," Jackson replied, his voice a bit cryptic as he joined the men grill-side.

Soon the three were debating loudly the finer points of cooking over an open fire, with both an oversize spatula and tongs being used for emphasis.

"Come on, doc," Cade said, grabbing a beer for himself. "We should probably join them. Just in case medical attention is needed."

Thomas took his iced tea with him just so he'd have something to do with his hands, and walked across the patio with Cade.

Minutes later, the noise level grew as the conversation switched from cooking to the current standings of their favorites baseball teams. Jackson was the lone holdout with his assurance of the Texas Rangers being play-off bound, but his opinion was voted down so boisterously that Thomas decided just to keep his mouth shut where his Dodgers were concerned.

The men shot statistics and scores back and forth until finally Jackson bet a prized saddle against one of Zeke's horses on the outcome of the World Series.

"I won't hesitate to take that beauty off your hands," Zeke said. "Doesn't matter if you're married to my daughter or not."

"And I'm looking forward to adding that stallion to my growing collection," Jackson shot back. "In fact, I might take him out for a run after dinner. Thomas, do you ride?"

Surprised at the question, Thomas glanced quickly at the feet of all four men. All wore cowboy boots that looked well loved and lived in. Not quite the same as his Italian leather loafers.

"Ah, I haven't in a while," he finally said, realizing he still hadn't answered the question. "Not since my days at boarding school."

Silence filled the air for a moment before Evelyn called out, asking for the status on the meat as everything else was ready. Thomas stepped back as the men all turned to the grill and in fluid movements that showed they'd worked together before, quickly gathered the food that was fully cooked.

Soon everyone was seated around the largest

table; a radio perched nearby was tuned to the local country-music station. After shooing Smiley out of the way, Annabel patted a chair next to her for Thomas to take, handing him a plastic plate and a matching set of silverware. Platters of meat and bowls of salads were passed around and he was encouraged to take whatever he wanted as arms reached back and forth across the table.

Someone spilled a drink, good-natured insults followed and a couple of flying pretzels joined in the mix. The banter flowed from sports to the economy to politics. Everyone talked at once, speaking over each other with no one afraid to voice their opinion no matter what the topic.

Thomas didn't know what to make of it all.

His childhood family dinners had been made up of classical music playing softly in the background, artfully arranged food served on the finest china and dinner conversation with one person speaking at a time. Even now when he dined with his parents and grandmother the evenings were exactly the same.

This…this was chaos.

"Hey, we're going to pull together a game of flag football after dinner," Brody said, elbowing Thomas from where he sat on the other side of him. "You want to join us?"

"Somehow I don't think rolling around in the grass chasing a leather-covered ball is something

Thomas would be interested in," Jazzy said, with a wink.

"Do you like football, Thomas?" Jordyn Leigh asked. "I warn you, it's pretty much a prerequisite to joining the family."

"No, it's not," Annabel protested. "Besides, his favorite team is the Broncos."

"Is that right?" Zeke asked, his eyes bright.

Thomas nodded, feeling as if he'd finally scored points with the man. "Yes, sir."

"Hey, do you feel that?" Cade lifted his beer in a mock salute. "I think the balance of power has shifted ever so slightly."

"What are you talking about?" Laila and Abby asked in unison.

"There's always been six women sitting around the Cates family table, but now we're up to five men." Cade leaned over and clinked his bottle against his father-in-law's. "All we need now is to get your last two daughters married off and the majority power will be all male."

"Amen to that," Zeke offered with a wide smile.

Laughter, jeers and catcalls filled the air but all Thomas felt was the rising panic at how everyone at the table already had him walking down the aisle while Annabel said nothing to ebb their train of thought.

Suddenly, he couldn't breathe, his chest and throat tight. The need to escape was so overwhelming Thomas almost missed the ringing of his cell phone. He reached for it, trying to ignore the hard lump in his gut, and peered at the display.

"I need to answer this," he gasped in Annabel's ear. "Is there somewhere I can go that's a bit quieter?"

"Of course." She wiped her hands and rose to her feet.

Thomas did the same and addressed the table. "Please excuse me. I need to make a call to the hospital."

The lively talking paused for a moment, then started back up as they walked away, diminishing slightly as they entered the cool interior of the house.

Annabel waved him into the kitchen, but stayed by the door as he walked farther away and hit the button that would connect him directly to TC General. As he listened to the call, the lump in his gut grew.

Damn, not the news he was hoping for.

After a few minutes he ended the call and walked back to her. "I'm sorry. I have to leave."

"What's wrong?"

He paused, weighing exactly what he should say. "It's Maurice Owens."

"Oh!" Her eyes filled with concern. "That poor, sweet man. Is it bad?"

Thomas knew Annabel had come to care for his patient over the past week, often stopping in to see the old man even without Smiley, but he couldn't go into the details with her. "Serious enough that I need to say my goodbyes and get to the hospital right away."

They went back outside. Thomas explained he'd had an emergency come up and offered his apologies for having to leave early. He returned her father's handshake, thanking the man for having him in his home and again read concern in her mother's eyes when Annabel grabbed his hand and insisted on walking him to his car.

"Will you call me later?" she asked and hurried to keep up with his quick strides. "I'd like to know how Maurice is doing."

Thomas glanced at his watch as he opened the driver's side door. It was after six already. "I don't have any idea how late that might be."

"I'll be up." She leaned in and gave him a quick kiss. "I can come over, too, you know, later on. If you need me."

He didn't know if it was her offer or the heat of her lips on his that caused that hard lump in his gut to rise up to his throat.

Unable to spare the time to figure out which the correct answer was, he shoved the thought from his head and slid behind the wheel. His focus right now had to be solely on his patient. "I can't make any promises."

"I know that, I was just…" Her voice trailed off as she stepped away from the car. "Please drive safe."

Eight hours later, Thomas finally dragged his tired self inside his home. Alone. It was after two in the morning and he was dead on his feet.

Maurice Owens had suffered a series of seizures and they were still trying to find the cause. The last one had been so strong they had no choice but to place the man in a medically induced coma to prevent brain damage.

The elderly gentleman had been doing so well ever since Smiley had started to visit, his recovery progressing much faster than estimated that Thomas had almost been willing to admit—

No. He shut down that thought, refusing to go there.

Not now. Not tonight.

Thomas had sat in his office for the past two hours going over the man's medical records and test results, certain that he'd missed something. A leg with multiple fractures wasn't good for anyone, least of all a man who was close to celebrating his one hundredth birthday. And the chances of someone Maurice's age not suffering any additional side effects from the seizures or the coma were slim at best.

Eyes glazed over and a headache on the edge of erupting, Thomas had finally noticed the time. Realizing he'd never called Annabel, he decided to head home. His place was so quiet after the craziness at Annabel's and the constant noise of the hospital. The silence seeped into his bones and he realized just how tired he was.

Heading upstairs, he toed off his shoes and socks and stripped off his shirt. He undid his belt and yanked down the zipper on his pants, pausing when his gaze landed on the multicolored quilt folded neatly over the back of a chair in the corner of his bedroom.

It was the same quilt he'd found in his living room the morning after they'd made love the first time. Annabel had brought it back with her last night, insisting he keep it as the blanket's muted shades fit perfectly in his home's color scheme.

Besides, she'd said, she was always cold, despite the warm summer night, and they'd cuddled beneath the quilt until soon the soft material was the only thing protecting their bare skin from the cool air-conditioning.

Thomas grabbed the blanket off the chair, brought it to his face, and breathed deeply. Annabel's scent filled his head, but soon memories of this afternoon and tonight did, as well.

Her family's comments linking him and Annabel, the sight of Maurice's body flailing uncontrollably, the soft blue eyes offering to come to him when he called, the aged, unseeing gaze, clouded with confusion, pain and then no expression at all....

Thomas still didn't know what he missed when it came to his patient's health, but he knew one thing.

If he hadn't been spending so much time over the past three days with Annabel, thinking about her when they weren't together, and anticipating when he was going to see her again, he would have seen this coming. He should have known his patient was heading down the wrong path, a path that could take the man's life.

Tossing the blanket down, Thomas turned and headed for his bed, ignoring the urge to call Annabel even at this late hour.

He was not going to pick up that phone.

No matter how much he wanted to.

Chapter Eleven

"Please, I need to see him." Annabel leaned over the counter, doing her best to persuade the nurse on duty, who happened to be an old high school friend, to bend the rules just a little bit. "I need to know if he's okay."

After waiting for hours with no phone call from Thomas on Maurice's condition, she'd finally fallen asleep around two this morning. When she'd woken up and still didn't have an update, she'd taken a quick shower and headed for the hospital, determined to find out what was going on.

"I'm sorry, but only family can visit patients in intensive care," Jody replied, her voice a low whisper. "You know that, Annabel."

"Maurice Owens doesn't have any family." A sense of hopelessness weighed heavily on her shoulders. She glanced at her watch, noting she needed to be at the library in forty-five minutes for a mandatory budget meeting. "He's over ninety years old and he's all alone in this world. Smiley and I have been by to visit him a few times last week and I've come by myself even more often. He was doing so much better. I don't understand—"

She broke off when the tears threatened, but pulled in a deep breath instead of letting them overpower her and forced herself to continue. "Jody, please. Can you at least tell me how he'd doing? Why he was moved here from his regular room?"

Jody's fingers flew over the keyboard in front of her for a moment, then her expression changed from stern to surprised. "If you'll follow me, I'll take you to his room."

"You will?" Shock radiated through Annabel. "But how? You just said I couldn't go in."

Her friend smiled as she rose and walked around the desk. "Your name just appeared on the approved visitors list. Believe me, it wasn't there a few minutes ago when you first asked. The attending physician must have made the change. Doctor's orders."

Doctor's orders.

Thomas's orders.

He had to be the one who granted permission for

her to follow the petite nurse through the security doors into the hush of the intensive-care area.

Did he somehow know she was here this morning? Was he here?

The urge to look around and see if he was nearby flowed through her, but she kept her gaze firmly on her friend as they walked down the long corridor.

"Okay, here we are." Jody stopped outside a glass door, her voice a hushed whisper. "All I can tell you is Mr. Owens suffered a series of seizures last night. As far as I know the doctors don't know why yet, but he is currently in a coma in order to keep him stable."

The tears threatened again, but Annabel held them off as she nodded her understanding.

"You only have fifteen minutes until the morning's visiting hours are over," Jody continued. "But you can come back later."

Annabel leaned in and gave her friend a hug. "Thank you, Jody, so much."

Entering the room, Annabel's eyes were drawn right away to the elderly man lying so still in the bed. She walked to a chair next to him and sat down, instinctively reaching out to grasp Maurice's hand. His skin was almost gray in color, wrinkled, and covered with age spots, but until now his grip had been strong whenever she'd held his hand.

"Hey there, Maurice." Annabel's heart ached for her new friend, but she kept her voice light. "Boy, when you said you were ready to get out of that room upstairs I don't think this is what you meant."

She swallowed hard and kept talking. "You know, they'll never allow Smiley to come into the ICU. You're going to have to get better so you two can spend some time together again. You promised to play catch with him, and Smiley just loves to chase a ball…."

Pressing a hand to her mouth as her voice faded, Annabel closed her eyes and offered a quick prayer for this very special man. A man who'd fought valiantly for his country during both the Second World War and the Korean Conflict. A man who often spoke of his wife, who he'd fallen in love with long after he thought his chance at happiness had passed him by, and how much he missed their simple home while being stuck in the hospital.

"You rest and get better, Maurice," she whispered. "I'll be back to see you very soon."

Rising, Annabel released his hand and leaned over to place a light kiss on the elderly man's forehead. After leaving his room, she walked out to the main corridor, her mind once again filled with thoughts of Thomas.

She still didn't know why he hadn't called her last night to give her an update on Maurice's condition. Not even a message on her cell phone. He had to know how worried she'd be…how much she'd wanted to make sure that Maurice was okay.

That he, too, had been okay.

As thankful as she was that he'd added her to Maurice's visitors list this morning, she still had no idea what was going on with Thomas. Deciding there was no time like the present to find out, Annabel quickly took the stairs up to the second floor, her high heels echoing on the polished linoleum as she made her way toward his office.

She had no idea what she would say to him once she got there, but she wasn't worried. The words would come. They always did. Except for yesterday when her family had so easily lumped her and Thomas together.

Heck, the way they'd carried on during the barbecue, they practically had them married!

While she had pleaded with them beforehand to make Thomas feel comfortable and at home, she'd never expected her brothers-in-law to go as far as they did.

As much as she liked the tingling that filled her bones at the idea of someday being Mrs. Thomas North, she'd known she needed to say something to downplay their teasing. Something along the lines of how she and Thomas had only been on a few dates, while leaving out the part about the great sex over the past three days for her parents' sake.

She'd been about to do just that when Thomas had gotten the call that forced him to leave early.

And yes, he did seem intently focused on Maurice

when he'd left, but she was smart enough to pick up that a small part of him was relieved to be out of the line of fire where her family was concern.

Not that she blamed him, because despite how easily the subject matter had changed from the two of them to something else once he'd left, she had to put up with the "I told you so" look and a few underhanded remarks from her mother about what life would be like married to a doctor.

Not that any of that excused him from not calling and letting her know about Maurice.

Confusion swamped her as she entered his office area, surprised to find both Marge's desk and Thomas's inner office empty. From the half-empty mug of coffee and paperwork scattered across his desk, she could tell he'd arrived already, he just wasn't here.

She checked her watch again and then grabbed a small pad of paper, determined to leave him a quick note. Three tries, three crumpled balls of paper later and she still didn't know what to say.

Why didn't you call?

I miss you.

When will we see each other again?

Oh, all of those openings seemed so…so…desperate? And Annabel didn't want him to think of her that way.

Yes, she was in love.

Yes, he was the one for her.

Two amazing and wonderful facts she'd carried in

her heart since the first time they'd made love. But she wanted Thomas to come to those same conclusions on his own, in his own way and time.

Deciding it was best to just call his office later and speak to him in person, she tossed the pad back onto Thomas's desk and headed for the doorway when voices from the outer office stopped her.

"And who would've thought the guy had enough time on his hands to steal my wife."

What?

Annabel's hand stilled on the door knob. Instead of moving to the other side of the door, she stood there, frozen.

"I mean, we've only been married a year," the man continued. "Aren't we supposed to still be in some damn honeymoon phase?"

"That's rough. Sorry you're going through all that."

Okay, that voice she recognized as Thomas's. The other man must be a friend of his.

"You know, people warned me about getting married during my residency, but we'd been together since college. I loved her. I thought she loved me," the friend went on. "Then I find out she's been spending time with some hot-shot lawyer while I'm busting my ass working long shifts here." The man sighed. "Sorry I'm unloading my problems on you."

Annabel's heart ached for the poor guy's obvious pain over his wife's infidelity. She should make her presence known, but the last thing she wanted was to embarrass the man, or Thomas. Better to step back and give them as much privacy as—

"I understand it's tough, but you can't let your personal life get in the way of your work here. That minor slip you had earlier with your patient could have become a major issue, if you hadn't caught it in time." Thomas's voice was low, but strong and filled with certainty. "Love and medicine don't mix. I found that out the hard way."

His last statements stunned her and Annabel found it impossible to move.

"Look, I'm the last person who should give out advice on something like this," Thomas continued.

"No, please," his friend pushed. "I want your opinion."

Silence filled the air for a long moment and Annabel found herself holding her breath waiting to see how Thomas would respond.

"I've learned that being one hundred percent committed to your career is a prerequisite for our profession. Anything less and people's lives are at stake," he finally said. "Some can find a balance between a personal life and a professional one, some can't. You need to find out which group you belong to."

"Have *you* figured that out yet?"

She pressed a hand to her mouth to stop herself from blurting out how wrong he was, how finding a balance was a part of being in love no matter what someone's line of work. Annabel closed her eyes, her heart pounding in her chest as she waited for Thomas to answer.

"All I know is you have to weigh the facts against the evidence. In my experience, trusting in love is crazy and I— Ah, hello, Marge."

Thomas cut off his words as his secretary arrived, ending the men's discussion. Turning away, Annabel walked to the windows, brushing away the tears before they could fall. She wrapped her arms tightly around herself, suddenly very cold despite the suit jacket she wore.

Wishing a hole in the floor would open up and swallow her would do no good. All she could do was wait and—what?

Hope that Thomas and Marge left again so she could sneak out unseen? Where would that leave her?

Still waiting for Thomas to come to her?

No, what she needed was to make a few things clear to him. At least one thing in particular. She knew what was in her heart and now seemed like the perfect time to share—

"Annabel?"

She whirled around.

"What are you—" Thomas stood in his doorway, shock on his face. He quickly glanced back out at the outer office before closing the door behind him. "How long have you been in here?"

"Long enough. I'm sorry. I didn't mean to eavesdrop." She waved one hand toward his desk. "I stopped by to see you, but you were gone. I was going to leave a note. Then I heard... I didn't want to interrupt a private conversation."

"So you just listened instead?"

"It was pretty hard not to. Oh, Thomas, I can't believe you really feel that way about love."

He moved to the other side of his desk, his attention on the paperwork in his hand. "Now is not the time to talk about this."

"I think this is the perfect time." Annabel reached deep inside for that certainty she'd been so sure of just a moment ago. "Thomas, I—"

"I'm guessing you came here to check on Maurice," he interrupted her. "I didn't call you last night because it was late when I finally got home. Actually it was very early this morning." Thomas dropped the folder to his desk. "I can't go into any detail about my patient's care—"

"I know he's in intensive care and I know I have you to thank for allowing me to see him." Annabel waved off his explanation, determined not to let him pull away from what they really needed to talk about. "Thank you for that. I'm sure you and the rest of the staff are doing all you can for him."

His gaze remained focused on his desk. "Yes, we are."

Annabel remained silent, but when he didn't say anything more, she purposely walked to him, invading his personal space as she slid between him and his desk.

He tried to step back, pushing his chair to one side, but the credenza behind him stopped him.

"Do you really believe it's crazy to trust in love?"

Thomas purposely kept his gaze away from her. "Annabel…"

"I don't, and do you want to know why?" She placed her fingertips at his jaw and gently forced him to look at her. "Because I love you, Thomas."

He closed his eyes and pressed his mouth into a hard line before he spoke. "No, you don't."

Yes, she did. Saying the words aloud for the first time made her even more certain of her feelings for this man.

"Yes, I do."

He opened his eyes again, the glacial chill in their blue depths surprising her. "You can't know that."

"Of course I can and I wanted you to know." Undeterred, she dropped her hand to his chest, the steady beat of his heart beneath her fingers reminding her of those nights when he'd held her close. "This may seem a bit sudden considering—"

"Sudden?" Thomas turned away from her, moving out from behind his desk. "Yes, I would say so. We've only known each other a couple of weeks."

"I'm sure of my feelings, Thomas, but knowing that I love you doesn't mean I have the future all planned out." Pushing aside the panic that the distance he was putting between them was more than physical, Annabel followed him. "Goodness knows, I'm very much a live-in-the-moment kind of person, but what I'm certain of is that I want you in every one of those moments."

"After such a short period of time?" The disbelief was evident in his voice as he crossed his office; this time he was the one staring out the windows. "How is that possible?"

"I don't know how." She wanted to reach out, to make him turn and look at her, but the stiffness of his posture held her back. "I just know that what we have is special and worth all the craziness that might come our way as we muddle through this."

"Worth it to whom? My patients? I can't allow my personal life to get in the way. To distract me from…" Thomas's voice trailed off as he pinched the bridge of his nose hard and sighed.

"Is that what you think?" Annabel quickly connected the dots. "That because you and I have been spending time together over the past few days you missed something in Maurice's treatment—"

"It doesn't matter what I think." Thomas spun around. "What I rely on are facts, while you place all of your trust in your feelings."

"Yes, I guess I do. And from what I overheard, you've been hurt in the past, but please don't let that affect what's happening now between us. You must know what we have is wonderful…"

"What I know is that I have a lot of work to do." Thomas's gaze traveled the length of her. "And you look like you're on your way to an important meeting."

Annabel glanced down at her business suit. "Yes," she finally admitted. "I need to get to the library."

"Well, please don't let me keep you."

The distance on his face spoke volumes at how far apart they were despite standing right in front of each other. For the first time, the words wouldn't come and Annabel had no idea how to reach him.

"I'm free tonight." She pushed the invitation past her lips, already knowing deep inside the reception her words would receive. "If you want to get together?"

"I'll probably be working late again." Thomas grabbed a white medical coat off a nearby hook. Sliding it over his shoulders, he pulled it on like a suit of body armor, leaving Annabel standing there alone and defenseless.

"Thomas, I—"

"Annabel, please." He started to reach for her, but curled his fingers into a tight fist and jammed it into his pocket. "I can't talk about this right now, and I really need to get back to work."

Pressing her palm hard against her chest as if she

could actually stop her heart from breaking, Annabel could only nod before she turned and walked away, certain that this time he wouldn't be coming after her.

Chapter Twelve

It amazed Thomas how much life could change in a mere seventy-two hours.

On Monday morning he had no clue as to the reason for Maurice Owens's seizures. Today the man was scheduled to be released from intensive care. They'd finally determined a blood infection was the source of the problems. After a heavy dose of IV antibiotics, the man now fully awake, alert and, according to his nurses, asking when that rag mop of a dog and his pretty owner were coming back to see him.

Annabel and Smiley.

Thomas's fist tightened on the bag he carried as he crossed the parking lot and headed inside the hospital.

Yeah, life had certainly changed since that Monday morning when he'd done the one thing he'd wanted to avoid from the moment he'd met Annabel.

Hurt her.

After he'd made it clear he didn't believe her declaration, the pain and disappointment in her eyes before she'd turned and walked out of his office had filled him with such remorse he'd actually started after her. Then common sense took over. Even so, stopping himself from chasing after her had taken every ounce of strength he had.

Let her go. Let her go. Let her go.

The words had echoed in his head, a resounding anthem that told him he'd done the right thing.

He hadn't seen her since.

His daily rounds and Maurice's unstable condition had kept him occupied for the next twenty-four hours until his boss ordered him to go home and not return until he'd gotten some much-needed rest. He'd obeyed and fell into a dreamless sleep for over fifteen hours, woke long enough to choke down some food, check in with Marge and then slept again.

But this time he'd dreamed of Annabel.

Her looking at him smiling and happy, her beautiful blue eyes filled with joy as she chatted about her work at the library, the therapy dog program, her family.

But then the joy faded, replaced with the same bewilderment and hurt that *he'd* put there as she faded farther and farther from his outstretched hands until she disappeared in swirling mist....

He'd shot awake, drenched in sweat and tangled in the sheets of his empty bed, his heart pounding in his chest. The urge to call her, to hear her voice, had been so powerful he'd grabbed his phone and held it in a grip so tight his knuckles ached.

But he couldn't do it. He couldn't put her through that again.

She'd laid her heart in his hands, and he'd all but thrown it back at her. He hadn't believed her when she poured out her feelings about how she felt about him, about *them*.

He couldn't do it because he hadn't changed his mind.

No matter how hollow and empty he might feel at the moment, making the choice of his patients over a personal life had been the right one.

He meant what he'd said to the young resident on his staff. Some in their profession managed to balance both a career and a life outside of the hospital, but others, the majority, tried and failed.

The consequences could be much worse than a broken heart.

He couldn't take that chance.

After his shower this morning, he'd dressed and started to leave his bedroom when the quilt Annabel had given him caught his attention.

He'd reached for it, ignoring how his fingers

shook as he grabbed the soft material. Marching downstairs and into the kitchen, he quickly stuffed the blanket into a paper sack.

Returning the gift was a necessity for the both of them.

Annabel had her Thursday session with Smiley this afternoon at the hospital. He was certain she would be there, just like she'd been every day this week visiting with Maurice, her name scrawled on the visitors' log in her loopy handwriting, which made his chest hurt every time he saw it.

He didn't have any idea what he was going to say when he came face-to-face with her, but he would think of something over the next six hours.

Even if it was only goodbye.

Exiting the elevator, he walked down the hall to his office and had to swallow the hard lump in his throat before he greeted Marge, who sat at her desk, the phone receiver in her hand.

"Morning, Marge."

"Oh, Dr. North." She looked up at him, surprise in her eyes. "I'm glad you're here. I was just about to page you."

He disregarded the natural quickening of his pulse. "What is it?"

"Mr. Owens is being a bit cantankerous this morning." She placed the receiver back in its cradle. "The head nurse in ICU just called to say he's insisting on seeing you *before* they move him."

Thomas dropped his briefcase and the bag into the closest chair. "I'll go right now. Can you please put these in my office?"

"That's quite a big lunch you're brown bagging today."

Turning to grab some much-needed coffee, he snapped a lid on the disposable cup and kept his gaze from returning to the bag. "That's not food."

"Is it something I can take care of for you?"

For a split second Thomas almost agreed to Marge's request. He could easily ask her to take it down to the session or even mail it to Annabel at her home, but he quickly squashed the idea. "No."

He softened his tone when the woman offered him a raised eyebrow. "Thank you, but that's something…it's something I need to handle on my own."

Three hours later Thomas returned to his office.

He'd gone ahead and completed his morning rounds after making sure Maurice was settled in his new room, which wasn't the same one he'd been in before. A fact the elderly man found very unsettling until Thomas had promised him the staff would make sure the new room number was available for anyone who asked for it.

Anyone meaning Annabel.

He hated to admit it, but he'd been disappointed to find out she hadn't made it in yet to see Maurice this morning unlike the past two days when she'd come by during the early visiting hours.

Another reason Maurice had been upset.

Thomas met up with Marge in the hallway just as she was leaving. "On your way out for lunch?"

"Yes, I need to pick up my cats from the vet." She pulled her keys from her purse. "They went in this morning for their checkups and the poor things hate it there. I want to get them home as soon as possible."

He peeked at her desk, noting the bag and his briefcase were gone, but he asked anyway, gesturing toward the still-closed door to his inner office. "Did you put my things inside?"

"I started to, but she insisted on taking that beautiful quilt into your office herself."

He stilled, his feet suddenly rooted to the floor. "She?"

"The bag tipped over when she bumped the chair and we couldn't help but see what was inside," Marge called out over her shoulder as she kept walking. "I tried to put it back, but she insisted and I knew it was useless to argue. Oh, and she was also adamant about waiting for you, too. Be back soon."

Before Thomas could say another word, Marge disappeared with a quick wave.

He remained standing there, staring at the door, trying to grasp the fact that Annabel was waiting for him on the other side.

Her coming back here to his office was the last thing he'd planned on, the last thing he expected. It was too early for Smiley's session. She must have come to see Maurice.

And him.

He pulled in a deep breath and moved forward, regretting that he didn't have the afternoon to figure out exactly what he was going to say to her. That he'd brought the quilt to the hospital was probably explanation enough, but still she'd persisted on waiting for him.

Determined to keep his focus completely on the facts and not the wild beating of his heart, he straightened his tie, turned the latch and stepped inside. His gaze was immediately drawn to the woman sitting at one end of his couch, the quilt spread over her lap, her fingertips tracing the mutely shaded blocks and the intricate stitching.

"Grandmother?"

Ernestine's hand stilled as she raised her head. "Good morning, Thomas. Or should I say good afternoon. You know, this quilt is a beautiful piece of work."

He walked farther into the room, bombarded with regret when he realized it wasn't Annabel who was waiting for him.

He tried to control the emotional roller coaster he was riding, knowing the fact he was on this ride in the first place was of his own doing. "Ah, yes, it is."

"The time and attention to detail it took to create such a lovely work of art." She returned her attention to the quilt, her hands again moving lightly over the fabric. "Someone must have been working on this for a very long time."

"Almost two years."

The words left his mouth before he'd even realized he spoke, remembering Annabel telling him about how she'd started the quilt as a way to keep busy during a crazy winter storm that dumped almost two feet of snow on Thunder Canyon.

He'd spent that same long weekend holed up in his empty condo with nothing but a home designer's catalog to flip through. It still amazed him how the colors she'd chosen had perfectly matched the furniture, carpeting and drapes he'd picked for his place that first weekend he'd been back in town.

Deciding he'd better sit before his shaky legs gave out on him, Thomas moved to the chair behind his desk.

"And it fits so perfectly with both your office and your home. Wherever did you have it made?"

"I didn't. I mean, it wasn't created specifically for me. For my place. The fact it matches is…just a fluke."

"Oh?" His grandmother slightly tilted her head, a familiar motion that spoke volumes despite her abbreviated question.

"It was a gift, actually." He paused and cleared his suddenly tight throat. "An unplanned gift. From a friend."

That caused his grandmother's gaze to sharpen with curiosity. "A lady friend?"

Thomas remained silent.

"A very special lady friend." Her words were spoken as a statement of fact as she answered her own question. "Well, that's even better."

"No, it's not."

She laced her fingers together and rested them primly on her quilt-covered lap. "I'm intrigued. Please go on."

"There is nothing to be intrigued about, Grandmother." He leaned back in his chair, forcing himself to appear relaxed as he returned her direct stare. "There is no special lady friend."

"But there was."

A heartbeat passed. "Yes, but it's over."

This time her head tilted ever so slightly in the opposite direction. "And does Miss Cates share in that assessment of your relationship?"

Thomas couldn't contain his shock. "How did— How did you know it was Annabel Cates?"

"Oh, my darling, you'd be surprised at the things I know." Ernestine gently folded the quilt into a neat package and laid it next to her on the couch. "With age comes wisdom, as the saying goes."

"What exactly does that mean?"

"It means I was hoping you would find more here in Thunder Canyon than just a brilliant career that you've worked so hard for and deservedly so."

Then it hit Thomas that his grandmother knew everything that happened back in California. "How did you find out?"

"Haven't you learned by now that there's little that goes on in this hospital that I don't know about? Including the professional backgrounds of our staff?" She held up a hand when he started to speak. "And when one of those staff members is related to me you can be certain my fellow administrators made sure I was aware of what exactly led to you looking for work away from Santa Monica."

Thomas leaned forward, bracing his elbows on his knees. "I'm sorry. I should've told you about all of that myself—"

"No apologies necessary, Thomas." She cut him off. "The way your personal and professional lives collided, and the fallout it created, was not something you could control."

"It was my fault."

"You were lied to. Your feelings were manipulated. How can you take responsibility for that?"

"I have to." Thomas rose and walked to the window, unable to take the sympathy he saw in his grandmother's eyes. "I have to make sure that 'collision,' as you called it, never happens again."

"By closing off your heart?"

"By choosing to focus all of my attention on my patients." Despite the rudeness of the gesture, he kept his back to her. "I missed something last weekend that could've cost a man his life."

"But it didn't."

"No, but to take that chance again…" He turned and looked at his grandmother. Pride welling inside him at all she'd accomplished here at the hospital, at what his family has achieved in this town. "To do anything that would result in a repeat of what happened in the past, to bring shame to this hospital, our family…to you. I won't take that risk."

"Thomas—"

"Besides, love and marriage and medicine aren't a good mix. Look at all the people here at TC General going through breakups and divorces."

His grandmother smiled as she stood, using her cane for balance as she walked toward him. "Thomas, you could say the same thing about any profession. Love and marriage take a lot of hard work, commitment and attention to keep it strong and healthy, just like any career does."

"Mother and Father haven't had to work that hard."

"Yes, they have," she countered. "Children don't always see all that goes into their parents' relationship, especially you because you were away so often at school and such. Believe me, with the two of them being hardheaded lawyers, like your grandpa Joe, they made some of their arguments more entertaining than most federal court cases."

His grandmother's assessment of his parents' stable and rather sedate marriage surprised him. Even more so was the hint that her own marriage had suffered its share of ups and downs. "You and Grandpa Joe?"

"We had our troubles as well, darling." She reached out and laid a hand on his arm. "Both long before and after that horrible accident. When we first met, your grandfather told me on our third date that we were going to spend the rest of our lives together. To an eighteen-year-old girl that sounded crazy, but he was so sure we were meant to be together."

Thomas did the math quickly in his head. "But you were married just before your nineteenth birthday."

"Yes, we were. With a lot of promises of forever from him and a big leap of faith on my part." Her eyes filled with long-ago memories. "Your grandfather told me he loved me enough for the both of us and that would carry us through until I was sure. And he was right. When he lost his legs all those years later, it was my turn to be the one to convince him our love was strong enough, that I could be strong enough, for the both of us."

"But you'd been married over three decades when that happened." Thomas remembered his own devastation at what his grandfather had suffered through when Thomas was a child. To picture those events again from his grandmother's point of view put a totally new spin on things. "Looking back now, as an adult and a doctor, I can see all he had to deal with, both physically and mentally, but I honestly never thought your marriage—"

"Our marriage lasted another twenty years because we found a way to make our love strong again, a feat achieved many times over." Her attention was back fully on him. "The ups and downs, the good times and bad, the strengths and weaknesses…when you find the right person, when you're that lucky, you need to grab ahold of that love and never let go. Fifty-five years or fifty-five days…I would've been happy with either because I was with the man I loved."

Thomas turned back to stare out the window again, folding his arms over his chest after his grandmother released her hold on him. His head swirled with everything she'd said, making sorting it into logical steps and facts difficult.

Falling back on his training, he started compartmentalizing, pushing away his emotions even as the desire to find Annabel, to go to her, surged inside of him.

The gentle cuff to the back of his head caught him completely by surprise.

He turned to stare at his grandmother, his mouth rising into a grin that matched hers. It'd been years since she'd swatted him one.

"What was that for?"

"I know you're going to think and reason and debate all we've talked about, because that's who you are and that's what you do, but don't take too long." She turned and headed for the door. "Your young lady doesn't seem to be as naive as I once was. I think it might take a lot more than fancy words and heartfelt promises to show her how wrong you were."

"I didn't say I was wrong."

"Not yet, you haven't." She glanced back and gave him a quick wink. "You're a smart boy. You'll get there eventually."

Thomas turned back to the window after his grandmother departed, closing the door behind her.

He didn't know how long he stood there, reflecting on the past few days, weeks and years. Thinking about all he'd gone through in California thanks to both his own choices and the things that had been out of his control.

Yes, he'd fallen hard and fast for Victoria and he'd overlooked—or just didn't want to see—the obvious signs that something was wrong with their relationship from the start. All the hiding and secrecy over the months they'd spent together should've been red flags that everything wasn't as it seemed.

She wasn't all she seemed.

While his day-to-day work at the hospital hadn't been affected, his career had suffered because of his own actions, even more so, by all that Victoria had done. Not just to him but to the poor schmuck still married to her.

Annabel wasn't Victoria though.

Yes, they'd only known each other a few weeks, but the way he felt when he was with her was so much more than he'd ever experienced with Victoria. With anyone, for that matter.

And the only one trying to keep their crazy and wonderful courtship a secret had been him, because of the past.

When he'd finally admitted to himself—and to her—how much he wanted her, wanted to be with her, everything fell in place so easily. It was almost scary at how perfect they fit.

Another reason why he'd tried to run.

Not that everything would always fit so flawlessly. They came from two different worlds. Her loud and adoring family, so different from his small and demure one, would require some getting used to. His demanding career, her devotion to her dog and their equally strong commitment to both would also require a lot of give and take.

The bottom line?

Finding a way to bring his world and hers together would be challenging and fun and well worth the effort.

Thomas moved back to his desk and sat, thinking about everything his grandmother had said about the hard work and commitment that came with making a relationship last.

He kept coming to the same conclusion.

Why was he running away from the best thing that ever happened to him? Fighting his feelings, hiding from them was useless because they weren't going to change.

Not now. Not ever.

But what to do to show that he'd finally understood? That he was finally sure?

The idea came to him quickly and while it might be a small first step, it was an important one.

He quickly booted up his computer, typed a simple request in the search engine and waited. As soon as the website appeared he scanned the images, one after the other, until he found the perfect one. Blonde, bubbly and a face that showed all the love in the world to give.

With one click he checked his calendar, relieved to find it empty for the afternoon. Rising, he rounded his desk and headed for the door.

"I'm out of here for the day, Marge," he said to his secretary, glad to see she'd returned. "I'll have my cell phone on if any emergencies arise."

"Has your grandmother left?" she asked.

"Yes, she did." He didn't even slow down as he hurried past her desk.

"Where are you going?" she called after him.

"To see a woman about a dog."

Chapter Thirteen

Forcing a smile had never been something Annabel needed to do, but today, despite stopping in and finding Maurice sleeping comfortably in his new room, it took all the energy she had to remain positive during this afternoon's Smiley session.

She'd left behind a note and an arrangement of brightly colored daisies for Maurice to find when he awoke, ushering Smiley away from the bed after he'd nudged at the sleeping man's hand.

Once they arrived at the therapy area, they'd found a roomful of patients already waiting, with more coming and going as the two hours passed. Annabel had already contacted a few members of her therapy group with the idea of adding more dogs to this weekly open session. Having two or three additional animals would allow each person to have more one-on-one time as many were often reluctant to allow Smiley to move on.

Of course, she still needed to get approval from—Thomas.

Still on bended knee, Smiley at her side after they'd said goodbye to the last child, Annabel bowed her head, blinking hard against the endless supply of tears.

Would they ever stop?

After the past three days one would think she'd exhausted her supply. But after Annabel had responded to her mother's innocently asked "how was your day" on Monday night by bursting into wrenching sobs, her mother had lovingly pointed out to her that the tears would end when the healing began.

Annabel wasn't sure that would ever happen.

Something deep inside told her that while the crippling ache in her heart might one day ease, the empty space left behind would always belong to the one man she'd been so sure was the love of her life.

A man who couldn't—wouldn't—accept her love.

Smiley's snout nuzzled her shoulder, his nose cool against her neck. Annabel sighed and her pet moved even closer, instinctively knowing how much his owner needed his faithful and unconditional love.

"Thank you, sweetie." Annabel wrapped her arms

around the dog's shoulders and gave him a gentle hug. Smiley had rarely left her side since greeting her at the door on Monday. "I don't know how I'd get through all of this without you."

"I was just thinking the same thing."

The low masculine voice caused Annabel to look up.

Shock filled her at the sight of Forrest Traub standing in front of her. Rising, she brushed the tears off her cheeks. "What are *you* doing here?"

The tall man leaned heavily on his cane as he held out one hand for her dog to inspect. "I'm here to see you. And Smiley."

Seconds later, Smiley offered a quick lick to the man's fingers and was rewarded with a firm scratch behind his ears.

Forrest leaned over and spoke gently to her pet. Annabel silently thanked him, sure he'd seen her crying, and used those few moments to pull in and then release a deep shuddering breath.

She had no idea why Forrest Traub was back in town or why he'd come looking for her. "No, what I meant was what are you doing back in Thunder Canyon? I was told you'd returned to your family's ranch."

"I did, for a while." Forrest straightened. "But my brother Clay and I have decided to move to Thunder Canyon on a permanent basis."

Her gaze flickered for a moment to his leg and

the brace still visible beneath his faded jeans. "For your treatment?"

His grip again tightened on the curved handle of his cane. "Among other reasons."

"Ah. Would you like to sit?" Annabel waved at a pair of nearby chairs, already inching toward the one farthest away. "Smiley's session ended a few minutes ago, but I don't think they'll kick us out just yet."

Forrest sank into the chair, his injured leg stretched out in front of him. Smiley moved in, placing his chin immediately on the man's good knee, just like he'd done that first day.

"I've been standing in the corner for the last few minutes, watching you work," Forrest said, his lips rising into a small grin when Smiley lifted his head and looked up at him. "Watching both of you work. I'd heard from my cousin about how popular your sessions have become. I guess you were able to convince Dr. North to give your idea a go."

Annabel ignored the kick to her gut at the memory of how she and Thomas first met, just a few short weeks ago. "Yes, I did."

"Do you have any interest in expanding them?"

Pushing aside her heartache, Annabel was happy for the distraction and equally surprised at how Forrest's question echoed her own thoughts from a moment ago. "I have been thinking of bringing in more dogs to spread the attention around."

"My idea is different."

"What's that?"

"I'd like to start a support group just for veterans."

Annabel thought back to the two servicemen, both recently returned from Afghanistan, who'd come to the first private session she held on Tuesdays. Despite the small size of the group, neither had been back since even though both were still patients here in the hospital.

They'd admitted to being strangers to one another during introductions, but had instinctively sat next to each other that first time. The chairs had formed a large circle, but the two men had remained emotionally, if not physically, separated from the other patients, both choosing not to speak, even during their turn with Smiley.

"That's an interesting idea," she said, watching as Forrest finally reached out and began scratching Smiley's ears again. "What made you think of it?"

Silence filled the room. Annabel waited, hoping he would share his inspiration when he was ready.

"I often thought about Smiley over the last few weeks. Just that short amount of time I spent with him really had an impact on me." Forrest kept his focus on her pet as he talked. "Being back on the ranch was harder than I'd thought it'd be. I honestly don't think I would've gone down to the barn to see the horses I still can't ride if I hadn't felt—if Smiley hadn't made me realize how much I missed…"

Annabel remained silent, watching the array of

emotions that crossed the man's handsome features. It was almost as if she could see his attempts at gathering his thoughts after his voice had faded with his last words.

"Animals offer an unrestricted love, don't they?" he finally said, his attention still focused on the repeated motion of his hand moving easily over Smiley's fur. "No questions, no divided loyalties, no demands or restrictions."

Everything Forrest said resounded deeply inside Annabel and made all her hard work with Smiley worthwhile. "You've obviously thought a lot about this."

"I haven't had much to do with my time lately but think."

"And heal," Annabel added.

Forrest lifted one shoulder in a shrug. "Physically, maybe, although that's taking longer than everyone, including myself, ever thought it would. But it's what's going on inside, the learning to let go of...certain behaviors, certain memories, that I think Smiley could help with. Not just for me, but others who have served their country, as well."

She could easily understand how letting go or at least learning to live with the memories of serving in a war might be difficult. From the straightforward hurting of being away from their loved ones to the unimaginable horror of living day to day, moment to moment, in a place where each decision could mean life or death, these men and women had been to hell and back.

"What do you mean by certain behaviors?" she questioned. "If you don't mind me asking."

"Soldiers tend to keep their problems to themselves. It isn't easy for them to rely on other people." Forrest's voice was low, his gaze now focused straight ahead at the large expanse of windows across the room. "Even the men and women we serve with, people who know better than anyone else what you've gone through—even talking with them isn't easy. Throw in family members who are often eager to help, but they sometimes don't realize how difficult answering even the simplest question can be.

"We're trained to lock away our emotions, to focus on the task at hand, to get the job done. Use your head and keep your heart out of it." Forrest punctured his last words with imaginary quotation marks drawn in the air. "Simple to do during the extreme moments when everything you've been taught comes as naturally as breathing, but when the job is done and things get quiet, when you're alone with your thoughts…it's a lot harder to keep your feelings under control. For some people denying any sentiment is the only way they can survive."

Annabel couldn't stop comparing Forrest's words to what Thomas had said to her as they stood in his office just a few days ago.

He'd been so adamant that there was no room in

his life for anything but his work. Somewhere along the way, he'd come to believe he couldn't have both love and his career.

In my experience, trusting in love is crazy.

Had someone taught him that? Was that why he refused to believe her when she told him how sure she was of her love for him?

"So learning to allow your feelings to be a part of your life again, that it's okay to even acknowledge the everyday emotions most people take for granted—is that what you mean?"

Forrest nodded. "I think it's a good place to start."

"So do I." For the first time in days, Annabel allowed her own emotions to flow freely, the pure joy of what she felt for Thomas to once again fill her heart.

"I'm sorry, I didn't mean to turn our talk into a personal session just for me." Forrest offered her that same slight grin as before. "See how easy it is to start jawing when this mutt of yours is around?"

"That is exactly why Smiley and I are here." Annabel reached for Forrest's hand and gave it a quick squeeze. "And I think your idea is wonderful."

"So you'll work with me on this?"

"I'd love to. We'll need to talk to people here at the hospital in order to pull it together, but I don't think that'll be a problem."

Forrest pushed himself to his feet. "You didn't let it stop you before."

"Nope." Annabel stood as well, her smile reflecting her renewed sense of confidence. Hadn't she told Thomas the first time they'd met that she could be persuasive when she wanted something? "And nothing is going to stop me this time, either."

The gravel drive crunched beneath the tires of her car as Annabel slowly pulled to a stop outside the oversize, tree-shaded building. There were only a few other vehicles in the Thunder Canyon Animal Shelter parking lot, but none that she recognized.

Was she too late?

Smiley pawed at the back of her seat when she turned off the engine. The sounds of their surroundings filtered in through the open windows.

"Yes, I know." She twisted around to look in the backseat. "You remember this place well, don't you?"

Smiley offered a low woof in response.

Removing her seat belt, Annabel got out of the car and freed Smiley, as well. She held tight to his leash as he eagerly headed for the front entrance. The office area was empty, but Annabel walked on through until they emerged back out in the bright sunshine as a familiar face met them.

"Hey there! It's good to see you two again." Betsy greeted them with a bright smile. "What brings you here this afternoon?"

"Hi, Betsy. I was hoping to find a friend of mine, but I didn't see his car out front."

"We only have one visitor here at the moment so I'm guessing that's who you're talking about. He parked around the other side in the employees' section." The woman smiled and gestured over her shoulder. "You'll find him right around the corner. Seems to be having a hard time making up his mind. Not everyone is as sure as you were that day."

Suddenly unable to speak, Annabel could only nod her thanks as she allowed Smiley to lead her to the familiar path. Rounding the corner, she stopped short at the sight in front of her.

Thomas, still dressed for work in dark slacks, a buttoned shirt now wrinkled with the sleeves folded back to his elbows, and his tie yanked halfway down his chest, sat on the grass inside a gated area, his lap overflowing with at least a dozen wiggling, happy puppies.

Three years ago, she'd come here to the Thunder Canyon Animal Shelter, drawn by a flyer advertising how a special pet could change a person's whole world. Finding Smiley within a few minutes of her arrival had been the most wonderful moment of her life…until the day the two of them walked into a certain doctor's office.

Her heart soared as she watched the ease of his smile and listened to his husky laughter as the playful pups vied for his attention. She had no idea exactly why he was here, but it was a sight she could've enjoyed for hours.

Except her pup had other ideas.

Smiley let loose with two happy yips of his own, causing Thomas and the dogs to jerk their heads their way.

"Annabel."

She offered a small wave, enchanted by the bright flush of embarrassment that crossed his features. "I'd ask if you're enjoying yourself, but that would be a silly question."

Thomas hurried to his feet, brushing at his clothes with one hand because the other cradled one petite pup in the crook of his arm. "Ah, yes. Well, you know...puppies."

"Yes, I know." She signaled for Smiley to sit. He obeyed, but that didn't stop his back end from wiggling back and forth in time with his swishing tail. "You seem to have found a new friend."

He took a few steps forward until only the wired fencing separated them, his gaze dropping for a moment to the surprisingly docile pup, whose tiny head rested contently against his chest. "I guess so."

"I didn't know you were interested in getting a dog."

His gaze returned to look at her, the icy blue coloring of his eyes reflecting a contentment she hadn't seen there before. "I guess it was a spur-of-the-moment decision."

Was that a good thing or not? Was he ready to

make more spontaneous choices in other areas of his life? And could she possibly be included in any way?

The questions filled her head, but engaging her mouth seemed impossible at the moment.

"How did you know I was here?"

Before she could answer Betsy came around the corner with a young family, complete with two boys, who seemed as excited as the puppies were to have someone new to play with.

"Hold that thought. I'd like to continue this conversation face-to-face." He waited until the shelter's director entered the gated area that allowed visitors to interact with the available pets before he slipped out and started toward her, the pup still in his arms.

To Annabel's trained eye the animal seemed to have at least some golden retriever in him, or her. She guessed the pup to be only a few months old, but the familiar coloring of its coat reminded her of Smiley when she'd first brought him home.

But it was the mixture of tenderness and purpose in Thomas's eyes that drew her gaze back to his face. Gone was the aloof detachment he'd so easily displayed in his office a few days ago.

He stopped right in front of her, leaning down to give Smiley a quick pat hello. "Hey there, Smiley." His attention returned to her. "Okay, now. How did you know where I was?"

"We were on our way to your office when we ran

into Marge at the elevator. She mentioned you'd left the shelter's website up on your computer when you left for the day." The words tumbled from her mouth, her eyes drawn to the ease with which Thomas stroked the pup's soft fur. "She, for whatever reason, thought I might like to know that."

"Of course she did."

Annabel couldn't stand it. She once again decided to jump in with both feet and trust in the love she felt in her heart and the warmth in Thomas's gaze.

"You know, I don't want to ruin a good thing. Correction, this great, amazing and wonderful thing that's happening right at this very moment, but to say I'm a bit confused is putting it mildly."

Thomas motioned toward a nearby bench. "Do you think we could sit for a moment?"

Annabel nodded, a thrill racing through her when Thomas laid his free hand at the small of her back as they made their way across the yard. Smiley sat again when she and Thomas did, his gaze moving between her, him and the pup that settled easily in Thomas's lap.

"Everything's okay, sweetie." She reassured her pet with a gentle pat, hoping the simple phrase would calm her, as well. "You can say hello."

Smiley quickly sniffed at the now-snoozing puppy then offered a low sigh before stretching out at her feet, his head resting on his paws.

"Wow, two quiet dogs. That's a bit unusual, isn't it?"

Thomas's words had Annabel returning her gaze to his. "Yes, it is, especially for a puppy. Do you have any idea what you're in for? Puppies demand a lot of time and attention. They need to be cared for, fed, bathed, trained, but most of all they need your love."

"I know all that." His smile was genuine. "I guess I've finally found the right one for me."

The whirlwind of emotions battling inside her was suddenly too much to contain. Annabel squeezed her eyes closed, but a single tear managed to escape anyway. "Thomas, you're driving me crazy here."

His touch was gentle as he cupped her jaw, his thumb brushing over her cheek to wipe the tear away. "Then the feeling is mutual. You've been nothing short of a beautiful, passionate and maddening presence in my carefully controlled world from the moment we met."

She opened her eyes. "What exactly does that mean?"

"It means my life changed in a way I never expected a few short weeks ago and as hard as I tried not to allow it to happen, you found a way past my defenses. And no matter how hard I pushed, you never gave up on me."

"I'd say that's pretty evident considering I followed you here," Annabel whispered, following her heart and all the love she carried inside for this amazing man. "I meant what I said to you three days ago. My feelings haven't changed. I love you."

This time it was Thomas who closed his eyes, his head dropping forward, pressing his forehead gently to hers. "I was so afraid I'd waited too long. That I was too late."

"Late for what?"

"To ask for another chance?" He pressed his kiss to her temple for a long moment, and then leaned back again. "Will you take a chance on me?"

Annabel's heart beat wildly in her chest. This was exactly what she wanted, what she'd hoped for when she'd decided less than a hour ago not to give up on him, but to believe in the sincerity of his words? "Thomas, you have to be sure of what you want, what you need in your life."

"I want you. I need you." He pulled her closer, his arm moving to wrap low around her waist. "I think I've known that all along. That's what was so scary, how easily you came into my life, as if you were meant to be here, with me. I love you, Annabel, and I'm going to for the rest of my life."

She laid a hand over his where it held the tiny bundle in his lap. "This…all of this is going to take a lot of hard work and commitment."

He smiled, his fingers lacing through hers. "And time, attention and love. Yeah, I got it. So, do you think you and Smiley have enough of all those things to share? For both of us? I think me and this little guy come as a package deal."

Annabel leaned forward and met Thomas's kiss while Smiley offered a resounding bark of approval. They broke apart with a shared laugh. "Two for one? How could we resist?"

* * * * *

So you think you can write?

It's your turn!

Mills & Boon® and Harlequin® have joined forces in a global search for new authors and now it's time for YOU to vote on the best stories.

It is our biggest contest ever—the prize is to be published by the world's leader in romance fiction.

And the most important judge of what makes a great new story?

YOU—our reader.

Read first chapters and story synopses for all our entries at
www.soyouthinkyoucanwrite.com

**Vote now at
www.soyouthinkyoucanwrite.com!**

HARLEQUIN®
entertain, enrich, inspire™

MILLS & BOON®

SYTYCW_3

A sneaky peek at next month...

Cherish™

ROMANCE TO MELT THE HEART EVERY TIME

My wish list for next month's titles...

In stores from 19th October 2012:

☐ Single Dad's Christmas Wish — Patricia Thayer

& Taming the Brooding Cattleman — Marion Lennox

☐ Nanny for the Millionaire's Twins — Susan Meier

& That New York Minute — Abby Gaines

In stores from 2nd November 2012:

☐ A Week Till the Wedding — Linda Winstead Jones

& The Doctor's Do-Over — Karen Templeton

☐ Real Vintage Maverick — Marie Ferrarella

& The Maverick's Ready-Made Family — Brenda Harlen

Available at WHSmith, Tesco, Asda, Eason, Amazon and Apple

Just can't wait?

Visit us Online

You can buy our books online a month before they hit the shops! **www.millsandboon.co.uk**

1012/23

MILLS & BOON

Book of the Month

SARAH MORGAN
A Night of No Return

BOOK OF THE MONTH
MILLS & BOON

We love this book because...

RT Book Reviews said of Sarah Morgan 'Morgan's love scenes should come with a warning: Reading may cause hot flashes'—and the hero of *A Night of No Return* is darker, sexier and more dangerous than ever. Consider yourselves notified!

On sale 19th October

Visit us Online

Find out more at
www.millsandboon.co.uk/BOTM

1012/BOTM

MILLS & BOON®
Book Club

2 Free Books!

Join the Mills & Boon Book Club

Want to read more **Cherish™**
books? We're offering
you **2 more** absolutely **FREE!**

We'll also treat you to these fabulous extras:

- 🌹 **Books up to 2 months ahead of shops**
- 🌹 **FREE home delivery**
- 🌹 **Bonus books with our special rewards scheme**
- 🌹 **Exclusive offers and much more!**

Get your free books now!

Visit us Online

Find out more at
www.millsandboon.co.uk/freebookoffer

SUBS/ONLINE/S

Special Offers

Every month we put together collections and longer reads written by your favourite authors.

Here are some of next month's highlights— and don't miss our fabulous discount online!

On sale 19th October　　　On sale 2nd November　　　On sale 2nd November

Save 20% on all Special Releases

Find out more at
www.millsandboon.co.uk/specialreleases

Visit us Online

1012/ST/MB389

The World of Mills & Boon®

There's a Mills & Boon® series that's perfect for you. We publish ten series and, with new titles every month, you never have to wait long for your favourite to come along.

Blaze
Scorching hot, sexy reads
4 new stories every month

By Request
Relive the romance with the best of the best
9 new stories every month

Cherish™
Romance to melt the heart every time
12 new stories every month

Desire™
Passionate and dramatic love stories
8 new stories every month

Visit us Online
Try something new with our Book Club offer
www.millsandboon.co.uk/freebookoffer

M&B/WORLD2

What will you treat yourself to next?

*Ignite your imagination,
step into the past...*
6 new stories every month

INTRIGUE...

Breathtaking romantic suspense
Up to 8 new stories every month

*Captivating medical drama –
with heart*
6 new stories every month

MODERN™

*International affairs,
seduction & passion guaranteed*
9 new stories every month

n o c t u r n e™

*Deliciously wicked
paranormal romance*
Up to 4 new stories every month

*Live life to the full –
give in to temptation*
3 new stories every month available
exclusively via our Book Club

You can also buy Mills & Boon eBooks at
www.millsandboon.co.uk

*Visit us
Online*

M&B/WORLD2

Mills & Boon® Online

Discover more romance at
www.millsandboon.co.uk

🌹 **FREE** online reads

🌹 **Books** up to one
month before shops

🌹 **Browse our books**
before you buy

...and much more!

For exclusive competitions and instant updates:

 Like us on **facebook.com/romancehq**

 Follow us on **twitter.com/millsandboonuk**

 Join us on **community.millsandboon.co.uk**

Visit us Online | Sign up for our FREE eNewsletter at
www.millsandboon.co.uk

WEB/M&B/RTL4